Lambeth
Libraries

Items must be returned on or before the last
date stamped below, or over due charges will
be made.

Published in Great Britain 2014
by Mills & Boon, an imprint of Harlequin (UK) Limited,
Eton House, 18-24 Paradise Road, Richmond, Surrey, TW9 1SR

KINGS OF CALIFORNIA © 2014 Harlequin Books S.A.

Bargaining for King's Baby, Marrying for King's Millions and *Falling for King's Fortune* were first published in Great Britain by Harlequin (UK) Limited.

Bargaining for King's Baby © 2008 Maureen Child
Marrying for King's Millions © 2008 Maureen Child
Falling for King's Fortune © 2008 Maureen Child

ISBN: 978 0 263 91180 0
eBook ISBN: 978 1 472 04475 4

05-0414

Harlequin (UK) Limited's policy is to use papers that are natural, renewable and recyclable products and made from wood grown in sustainable forests. The logging and manufacturing processes conform to the legal environmental regulations of the country of origin.

Printed and bound in Spain
by Blackprint CPI, Barcelona

BARGAINING FOR KING'S BABY

BY
MAUREEN CHILD

Maureen Child is a California native who loves to travel. Every chance they get, she and her husband are taking off on another research trip. An author of more than sixty books, Maureen loves a happy ending and still swears that she has the best job in the world. She lives in Southern California with her husband, two children and a golden retriever with delusions of grandeur.

You can contact Maureen via her website: www.maureenchild.com.

To Carter, for bringing so much love into our lives.
We wish for you all the good things life holds,
and we're grateful to be able to watch you
discover the world around you.

One

"You're obsessed." Travis King looked at his older brother and smiled. "And not in a good way."

"I agree," Jackson King said, with a shake of his head. "Why is this so important to you anyway?"

Adam King looked from one of his brothers to the other and paused for a few seconds before answering them. When he did, he used the tone he usually reserved for his employees—the tone that precluded arguments. "We agreed when we took over the reins of the family businesses from Dad that we'd each be in charge of our own areas."

Then he waited, because Adam knew his brothers weren't finished. Every month, the King brothers held a meeting. They'd get together either here at the family ranch, at the vineyard Travis operated or on one of the executive jets Jackson owned and leased to the mega-wealthy of the world.

The King family had holdings in so many different areas, the monthly meetings helped the brothers keep up with what the tangled lines of the King dynasty were up to at any given moment. But it also gave the brothers a chance to catch up on each other's lives. Even if sometimes, Adam thought, that meant putting up with inter-ference—no matter how well meant.

Picking up his Waterford crystal tumbler of brandy, he swirled the amber liquid in the bottom of the glass and watched the firelight from the hearth wink in its depths. He knew it wouldn't take long to get a comment from his brothers and he silently bet himself that it would be Travis who spoke first. A moment later, he was proven right.

"Yeah, Adam, we each run our own areas," Travis said, taking a deep sip of a King Vineyard Merlot. Travis preferred drinking the wines his vineyard produced to the brandy Adam enjoyed. He shot a look at Jackson, who nodded at him. "That doesn't mean we won't have a question or two."

"Have all the questions you like," Adam told him. He stood up, walked to the massive stone hearth and stared down into the crackling fire. "Just don't expect me to answer them."

Jackson spoke up as if to head off a budding confron-tation. Holding his glass of Irish whiskey, he said, "We're not saying that the ranch isn't yours to do with as you want, Adam. We're only trying to figure out why it means so damn much to you to get back every inch of land we used to hold."

Adam turned his back on the fireplace, looked at his brothers and felt that tight bond they'd always shared. Only a year separated each of them and the friendship they'd formed when they were kids was every bit as strong now. But that didn't mean he was going to explain his every move to them. He was still the oldest, and Adam King didn't *do* explanations.

"The ranch is mine," he said simply. "If I want to make it whole again, why should you care?"

"We don't," Travis said, speaking up before Jackson could. Leaning back in the maroon leather chair, he kicked his feet out in front of him, balanced the fragile wineglass on his flat stomach and looked at Adam through slitted eyes. "I just want to know why *you* care. Hell, Adam, Great-Grandpa King sold off that twenty-acre parcel to the Torinos nearly sixty years ago. We already own nearly half the county. Why's that twenty acre plot so important?"

Because he'd set out to do this and Adam had never given up on anything. Once he'd made up his mind to do something, it got done, come hell or high water. He glanced from his brothers to the wide front windows overlooking a stretch of neatly tended lawn and garden that stretched for almost a quarter of a mile before feeding into the road.

This ranch had always been important to him. But in the last five years, it had become everything to him and damned if he'd stop before it was complete again.

Outside, the night was thick and black, broken only by tiny puddles of decorative lights positioned along the wide, curved driveway. This was his home. *Their* home. And he was going to see to it that it was once again completely in King hands.

"Because it's the last missing piece," Adam said, thinking of the last five years. Years that he'd spent buying back every piece of land that had been in the original King land grant more than a hundred and fifty years ago.

The King family had been in central California since before the gold rush. They'd been miners and ranchers and farmers and ship builders. Over the years, the family had changed with the times, moving into different fields, expanding their dynasty. Generations of them had worked to broaden the family's holdings. To grow and build on the previous generations—with one exception.

Their great-grandfather, Simon King, had been more of a gambler than a family scion. And to support his gambling habits, he'd sold off pieces of his heritage. Thankfully the Kings who'd come after Simon had held on to their family history with both hands.

Adam didn't know if he could make his brothers understand—didn't know that he cared to try. All he knew was that he'd devoted the last five years to putting the jigsaw pieces of this ranch back together and he wasn't going to stop until he'd completed the task.

"Fine," Jackson said, shooting Travis a quick *shut-up* look. "If it's that important to you, go ahead."

Adam snorted. "Your permission isn't necessary. But thanks."

Jackson smiled. As always, the youngest of the King boys was almost impossible to rile. "Good luck getting that land away from the Torinos, though," he added, taking a sip of his whiskey and giving a dramatic sigh. "That old man holds on to everything that's his with both hands." His mouth twisted into a smile. "Like you, big brother. Sal's not going to just up and sell it to you."

Adam smiled now, and lifted his brandy snifter in a salute. "What was Dad's favorite saying?"

"Every man's got his price," Travis said, and lifted his glass, too, as he finished their father's quote, *"the trick is to find it the quickest way you can."*

Jackson shook his head, but lifted his glass to his brothers. "Salvatore Torino may be the exception to that rule."

"Not a chance," Adam said and he could already taste the victory he'd worked five years for. He wasn't about to let one stubborn neighbor stand in the way of success. "Sal's got a price. *Somewhere.*"

Gina Torino hooked the heel of her scuffed boot on the bottom rung of the weathered wooden fence. She crossed her arms on the top rail and looked out at the field in front of her. The sun was shining out of a clear blue sky, the grass was thick and green and a brand-new baby was trotting alongside his mother.

"See, Shadow?" she whispered to the contented mare, "I told you he'd be fine."

Of course, last night Gina hadn't been so sure. Playing midwife to a Gypsy horse she'd raised from infancy had absolutely terrified her. But today, she could smile and enjoy the moment.

Her gaze followed the black-and-white mare as she moved lazily around the enclosure, new baby at her feathered heels. The Gypsies were the most beautiful horses Gina had ever seen. Their broad shoulders, proud neck and the "feathers," or long, delicate hairs flying around their feet, looked exquisite. Most people, of course, took one look at the breed and thought…miniature Clydesdales. But the Gypsy horses were something else entirely.

Relatively small, but sturdy, the Gypsies had at first been bred by the roaming people who gave them their name. They were bred to be strong enough to pull loaded carts and wagons and gentle enough to be considered part of the family. They were exceptionally gentle with children and incredibly loyal to those they loved.

The horses, to Gina, were more than animals to be bred and sold…they were family.

"You baby them."

Gina didn't even turn when her mother spoke up from behind her. This was a long-standing argument—with her mother claiming that Gina spent too much time with the horses and too little time looking for a husband. "There's no harm in that."

"You need your *own* babies."

Gina rolled her eyes, grateful her mother couldn't see the action. Teresa Torino didn't care how old her children were. If they sassed, they were just as likely to get a swat on the back of the head as they had been when they were children. If she'd had any sense at all, Gina told herself, she'd have moved away like two of her three older brothers had.

"I know you're rolling your eyes...."

Grinning, Gina glanced back over her shoulder. Teresa Torino was short, curvy and opinionated. Her black hair was going gray and she didn't bother dyeing it, instead reminding everyone in the family that she'd *earned* those gray hairs. Her chin was stubborn and her brown eyes were sharp and didn't miss much.

"Would I roll my eyes at you, Mom?"

One dark eyebrow lifted. "If you thought you could get away with it, yes."

Gina lifted her face into a soft wind blowing in off the nearby ocean and changed the subject. Safer that way. "I heard you talking on the phone to Nick this morning. Everything all right?"

"Yes," Teresa said, walking up to join her daughter at the split rail fence. "Your brother Nickie's wife is pregnant again."

Ah. So this explained the *let's get Gina married and pregnant* theme of the morning. "That's great news."

"Yes. That will be three for Nick, two children for Tony and four for Peter."

Her brothers were really doing all they could to re-populate the world with Torinos, Gina thought with a smile. She loved being an aunt, of course. But she wished they all lived closer, so they could take more of the heat off of *her.* Yet of the three Torino sons, only Tony lived here on the ranch, working it with their father. Nick was in Colorado, coaching high school football and Peter was in Southern California, installing computer software for security companies.

"You're a lucky nana to have so many grandbabies to spoil," Gina said, sliding a glance at her mother.

"Could be luckier," Teresa countered with a sniff.

"Mom…" Gina couldn't stop the sigh that slipped from her. "You've got eight and a half grandchildren. You don't need me to produce one."

Her mother had always dreamed of Gina's wedding day. Of seeing her only daughter walk down the aisle on her father's arm. The fact that Gina hadn't complied didn't sit well with Teresa.

"It's not good for you to be alone, Gina," her mother said, slapping one hand against a board hard enough to make the fence rattle.

"I'm not alone," Gina argued. "I've got you and Papa, my brothers, their wives, their kids. Who could ever be alone in this family?"

Teresa, though, was on a roll. The music of her still-thick Italian accent colored her words when she spoke again. "A woman should have a man in her life, Gina. A man to love and be loved by…"

Gina felt her back go up, even though a part of her agreed with her mother. It wasn't as if she'd gone out of her way to decide to *never* get married. To *never* have children. It's just the way things had worked out. And she wasn't going to spend the rest of her life being miserable because of it.

"Just because I'm not married, Mom," Gina interrupted, "that doesn't mean I don't have men in my life."

Teresa sucked air in through her nose in a disapproving sniff that was so loud, one of the horses in the meadow turned its head to investigate. "I don't want to know about that."

Good, because Gina didn't really want to talk about her love life—or lack thereof—with her *mother*. She loved her parents dearly, she really did. Teresa had been born into a huge Sicilian family and had come to America more than forty years ago to marry Sal Torino. And despite the fact that Sal had been born and raised in America, he tended to side with his wife when she clung to Old World values—namely, that daughters who hadn't found husbands by their thirtieth birthday were destined to be old maids.

Sadly, Gina's thirtieth birthday had come and gone two months ago.

"Mom…" Gina took a breath, blew it out and prayed for patience. She'd hoped that having her own small house built on the family ranch would give her more privacy. Would make her parents think of her as a capable adult. She should have known better. Once a Torino child, *always* a Torino child.

Maybe she should have just moved away from the ranch entirely. But even if she had, she'd have been spending every day here anyway, since the Gypsy horses she raised and trained were her life. So she'd simply have to find a way to deal with being her mother's great disappointment.

"I know, I know," Teresa said, holding up one hand as if to stave off a familiar argument. "You are a grown woman. You don't need a man to complete you." She gave an impatient huff. "I should never have let you watch those talk shows when you were growing up. They fill your head with—"

"—sense?" Gina offered, smiling. She did love her mom, it was just so aggravating having to apologize for not being married and/or pregnant all the damn time.

"Sense. Is it sense to live alone? To not have love in your life? No," Teresa snapped, not waiting for an answer. "It is not."

It would be easier to argue with her mom if a part of Gina didn't agree. Okay, a small part. But a tiny voice in the back of her mind whispered that she wasn't getting any younger. That she should give up on old fantasies that should have died years ago.

Yet somehow…she couldn't quite manage it.

"I'm fine, Mom," she said, willing herself to believe it.

Teresa laid one hand on her daughter's forearm and gave her a pat. "Of course you are."

Okay, Gina was willing to accept that, even if her mom was placating her. At least it had stopped the conversation. "Where's Papa?" she asked. "He was going to come look over the new baby this morning."

Teresa waved one hand. "He has a 'meeting' he said. Very important."

"Yeah? With who?"

"You think he tells me?" Teresa huffed out a frustrated breath and Gina smiled.

Nothing her mother hated more than not knowing what was going on at all times.

"Well, while Papa's in his meeting, you can meet the new baby."

"Horses," Teresa muttered. "You and your horses."

Gina laughed and took her mother's hand. "Come on."

As they walked to the fence gate, a rumble of noise drifted to them and Gina turned to watch a car approach down the long driveway leading in from the main road. Dust billowed behind the black luxury SUV and Gina felt a stir of something deep inside her when she recognized the car. Despite trying to ignore that feeling, her breath caught and held in her chest and her mouth suddenly went dry.

She didn't even need to read the license plate… KING 1 to know without a doubt that Adam King was in that car. She felt it as surely as she felt the rocky ground beneath her feet. What was that, anyway? Some sort of inner radar that leaped into life whenever Adam got close?

"So, Adam King is the important meeting," her mother mused. "I wonder why."

Gina wondered, too. She knew she should just go about her business, but somehow, she couldn't make her feet move. She just stood there and watched as Adam parked his car and opened the door. When he stepped out and looked around, his dark-eyed gaze sliding across the ranch yard, something inside her jumped in reaction. Stupid, she told herself. Stupid to feel anything for a man who didn't even know you existed.

Adam's gaze kept moving, as if he were cataloging the Torino ranch and would be given a test on it later.

Finally, his gaze moved over Gina. She stiffened. Even from a distance she felt the power of his stare as if he'd reached out and touched her.

He nodded at her and her mother, and Gina forced herself to lift one hand in a halfhearted wave. Almost before her fingers had stopped moving, though, Adam had turned for the house.

"A cold man, that one," Teresa said in a quiet voice from right beside Gina. Crossing herself she added, "There is a darkness in him."

Gina had felt the darkness, too, so she couldn't really argue the point. But she'd known Adam and his brothers all of her life. And she'd always wanted to be the one to ease the darkness back for him.

Stupid, she supposed. What is it with women that we all want to be the one to "save" a guy? she wondered.

She was still standing there, watching after Adam, even though he'd already gone into the ranch house for his meeting with her father. And finally, Gina felt her mother watching her. "What?"

"I see something in your eyes, Gina," her mother whispered, worry tightening her mouth and flashing in her gaze.

Gina immediately turned away and started walking toward the horses in the meadow. She still felt a little shaky so she made sure her steps were long and steady. Lifting her chin, she whipped her hair back out of her eyes and said, "I don't know what you mean, Mom."

Teresa wasn't so easily put off, however. She hurried after her daughter, took hold of Gina's arm and dragged her to a stop. Looking into her eyes, Teresa said, "You cannot fool me. There is something there in you for Adam King. And you must not surrender to it."

Surprised, Gina laughed. "Excuse me? This from the woman who not five minutes ago was telling me to get married and start having babies?"

"Not with him," Teresa said. "Adam King is the one man I do not want for you."

Unfortunate.

Since Adam King was the only man Gina wanted.

Two

Adam knocked on the front door, waited impatiently and then jerked to attention when a shorter, older man opened it and smiled out at him.

"Adam," Sal Torino said, stepping back and waving him inside. "Right on time, as always."

"Sal. Thanks for seeing me." Adam stepped into the house and glanced around. It had been a long time since he was last here, but he noticed that the place hadn't changed much.

The entryway was wide and lit from above by a skylight that spilled sunshine in a wash of gold across the gleaming pine floors. The hall leading to the back of the house was covered in framed family photos of smiling kids and proud parents. The high, arched doorway that led into the living room where Sal gestured for Adam to follow had been unchanged, as well. The walls were still a soft, warm yellow, the furniture was oversize and comfortable, and a stone hearth, cold now, held a copper urn filled with fresh flowers. Sal took a seat on the sofa and reached for a coffeepot sitting on a tray atop a wide, scarred pine table.

While Sal poured coffee Adam didn't want, he wandered the room and stopped at the curved bay window. The glass gleamed in the morning light and provided a sweeping view of the neatly trimmed lawn ringed by ancient oak trees. Adam hardly noticed, though. His mind was already focused on the task at hand: How he would convince Sal to sell him the land he needed.

"So, what brings Adam King to my house first thing in the morning?"

Adam turned around to look at his neighbor. Sal stood about five foot eight, had thick black hair streaked with gray, skin as weathered and tanned as old leather and sharp brown eyes.

He walked over to take the coffee cup Sal offered him and then had a sip just to be polite. Sitting down opposite the other man, Adam cupped the heavy mug between his palms and said, "I want to talk to you about that twenty-acre parcel in your north pasture, Sal."

The older man's face split in an understanding smile as he leaned back into the sofa cushions. "Ah."

It wasn't good business to let your opponent know how badly you wanted something. But Sal Torino was no dummy. The King family had made offers for that land several times over the last couple of decades and Sal had always turned them down flat. So, he already knew how important this was to Adam. No point in trying to pretend otherwise.

"I want that land, Sal, and I'm willing to make you a deal that'll give you a hell of a profit on it."

Shaking his head Sal took a gulp of coffee, swallowed and sighed. "Adam…"

"Hear me out." Adam leaned forward, set his coffee cup down on the tray and sat back again, bracing his forearms on his thighs. "You don't use that piece of land for grazing or pasture. It's just sitting there."

Sal smiled and shook his head again. Fine. He was stubborn. Adam could appreciate that. He bit down on the impatience scratching at his insides and forced a congenial tone to his voice. "Think about this, Sal. I'm willing to make you another substantial offer for the property."

"Why is this so important to you?"

Now we play the game. Adam wished this were all somehow easier. Sal knew damn well about Adam's quest to make the King ranch whole again, but clearly he was going to have to spell it all out.

"It's the last piece of the original King family holdings," Adam said tightly. "Which you already know."

Sal smiled again and Adam thought the older man sort of looked like a benevolent elf. Too bad he didn't look like an elf who wanted to sell. "So let's get down to business here. You don't need the land. I want the land. Simple as that. So what do you say?"

"Adam," Sal started, pausing for another sip of

coffee, "I don't like selling land. What's mine is mine. You know that. You feel the same way I do."

"Yes, and that parcel is *mine,* Sal. Or it should be. It started out King land. It should be King land again."

"But it isn't."

Adam quietly seethed with frustration.

"I don't need your money." Sal sat forward, set his coffee cup down and then stood up to wander the room. "You know that, and yet, you come to me anyway, thinking to sway me with an argument for profit margins."

"Making a profit's not a sin, Sal," Adam countered.

"Money is not the only thing a man thinks about, though."

Sal stopped at the hearth, leaned one arm on the heavily carved mantel and looked down at Adam.

Adam wasn't used to being the one on the defensive in a negotiation. And looking up at Sal from the comfort of a too-soft chair made him feel at a disadvantage, so he stood up, too. Shoving both hands into the pockets of his jeans, he watched the older man and wondered what Sal was up to.

"I hear an implied 'but' in there somewhere," Adam said. "So why don't you just tell me what you've got in mind and we can decide if we're going to be able to make a deal."

"Ah," Sal said. "So impatient. You should learn to enjoy life more, Adam. It's not good to build a life solely on business."

"Works for me."

Adam wasn't interested in listening to advice. He

didn't want to hear about "enjoying" life. All he wanted was that last piece of land.

"There was a time when you didn't feel that way," Sal mused and the smile slipped off his features even as his dark eyes went soft and sympathetic.

Adam stiffened perceptibly. The worst part of living in a small town was having everyone for miles around knowing your personal business. Sal, he knew, was trying to be nice, so he kept a lid on the simmering knot of something ugly inside him. People thought they knew him. Thought they could understand what he was feeling, thinking. But they were wrong.

He wasn't interested in sympathy any more than he was looking for advice. He didn't *need* anyone's pity. Adam's life was just as he wanted it.

Except for owning that damned piece of land.

"Look, Sal," Adam said slowly, quietly, "I'm not here to talk about my life. I'm here to make a deal. So if you don't mind…"

Sal clucked his tongue in disapproval. "You are a single-minded man, Adam. And while I admire that, it can also make one's life harder than it has to be."

"Let me worry about my life, okay?" That sizzle of impatience he'd felt earlier had begun to bubble and froth in the pit of his stomach. "What do you say, Sal? Are we going to be able to come to an agreement?"

Sal braced his feet wide apart, folded his arms across his chest and tipped his head to one side, studying Adam as if looking for something in particular. After a long moment or two, he said, "We might be able to strike a deal. Though the terms I have in mind are somewhat different than you were expecting."

"What're you talking about?"

"Simple," Sal said with a shrug. "You want the land. I want something in return. And it's not your money."

"Then what?"

The older man nodded, walked back to the sofa and sat down again, getting comfortable. When he was settled, he looked up at Adam and said, "You know my Gina."

"Yeah…" Suspicion rattled through Adam.

"I want to see her happy," Sal said.

"I'm sure you do." And what the *hell* did Gina have to do with any of this?

"I want to see her married. Settled. With a family."

Everything in Adam went still and cold. He suddenly became hyperaware. He heard the ticking of the clock that hung over the fireplace. He heard a fly bumping against the bay window. He took a long, slow, deep breath and dragged in the enticing aroma of spaghetti sauce bubbling in the kitchen. Adam's skin felt too tight and every nerve ending in his body was standing straight up.

He took another breath, shook his head and stared at Sal, hardly able to believe what he'd just heard— realization at what Sal could be insinuating hitting him like a ton of bricks. But the older man was staring at him through steady, determined eyes, allowing Adam time to absorb what he'd said. But how could he possibly believe the old man was serious?

Adam had faced tough negotiators before and come out on top, though. Today would be no different.

"I don't see what Gina getting married has to do with me *or* this conversation."

"Don't you?" Sal smiled. "You're a man alone, Adam. Gina is alone, as well…"

This was *not* going the way he'd planned.

Gina?

Married?

To *him?*

No way. He looked into Sal's eyes and saw that the older man was absolutely sincere. No matter how whacked it sounded. Adam ground his back teeth together and took a couple of long, hopefully calming, breaths. Didn't help.

"Let me be clear," Sal said, shifting to rest one arm along the back of the sofa, like a man completely at ease with himself and his surroundings. "I offer you a deal, Adam. Marry my Gina. Make her happy. Give her one or two babies. And I give you the land."

Babies?

Fury erupted within and turned Adam's vision red at the edges. His lungs labored for air. His brain was covered in a mist of temper that made thinking nearly impossible. Which was probably for the best. Because if he took the time to actually consider what Sal was saying, who the hell knew what he might say?

He couldn't even remember being that angry before. Adam wasn't manipulated—he was the one who did the manipulating. *He* was the one who was a shark in negotiations. He didn't get surprised. He didn't feel at a loss. He was *never* at a loss for words, damn it.

And looking at Sal now, he could see the old guy was

really enjoying him being confounded, which only made Adam more furious.

"Forget it," Adam said, the words hardly more than a hiss of sound. Unable to stand still, he stalked over to the bay window, glared at the outside world for a second or two, then spun back around to face the man still seated on the couch. "What the hell's wrong with you, Sal? Are you delusional? People don't bargain their daughters for gain anymore. This isn't the middle ages, you know."

Slowly the older man stood up, narrowed his eyes on Adam and pointed his index finger, stabbing at the air with it. "This is not for my gain," Sal pointed out. "This is for *your* gain. You think I would accept *any* man for my Gina? You think I value her so lowly that I do this without thinking? Without considering?"

"I think you're *nuts.*"

Sal snorted a laugh that had no humor in it. "You want the land so badly? Do this one thing and it's yours."

"Unbelievable." This was crazy. Plain and simple. He'd always liked Sal Torino, too. Who knew the old guy was off his rocker?

"Why does this seem so unreasonable to you?" Sal demanded, coming around the sofa to stand beside Adam at the window. Sunlight speared in through the leaded glass panes, dotting the two men and the wood floor with diamond-shaped splotches of gold. "Is it crazy for a father to look to his daughter's happiness? To the happiness of the son of a man I called friend? You're a good man, Adam. But you've been alone too long. Lost too much."

"Sal—" His tone filled with warning.

"Fine." He held up both hands. "We won't speak of the past, but of the future." Sal turned his head, looked out the window and stared into the distance. Nodding his head, he said, "My Gina needs more in her life than her beloved horses. You need more in your life than your ranch. Is it so crazy to think the two of you could build something together?"

Adam just stared at him. "You want your daughter to marry a man who doesn't love her?"

He shrugged. "Love can grow."

"Not for me."

"Never say never, Adam." Sal slid a glance at him. "A life is long and not meant to be lived alone."

Life wasn't always long and Adam had discovered that it was better lived alone. He had no one's interests but his own to look after. He lived the way he wanted and made no excuses or apologies for it. And he had no intention of changing any part of his life.

Irritation spiked inside him. He *did* want that damned land. It had become a Holy Grail of sorts for him. The last square to place in the King family quilt of holdings. He could almost taste the satisfaction of finishing the task he'd set for himself. But now…looked like he'd be tasting failure instead and that knowledge notched his irritation a little higher.

"Thanks, Sal. But I'm not interested." In any of it. He wanted the land, but he wasn't willing to marry again. He'd tried that once. And even before the crashing end, it hadn't worked out for him or for his wife. He just wasn't built to be a husband.

"Think about it," Sal said and pointed out the window.

Adam glanced in the direction indicated and saw Gina and her mother out in the pasture. While he stood there, Teresa walked off, leaving her daughter alone in the field, surrounded by small, sturdy horses.

Sunlight dropped down on Gina like a cloud of light. Her long, dark hair whipped around her shoulders and when she tipped her head back to laugh, she made such an intriguing picture Adam gritted his teeth even harder.

"My Gina's a wonderful woman. You could do worse."

Adam tore his gaze from the woman in the meadow, shook his head and looked at the older man beside him. "You can let this idea of yours go, Sal. So why don't you do some realistic thinking and come up with a price for the land that we can both live with?"

This whole situation had gotten way out of hand and Adam felt as if the walls were closing in on him. Looking at Sal, you'd never guess he was crazy as a loon. But clearly he was. Who the hell bartered their children these days?

Giving reasonable one last shot, Adam asked, "What the hell do you think Gina would say if she could hear you?"

Sal shrugged and smiled a little. "She doesn't have to know."

"You live dangerously, Sal."

The older man snorted. "I know what's good for my children. And, I know what's good for you. This is the best bargain you could ever make, Adam. So *you* are the one who should think carefully before you decide."

"Decision's already made," Adam assured him. "I'm not marrying Gina or anybody else for that matter. But if you change your mind and want to actually talk business, you give me a call."

Adam had to get out of there. His blood was buzzing in his veins and he felt like his skin was on fire. Damned old man, throwing something like this at him out of the blue. Turning for the foyer, Adam crossed the room in a few long strides and yanked open the front door just as Teresa Torino was stepping inside. She jolted.

"Adam."

"Teresa." He gave her a nod, shot another incredulous look at Sal, then walked outside, closing the door behind him.

Instantly he felt as if he could breathe again. The sharp, clear air carried the scent of horses and the far-off sea. A cool wind brushed past him and almost without thinking about it, Adam turned his head and thoughtfully looked at the meadow where Gina Torino was communing with her horses.

Even from a distance, he felt the tug of an attraction he hadn't felt in too long to count. The last time he'd seen Gina, it had been at his wife and son's funeral. He'd been too numb that day to notice and since then, he'd mostly spent his time working the ranch.

And rather than heading for his car, he surprised himself by heading toward the fenced meadow.

Gina watched Adam approach and told her hormones to take a nap. Apparently, though, they weren't listening. Nope, instead of lying down and keeping quiet, her hormones were instead tap dancing on every one of her nerve endings. Heck, she was surprised she wasn't actually *vibrating*.

"Oh, Shadow," she whispered, stroking the mare's velvety neck, "I am *such* an idiot."

"Morning, Gina."

She braced herself, turned to face him and with one look into Adam's dark eyes, Gina knew she could never be "braced" enough. Why was it this one man absolutely lit up her insides like a fireworks display on the Fourth of July? Why did it have to be Adam King her heart yearned for?

"Hello, Adam," she said and silently congratulated herself on keeping her voice so nice and steady. "You're out early this morning."

"Yeah." His features twisted briefly, then he made an obvious effort to ease them before saying, "Had a meeting with your father."

"About what?"

"Nothing," he said so quickly that Gina knew something was definitely going on. And knowing her father as she did, it could be *anything*.

Still, it was clear Adam wouldn't be talking about whatever it was, so she'd save her curiosity for later. When she could pry it out of her father. For now, it was all she could do to keep from gibbering like an idiot. Adam walked closer, leaned his forearms on the top rung of the fence and squinted into the morning light. And wouldn't you know it, the wind shifted directions, just so it could tease her by drifting the scent of him toward her.

Nothing so prosaic as aftershave, though. Nope, the only scent she picked up was soap and man. Which only made it harder to draw a breath. Oh, yeah. This was going really well.

"Looks like you've had a new addition to your herd," he said with a nod at the foal.

Instantly Gina grinned and looked at the sturdy baby nuzzling his mother. "He arrived last night. Well, the middle of the night, really. I was up until nearly four this morning—hence my close resemblance to Franken-stein's Bride."

God, idiot. Make sure you point out to the man how haggard and hideous you look. First time you've seen him since his family's funeral and you have to look like the wrath of God? Just fabulous.

"You look great," he said and almost sounded grudg-ing about it.

"Yeah. I'm sure." Gina laughed, gave Shadow one more caress, then climbed through the fence. She knew right away that she should have just taken a short walk and opened the gate. She was too tired and strung a little too tightly to gracefully maneuver slipping between the rungs of the fence.

The toe of her boot caught on the bottom slat and she only had a second to think, *This is perfect. I'm about to fall on my face in the dirt, right in front of Adam. Can this get any better?* Then Adam's hand curled around her upper arm and he held on to her until she found her balance again.

Flinging her hair back out of her face, she looked up into dark-chocolate eyes and said, "Thanks—" Whatever else she might have added died unspoken because her mouth dried up completely.

The heat in his gaze was nearly overpowering. She felt blasted by it, as if she were being hit by a flamethrower. Blood sizzling, breath straining in her lungs, stomach spinning in wild circles, she could only stare at him. The feel of his hand on her skin only added to the sensation of heat pouring through her.

And just when she wondered what in the hell she could possibly say to explain why she had suddenly become dumb as a post, Adam said, "Have dinner with me."

Three

The words were out before he could stop himself and once they'd been said, Adam thought—*why the hell not?*

Yeah, he'd surprised himself and judging from the expression on her face, he'd surprised Gina, as well. But damned if he'd expected this rush of something hot and needy pulsing inside him. She'd caught him off guard, that was for sure.

Gina Torino was luscious. He hadn't noticed the last time he'd seen her. But now, just looking at her made him feel something he'd thought himself immune to. And he was male enough to enjoy the rush of lust crowding his system.

While she stared up at him out of golden eyes, he heard her father's offer repeat again and again in his mind. And as desire pumped fast and fiercely through his bloodstream, he told himself maybe he should re-think his instant rejection of her father's idea. It wouldn't be too much a hardship to make Gina Torino his wife.

And God knew he could hardly believe himself that he was considering this. But after all, it didn't have to be forever. There didn't have to be a baby. All he had to do was marry Gina and he'd get the land he wanted so badly. Then he'd divorce her with a good settlement and everybody's happy.

Was he as crazy as Sal? Possibly. On the other hand, Adam had always been able to look at a situation, see it from every angle and then make the moves neces-sary for him to come out on top. Why should this be any different?

It wasn't as if he was going into the deal with an idea to cheat Sal. The old man had come up with this bizarre plan all on his own. And Gina?

Well, hell. His gaze swept her up and down in a heart-beat of time. He took in her bright, golden eyes, her full mouth tipped into a smile, her lush breasts pressing against the faded fabric of a denim shirt and her rounded hips and long legs encased in worn jeans. She was enough to make any man's mouth water. And the fact that she was getting to him was enough to have him con-sidering Sal's proposal.

"You look surprised," he said when he realized that seconds of silence were ticking past.

"Well, I am." She brushed her palms against her thighs but it was clearly more about nerves than cleaning her hands off. "I haven't even spoken to you in the last five years, Adam."

True. He'd never been a social type, like his brothers were. And in the last few years, he'd cut himself off even further from his neighbors. "I've been busy."

She laughed and somehow the rollicking music of it seemed to slice through him, cutting him so deep his breath caught in his chest. What was this? Lust he could deal with. Use to his own advantage. But he wasn't looking to be intrigued or captivated by her.

Yet he wanted her. And after years of feeling *nothing,* this rush of lust felt damn good. All he had to do was remind himself why he was considering this. The land. Marry Gina, enjoy himself, and when he was finished with her, they'd divorce and then this *lust* would be over with and he would have the land he required.

"You've been busy." Nodding, she shot him a smile. "For five years."

He shrugged. "What about you?"

"What about me?"

"What've you been up to?"

Her eyebrows lifted and she tipped her head to one side to look at him. "Five years of news is going to take a little while to tell."

"So, do it at dinner."

"First a question."

"Of course." Women always had questions.

"Why?"

"Why what?"

"Why ask me to dinner?" She pushed her hands into the back pockets of her jeans, arching her back a little, making her breasts push against the fabric of her shirt. "Why now all of a sudden?"

Adam frowned a little. Figured she'd make him work for this. "Look, it's no big deal. I saw you, we talked, I asked. If you don't want to go, just say so."

She stared at him for a long moment or two, but Adam knew she wasn't going to turn him down. She was intrigued. She was interested. And more than that, she was feeling the same sort of physical buzz he was. He could see it in her eyes.

"I didn't say that," she said a moment later, proving that he could still read people pretty well. "I was just curious."

He gave her a casual shrug. "We both have to eat. Why not do it together?"

"Okay…where are you taking me?"

He offered the first place that came to him. It wasn't as if he'd planned this all out. He'd come to the Torino spread looking to make a deal. Now, it appeared that he was going to make that deal after all—just not the one he'd counted on.

Gina's insides were doing a happy skip and dance. She couldn't believe that Adam King had finally noticed her. And for a few minutes, that was the only thought she concentrated on. But finally, dumb ol' reality crashed in. Why now? She had to ask herself the question. She'd known Adam all her life and up until five minutes ago, he'd never acknowledged her existence beyond the occasional "hi."

Since the death of his family five years before, Adam had pretty much been a recluse. He'd shut himself away from everything but his ranch and his brothers. So why all of a sudden was he Mr. Charm? A tiny nugget of suspicion settled in the pit of her stomach, but it didn't do a thing to ease the thumping of her heart.

"What about Serenity?"

Ah. The almost impossible to get into place on the coast. He really was pulling out all the stops.

"Sounds good," she said, even though what she really meant was, *sounds fabulous, can't wait, what took you so long?*

"Tomorrow night? Seven?"

"Okay. Seven." The moment she agreed, she saw satisfaction glitter in his dark-chocolate eyes and the suspicion crowding her jumped up in her brain and started waving hands, trying to get her attention. Well, it worked. "Though I really would like to know what actually prompted this out-of-nowhere invitation."

His features tightened briefly, but a moment later, he gave her a small smile again. "If you're not interested, Gina, all you have to do is say no."

"I didn't say that." She pulled her hands from her pockets and folded her arms across her chest.

"Glad to hear it," he said and reached for one of her hands, holding it in his, smoothing his thumb gently across her skin. He looked into her eyes, gave her a small smile and said, "So, I'll pick you up at seven tomorrow? You can tell me all about what you've been up to for the last five years."

When he let go of her hand, Gina could have sworn she could actually *smell* her skin sizzling from the heat he'd generated. Oh, she was sliding into some seriously deep waters here.

Adam was charming. Friendly. Smiley. Flirty.

Something was definitely going on here. Something he wasn't telling her. And still, she wouldn't turn down this invitation for anything.

"I'll be ready."

"See you then." With one last smile, he turned around and walked with determined steps across the yard to the SUV he'd left parked near the house.

Gina stood stock-still to enjoy the view. His excellent butt looked great in the dark blue jeans. His long legs moved with a deceptively lazy stride and the sun hit his dark brown hair and gleamed in its depths.

Her heart actually *fluttered* in her chest. Weird sensation. And not a good sign. "Oh, Gina," she whispered, "you are in very deep trouble, here."

Just being that close to Adam, having him focusing his attention on her, had been enough to stir up all of the old fantasies and dreams. She felt shaky, like the time she'd had three espresso drinks in an hour. Only Adam King was a way bigger buzz than too much caffeine.

Her breath left her in a rush as Adam steered his car down the driveway and away from the ranch. She rubbed the spot on her hand where Adam had touched her. When the cloud of dust behind his car had settled back down onto the driveway, Gina thoughtfully turned her gaze on the house behind her. Adam might not be willing to tell her what was going on, but she had a bone-deep feeling that her father had the answers she needed.

"I can't believe it," Gina muttered, stalking around the perimeter of the great room. She must have made thirty circuits in the last twenty minutes. Ever since her father had confessed what his meeting with Adam King had really been about. Gina's temper spiked anew every time she thought about it. She couldn't seem to sit down. Couldn't keep still.

At every other clomp of her boots against the wood floor, she shot her father a look that should have frizzed his hair. When she thought she could speak without screaming, she asked, "You tried to *sell* me?"

"You make too much of this, Gina." Sal sat on the sofa, but his comfy, relaxed position was belied by the glitter of guilt and caution in his eyes.

"Too much?" She threw her hands high and let them slap to her thighs again. "What am I, a princess in a tower? Are you some feudal lord, Papa? God, this is like one of the historical romance novels I read." She stopped dead and stabbed her index finger at him. "Only difference is, this is the *twenty-first century!*"

"Women are too emotional," Sal muttered. "This is why men run the world."

"This is what you think?" Teresa Torino reached over and slapped her husband's upper arm. "Men run the world because *women* allow it."

Normally Gina would have smiled at that, but at the moment, she was just too furious to see the humor in anything about this situation. Oh, man, she wanted to open up a big, yawning hole in the earth and fall into it. What must Adam have been thinking when her father faced him with this "plan"?

God. Everything in her cringed away from *that* image. Could a person die of embarrassment?

"You said yourself Gina should get married and have babies," Sal told his wife.

"Yes, but not like this. Not with him."

"What's wrong with Adam?" Sal wanted to know.

Nothing, as far as Gina was concerned, but she wasn't about to say *that*.

"There is…*something*," Teresa said with a sniff.

Gina nearly groaned.

"You don't know Adam well enough to think there's something wrong with him," Sal told his wife.

"Ah," Teresa argued. "But you know him well enough to *barter* your daughter's future with him?"

And the argument was off and running. Gina only half listened. In her family, yelling was as much a part of life as the constant hugs and laughter. Italians, her mother liked to say, lived life to the *fullest*. Of course, Gina's father liked to say that his wife lived life to the *loudest*, but basically, it was the same thing.

She and her brothers had grown up with laughter,

shouts, hugs, more shouts and the knowledge that they were all loved unconditionally.

Today, though…she could have cheerfully strangled the father she loved so much. Gina's gaze shifted around the room, picking out the framed family photos sprinkled across every flat surface. There were dozens of her brothers and their families. There were old, sepia prints of grandparents and great-grandparents, too. There were photos of children in Italy, cousins she'd never met. And there were pictures of Gina. With her first horse. As the winning pitcher on her high school softball team. Getting ready for her prom. Her graduation. And in all of the pictures of Gina, she was alone. There was no husband. No kids.

Just good ol' Aunt Gina.

Old maid.

The Torino clan was big on family. And she was no exception to that rule.

Gina had always wanted a family of her own. Had always expected that she would be a mother, once the time was right. But in the last couple of years, as she'd watched her brothers' families grow while she remained alone and single, she'd begun to accept that maybe her life wouldn't turn out the way she'd always hoped.

And on that depressing thought, she stopped walking crazily around the room, closed down her racing brain and focused her gaze on the slant of sunlight beaming in through the wide front windows and the dust motes dancing in the still air. The scent of her mother's sauce spilled from the kitchen and wrapped itself around Gina like a warm hug.

Sal scowled at his wife, shot his daughter a cautious look and said, "Besides, all of this is wasted effort. You're angry for nothing, Gina. Adam turned me down."

"He did?"

"Of *course* he did," Teresa said, reaching out to give her husband another smack.

"Hey!" Sal complained.

"Adam King is not a man to be trifled with this way," Teresa said, lifting one hand to wag a warning finger. "There is a darkness there…."

Sal rolled his eyes and even Gina had to stifle a snort. Any man who didn't like pasta wasn't to be trusted in Teresa Torino's world.

"There's nothing wrong with Adam," Sal argued. "He's a good businessman. He's steady. He's wealthy so we don't need to worry about a man marrying Gina for her money—"

"Oh," Gina snapped, feeling the insult jab its way home, "thanks very much for that!"

"And," Sal continued before either his wife or his daughter could interrupt again, "he needs a wife."

"He had a wife," Teresa pointed out.

"She's dead," Sal argued.

"So you sign me up as a pinch hitter?" Gina demanded.

"It's not good to be alone," her father said.

"God." Gina slumped onto the arm of the closest sofa and stared at her father. "Did you and Mom rehearse that little ditty? Maybe we should put it to music!"

"There's no reason to be smart," Teresa said.

"No reason?" Gina slid her gaze to her mother in astonishment. Typical. A minute ago, Teresa had been furious with her husband. But the moment she felt he was the underdog, she jumped onto his side of the debate.

"Mom, I know Papa meant well, but this is…is…" She stopped and shook her head. "I don't even have a word for what this is. Beyond the usual. You know… humiliating. Embarrassing. Demeaning."

Teresa blew out a breath. "So dramatic."

Gina just goggled at her. How did a person argue with parents like this? And *why* was she still living on this ranch?

Oh, she wanted to scream. How mortifying was this? She was so pitiful, so unwanted that her father had to try to *buy* her a husband?

Her head was pounding and her chest felt tight. Vaguely she heard her mother's whispered mutterings as she continued her tirade. But Gina couldn't even think about her parents at the moment.

What must Adam have thought? Oh, God, she didn't want to know. Way better to just push that little question right out of her mind. How would she ever face him again? How would she be able to keep that dinner date with him tomorrow night?

And with that thought, everything inside her stopped.

He'd turned her father down.

He wasn't willing to marry her for the land he wanted so badly. So why, then, had he stepped outside and asked her to dinner? Was this a pity date? Poor little

Gina will never get married, why not toss her a bowl of soup and a nice night out?

No.

Adam wasn't the doing-good-deeds kind of guy. She didn't agree with her mother about the darkness in him, but he also wasn't the kind of guy who went out of his way for people.

So what did all of this mean?

Her headache erupted into migraine territory.

"So what?" Sal asked. "How long am I going to be in trouble?"

Gina glared at her father.

"Long time, I guess," he muttered.

"You want me to call and talk to Adam? Explain?" Teresa asked.

"Good God, no!" Gina hopped up off the arm of the couch. "What am I? In third grade?"

"Only to help," her mother soothed. "To tell him that your papa is crazy."

"I'm not crazy," Sal argued.

"Matter of debate," Gina said wryly and her father had the grace to flush.

"I meant no harm," Sal told her.

Gina's heart melted a little. No matter how furious he made her, she'd loved him too long to stay mad forever. "I know that, Papa. But *please* stay out of my love life."

"Yes, yes," he said.

When her parents started arguing again, Gina left them to it. She was just too tired to hold up her end of the battle. Walking across the ranch yard, she went straight to her own small house and stepped inside. It was quiet. Empty. She didn't even have a pet. Since she spent so much time with her horses, it seemed silly to have another animal around.

She stopped just inside the living room. Her gaze swept quickly around the familiar space but it was as if she were seeing it with new eyes.

Here, too, just like up at the main house, there were framed photos. Pictures of her nieces and nephews. Laughing kids with gap-toothed smiles. Snapshots of days spent at amusement parks, on the Gypsy horses, eating at her kitchen table. There were drawings taped to the wall, too, each signed by the young artist.

And there were toys. Some scattered across her coffee table, others in a chest she kept under her front window. Baby dolls and fire trucks. GameBoys and coloring books.

In a blink, Gina knew that this was the pattern of her life. As it was. As it would always be. She would forever be the favorite aunt. The children she loved would never be her own. And she would no doubt end up an old woman, alone, with a houseful of cats.

Tears stung the backs of her eyes as she imagined it, the years spilling out in front of her so clearly, it made her head spin. Her house wasn't a home. It was a place where she slept. It was a place that children visited and never stayed. It was a place that would forever be haunted by the ghosts of the children she *might* have had.

Unless she did something outrageous.
Something no one would expect.
Least of all Adam King.

Four

A dinner date with Adam King—especially this one—required nothing less than a new dress.

Turning in front of her mirror, Gina took a long, critical look and decided she looked pretty good. The black dress hit just above her knee and the full skirt swirled out when she turned. The bodice dipped low enough to give a peek at what was hidden beneath the silky fabric, and the sleeveless straps over her shoulders were narrow, delicate.

Her hair hung in a cascade of curls down her back and her new high-heeled sandals gave her an extra three inches of height.

"Okay," she said, smiling at the woman in the glass. "I can do this. Everything's gonna be great. I am sooooo ready."

Her reflection was not convinced. Frowning a little, Gina jolted at the knock on her front door. "Oh, yeah. You're ready."

Shaking her head, she snapped up her black clutch bag and headed for the front of the little house. When she opened the door, though, she found not Adam, but her brother Tony standing on the porch.

Hands on his hips, he said, "I just talked to Mom and thought I'd better come see you."

"No time," she said, looking past him at the driveway to the road.

"Why not?"

"I have a date." She waved one hand at him in a "shooing" motion. "Me. Going out. Thanks for stopping by. Bye now."

He paid no attention to that at all, just stalked past her into the house. Gina sighed at the dust his boots left on the floor, then she turned and said, "What're you doing here?"

"Mom told me what Pop did."

"Fabulous." Had her mom called Peter and Nicky, too, to bring them up to speed on the pitiful wasteland that was Gina's love life? Was she going to take out an ad in the Birkfield paper, too?

"I just want to say, Pop was out of line. You don't need him to find you a man."

"Thanks for the vote of confidence," she said and waved at the still open front door, trying to get her brother out of there before Adam showed up.

"Because, if you want a guy, I can find one for you."

"No."

Tony shrugged. "I'm just saying…Mike over at the bank? Great guy. Good job…"

"Did you learn *nothing* from Papa?"

"Pop's mistake was going for Adam. Adam's a bad bet," Tony said. "He's a good guy, but he's shut down emotionally."

"Huh?" Gina shook her head. "You've been reading Vickie's magazines again, haven't you?"

He grinned and the Torino golden eyes twinkled at her. "Gotta keep up. Don't want the wife thinking I'm just a dumb ranch hand."

"Uh-huh. How about you go home and tell her that?"

"What's the rush?" Then he seemed to notice her for the first time. He gave a long, slow whistle. "Wow. You look…did you say you have a *date?*"

Insulted, she demanded, "Why do you sound so surprised?"

"You never go out."

"Not true." Okay, semitrue. She wasn't a shy little wallflower virgin, but she wasn't exactly party central, either. And why couldn't she have had sisters instead of three well-meaning, but interfering older brothers?

"Who's this date with?"

"None of your business. Gee, look at the time."

"Why don't you want to tell me who this guy—"

"Hi, Tony."

They both turned at the sound of the deep voice. Adam stood on her porch, the wash of lamplight spilling out of the house to welcome him. He wore a well-

tailored black suit with a dark red tie and he looked as
at home in the elegantly cut suit as he did in his jeans
and boots. As he looked from her to Tony and back
again, his dark eyes shone with interest and what Gina
suspected was humor.

So how long had he been standing there?

"Adam," Tony said with a nod, stepping out in front
of his sister to hold out one hand.

Adam shook his hand, then shifted his gaze to Gina.
The power of his stare was enough to make her head go
light and her heart jitter in her chest.

"You look lovely," he said.

"Thanks. Um, Tony was just leaving."

"No, I wasn't."

"Well, we *are*," Adam countered and held out one
hand to Gina.

The look on Tony's face was priceless. Gina smiled
as she slipped past her brother to join Adam on the
porch. Then she threw Tony a look over her shoulder.
"Lock up when you leave, okay?"

The restaurant was amazing. Sitting atop a cliff overlooking the ocean, one entire wall of Serenity was glass,
providing a breathtaking view of moonlight, waves
crashing against the rocks below. Overhead lighting in
the sprawling building was deliberately faint, as if each
wall and ceiling sconce had been chosen to define the
darkness rather than defeat it.

The musical clink of crystal and the whisper of
muted conversations were flavored with soft jazz piping

from the three piece band. Completing the atmosphere, each round table boasted a single votive candle and the effect of dozens of flickering flames was nearly magical.

All in all, it had been a perfect evening. Adam was considerate, charming and never even hinted at the deal her father had broached to him. And while Gina was enjoying herself, she'd been dealing with a twist of nerves in her stomach since the hostess had first seated them. Now that dinner was over and they were sipping a last cup of coffee before leaving, time was up.

She either faced Adam with her own deal—or came to her senses and forgot the whole thing. Gina stared out the glass wall beside their table and watched as waves rolled ceaselessly into shore, slamming into the rocks, sending white spray into the air.

"What're you thinking?"

"What?" She turned her head to find Adam watching her with a bemused smile on his face. "I'm sorry. Mind wandering."

"To where, exactly?"

Here it was, she told herself, fingers curling around the fragile handle of her coffee cup. Speak now or forever hold your peace. Funny *that* was the phrase that sprang to mind.

"Adam," she said before she could talk herself out of it, "I know what my father said to you."

His features tightened. "Excuse me?"

Now it was her turn to give him a small smile. Shaking her head, she said, "Forget it. Papa confessed all."

He shifted on his chair, scowled a little and picked

up his coffee cup. "Did he also mention that I turned him down?"

"Yeah, he did." Gina swiveled in her seat, turning her back on the wide vista of ocean and cliffs to face him. "And by the way, thanks."

"No problem." Sitting back in his chair, Adam watched her. Waiting.

"But," she said, "I had to wonder about you asking me out to dinner. I mean, if you weren't interested in buying a bride, why the invitation?"

His mouth flattened into a thin line. "One has nothing to do with the other."

"I don't know," Gina said softly, running the tip of her index finger around the outside rim of the cup. "See, I've had some time to think about all of this…"

"Gina."

"I think that when Papa first—" she paused as if looking for the right word before continuing "—*proposed*, if you'll pardon the pun, his little deal, your first reaction was no. Of course not."

"Exactly," Adam agreed.

"And then…" She smiled when he frowned. "You started thinking. You came outside. You saw Mom and I and you told yourself that maybe it wasn't such a bad idea after all."

Adam straightened in his chair, then leaned over the table, peering directly into her eyes with a hard stare. "I did *not* bring you here so that I could propose to you."

Gina actually laughed at that. "Oh, you wouldn't have done that. Not right away, anyway. You brought me here on a date." She stopped and grinned, looking around the restaurant in approval. "And it's been lovely, by the way. Anyway, after tonight, there would have been other dates. And after a couple of months, you would have proposed."

He stared at her for a long, silent minute and Gina knew that she was right. For whatever reason, Adam had reconsidered her father's offer. Which was good. In a way. Of course, she didn't like the idea that he'd been seriously willing to marry her for his own gain. Actually it made her heart hurt to think about that too long. After all, she'd been in love with Adam King since she was fourteen years old. But at least it made her own plan seem more reasonable.

"Okay, that's enough." He lifted one hand in a silent signal to their server, requesting their check. "I'm sorry you feel this way, but since you do, there's no point in continuing this. I'll take you home."

"Not ready to leave yet," she said, leaning back into her own chair to watch him. "I know you, Adam. And right now, you're a little embarrassed and a lot on the defensive."

"Gina, what I am is sorry that you misunderstood."

"But I didn't," she said. "In fact, I completely understand."

"Understand what?" His tone was clipped, impatient.

"Look, I know how much getting the King holdings back together means to you," Gina said and felt a tug of satisfaction when his eyes flashed at the thought. "I know that you would do just about anything to ensure that happens."

"Believe what you will," Adam said, then paused as the waiter delivered their bill in a sleek, black leather folder. Once the waiter was gone, he continued, "But there are limits to what I'm willing to do. Lines I won't cross."

"Well, if that's true, it's a shame."

He blinked at her. "I beg your pardon?"

"Adam, I know you want the land. I know you don't want to be married. And I know you don't like being manipulated any more than I do."

He nodded. "Go on."

"See, I've had a little time to think about this and I'm pretty sure I've come up with a solution that'll work for both of us."

Still scowling, he folded his arms across his chest. "Now, this I've got to hear."

She smiled and realized that the flutter of nerves that had been irritating her all night were suddenly gone. Because she'd finally brought everything into the light? Because she knew that what she was doing was the right thing? Or was it the wine they'd had with dinner?

Didn't matter now, she thought. She was in way too deep to quit at this point.

"Well," she said, letting the words tumble from her mouth in a rush, "the thing is, I'm willing to discuss my father's offer to you."

Adam was stunned. He couldn't believe she was saying any of this. First off, that she *knew* about Sal's offer was bad enough. The fact that she'd guessed Adam had reconsidered the deal was disquieting. Did she really know him as well as she seemed to? And why in the hell would a woman like Gina be willing to consider such an insulting bargain?

In the candlelight, Gina's eyes seemed to shine with the deep, rich glow of antique gold. Her skin was soft and smooth and lightly tanned. He'd hardly been able to look away from her all night. His gaze caught in the tumble of thick, dark curls that hung down her back in waves so silky they invited a man's hands to delve into them. Her black dress hugged every curve—and she had good ones—and her long, tanned legs looked amazing in high-heeled sandals that should have been impossible to walk in.

All night, she'd tormented him, simply by being Gina. How had he not noticed years ago just how beguiling she was? Had he really been blind enough to dismiss his little neighbor because he'd once known her as a pigtailed child? Well, she was all grown-up now and surprisingly enough, was damn calm and accepting about the bargain her father had offered.

And somehow, that worried him more than anything else.

"Why would you want to do that?" he asked and watched as something not quite identifiable flashed in her eyes.

"I have my reasons," she said, then smiled at him again.

Adam hissed in a breath. She really was beautiful—but it was more than that. It was something indefinable. Something that tugged at him. Prodded him. Why else would he have considered Sal's proposition for more than an instant?

"What are these reasons?" he asked.

"Mine," she said and didn't offer any more.

This wasn't going at all the way Adam had expected. What was it about the Torinos that could keep him off balance? First her father, now her. *He* was the one in charge of situations. On top of everything. He knew what the other guy was thinking, what his next move would be and exactly the right countermove to ensure that Adam King got exactly what he set out to get.

Having the tables turned on him wasn't something he appreciated. And it was damned uncomfortable to have someone know him as well as Gina seemed to. At the moment, she was watching him with patient understanding glimmering in her eyes and it irritated him that she was so damned complacent while he felt off balance.

Clearly then, it was time to take charge again. Time to let her know that he wouldn't be twisted around and made to feel as if he'd taken a wrong step. Time to let her know that this date was over.

"Gina…" He flipped open the check folder, tucked a credit card into the pocket, then closed the whole thing and set it on the edge of the table. Their waiter rushed by a moment later and took it away. "I don't know what you're getting at, but I won't be maneuvered. By you… or your father."

She laughed, damn it, and he was both annoyed and charmed. "I don't see what's so funny."

"Of course you don't," she said and reached across the table to pat his hand as she would have an excitable kid. "But come on, Adam. We've known each other way too long for you to put on the big crabby attitude and expect me to either salute or slink away!"

He ground his back teeth together and hissed in a breath. "Fine. Say what you want to say, then I'll take you home."

She shook her head and smiled again. "Charming to the last." Before he could say anything to that, she spoke up again, quickly. "Okay. To the point. I'll marry you, Adam, so you can get the land. But I have a condition."

"I can't wait to hear it."

"I want a child."

Adam felt the slam of those words crush into his chest and he could have sworn he felt his heart actually stop. Her eyes were clear and steady. Her features calm. Her manner at ease. All the while, his insides were churning and it felt as though the air was on fire. Otherwise, why would his lungs be burning with every breath?

"You can't be serious."

"Completely," she assured him and her face softened, her mouth curving gently. "I know what you went through with the loss of your son and—"

While he was reeling, the waiter brought their check back to be signed. Adam took it, glanced at it, added a hefty tip and signed his name. Taking his credit card and the receipt, he tucked them into his wallet and only when he was finished did he look up at Gina again.

"I don't discuss my son. Ever." His loss was just that. *His* loss. He'd survived. Put the past behind him and that was where he intended to keep it. Those memories, that pain had nothing to do with his life or his world today.

"Fine."

"And I'm not interested in being a father again."

"I don't need your help in parenting my child, Adam," she said and her voice went suddenly as chill as his own. "All I need from you is your sperm."

"Why are you doing this?"

"Because I want to be a mother." She leaned back in her chair, fiddled with the handle of her coffee cup and lowered her gaze to the tabletop. "My brothers' kids are beautiful and I love them with all my heart. But I don't want to spend the rest of my life being the favorite auntie. I want a child of my own. I don't want to be married any more than you do—don't worry about that. But I do want a baby. The way I see it—" she lifted her gaze to his "—this bargain satisfies both parties. You get your land. I get the baby I want."

He was already shaking his head. Instinct, he supposed, when she spoke again.

"Think about this before you turn me down. I'll marry you. Be your wife in every way. As soon as I'm pregnant, you get the land and we get a divorce. And I'll sign whatever you want me to sign, exempting you from any responsibility toward me or my child." Her gaze was steady on his as she added, "It's a good deal, Adam. For both of us."

She had him in a corner. He hadn't expected her to know about her father's proposition—let alone come up with one of her own. The tantalizing idea that he could, in a few short months, have the King family ranch whole and secure again was a tempting one.

He had to give Gina credit. She'd thought this out and had come up with a bargain sure to be tempting to him. And the fact that she, too, was getting something out of the deal made him feel less like some robber baron.

Yet the thought of fathering another child wasn't something he'd even considered. A pain he refused to recognize thrummed inside him for a long moment. Then it was gone, because he'd had years to learn how to distance himself from emotional distress.

Besides, it wasn't as if this would be a real marriage. A genuine family situation. This was something completely different and apart from the norm. Gina knew him. And she didn't want a husband any more than he wanted a wife. She wanted a child, he wanted his land. A win-win bargain. All it would take was being married to a desirable woman for a few months.

How bad could that be?

"Well, Adam," she said softly, her voice nearly lost in the quiet rhythm of the jazz spilling through the restaurant. "What do you say?"

He stood up and held out one hand to help her from her chair. When she was standing, too, he shook the hand she held out and said, "Gina, you've got yourself a bargain."

Five

Things happened pretty quickly after the proposal.

Within a few days, Adam had arranged for a marriage license—apparently it paid to be one of the wealthiest men in California. And, since Adam was anxious to get their bargain up and running, there was no time for the big, fancy wedding Gina's mom had always dreamed of.

Instead Adam, Gina and her parents took one of the King family jets to Vegas.

"Not exactly the wedding every little girl dreams of," Gina whispered to herself as she looked around the interior of the luxury garden the ceremony was taking place in.

The walls were painted a soft summer-blue, with white clouds sponge-painted on as accents. There were tall pedestals holding elegant sprays of silk flowers and the white carpeted main aisle still held the footprints of the couple who had been married before them. Classical music piped in from overhead speakers and Gina's fingers tightened on the handle of her complimentary bouquet.

Gina's heart did a bump and roll in her chest and she was very glad she'd insisted on doing some prewedding shopping in San Jose. The deep yellow dress she wore made her feel beautiful and Gina had known instinctively that she would need all the confidence she could find.

"You're sure about this, Gina?"

She turned her head to look at her father and swallowed hard before answering. "Yes, Papa. I'm sure."

Of course she was sure. She'd been in love with Adam King for what felt like forever. She'd dreamed of this day for years. Of course, in all of those dreams, Adam had loved *her,* too. Her dream groom was happy and smiling, surrounded by his brothers, looking at Gina with desire flashing in his eyes.

So okay, the reality was a little disappointing. Still, she thought, shifting her gaze to the head of the aisle where her groom waited. She was marrying Adam.

And Gina'd had a few days to completely rethink this bargain she'd made with her about-to-be husband. This was a business deal, certainly. Adam was getting what he wanted out of it and she would be getting the baby her heart craved.

But over the last couple of days, she'd begun to imagine a slightly different outcome to this bargain. If she were willing to take a chance, to risk her heart, she might find a way to get everything she'd ever wanted.

All she had to do was find a way to break Adam's defences. Her insides fisted and released at the daunting prospect. She'd come this far, why not take that extra step? She only needed time. Gina was sure that once Adam and she were married, he would see the truth she'd always known. That they could be a great couple.

She sucked in a deep breath as that thought shot through her brain and sent a current of adrenaline to the pit of her stomach.

"You don't look so good, honey," her father said.

"I'm fine, Papa. Really. It's all good. See?" She gave her father a wide, phony smile that, thankfully, he accepted at face value. "Let's get this done, okay?"

"Yes," he said. "Your mother looks anxious."

She did, Gina thought, sliding a quick look at her mom. Actually her mother looked as though she wanted to give Adam a stern lecture about how to treat her daughter. Best to head that off at the pass. Teresa Torino was already a little snippy about Gina marrying a man she didn't think loved her.

The string quartet suddenly began playing the solemn strains of the Wedding March. Gina's stomach lurched, but she fought down the last bits of hesitation she felt and started down the aisle on her father's arm.

Not a very long walk, really, but with every step, she moved further away from the life she knew and closer to the life she'd always wanted.

Adam's dark chocolate eyes were narrowed on her. His features were stiff and the smile she'd hoped to see didn't appear. But then, this wasn't a love match, was it? His gaze was steady, but blank, giving away no hint at all of what he was feeling, thinking. And Gina could only hope he wasn't able to read her emotions any better than she could his.

At the head of the aisle, Sal laid Gina's hand in Adam's and stepped back to join his wife.

Adam gave her a brief smile that didn't do a thing to ease the cool indifference on his features.

When the minister started talking, she found it hard to hear him over the thundering of her own heartbeat. She was only able to catch every other word, but they were the important ones. The ones that would change her life. At least for now.

"I will," Adam said and Gina swayed a little at the impact of two small words. And her heartbeat seemed to pound out, *if only.*

Then it was her turn. She felt Adam's big hand enveloping hers and focused on the minister. Here it was. Her last chance to back out. Or, she thought, the beginning of the biggest gamble she would ever make.

There was a long pause when the minister stopped speaking and the silence in the chapel was nearly deafening. She felt Adam watching her, waiting for her answer.

"I will," she said finally and it was as if the room took a relieved breath and let it out again.

Adam slipped a ring on her finger and as the short, round minister finished up the brief ceremony, Gina looked down at her hand. A wide, thick gold band glittered up at her. There were no stones set into the precious metal. No delicate carvings or etchings that proclaimed a deeply felt connection between two people.

It was plain.

Impersonal.

Much like her marriage.

Then Adam held her shoulders, pulled her in close and gave her a quick, hard kiss, sealing the bargain Gina really hoped wouldn't come back to haunt them both.

For the first time in far too long, Adam felt as though he'd somehow lost control of a situation. And he didn't like the sensation.

Yet somehow, he'd ended up here, in the Presidential Suite of Dreams, the newest, most opulent hotel yet to be built in Las Vegas, waiting for his bride to join him.

"Bride." He shook his head and poured himself a glass of the champagne chilling in a sterling silver ice bucket atop the table set up for them on the suite's private balcony. If ever a man needed a drink, it was now.

Taking a sip, he looked out over the view sprawling for miles. In the distance, he saw the purple smudge of mountains, crowned by the first stars blinking into life in the night sky. The setting sun still provided an orange glow on the horizon and in the streets far below him, other lights in dizzying colors and patterns glittered and shone like jewels in a treasure chest.

From thirty stories up, Las Vegas was beautiful. Up close and personal, Adam knew that the tattered edges of the city were much easier to spot. Much like his marriage, he thought wryly, taking a long sip of the cold, bubbly wine. From a distance, people would assume that he and Gina had been swept away by passion. Only they would ever know the cold, hard truth.

Which was what, exactly?

"That you're a hard ass," he muttered. "Willing to use a woman to get what you want. Ready to create a child and walk away from it without a second thought."

Surprisingly enough, that little jolt of reality bothered Adam more than he'd thought it would. He scrubbed one hand across his jaw, stared off into the night and reminded himself that this had been Gina's idea. She wasn't a victim in this but a willing conspirator.

When his cell phone rang, though, Adam grabbed it, grateful to have something besides his own thoughts to concentrate on. A glance at the screen had him sighing. Flipping the phone open, he asked, "What is it, Travis?"

"What is it?" his brother echoed. "You're not serious. I just talked to Esperanza and she told me you were in Las Vegas getting married."

Adam sighed. His housekeeper had a big mouth. "That's right."

"To *Gina.*"

"That's right."

"So my invitation got lost in the mail?" Travis demanded.

Setting his champagne glass down on the stone balcony railing, Adam shoved his free hand into his pants pocket and tightened his grip on the phone. "It was a small ceremony."

"Yeah? I hear her parents were there."

"And now they're gone. The jet took them home this afternoon."

"Uh-huh. Any reason why you didn't want *your* family there?"

"It's not what you think."

"Really? Because what I think is you just married a kid we've known all our lives without bothering to tell your brothers."

"She's not a kid," Adam said tightly, his fingers clenching down hard on his phone. "Hasn't been one for a long time. And since when do I report to you and Jackson?"

"You don't," Travis countered. "But there's something fishy going on here, Adam. This 'marriage' of yours wouldn't have anything to do with getting that damned land, would it?"

There was a long, silent moment as Adam got a tight rein on the temper screaming inside, then Travis muttered, "You really are a son of a bitch, aren't you?"

"She knew what she was doing." Hadn't he told himself that over and over again since agreeing to the bargain Gina had offered him?

"I doubt it."

Shoving his free hand through his hair, Adam shot a look behind him to assure himself that Gina hadn't come out of the bathroom yet. Then he argued, "You know, Travis, you're not exactly the poster child for the better treatment of women."

"That's not the point," his brother snapped.

"It's exactly the point. I don't tell you to stop squiring bimbos around—or to avoid the damn paparazzi that follow you everywhere. So butt the hell out of my life, little brother."

"You screw with Gina and her father will make your life a living hell," Travis warned.

"Because my life now is just rainbows and kittens, right?"

"Damn, Adam," his brother said on a sigh. "When the hell did you get so cold?"

"When wasn't I?" Adam asked and snapped the phone closed before Travis could get started again. Then he turned the phone off before Jackson could call and have his say. He didn't need to hear his brothers' opinions. He knew going into this what they'd think. And it didn't matter a damn.

He and Gina were two consenting adults. Their marriage—such as it was—was nobody else's business.

"Well," Gina said from behind him. "You look like you want to take a bite out of somebody."

He turned, schooling his features into the calm, unreadable mask he used with everyone but his brothers. But even as he fought for distance, the sight of her had a hot ball of lust pooling in his belly.

In the pale wash of the soft balcony lights, she looked almost otherworldly. Her nightgown was short, stopping midthigh. A deep, rich red, the satin fabric clung to her skin, outlining every curve and exposing what looked like a mile of leg. The bodice was red lace and it cupped her breasts like a lover's hands. Her hair hung loose and thick over her shoulders, the untamed curls enticing him. She smelled like heaven—peaches and flowers and the smile she gave him was knowing and nervous at the same time.

"You look," he said, "beautiful."

Her smile brightened. "I feel silly." Then she smoothed one hand over her stomach as if trying to calm butterflies and he wondered if she was regretting making the offer that had brought them to this place.

Adam poured her a flute of champagne and when she took it from him, her fingertips grazed his skin and heat exploded. He ignored it for the moment. "Why silly?"

She waved a hand at her negligee and shrugged. "I went out and bought this, especially for tonight and I probably shouldn't have. It's not like this is an ordinary wedding night, is it?"

"No," he conceded and found he couldn't take his gaze from her. From the curve of her breasts. From the hard tips of her nipples, pressing against the dark red lace. "It's not. But it *is* the beginning of our bargain."

"True," she said and took a sip of champagne. Then she licked her bottom lip and everything in Adam tightened painfully.

"And," he said, taking a swallow himself, "for myself, I can tell you I appreciate your shopping talents."

Her eyes widened, then she smiled more easily. "Thanks." Stepping out onto the balcony, heedless of the negligee she wore, she looked out at the view and sighed. "It's gorgeous, isn't it?"

"Yeah, it is." But he wasn't looking at the neon-lit desert or the mountains beyond. He was staring at her. He took another drink of champagne, hoping the icy wine would spill into his blood and cool it off a little. No such luck.

She glanced at him over her shoulder. "Thanks for flying Mom and Dad here and home again."

He shrugged. He hadn't minded bringing Sal and Teresa along, though he also hadn't been sorry to see them go. Teresa especially. The woman had looked daggers at him all day. "Seemed important that they be there for you."

"But you didn't want your brothers?"

He leaned back against the stone railing. "I thought it would be easier all around if we kept it simple."

"Right," she said. "Simple. Do they know?"

"About us?" he asked. When she nodded he said, "They do now. Esperanza told them."

She smiled. "How'd they take it?"

He looked at her and lied. It didn't matter a damn to him what his brothers thought about this. "Fine. Talked to Travis a few minutes ago."

A desert wind sailed past them and Gina shivered.

"You're cold."

"A little."

He set his glass down on the table and went to her. A short walk and yet Adam felt as if each step were measured. He was about to seal their bargain. There would be no going back. And if he woke up tomorrow regretting what he'd done tonight, then he'd have to live with it.

But then, he'd had plenty of practice living with uncomfortable realities.

"Come here." Pulling her close, he wrapped both arms around her, drawing her in, her back to his front. Heat pooled between them, seeping into his bones, firing his blood. Adam felt that sweet rush of need fill him and he gritted his teeth to maintain control. He wouldn't be led around by his groin. This bargain was one thing.

Releasing control was something else. Something he wouldn't allow to happen.

"Adam," Gina said, her voice so soft, he almost missed it. "I know this was my idea, but I suddenly don't know what to do next."

"We do what we planned to do. We make a child together."

She shivered again and pressed harder against him. "Right. I mean, that is what this is all about. So," she said, turning in his arms to look up at him, "no point in wasting time, is there?"

She lifted her arms and hooked them behind his neck. Then she went up on her toes, tilted her head and kissed him. The soft, almost hesitant touch of her mouth to his lit up Adam's insides brighter than any of the neon stretching out across the desert beneath them.

He'd spent the last five years alone. Pushing aside wants and needs he didn't have the time or patience to deal with. Now, there was no reason to hold back. So he didn't. Wrapping his arms around her middle, he held her to him with a fierce grip and took her mouth with all the pent-up hunger he felt surging within.

She groaned a little as he parted her lips with his tongue

and tasted her warmth. She sighed and fed the fires racing through his blood. He held her tighter to him, grinding his hips against hers, needing that sweet pressure.

Again and again, his tongue delved inside, claiming her, taking all she had to give. He allowed his control to slip and he surrendered to the waves of desire crashing inside him. He slid his hands up and down her back, cupping her bottom, stroking her spine, threading through the thick mass of curls that fell in a dark curtain around her.

Her scent filled him. Her taste enflamed him. And his body physically ached to have her under him.

He tore his mouth from hers, like a man struggling for air before he drowned. Gina swayed unsteadily, but Adam's arms were like steel bands, supporting her, holding her. She tipped her head back to stare up at the desert sky while Adam's mouth moved up and down her neck, nibbling, licking, tasting. She felt like a banquet laid out before a starving man.

She felt needed. Wanted.

If only she also felt loved.

But when that thought appeared in her mind, she shut it off instantly. For now, it was enough that *she* loved. It was enough that she finally knew what it was to have Adam King's legendary focus directed at *her*. And she wanted more. She wanted it all. Tomorrow, she would begin the pretense of a marriage they'd decided on. But tonight was her wedding night and she wanted to remember every moment of it.

When Adam swept her up into his arms, she gasped.

Then she looked into his dark, dark eyes. She smiled at him, but there was no glint of humor or warmth in his gaze.

Only need.

A part of her saddened at that knowledge, but she fought that sensation back, cupped his face in her hands and said, "We can do this, right?"

His mouth quirked. "Oh, we're *going* to do this, Gina. Now."

A swirl of something delicious swept through her, heating her core, making her blood run thick. She took a deep breath as he started to carry her back into the suite. "I wasn't talking about sex, Adam. I was talking about our bargain."

He stopped dead just inside the French doors. Looking down at her, he asked, "Second thoughts?"

And thirds. And fourths, she thought, but didn't say. "No. Just making sure you're not having any."

He held her tighter, his right hand sliding up her thigh. "Once I make a deal, I stick with it."

"Of course you do," she said, nodding even as she let one hand slide from his neck, down his throat to his chest. His heartbeat thudded beneath her hand and she knew, whether his features were stoic or not, he wasn't as calm as he pretended. "And so do I," she added.

"Good to know. Now, how about we start taking care of business?"

"That might be easier for me if we didn't call it business," she pointed out, unbuttoning the front of his shirt.

He shook his head and his eyes seemed to swallow

her. "This is business, though, Gina. Nothing more. Don't fool yourself. Don't pretend that this is a real marriage. You'll only be hurt in the end."

Well, nothing like a cold flood of reality to warm you up for the night's festivities. He was making sure she didn't put too much of herself into this bargain they'd struck. And maybe assuring himself that there wouldn't be any hard feelings when it was done.

That was fine with Gina. He could think what he wanted. Her thoughts she would keep to herself. Her dreams would remain hidden and secret, locked away in her heart. For now, she had the man she'd always wanted and she wasn't going to let doubts or fears about the future ruin the night she'd been waiting for all of her life.

Six

His hands on her bare skin felt wicked. Felt…right. She felt as though she'd been waiting for this one particular moment all of her life. The moment when she would have Adam to herself. When she would take him into her body and hold him there.

Her stomach was spinning, a weird combination of nerves and champagne. Her brain was racing, alternately shouting out warnings and egging her on. But Gina didn't need urging. She unbuttoned his shirt and slid one hand across his bare chest. She felt his body jerk at the slight touch and knew that he wanted her as badly as she wanted him.

The plush, gigantic bedroom was dark, but for the desert moonlight streaming through the open balcony doors. The white sheers hanging there fluttered and swayed seductively in a soft wind and the scent of desert sage wafted into the room.

The bed was wide and high and covered in a luxurious white silk duvet that had already been turned down for the night. A mountain of pillows were stacked against the black iron headboard. Adam carried her with quick steps, right to the edge of the bed. Then he set her on her feet, grabbed the edge of the duvet and tossed it heedlessly to the foot of the mattress.

Gina's knees went a little wobbly, so she locked them just to make sure she didn't do anything totally stupid like topple over. In the semidarkness, Adam's chocolate-brown eyes looked nearly black as he stared down at her. His mouth was thin, tight, as if he were holding on to the ragged edge of control.

Well, she didn't want him controlled.

She wanted him wild and eager and spontaneous. Biting down on her bottom lip, Gina lifted her hands to the front of his shirt and undid the rest of the buttons. While he stood there, unmoving, she pushed the shirt off his shoulders and down his arms, to drop to the floor. Then she let her hands slide across his hard, warm chest. Felt the soft brush of the dark hair that whorled across his tanned skin. Felt him flinch when her thumbnail stroked the tip of one flat nipple.

He grabbed her waist, his hands big and hard and strong. Then he yanked her close, holding her to him so that she felt the thick ridge of his arousal. Looming over her, he stared into her eyes and Gina felt the heat of that gaze fire up her insides like a match to a pool of gasoline.

His mouth came down on hers with a fierceness she hadn't expected. His tongue parted her lips and she opened for him, inviting his exploration. Their tongues twisted together in a heated dance that was only a prelude of things to come. Gina's breath caught in her chest and her head began to swim.

Her body alive with sensation, she groaned from the back of her throat when Adam's hands slid up to cover her breasts. He stroked her, causing the lace to rub across her already sensitized nipples with a delicious friction that heated her core and drove her to the edge of madness. Each touch was a fire. Each touch only made her want the next. Each stroking caress tautened the tension already coiled inside her.

When he tore his mouth from hers to lick and nibble his way down the length of her throat, Gina tipped her head back to give him more access. His mouth was a wonder. His hands at her breasts a lovely torture.

Then he shifted position, lifting his hands to the thin, ribbonlike straps of her nightgown and he slid them down over her shoulders. Gina shivered a little at the cool glide of his fingertips against her skin, then shivered harder as he pushed the nightgown down and off to puddle at her feet.

The desert wind was cool as it brushed into the room and danced across her skin, but Adam's gaze kept her too warm to notice. He looked her up and down, then looking directly into her eyes, he lifted her again and dropped her onto the mattress.

She bounced once, then settled back against the backdrop of pillows, a lavender scent drifting to her like a lost memory of summer. Her center, hot and aching, had her shifting on the smooth, cool sheets, looking for the release her body already clamored for.

Gina watched as Adam stripped quickly out of his clothes. Her mouth went dry when he was naked and her gaze dropped down to the incredible, hard length of him.

Gina forced herself to relax, ordering her legs to loosen and the hard knot of worry to dissolve in the back of her mind. She'd known him her whole life practically. She knew he wouldn't hurt her. Knew that even if he didn't love her, he would take care of her.

Then he was moving over her and her brain shut down. All she had the strength to focus on were the sensations rippling through her body in relentless waves. His hands, his mouth, his body, lavished attention on her. Every inch of her felt alive and tingling.

He closed his mouth over one nipple and Gina nearly leaped off the bed. His lips and tongue and teeth tormented her until she whimpered and shifted beneath him, trying to get closer. Her hands slid up and down his broad, muscled back and her short, neat fingernails scraped over his skin.

He groaned against her and Gina's hips rocked into him. She lifted one leg, trailing the sole of her foot along his leg, desperate to touch him. To feel all of him.

"You smell incredible," he whispered, moving his mouth from one nipple to the other.

Gina made a mental note to buy more of the citrus/flowery body lotion she preferred.

She stared up at the moonlit ceiling above them and stared blindly as shadows shifted and waved against the pale lemon paint. Her breath struggled in and out of her lungs. Her body burned and when he moved lazily and she felt that hard, thick length of him rub her core, she gasped and arched higher. "Adam…"

"I know," he whispered, lifting his head to look into her eyes.

She met his gaze with a dazed look, and saw the wildness in his eyes. Gina took his face between her palms and drew his head to her. She wanted to kiss him. To feel that connection of want and desire build between them. To have his body atop hers, his heartbeat thundering in time with her own.

The kiss seared them both. Heat and passion trembled in the air and Gina put all she had into it. She gave him her heart in that kiss, whether he knew it or not. She poured the feelings she'd so carefully banked for years into that one instant of mouths and hearts blending and when she felt him shift, positioning himself between her legs, she kissed him even harder.

She wanted his mouth on hers when he entered her and so she moved with him, spreading her thighs, lifting her hips while at the same time keeping her lips firmly attached to his. His tongue swept across the inside of her mouth as he pushed his body into hers.

He lifted his head, looked down into her eyes and held perfectly still, allowing her body to adjust to the presence of his. Gina groaned, digging her head into the mound of pillows behind her. She wriggled her hips, lifting, shifting, feeling him slowly sink deeper within and as he claimed her, inch by inch, she felt her body stretching to accommodate him.

"Oh, my…" She let out a breath on a sigh and looked up at him smiling down at her.

She smiled, then gasped as he rocked his hips, pushing higher within.

He eased back, sitting on his haunches, scooping his hands under bottom, lifting her hips a little, pulling her body down harder on his. "We're just getting started."

"Oh, boy."

His thumb stroked the hard, hot nub of flesh at her center and Gina's back arched high off the mattress. Her hands scrabbled for something to hold on to and her fingers curled into the silken sheets beneath her. It didn't help; she still felt her world swaying and tilting weirdly around her as he moved, withdrawing only to plunge inside her again.

His fingers continued to rub and stroke her most sensitive spot, until Gina was writhing in his grasp, twisting her hips, unconsciously drawing his body deeper into hers. *Too much,* she thought. *It was all too much. She couldn't handle so many sensations. So much pleasure. Surely there was a saturation point where her body would simply dissolve and her mind become a puddle of goo.*

And then he showed her differently. Reaching for her,

he took hold of her waist and lifted her off the bed, settling her down on his lap, so that his length was deep inside her. Gina looked directly into his eyes as he guided her in an easy rhythm that had her rocking on him, tantalizing them both.

The wind slid into the room, and the scent of sage melded with the scent of their heated bodies and the bloom of sex. Skin met skin, breath intermingled and their sighs became a symphony of want and desperate need.

Moving on him, sliding her body onto his, Gina found a magic she'd never expected. Her body quivered, her insides straining, reaching toward the release that built within. Her heart swelled, filling with the thrill of being a part of Adam at long last. And her mind raced with images she couldn't allow herself to indulge in. Images of Adam's eyes shining with love for her. Images of the two of them, together. Always.

But even though a part of her mourned, she relished the feelings coursing through her. She looked into Adam's eyes, lost herself in those dark, dark depths and watched as passion ignited, firing sparks she knew *she* had brought him.

Tension coiled tighter, tighter. Her body trembled. She held her breath and when she slid down his length one more time, the first explosion smashed into her.

"Adam!" She gripped his shoulders hard, trying to keep herself stable in a suddenly wildly *un*stable world.

"Let go," he ordered, his voice a low rush of sound, scraping from his throat. "Let yourself go, Gina."

She did. She couldn't help it. Didn't want to try.

Instead she gave herself up to the incredible sensations coursing through her. Riding wave after wave of tremors that continued to ripple through her long after that first tremendous burst had diminished.

And when Gina thought she couldn't take another moment, there was more. Adam dropped one hand to the spot where their bodies joined. Once again, he rubbed that tender piece of flesh that seemed to hold a store of electrical-like nerve endings. She jolted in his embrace and instinctively ground her hips against him.

"Adam..." She whispered his name now, a sigh of pleasure.

"Again," he said, pushing her even higher than she'd been before. Her mind splintered, her body shattered and when she felt herself falling, she heard Adam groan and knew he was taking the fall with her.

Adam's heart was racing and his body felt more lax than it had in years. He turned his head on the pillows to look at the woman lying beside him. Her eyes were closed, and she lay, one arm flung back behind her head, the other reaching toward him across the wide expanse of mattress.

Her skin was softer than the silk they lay on and her hair was a tumble of curls he couldn't seem to touch enough. Her sighs, her pleasures, tempted him to take her again and again. Even now, he felt himself stir, his body already hardening for her.

"You're watching me."

"Your eyes are closed," he pointed out. "How do you know?"

"I can feel it," she said and turned her head on the pillows to look at him. A smile curved her delectable mouth and Adam felt another jolt of desire slam into him. Maybe this bargain between them hadn't been such a good idea after all, he thought, at the realization that in the last hour with her, he'd *felt* more than he had in the last five years.

"Now you're frowning," Gina said, rolling to her side, unabashedly naked, her tanned, smooth skin nearly glowing in the moonlight. "No frowns allowed."

"Don't know if I can accommodate that request," he said.

She sighed, pushed one hand through her hair, throwing the thick mass over her shoulder. "Adam, you don't have to be worried."

"What makes you think I'm worried?"

She laughed and the sound of it sang through the otherwise quiet room. "Please. I know exactly what you're thinking."

"Is that right?" Turning to face her, he went up on one elbow. "Then what am I thinking?" he said with a slight smile.

She stroked the tips of her fingers across the sheet covered distance separating them and Adam wished she were touching him.

"That's easy. You're worrying that you made a mistake by agreeing to this little bargain."

He opened his mouth to argue, more because he hated knowing that she could read him so well than anything else, but she spoke up again.

"You're worried that I'm building up romantic notions. Hoping you'll fall in love with me."

He frowned harder, because damn it, she was right. He had been worrying about that, too. But he wouldn't admit it. "Wrong. I know you're not doing anything that foolish." At least, he hoped not. "After all, this was your idea."

"True." She smiled and rolled onto her stomach, coming closer to him. Close enough that he couldn't keep himself from reaching one hand out to stroke the line of her spine, the curve of her bottom. And he wondered how in the hell she'd managed to get a tan all over.

Shaking his head to get rid of the image of her stretched out naked in the sun, Adam asked, "Why?"

"Why what?" She looked at him, her golden eyes shining in the darkness.

"Why'd you offer me this bargain? I mean, I know you want a baby. I understand that. What I want to know is why me?"

She stretched lazily, moving that tanned, toned body on the white silk sheets until blood vessels started popping in Adam's brain.

"Easily enough explained, Adam," she said, glancing at him. "You wanted the land, so that gave me some leverage…."

"Yes…" He wanted the rest of her reason.

"And, I've known you forever, Adam. I like you. I think you like me—"

He nodded. He did like Gina. He'd just never paid much attention to that fact over the years. She was younger than he was, so they hadn't spent much time together when they were kids. Then, when they were grown, he'd had other priorities.

"—it seemed like the perfect answer to both of our problems." She lifted one hand to him and stroked her palm across his chest. Adam sucked in a gulp of air at the heat that instantly shot through him. "And…I think the two of us will make a beautiful baby."

A slice of something cold and dark cut through his mind at those words. He'd once made a vow to never have another child. To never open himself up to that kind of risk again. But this was different, he reasoned, so he pushed those thoughts into a corner of his mind. He'd made this bargain and he'd honor it. The child he and Gina made between them wouldn't be a part of his life. He wouldn't know it. Love it. Or lose it. In fact, best to not think about it at all.

"I'm sorry," she whispered and Adam cut her a look. "About what?"

"Talking about the baby I want must make you remember your son."

Adam froze. He felt his features tighten and everything in him go hard and still as glass. Memories jumped into his mind, but he refused to acknowledge them. He turned them off as easily as punching the remote button aimed at a television. He'd had a lot of practice.

He wasn't open to talking about the son he'd lost five years before and they might as well get that straight right up front. "I don't talk about him. Ever."

Her eyes went soft in sympathy and Adam resented it. He didn't need her feeling sorry for him.

"I understand."

"You couldn't possibly," he told her.

A silent second or two passed before Gina said, "Fine, you're right. I don't understand. I hope I never learn the kind of pain you experienced and—"

He caught her hand in his and gave it a hard squeeze. Just enough to get her to stop talking. How the hell had they gotten onto the subject of his lost family anyway? Wasn't their bargain supposed to be about sex, plain and simple? "What part of 'I don't talk about it' didn't you get?"

She pulled her hand free of his, pushed herself up on the bed and leaned in close to him. Staring into his eyes, it looked as though she were searching for something, some sign that there was warmth hidden somewhere inside him. Adam could have told her to not bother looking.

After a long moment, Gina leaned in even further and kissed him, briefly, softly. "I get it, Adam. The subject's off-limits."

"Good."

"I don't want to talk anyway." Gina stroked his cheek with her palm and drew his head closer to hers.

"That's good, too." At her touch, his body heated and was instantly ready for her again. He'd been too long without a woman, that was all. He'd been a damn recluse for five years, with only the occasional, temporary woman to ease needs that couldn't be denied any longer.

That explained why his response to Gina was so overwhelming. It was just biological, that was all. It wasn't about her. It was about sex. Need.

And when she moved into him, he kept telling himself that, even as he inhaled her scent, drawing it deep inside him. Even as he twisted his hand into her hair, letting the silky feel of it slide over his skin. Even as he took her mouth and tasted the sweetness that was Gina alone.

He couldn't—wouldn't—allow anything else.

She tried to roll over in his arms, but he kept her on her stomach and shifted enough that he could trail kisses along the length of her spine. Such soft, honey-brown skin. Such long lines and rich curves. He heard her sigh and felt her tremble as his left hand swept down to stroke her bottom. He glanced at her, saw her eyes closed, her hands fisted in the bank of pillows.

"Adam…"

"We have all night, Gina," he said and suddenly knew that he wanted every moment of the night. He wanted her over him, under him. He wanted to taste and explore every glorious inch of her and then he wanted to start all over again.

Fire erupted in his blood as she moved on the sheets and he knew he had to have her. No more thinking. No more worrying about tomorrow or the day after that. For now, he would waste no more time with her.

Flipping her over with a quick twist, he grinned when she smiled up at him and lifted her arms in welcome. He slid into her embrace, covering her body with his and when he entered her, she arched her hips to take him completely. To hold him deep inside her heat. And Adam closed his mind to everything but her.

They moved together in a rhythm that left them both breathless. Bodies sang, minds emptied and when the first flash of release slammed into Gina, Adam held on to her, watching her eyes, dazzled with pleasure as he surrendered himself to the glory waiting for him.

Seven

Thanks to Esperanza Sanchez, Adam's longtime housekeeper, Gina was pretty sure she'd gained five pounds in four days. The older woman was so happy to see Adam married again, she hadn't stopped cooking all week. And every time Gina tried to help out in the kitchen, straighten up the living room or even to dust, she was shooed out of the room and told to go spend time with her new husband.

Not as easy as it sounded.

Esperanza was determined to see that Gina felt at home. Even if Adam was a little less than welcoming. Staring into a full-length mirror in the bedroom she now shared with Adam, Gina wasn't looking at her own reflection so much as at the gigantic bed behind her.

That was the only place she felt as though Adam was glad to have her in his home.

"Happy to have me in his bed anyway," she muttered and tried to find the bright spot in that statement. At least they shared passion. At least they connected occasionally. Even if it was only physically.

"Pitiful, Gina, just pitiful." She shook her head, met her own gaze in the mirror and gave her reflection one last glance. Not exactly a femme fatale, she admitted. In her pink T-shirt, worn jeans and boots, she looked more like a ranch hand than a newlywed. Her long dark hair hung down her back in a single braid and her eyes looked huge in her face.

She'd had a lot of hopes for this bargain. Had counted on Adam being a little easier to maneuver than he was proving. Instead he seemed determined to keep to himself. To keep their relationship as superficial as possible, despite the fact that they were married and living together.

Gina turned away, opened the French doors to their bedroom terrace and stepped out onto the glossy wood floor. The early morning sky was deep blue, but there were storm clouds banking out over the ocean. Now why, she wondered, did that sound like a perfect metaphor for her marriage?

They'd been back from Vegas for nearly a week, and it was as if that brief "honeymoon" had never happened. She leaned both hands on the second-story balcony railing and curled her fingers over the sun-warmed decorative iron. The minute they'd arrived back at the ranch,

Adam had closed himself off. She actually felt like they were a couple those days and nights together. It was as if a switch inside him had been flipped. He'd become the recluse he'd been for five long years. She hardly saw him during the day and when she did, he was distant, if polite. The only time he warmed to her was at night.

Then, he was the man she'd always dreamed he would be. Then, he gave himself and took from her. Every time they came together was better than the time before. Frankly the sex was incredible. Gina'd never known anything quite like it. But at the bottom of it, if all they shared was great sex, was there anything between them worth fighting for?

"Way to go, Gina," she muttered. "Depress yourself."

She squinted into the sun and watched Adam walk with long, determined steps into the barn. Once he'd been swallowed by the shadows, Gina sighed. She wondered what he was doing. What he was thinking. He didn't talk to her. Didn't share his plans for the day. Didn't let her into what was going on in his head. It was as if she were a boarder here at the ranch. Nothing more than a guest who would be moving on shortly.

Another sigh escaped before she could stop it. Bending slightly, she leaned her elbows on the railing and studied the shiny new gold band on her ring finger. She wasn't a guest. She was his wife. For now.

At least, for as long as it took her to get pregnant.

Which, she thought, explained why she was still using her diaphragm. A tiny thread of guilt whipped through her like summer lightning. She admitted at least to herself that what she was doing wasn't technically fair. But she was willing to risk everything for the chance at real love. Even if that meant Adam one day finding out what she'd done. If that day came, she'd confess all and hope that he understood.

Every night, he did everything he could to impregnate her, no doubt so that he could end the marriage quickly and send her on her way.

He just had no idea that she was sabotaging the bargain she had proposed in the first place.

"Gina, this might turn out to be a lot harder than you thought it would be." And maybe, she admitted silently, it would be impossible.

But even as that thought niggled away in her brain, she vowed she wouldn't give up so quickly.

She'd made the decision to keep using her diaphragm before the wedding. Yes, she wanted a baby. Adam's baby. But she also wanted a chance to make Adam want her for longer than the duration of their arrangement. She wanted time for them to get used to each other. Time for him to realize that they could have something special together.

Time to make him fall in love with her.

Risky?

Oh, yeah.

But if she could pull it off, so worth it.

While her mind wandered down the "what if" paths it was getting so used to lately, she noticed a bright red sports car turning into the driveway. Before she could even wonder who their visitor was, though, another vehicle turned onto the ranch road right behind the zippy little car. This one was a huge horse trailer. Instantly excitement shot through her.

"They're here!" She grinned, turned and ran back into the bedroom she shared with Adam. She raced through the big room, hardly looking at it, then down the hall and took the stairs two at a time. She was already standing in the driveway when the car and then the horse van pulled up in the yard and stopped.

A tall, gorgeous man stepped out of the car, took one look at Gina and said, "I'm guessing that eager welcome isn't for me?"

Gina gave Adam's brother a quick smile. Travis was so easygoing. So relaxed. So ready to smile and quick to laugh. How much easier would her life had been if she'd only fallen in love with him? Unfortunately, though, when she looked at him, she didn't get that "zing" of something hot and sweet inside her. It was just pure female admiration for a gorgeous man.

"Hi, Travis. Nice to see you." She waved a hand at the trailer. "My horses are here."

"Upstaged by a truck full of horses?" Travis walked around the front of his car, then leaned lazily against the front fender. "Must be losing my touch. Came by to see my new sister-in-law and say welcome to the family."

She knew that Travis and Jackson had a feeling of the true circumstances of her marriage, but he'd come anyway. Wanted to welcome her, however briefly, into the King family. For that, she wanted to kiss him. She walked to him and gave him a brief hug. "Thanks. I appreciate it, really."

He gave her a hard squeeze and held on to her when she would have backed away. Looking down into her eyes, Travis asked, "How's it going, Gina? Adam making you nuts yet?"

"Not completely." She smiled, grateful for the understanding.

"Give him time," Travis said with a wink. Then the smile faded from his face. "Gina, I just want you to be careful, okay? I don't want to see you get hurt and—"

"Why're you hugging my wife, Travis?" Adam's voice boomed as he walked out of the barn.

"Well, she's just so damn huggable, isn't she?" Travis sounded amused as he gave her another squeeze. He winked down at her before letting her go.

Adam's features were tight and his eyes were narrowed. Gina wished she could pretend he was actually a little jealous, but she had the feeling it was more about Travis showing up unannounced than about a hug.

Adam looked at her, then shifted his gaze back to his brother. "What're you doing here?"

"And hello to you, too, big brother," Travis answered.

Gina looked at her husband and tried to rein in her instant physical response. But it was way too late. No matter how she tried to control it, her body lit up the moment she saw Adam. Where she could look at Travis or Jackson, for that matter, and see a handsome man with a great body and lots of charm, that's as far as it went. When she looked at Adam, though, her stomach fluttered with the nervous clip of butterfly wings and her heartbeat quickened into a fast gallop.

Even with his crabby nature and tendency to shut out anyone who threatened to get close, she loved him. Somewhere inside that perpetual crab, there was still the guy who at sixteen had helped her home after she'd fallen off her horse. Inside Adam, there was still the young hero who'd come to her rescue at a school dance when her date had gotten too grabby.

She looked at him and saw not only the past, but their possible future and the love for him she'd carried around inside her for years was alive and well. God help her. She took a deep breath, waited for him to look at her and then said with a forced brightness, "My horses are here."

"I see that," he said, shooting a glare at the trailer as it parked close to the corral. "Why?"

That she hadn't expected. "What do you mean, why?"

"Simple question, Gina," he said, folding his arms over his chest, planting his booted feet wide apart as if readying for battle. "Why are they here? Why didn't you just keep them at your folks' place?"

Gina stared at him. He was mad about her horses being shuttled to the ranch? "Because I live here now."

"Temporarily," Adam said.

Direct hit, she thought and inwardly winced.

"For God's sake, Adam." Travis straightened up and walked to Gina's side, clearly aligning himself with her.

"This is none of your business, Travis."

Gina appreciated Adam's brother's attempts at help, but she needed to take care of this herself. "He's right, Travis. This is between Adam and me."

She walked over to her husband, whose scowl looked fierce enough to strip paint and tipped her head back to look up at him. "Adam, we're married. I live here. I work with the Gypsies every day. It's not exactly convenient to drive over to my parents ranch every morning to do that work."

Adam did a quiet seethe. She could see it in his narrowed eyes and the tense lock of his jaw. Then she watched him flick a glance at Travis before turning his gaze back to her. Clearly there was more he wanted to say, but Travis being a witness wasn't something he was interested in.

Taking her upper arm in a firm grip, he steered her farther away from his brother and didn't stop until they were standing in the shade of the open barn doors. "You don't have to put on a front, Gina. We both know that this marriage isn't *real*."

Another barb that hit home with deadly accuracy. But damned if she'd let him know it. If she was going to make Adam see her, really see her, then she had to stand up to him. Let him know right up front that she wasn't going to be ignored or placated or pushed around.

"You're wrong," she said shortly. "This marriage is *very* real." She held up her left hand and wiggled her ring finger at him. "Whatever you'd like to think, Adam, we're legally married, for however long it lasts."

He released his grip on her arm, but her skin kept buzzing as if his touch had branded her. "I know it's legal, but it's not your ordinary marriage, now is it?"

"What marriage is ordinary, Adam?"

He blew out a frustrated breath. "You're purposely misunderstanding me."

"Oh, I understand just fine," she said and tapped the tip of her index finger against his chest. "You want to pretend that I'm not really here. The only place you want to see me is our bedroom. Well, get over it. I am here. And I'm not going anywhere just yet."

"I know that." He shot a look at Travis, lowered his voice and said, "I'm just saying it doesn't make much sense to uproot your horses. Besides, there's no room for them here. Not to mention the fact that you could have talked to me about this before arranging for their arrival."

Okay. Love him or not, Gina wasn't going to be walked on. "There's plenty of room on this ranch for the horses, Adam. You don't even use the front corral and the barn's half empty."

"That's not the point—"

"You just made it the point. Plus," she said, rushing on before he could get started again, "you knew going in that I work with those horses."

"I didn't think—"

"What?" Her eyes widened and she waved both hands in the air. "You didn't think I'd work with them here? Where I live?" She lowered her voice a little and leaned in. "What did you think, Adam? That I'd just stay tucked up in the bedroom waiting for you to service me? I said I wanted a baby, but I also have a life. One I'm not interested in giving up."

"You could have told me—"

"Maybe I should have. But I didn't realize I would

have to discuss every one of my decisions with you to get your approval."

"I didn't say that—"

"What did you say then?" She was almost enjoying this, Gina thought. Adam looked confused and off balance. But it was better than disinterested. At least he was looking at her. Talking to her. Actually, she thought, keeping him off balance might be just the answer.

He scrubbed one hand across his face in an impatient gesture. "Fine. I'm not going to argue about this."

"Too late."

"You want the damn horses here, then fine."

"Oh," she said, laying one hand on her chest. "Thanks so much."

His mouth worked, he pulled in a long breath and then said, "You're really starting to irritate me, Gina."

"Good," she said and gave him a smile. Irritated meant she was getting to him. Keeping him confused could only help her. "I like knowing that I can make you feel *something*."

When she turned to leave, he grabbed her arm again, spun her around and before she could ask what else he wanted to complain about, he kissed her. He covered her mouth with his in a fast, hungry kiss that left her knees wobbly. He let her go then took a step back as if even he were surprised by what he'd done. "Be careful what you wish for, Gina. Not all feelings are pretty."

She lifted one hand to her mouth, rubbed her lips

with her fingertips and looked up at him. "Even that would be better than feeling nothing."

"Now you're the one who's wrong," he said. Then he jerked his head at the trailer, where the driver was jumping down from the truck cab. "Go get your horses settled in."

He turned his back on her and walked away, stepping into the darkness of the van without another look her way.

Adam stalked to the rear of the barn and turned into the small ranch office that had been built into what had once been just another stall. He took a seat behind the battered desk his ranch foreman usually used. Today, though, he was damn glad that Sam was somewhere out on the ranch.

Travis stopped in the open doorway, leaned one shoulder against the jamb and looked in at him. "You really enjoy being a jackass?"

"Butt out." Adam propped one boot up on the corner of the desk and folded his hands atop his middle. He could still taste Gina and that wasn't good. He hadn't meant to kiss her. But she'd prodded him until damned if he could control the urge to touch her.

Since coming back home from Vegas, he'd done his damnedest to avoid spending much time with her. If he kept himself busy enough, it was almost possible to pretend that she wasn't living there. That nothing had changed in his life. He went about his normal routine during the day.

But every afternoon, his mind started drifting to thoughts of her. His body started yearning. And every night, he went to her like a man on fire.

He hadn't counted on this. Hadn't planned on being affected by Gina's presence at all. This was just one more deal made. One more bargain struck.

But she was wriggling her way into his thoughts, his life, with a surety that bothered him more than a little.

"Gina deserves better than the way you're treating her."

Adam shot Travis a look through narrowed eyes that should have fried him on the spot. Naturally Travis was unaffected. "What's between Gina and me is just that," Adam said. "Between Gina and me."

Travis pushed away from the doorjamb, walked into the room and pushed Adam's foot off the edge of the desk before sitting down. One eyebrow lifted and a corner of his mouth tipped into a half smile. "She's getting to you."

"No," Adam lied. "She's not."

"She could if you let her."

"And why would I do that?" Adam's fingers, laced together atop his stomach, tightened until the knuckles went white.

"Let me answer that with another question. Do you really like living like a damn monk?" Travis demanded. "Do you enjoy locking yourself away on this ranch? Shutting out everybody but me and Jackson?"

Adam inhaled slowly, deeply, getting a rein on the flare of anger that had erupted inside him. "I'm not shut away. I'm working. The ranch demands a lot of time and—"

"Tell that to somebody else," Travis said, neatly interrupting him. "I grew up here, too. I know what it takes to run this place. Didn't I watch Dad do it year after year?"

"Dad didn't have the same plans for it I do."

"Yeah," Travis agreed amiably. "Dad wanted a *life,* too."

"I have a life."

Smiling, Travis nodded. "After seeing that kiss, I'm guessing you've got a shot at one, anyway. If you don't screw it up."

Adam fixed him with a frown. "Is there a reason you came by here today? Or are you just here to be another thorn in my figurative paw?"

"The thorn thing appeals, I'll admit. But I did have a reason." Standing up, Travis stuffed both hands into the pockets of his black slacks. "I'm taking one of the family jets to Napa for a couple of weeks."

"Bon voyage," Adam said, standing himself. "But what's that got to do with me?"

"Just wanted to let you know. There's a winery there doing some interesting stuff with cabernets. Want to see what I can find out about their operation."

"So why is it when you do something related to the vineyard it's okay, but when I'm concentrating on the ranch I'm a recluse?"

"Because—" Travis grinned "—I make time for the ladies, too. I don't live and die by the grape, Adam. And now that you've got yourself married again, maybe it's time for you to remember that there's more to life than this damn ranch."

"You know exactly why I'm married. Don't make it out to be more than it is."

"Doesn't mean it couldn't work out. For both of you."

"Not interested."

"Just because you and Monica—" He stopped short when Adam flushed a dark red. "Fine. We won't talk about it. Even though you should—"

"I don't need to be psychoanalyzed, either."

"Wouldn't be too sure of that," Travis said, then continued. "Go ahead, Adam. Bury your future because of your past. But—" he half turned to point toward the ranch yard beyond the barn "—that's a fine woman out there. Too good for you to use and toss away. She deserves better." When his brother didn't say anything else, Travis added, "Hell, Adam, *you* deserve better."

He didn't want to talk about any of this. "Don't you have a winemaker to seduce?"

"I do indeed." Travis headed for the door and stopped on the threshold. "But do me a favor while I'm gone?"

"Depends."

"Try not to be such a complete ass all the time. Give Gina a chance. Give *yourself* a damn break, will you?"

When Travis was gone, Adam couldn't settle. He paced the narrow confines of the office and listened to the sounds from the yard. The clatter of hooves on a metal gate, the nervous whinnies, Gina's delighted laughter.

He stopped dead, concentrating on the near magical music of it.

And he told himself that no matter what he felt or didn't feel for Gina, once she was pregnant, deal done. Marriage over. She'd move out and he'd move on.

Despite what Travis seemed to think, there was no hope for a future here. Adam had already proven to himself that he simply wasn't the marrying kind.

Eight

Gina left Adam sleeping in their big bed. She grabbed her robe from a nearby chair, tugged it on and belted it at the waist before slipping out of the bedroom. She couldn't seem to fall asleep no matter how long she lay there in the darkness. So why not get up, make some tea and have a few of Esperanza's cookies?

At the doorway, she looked back at her husband and her heart turned over as she studied him in the dim light. Even in sleep, Adam managed to look powerful, aloof. As if his emotions were closed up so tightly they couldn't even find the surface when he wasn't actively guarding them. Apparently she would have to do battle with his subconscious, as well.

She sighed a little, shut the door quietly behind her and

wandered down the hall toward the stairs. The house was quiet, tucked up for the night, resting after a long day. Gina only wished she could rest, too. But her mind was just too busy. She couldn't stop thinking about Adam, their argument earlier and the way he'd watched her from afar as she settled the Gypsies into their new home.

Why had she thought she'd be able to reach him easily when he'd spent the last five years sealing himself off from the entire world? What if he didn't want to be reached? Would she be able to outlast him? Would he guess there was something going on when she didn't get pregnant right away? A headache burst into life behind her eyes and she blew out a breath as she headed downstairs.

There were no lights on, but moonlight shone through the skylights, illuminating the dark staircase in a pale silver glow. Her bare feet made no sound on the carpet runner and as she walked downstairs, she looked at the framed photographs lining the wall.

Pictures of the King brothers from infancy to adulthood stared back at her. There was a smiling Jackson, boasting a black eye, standing between his older brothers, each of them with an arm draped over his shoulders. There was Travis, holding the trophy the high school football team had won when he was the quarterback. There was even a twenty-year-old photo taken at a Fourth of July picnic. The King brothers were there, but so were Gina and her brothers. Adam was the tallest and he was standing right behind a ten-year-old Gina. As if even then, she'd been arranging things so she could be close to him. Had he noticed? Smiling to herself, her gaze continued over the faces frozen in time and as she looked, she noticed that there weren't any pictures of Monica, Adam's late wife. Or even of his lost son, Jeremy.

That made her frown thoughtfully for a minute and think about the other photographs she'd noticed throughout the house. Now that she was considering it, she realized there weren't *any* pictures of the family Adam had lost five years ago. Strange. Why would he not want to see them? Remember them?

Then she pushed those thoughts aside and went back to studying the framed photographs on the wall. She blurred her vision to all but the shots of Adam.

Gina studied them, one at a time, remembering some, wondering about others. There was Adam as a kid, with torn blue jeans and a baseball cap shading his eyes. Adam as captain of the high school baseball team. Adam at his prom. Adam with a blue ribbon won at a local rodeo. Adam smiling. God, he should do that more often, she thought.

Reaching out, Gina touched her fingertips to that captured smile and wished she could reach the man as easily. He was so close to her now, yet he felt even further away from her than ever.

A chill swept along her spine and she hunched deeper into the soft folds of the green cashmere robe. But this chill came from her heart, not the temperature of the room, so nothing she did helped with it. She took the last of the stairs and stopped in the foyer.

In the silence, she looked down the long hall toward

the kitchen and Esperanza's cookies—-then to the front door and the night beyond. She made up her mind quickly and opened the door to step outside.

The night air was cold and damp and still. Not a breath of wind moved. Overhead, the sky was clear and spatter-shot with bright stars. The moon was half-full and the light that shone down was bright enough to cast shadows across the ground.

Gina stepped onto the dirt driveway and walked quietly across the yard toward the corral where the Gypsies slept. Tomorrow, they'd be assigned stalls in the barn, but for tonight, they were here, getting used to their new home.

She leaned her forearms on the topmost rail and whispered, "I hope you guys catch on faster than I am."

One of the mares whickered softly and moved to her. Gina reached out, stroked the horse's nose with a gentle touch and smiled when the animal moved in closer for more. "Hi, Rosie. Did you miss me?" The horse shifted from foot to foot, the long, delicate feathers about its hooves waving lightly. Gina looked from Rosie to the other horses beyond and then back to the mare that had been her very first Gypsy.

"Feeling a little out of your element?" she asked, fingers stroking through the mare's silky mane. "Yeah, I know just how you feel. But we'll get used to it here. You know, Adam's not a bad guy at all. He just acts crabby."

"I *am* crabby."

His voice came directly behind her and Gina jolted so hard, the mare skipped away, dancing back from the fence to join the rest of the horses on the far side of the corral. Gina caught her breath and turned around to face him.

"You could have said something instead of sneaking up on me and giving me a heart attack!" Her hand slapped to her chest and she felt her heartbeat thundering hard and fast. "Jeez, Adam."

"What the hell are you doing out here in the middle of the night?"

Gina fought back the last of the adrenaline pumping through her and took her first good look at him. His naked chest gleamed gold in the soft light. His hair was rumpled from sleep and his jaw carried the shadow of a dark beard. Barefoot, he wore a pair of threadbare jeans that he'd apparently dragged on in a hurry. The top couple of buttons were undone and her gaze tracked the narrow line of dark hair that disappeared beneath the denim fabric.

He looked way too good.

Shaking her head, though, Gina asked, "Is this another rule, Adam? Do I have to ask permission to come outside, too?"

"That's not what I meant."

"Then what?"

He came closer and the scent of him, soap and male, drifted to her and seemed to coil in the pit of her stomach. She took a breath, hoping to steady herself, but all she succeeded in doing was dragging more of that scent deeper inside.

"I woke up and you were gone." He said it with a shrug.

A small note of hope lifted inside her. "You were worried about me?"

He glanced at her, then shifted his gaze to the animals wandering the corral enclosure. "I wouldn't go that far," he said. "I…wondered about you."

That was a start, Gina thought.

"You were sleeping and I couldn't," she said, turning to lean on the railing again and watch the horses moving through moonlight. "I was going to go for some of Esperanza's cookies, then I decided to come out and check on the Gypsies."

He shook his head and took up a spot beside her at the fence. Amusement colored his voice when he said, "What is it about these horses that's so damn special?"

She shot him a quick look, smiled and said, "Everything."

"Care to vague that up for me?"

"Wow. A joke?" She laid one hand on his forearm and when he didn't flinch and pull away, Gina considered it a win. "This is a real moment for me, Adam."

"Very funny." He turned to look down at her. "But that doesn't tell me why you're so nuts about these horses."

"They're gentle. And smart. And so good with kids, its nearly eerie." She blew out a breath and watched as one of the foals jolted into a one-horse race around the corral. Smiling as she watched the spindly legged baby run, she said, "They've been bred for centuries to become part of a family. They're strong and loyal. I admire that."

"Me, too," he said and when she looked at him, she noticed he hadn't been watching the horses, but her.

Nerves fizzed inside her, but in a good way. The night was quiet, but for the sounds of the horses. The wind was still, the sky brilliant with stars and it suddenly felt as though the world itself was holding its breath.

He was silent for so long, her nerves buzzed even harder, so she spoke to break the hush building between them. "I saw my first Gypsy about six years ago, at a horse show." Her gaze slid from his to the corral again. "They were so beautiful. Elegant somehow, yet their eyes were liquid and kind, as if there were very old souls looking back at me."

"If you love them so much, how do you bring yourself to sell them?"

She laughed. "It's not easy. And I'm very careful who they go to. I check out prospective buyers so thoroughly, the CIA would be impressed."

"I know I am."

"Really?" Gina turned her head to look up at him again and saw his dark eyes flash with something she couldn't quite read.

"Really," he said and leaned his bare forearms on the top railing of the corral fence, alongside hers. Jerking his chin at the horses milling around like wallflowers at a high school reunion, he continued, "I've seen my share of horse breeders who couldn't care less about the animals in their charge. They're only interested in the money they can make."

Gina's mouth tightened. "I've seen a few like that myself."

"Bet you have." Glancing down at her, he said, "Sorry about earlier today."

"Sorry?" Gina blinked at him, shook her head as if she hadn't heard him right and smiled. "Wow. A joke *and* an apology. This is a red-letter night for me!"

"You've got a smart mouth on you, that's for damn sure."

"True. My mom always said it would get me in trouble someday."

"Do you always listen to your mother?"

"If I did, we wouldn't be married right now," she pointed out, then wished she hadn't when he frowned.

"She was right, you know. About me. About warning you off."

"No, she wasn't. I love my mom, but sometimes she worries more than she should." Gina looked up at him and felt that maybe, just maybe, he was reaching out to her for the first time since their hurried wedding. Everything in her yearned for it to be true. She laid one hand on his forearm and tried not to notice that he nearly flinched from her gentle touch. "I know you, Adam…"

"No, you don't." He looked down at her hand on his arm and his stare was so steady, she finally pulled her hand away in response. When she had, he said, "You used to know me, Gina. I give you that. But I'm not that kid anymore. Time's gone by and things have changed. *I've* changed."

"You're still Adam," she insisted.

"Damn it." He pushed away from the railing, grabbed her shoulders and turned her around to face him. In the starlight, his features were hard and cold and his eyes were deep, dark, filled with shadows. Gina felt the strength in his hands and the heat of his skin, burning through the thick, cashmere robe right into hers.

"Don't mistake what's happening here, Gina."

She wouldn't be intimidated. And she wasn't afraid of him at all—even if that's what he was trying to do. "What's that supposed to mean?"

"You know exactly what I mean." His grip on her gentled slightly even as his eyes became darker, nearly black with the intensity of his gaze. "You're fooling yourself, Gina. You think I don't see it? Feel it?"

"Adam—"

"This bargain we made? That's *all* we share," he assured her. "We each want something from the other and when that bargain's fulfilled, it's over. Don't get comfortable here. Don't expect more from me than there is. And for God's sake, stop looking at me with those golden eyes of yours all soft and dewy."

"I don't—"

"Yeah, you do. And it's time to stop, Gina. For your own sake if nothing else. There is no *us*. There won't ever be."

Her heart *ached*.

Literally ached.

Her stomach churned and tears stung the backs of her eyes, but she fought them back, buried the swell of emotion that threatened to choke her. Everything he said, she knew he really meant, and yet, wasn't there more here than he would—or could—admit? Or was she just fooling herself as he thought? Was she setting herself up for a crashing fall at the end of their time together? Was she expecting to find the boy she'd once known inside a man too changed to remember him?

"We have now," she said, lifting both hands to lay her palms on his chest. The hard, sculpted muscles felt warm beneath her hands and the pound of his heart shattered something inside her. When he hissed in a breath, she took it as a sign to continue. "And for now Adam, there *is* an us."

"Gina…" He shook his head and blew out a breath riddled with frustration. "You're making this harder than it has to be."

"Maybe," she admitted. "And maybe you're making this far less fun than it could be."

She moved in toward him, closing the spare distance between them with a single step. Her hands moved over his chest, fingertips exploring, smoothing across his flat nipples until he took a breath and held it, trying not to surrender.

But she wanted his surrender and was willing to fight for it.

He caught her wrists and held them, staring down into her eyes like a man lost in unfamiliar territory. "You're playing with fire here, Gina."

"I'm not fragile, Adam," she said. "I don't mind a burn or two."

"This kind of fire consumes."

"And that's a bad thing?" she asked, smiling up at him despite the blackness of his eyes, the tight, grim slash of his mouth. Whether he wanted to admit it or not, the Adam she'd once known and fallen in love with was still there, hidden inside him, and she wanted to set him free again. To remind him that love and life and laughter were worth having. Worth cherishing. "We're married, Adam. This fire is what most people dream of finding."

"Fires usually burn out fast."

"Sometimes," she said with a short nod. "But while they burn, it's an amazing thing."

"You're not going to listen to anybody about this, are you?"

"No," she admitted.

"Thank God."

He released her wrists and without a word, reached for the cloth belt at her waist. Pulling it free, he silently swept the sides of the robe back, baring her naked body to his gaze.

Gina shivered a little as the cool, night air kissed her skin, but that minor chill dissipated under Adam's steady, heat-filled gaze. Her nipples peaked, tightening in the cold, aching for the touch of his lips, his mouth. His hands moved over her body, the hard calluses on his fingers scraping against her skin with an erotic friction that sent heat directly to her center.

Shifting from foot to foot in an unconscious attempt to ease the throbbing at her core, she let her head fall back against the fence post. Adam stroked her from breast to core and back again.

"Your skin glows in the moonlight," he said softly and leaned in to take one of her nipples into his mouth.

She gasped, arched into him and cradled the back of his head in the palm of her hand. He nibbled at her, scoring the tip of her nipple with the edges of his teeth. Ripples of something amazing rolled through her and Gina held her breath as she watched him suckle her. With each draw and tug of his mouth at her breast, Gina was swamped with more tenderness for this man who tried so hard to keep her at a distance for her own sake.

Holding him to her, she watched him as his mouth worked her body, teasing, tormenting, drawing out her pleasure as if he could taste her all night. She felt his connection to her, despite his warnings. His feelings were communicated in his touch. Tender strokes, gentle bites and licks. The brush of his breath across her skin and the sweep of his hands down her body, along her curves, down her hips and behind to cup her bottom.

In his touch, she felt everything she'd ever dreamed of.

Her hands fell to his shoulders and she reveled in the strength of him. The warm, solid feel of him beneath her hands. He lifted his head from her breast and she wanted to weep with the loss of him.

"I need to have you," he whispered and Gina quivered from head to foot.

"You *are* having me," she said on a choked-off laugh.

He smiled up at her and her heart stuttered in her chest. Those smiles of his, so rare, so breathtaking, tugged at her more than anything else.

"I want more," he said, sliding down the length of her body, trailing his lips and tongue along her skin as she leaned against the corral fence and hoped she didn't simply topple over.

"Yes, Adam." Two words, softly spoken, nearly lost in the quiet, moonlit darkness surrounding them, cradling them in the cool night air.

Then he was kneeling in front of her, pushing her thighs apart with his big hands and lowering his mouth to cover the very heart of her.

Gina groaned and gripped his shoulders tighter, her short nails digging into his skin to stabilize her hold on him. But even as she found her balance, the world tipped crazily around her. He stroked her damp heat with his tongue and had her gasping for air that never seemed enough to fill her straining lungs.

Wicked, she thought wildly. Here. Outside. In the ranch yard, she was naked and letting Adam have his way with her. More, *needing* him to have her. The thrill of being outside with him, beneath the stars, only added to the amazing feelings churning inside.

Again and again, he tasted her, torturing her with sweet, intimate caresses that sent waves of electrical-like surges moving through her. Then he lifted one of her legs, draped it across his shoulders and Gina was forced to reach back, grabbing hold of the fence behind her. She wanted this so badly she could hardly breathe anymore. Her world had shrunk to this one spot. Just she and Adam and what he could do to her.

The only sounds were her ragged groans, his steady breathing and the nervous stamping from the horses gathered at the other side of the corral. She stared blindly up at the stars, concentrating on what she was feeling, experiencing. The night was soft, and the magic of what Adam was doing to her was almost more than she could bear.

While his tongue and lips moved over her, he slid one hand around the curve of her hip and deftly slipped first one finger, and then two into her depths. He worked her with a steely determination that had Gina shaking unsteadily as a soul shattering climax coiled tightly within and prepared to spring.

His fingers explored her depths while his mouth continued its delicious torment. She wanted to keep him just like this. Forever. She wanted the orgasm that was just out of reach to stay poised where it was for eternity. She never wanted this moment to end.

Shifting her gaze from the sky to the man kneeling before her, Gina swallowed hard as she watched him take her. She looked at him and seeing what he was doing to her, watching as his mouth took her higher and higher, only seemed to intensify the very feelings he was stoking within. She couldn't look away now. Couldn't tear her gaze from Adam as he took her more intimately than anyone ever had before.

She felt him inside, outside. Her body shook. Her mind splintered. And when the first punch of release crashed through her, she called his name on a broken shout that trembled in the darkness.

Trembling, she rode that silky wave until it ended and when it was over, she swayed into him as he stood slowly, skimming his hands up her body as if memorizing the feel of her. "You taste sweet," he said, dipping his head to kiss her lips, her jaw, neck.

"Adam, that was—" Her forehead hit his chest as she struggled for air. Her body was humming and when he pulled her in close, she felt the hard length of him pressing into her abdomen. And fresh need erupted like a fireball.

Adam sensed her quickening desire as surely as he did his own. He hadn't come out here for this. Had only followed her into the yard to see if something was wrong. If she was all right.

He'd felt her leave their bed and told himself that he should let her go. But in moments, he'd been following her and when he'd seen her here in the moonlight, something inside him had fisted into a hard knot of pure lust.

Looking into her eyes now, he knew this was dangerous. He knew that she would be building on this encounter, turning it into something romantic. Something that might lead to a future for the two of them. But he'd warned her, hadn't he?

They'd gone into this with their eyes open, both of them. He was only doing what he could to keep his end of the bargain. Making love with her was just a part of the deal. That's all this was.

All it could be.

All he'd allow it to be.

He shook his head, letting thoughts and worries fly from his mind as he concentrated only on this moment with her. He wouldn't question this fire. Wouldn't try to define it.

As Gina had said, they had *now*.

Keeping his gaze locked on hers, Adam reached for the fly of his jeans, undid the last two buttons and freed himself. She sucked in a gulp of air and curled her fingers around him. Now it was Adam's turn to hiss in a breath through clenched teeth. Her touch was torment and pleasure rolled into one.

As she slid her hand up and down his thick length, he fought for control and knew he was losing.

Knew he didn't care.

Nine

She wrapped her legs around his waist and Adam turned, bracing his bare back against the fence post. The weathered, rough wood scraped at his skin but he couldn't care. All he felt, all he *wanted* to feel, was the woman in his arms.

He balanced her slender, curvy weight easily as he lowered her onto his body, inch by tantalizing inch. She slid over him in a slick heat that enveloped him in a rush of sensation like nothing he'd never known before.

Every time with Gina was like the first time.

And damn it, he didn't want to admit that. Not even to himself. But she was so much more than he'd expected. Her laughter filled him. Her temper challenged him. Her passion ignited his.

Adam held her, hands at her bottom, supporting her weight, easing her up and down on his thick erection. Every move dazzled. Every withdrawal was agony. Every thrust was victory. He filled her and her body opened and held him as if made to fit his.

Her head fell back as she rode him and arched into him. He could watch her all night. Listen to her sighs. Smell the sweet, slightly citrus scent of her skin. He watched every movement she made and saw the moonlight kiss her flesh with a silvery wash that made her seem lit up from within. And when she lifted her head to look at him, that same moon danced in her eyes.

He snaked one hand up her back, cradled her head in his hand and drew her mouth to his as his body tightened, fisting in anticipation. Again and again, she moved on him, rocking, swiveling her hips, driving him faster, harder than he'd ever gone before and still it wasn't enough.

He wanted.

He…needed…*her*.

Her tongue tangled with his and he took everything she offered. Her breath mingled with his. She trembled as her climax hit and when she groaned into his mouth, he swallowed it, taking that, as well. He wanted all of her. Needed all of her. And knew, bone-deep, that he would never get enough of her.

Then all thought ceased as he finally surrendered to a shattering release. And as he filled her with everything he had, he wondered if *this* was the night they would make the child that would end what was between them.

* * *

She still wasn't pregnant.

Gina'd worried a little after that night in the ranch yard two months ago. But the fates were apparently on her side, because her period had arrived right on time.

So she was still married and still trying to find a way to convince the man she loved that he loved her, too.

"You're thinking about Adam," her mother said. "I see it on your face."

Gina looked up from her place at the Torino kitchen table. She'd been assigned that chair when she was a little girl and she still headed straight for it whenever she came home again.

Sunlight speared through the wide windows her mother kept at a high gloss at all times. A clock on the wall chimed twelve times and in the backyard, Papa's golden retriever barked at a squirrel. Soup simmered on the stove, filling the air with the scents of beef and oregano.

Nothing in this room ever changed, Gina thought. Oh, there was fresh paint—same shade of bright yellow— every couple of years, new rugs or curtains and the occasional new set of pans, but otherwise, it was the same as it had always been. The heart of the Torino house.

The kitchen was where the family had breakfast and dinner. Where she and her brothers had complained and laughed and sometimes cried about whatever was happening in their lives. Her parents, the foundation of the family, had listened, advised and punished when necessary. And each of their children came home whenever they could, just to touch base with their beginnings.

Of course, if there was something they didn't want their parents to know, it was best to stay away. Especially from Mama. She didn't miss much.

Her mother was standing at the kitchen counter, putting finishing touches on the lunch she'd insisted Gina eat, while waiting for her daughter's answer.

"I must look happy then, huh?" Gina quipped and smiled too brightly.

"No, you do not." Her mother picked up the plate holding a sandwich and some homemade pasta salad. Carrying it to the table, she plunked it down, poured two tall glasses of iced tea and took a seat opposite her daughter. "I worry about you, Gina. Two months you're with Adam. You do not look happy. You think I don't see it in your eyes?"

"Mama…"

"Fine," her mother said, grabbing her glass to chug some of her tea. "You want a baby. I understand. How could I not? I, too, wanted babies. But you want them with the man you love. With a father who will also love the child you make."

"I do love him," Gina said and took a bite of the roast beef sandwich, because knowing her mother, she'd never be allowed to leave until she did. She chewed, swallowed and said, "Adam loved his son. He would love our child, too. He wouldn't be able to help himself."

Teresa crossed herself quickly at the mention of Adam's dead son and conceded, "He did love that boy. Such a tragedy. But you know as well as everyone else he changed when he lost his family."

Gina shifted uneasily on her chair and used her fork to move bow tie pasta around on her plate. "That's natural enough, isn't it?"

"Yes. It is. But he does not want to move on, Gina. The darkness in him is thick and heavy and he doesn't want it lifted."

"You don't know that."

Her mother snorted. "You do not want to see it."

Gina sighed, dropped her fork and said, "We've been over this."

Teresa Torino set her glass down, reached across the table and patted her daughter's hand. "And we will again. Until I make you see that you are making a mistake that will only cause you pain."

"Mama…"

The older woman sat back, folded her arms beneath her copious breasts and frowned. "So. You get pregnant. Then what? You leave? Then you walk away from your baby's father? You believe you can do this? With no pain?"

Just thinking about it was painful, but admitting that would probably be the wrong move. Besides, she was still hoping she wouldn't have to walk away. That Adam wouldn't want to let her go. "Adam and I made a deal."

"*Sì.*" Her mother sniffed in disgust. "So your papa tells me all the time. A deal. What kind of a way is that to start a marriage?"

"Um," Gina said, picking her fork up again to take a bite of her mom's pasta salad—only the best in the known universe, "excuse me, but didn't Papa go to Italy to meet you because his parents knew your parents and they thought you two would make a good couple?"

Teresa's big brown eyes narrowed on her daughter. "You think you're so smart, eh?"

"Pretty smart," Gina acknowledged with a smile. "I know my family history anyway."

"Yes, but you also know this," her mother said, sitting forward suddenly and leaning her forearms on the yellow-and-white-vinyl-cloth-covered table. "My papa told me I should marry Sal Torino and move to America. I argued with him. Told him I wouldn't marry a man I didn't love. Then I took one look at *your* papa and loved him in that instant." She lifted one hand and wagged her index finger at Gina. "One look. I *knew*. I knew it was right. That this marriage would last and be a good one. Can you say the same?"

Spearing another piece of pasta, Gina met her mother's worried gaze and said softly, "I've loved Adam since I was a kid, Mama. One look. I *knew*."

Teresa blew out an exasperated sigh. "Is not the same."

"No, it's not," Gina said wearily. "Papa wanted to get married. Adam didn't. But," she added, "we *are* married. And I know he cares for me."

"Care is not love," her mother warned softly.

"No, but it could be. Mama, Adam needs me. I love him and I'm going to try to make this work. For both of us. Can't you be on my side? Please?"

Astonishment crossed her mother's features as her brown eyes widened and her mouth dropped open. Standing up, Teresa moved around the kitchen table to stand beside Gina. She cupped her daughter's face between her palms, then drew her in close, wrapped her arms around her girl and held on tightly. "Of course I am on your side, Gina. I'm your mother. I want for you all that you want. Always. I only wish to spare you pain."

Gina held on and let herself be rocked for a while, taking comfort from the one source she'd always been able to count on. She thought of Adam, saw his face in her mind, felt his touch in her memory and her heart lifted, despite the odds being stacked against her. For two months, she'd lived with him, loved with him. She'd wormed her way into his house and could only hope she was worming her way into his heart, as well.

The chance she was taking was worth it. She had to believe that. She had to try. Otherwise, she'd always wonder if she'd given up on Adam too soon.

"I know that, Mama, I do," she said, her voice getting more determined with every word. "But sometimes, you can only get to happy by going through the pain."

"That wife of yours is a real hand with horses," Sam Ottowell said as he thumbed through a sheaf of receipts for ranch supplies.

"Yes." Adam smiled. "She is." Then he leaned over his foreman's desk and pulled a notebook toward him. Making a few quick notations, he dropped it again. "I want you to call Flanagan's. Get an extra order of oats out here. With Gina's horses here, too, we're going through twice as much."

"Right," Sam said, leaning back in his chair, propping his hands on his abundant belly. "She's really something, you know? Got those damn animals following her around like trained puppies or something. Girl's got a gift with horses."

She had a lot of gifts, Adam thought. Most particularly, she had a gift for throwing his perfectly organized life into turmoil. He'd hardly had a moment to himself since entering into this little wedding bargain. And the moments he *did* manage to find, his thoughts usually turned to her anyway.

"You hear those kids?" Sam asked, cocking his head as if to better hear the laughter drifting to them from the corral.

"Hard not to," Adam snapped. Though God knew he was trying.

Sam's features went stiff and blank in a heartbeat. He sat up, reached for the Rolodex and asked, "You going to call Simpson about the hundred-acre lot he wants to lease?"

"Yeah," Adam said, grabbing on to the change of subject with both hands. He checked his watch, then said, "I'll call his office tomorrow. We can work out—"

Whatever else he might have said was cut off at the sound of a scream shredding the air.

With Sam right behind him, Adam raced out of the barn, heart in his throat and skidded to a stop when that scream turned into peals of laughter. His gaze shot to the corral and everything in him fisted into a tight knot.

A boy, no more than four or five, was seated on the back of one of the Gypsy horses. The child's parents were standing outside the corral, watching the scene with indulgent smiles as a daughter, no more than ten, hopped up and down impatiently awaiting her turn on the horse.

Gina walked alongside the tiny would-be cowboy, her hand on the boy's thigh, holding him in place while she grinned up at him. The boy's delighted laughter spilled into the air like soap bubbles and Adam wrestled with the pain lodged in the center of his chest.

He couldn't move. Couldn't tear his gaze from Gina and the boy as they moved slowly around the inside of the corral. He noticed everything. The sunlight on the boy's blond hair, the steady gait of the horse, the patient smile on Gina's face. Again and again, the boy laughed as he petted and stroked the mare's neck, his tiny fingers getting lost in the thick, black mane.

"Uh, I'll just head on back to the office," Sam said, and slipped away unnoticed.

While his vision narrowed to that solitary child, Adam's mind filled with images of another boy. On another sunny day. Another lifetime ago.

"I want to stay with you, Daddy." Jeremy's big brown eyes were filled with tears and his lower lip trembled.

"I know you do," Adam said, checking his wrist-watch and inwardly wincing. He was already late for a meeting. There were offers to be made, documents to be signed, dreams to be crushed. Instead of that wince, he smiled to himself. Since taking over the family ranch, he'd already made a difference.

He'd found new buyers for their grain and cattle.

New tenants for the farmland and he had plans to rebuild the King stables.

If that meant spending less time with his wife and son than he would have liked, that's the price he would pay. He was doing this for their future.

"Please let me stay," Jeremy said and a single tear rolled down his cheek. "I'll be good."

"Jeremy," he said, going down on one knee long enough to look his son in the eye. "I know you'd be good. But I've got work. I can't play now anyway. You'll have more fun with Mommy."

Adam lifted his gaze to the woman standing behind his son. Monica didn't look any happier than Jeremy, but rather than tears in her eyes, there was fire. Anger. An expression Adam had become more and more used to seeing.

Jeremy's chin hit his chest and his narrow shoulders slumped in dejection. He rubbed the toe of his bright red tennis shoe in the dirt, sniffed loudly and ran one hand under his nose. "'Kay."

As the boy turned and walked with slow, miserable steps toward the silver sedan parked in the driveway, Adam stood up to face his wife.

"That's so typical of you, Adam," she muttered, shooting a look over her shoulder at their son to make sure he was out of earshot.

"Let's not do this right now, all right?" He checked his wristwatch again and Monica hissed in a breath.

"You never want to 'do' this, Adam. That's the problem."

"I don't have time for it, all right?"

"Why don't you schedule me in for a week from Tuesday, Adam? Will I get one minute? Or two?"

He blew out a breath, reached out one hand to her, but she skipped back to avoid his touch. Adam sighed. "You know as well as I do, I've got responsibilities."

"Yes, you do."

He was irritated, angry and just a little weary of this whole situation. Monica had less and less patience with what she saw as Adam's "preoccupation" with the King ranch. And as she pulled further away from him, he did the same. The ranch was his family's legacy. It took time. Dedication.

The car door closed behind Jeremy and he looked to see his son pull the seat belt across his chest and hook it securely.

Glancing back at his wife, Adam said, "Can we not do this now? I've got a meeting."

"Right." She shook her head, blond hair flying in a tight, short arc around her jawline. "Wouldn't want you to miss a meeting just because of your family."

"Damn it, Monica."

"Damn you, Adam." She turned and stalked to the car without another look at him. Just before she opened the car door, though, she allowed her gaze to lock with his. "Not that you'll notice or anything, but I thought you should know—we're not coming back. Jeremy and I are driving to my mother's in San Francisco. I'll let you know where to send our things once we're settled."

"Just a damn minute," Adam said, starting for her. But she hopped into the car, fired the engine and raced

down the driveway before he could get to her. He watched dust and gravel fantail up behind the wheels of her car. The sun beat down on his head and shoulders and despite the heat, he felt cold. Right down to his bones.

The dust settled and still he stood there, watching after the car carrying his wife and son away from him. Then the alarm on his watch beeped and he idly reached to turn it off. He had to leave for the meeting. He'd give Monica a chance to cool off. Then they'd talk. Work this out.

He headed for his SUV.

First things first. He had just enough time to make that meeting.

Twenty minutes later, Jeremy and Monica were dead.

Adam came up out of the past with a jolt.

It had been years since he'd allowed himself to remember that day. But now, it had all rushed back at him because of the child, still laughing, in the corral.

Adam felt as though a steel clamp was on his chest and it was tightening with every strangled breath he took. His eyes narrowed until he was looking at Gina and the boy as if down a long, dark tunnel. He might as well have been miles away. Sunlight splashed down on the two of them, as if defining the difference between Adam in the shadows, and his wife, in the golden rush of light.

Then Gina caught sight of him, smiled and waved. He stiffened at the warmth in her gaze, the welcome in her smile. He hadn't wanted this. Still didn't want it.

He could admit that over the last couple of months, he'd become too accustomed to her presence. The scent of her in the house. The feel of her in his arms. He turned to her in the night and listened for her during the day. This was a temporary arrangement that was beginning to seem far too permanent.

When he didn't answer her wave, only stared at her out of cold, empty eyes, Gina frowned slightly, then shifted her gaze back to the boy on the horse.

"She's good with kids, isn't she?"

Adam slowly turned his head to nod at Gina's brother Tony, walking toward him. He hadn't even known the man was on the ranch.

Tony pulled the brim of his hat down lower over his eyes to combat the glare of the sun. He stopped beside Adam and shot a look at his sister. "Mama sent me over with some of her homemade bread. Thought I'd watch Gina for a while before going back to the ranch." He turned an interested look on Adam. "Looks like I'm not the only one watching her."

Adam frowned at him. "Did you have a point?"

Tony grinned. "Only one. That look you were giving Gina just then makes me think that maybe this temporary arrangement might be coming to mean a little more to you."

"You're wrong." Couldn't have been more wrong. If anything, watching Gina with that child had just brought home to Adam the fact that he had to get her out of his life. The sooner the better. He wanted his old insular life back.

"See, I don't think so." Tony wandered to the barn, leaned back into a patch of shade and folded his arms over his chest. "I admit, I sided with Mom about this marriage. Seemed like a bad idea all the way around to me. But," he said, pausing to briefly look at his sister again, "Gina's happy here. And I think you're happier with her here, too."

Adam's features closed. He stared at Tony, deliberately keeping his gaze from the temptation of Gina. "You're wrong about that, too. Haven't you heard, Tony? I don't do happy."

"You used to."

"Used to do a lot of things," he said shortly, turning his back on his uninvited guest, as well as his wife, and heading back into the barn.

Tony, of course, followed him. "You just determined to be a miserable bastard, Adam?"

"Go with your strengths," he said, never stopping, never turning for a look back at the other man. He didn't want to make nice with Gina's family. He didn't want to watch Gina and feel a yearning. He wanted his world back the way it had been before Gina had become a part of it.

He walked straight to the rear of the barn and into the tiny office. Jerking his head at his foreman, an unspoken message was passed between them. The other man jumped out of the chair, nodded to Adam and Tony, then hurried out of the office, muttering something about seeing if Gina needed any help at the corral.

Adam didn't watch him go. If there'd been a door on the office, he'd have slammed it. But he had a feeling, that wouldn't have slowed Tony down anyway. Like his sister, the man refused to be ignored.

"So what's the deal, Adam? You too scared to admit you care for my sister?"

Adam's head snapped up and he shot Tony a glare with so much ice in it, the man should have been sliced to ribbons. Naturally Tony looked unmoved. "My brothers don't get away with talking to me like that. What makes you think you can?"

Tony shrugged indolently, then took off his wide-brimmed hat and ran one hand through his hair. Lifting his gaze to Adam's, he said, "Because I'm worried about my sister and I figure you can understand that."

Damn, he was right. Adam did understand all too well. Family loyalty. The instinct to defend and protect. These were things the Kings were raised with as well as the Torinos. So he was willing to cut Tony some slack in that department. But that didn't mean that he was willing to discuss his private life. Or his marriage to Tony's sister.

"I get it," Adam said. "But I'm still telling you to butt out. Gina and I will handle what's between us without your help or anyone else's."

"That may be the way you want it," Tony mused, stepping into the room. He put his hat back on, bent down and planted both palms on the edge of the cluttered desk. "But that's not how it works. Gina's family. My baby sister. I look after my own."

"So do I," Adam countered.

"That right?" Tony's eyebrows lifted. "Not how I remember it."

Adam flushed and felt the rising tide of anger rush up from the soles of his feet to fill his head and his vision until the very edges of it were a cloudy red. "You got something else to say, say it and get out."

Tony pushed up from the desk and scrubbed a hand over his mouth as if he could physically call back the words he'd just said. "That was out of line. I'm sorry."

Adam nodded, but he wasn't willing to give more than that.

"All I'm saying is, you're an idiot if you don't give what you've got with Gina a real chance, Adam. And I don't figure you for an idiot."

"Tony, *what* are you doing?"

Both men turned to face Gina, standing in the doorway of the small office. She looked from one man to the other, fury flashing in her eyes and Adam felt a solid punch of something that was much more than desire.

That's when he knew for sure he was in trouble.

"I thought you were with the horses."

She brushed that aside with a wave of her hand and narrowed her eyes on her older brother. "Not that it's any of your business, but Sam's taking Danny around and talking to his parents. I want to know what you're doing here."

"I'm having a talk with my brother-in-law," Tony told her easily, but being a wise man, he took a short step back.

"And you?" She shifted her look to Adam.

"Let it go, Gina," he said.

"Why?"

"Because it's over," Adam said with a glance at Tony as if to make sure of that fact. "Isn't it?"

"Yeah." Tony nodded and edged toward the door, clearly trying to slip past his sister before she could turn her fury directly on him. "It's over. Adam? Good to see you."

Adam nodded again and waited until Tony was gone before looking at the woman who was his wife. And only then did Tony's words reverberate through his mind.

It's over.

If only, Adam thought, staring into Gina's amber-colored eyes, it were that easy.

Ten

When Tony left, it was as if Gina were alone in the small, cramped office. Adam, though physically present, had shut himself down so completely, it was as if he'd forgotten she was even there.

"Adam," she said, moving in closer, despite the unwelcoming chill in the room, "what's going on? What were you and Tony talking about? And why do you look so angry?"

"Angry?" He glanced at her and his eyes were cool, dispassionate. "I'm not angry, Gina. I'm simply busy." To make his point, he picked up a sheaf of papers, straightened them and tucked them into a manila file folder.

"Uh-huh. Too busy to talk to me but not too busy to talk to Tony, is that it?"

He swiveled in the desk chair, propped his elbows on the narrow, cushioned arms and folded his fingers together. Tipping his head to one side, he said, "Your brother showed up, I had no choice but to talk to him. Just as I had no choice but to put my own work aside when I heard that boy screaming."

Gina shrugged and tried a smile. It didn't get a reaction out of him. "Danny was excited, that's all. His parents are buying the young mare for him and his sister and it was his first ride."

"I didn't ask why the child screamed," Adam said, then reached for a pen laying on the desk. Absently clicking the top of it, he continued. "I only said the noise is distracting. I'm not used to having all of these people coming and going from the ranch. And I don't like it."

Now Gina flushed a little with the small whip of anger that jolted her. The way he sounded, she might as well have been holding parades every day. One or two people a week was nothing. It was normal. And hey, if he'd come out of the barn or his office and talk to them, maybe he might not hate it so much. Instead he kept himself in solitude. He was always working. On the phone, riding the ranch on one of his horses, closeted in the office with buyers.

Fine for him to lose himself in his own business, but he didn't want to allow her the same privilege. Her business was as important to her as the ranch itself was to Adam. You would have thought he could appreciate that, at least.

Still, no point in arguing with a man whose expression clearly stated he was looking for a battle. She didn't really want to fight with him anyway. Instead she wanted to reach him. Reach the Adam she'd known as a girl. The one who'd always stood up for her. The one she knew was still locked away deep inside him.

So when Gina spoke, she kept her tone reasonable, despite the flare of what her mother liked to call the Torino Temper.

"I've only had a few people a week over, Adam. They have to come to see the Gypsies in person. I have to see the way they are around the horses. There's simply no way to avoid it even if I wanted to. Which, by the way, I don't."

"I don't want these people around."

"I'm sorry to hear that." She wouldn't give in. She loved him, but she wasn't going to stand still for having *Welcome* tattooed on her forehead, either.

His mouth flattened into a slash of disapproval. "This isn't working out, Gina."

"This?" she repeated, with a wave of her hand. "This what? The horses? The people?"

"The marriage," he said shortly.

She rocked back on her heels a little from the force of that smack down. Her stomach tightened and an ache settled around her heart. But through the pain, her mind started racing. What had brought this on? She thought back over the day and all she could find was little Danny's scream. Then something hit her and she felt badly that it hadn't occurred to her before.

"It was Danny, wasn't it?" Her voice was a whisper of concern. "Little Danny's scream started all this."

His face froze, so Gina knew she'd touched on the truth. She should have realized. He'd lost a son. Of course that child's scream would tear at him. Bring back memories of another child, that one lost to him forever.

"The boy has nothing to do with this."

"I think you're wrong."

"Of course you do," he said. "But that doesn't really matter."

"Adam, it does matter." She took a step closer to him, her momentary rush of anger dying in a swell of sympathy. "Hearing Danny made you think of Jeremy."

If possible, the scowl on his face deepened. His dark eyes shuttered and before she could say anything else, Adam stood up and faced her.

"This isn't about my son. Don't bring the past into this."

"The past colors everything we have now," she argued.

"Maybe in your world, but the past does not influence me." He glared at her and Gina knew he actually believed that lie. But she also knew the truth. She knew that when he'd heard Danny's joyful scream, it had touched something inside him. Something he kept locked away from everyone.

"This isn't about that boy. This is about the deal we struck. I realize we made a bargain," he said, his eyes as cold as ever, his words as unaffected by emotion as the robotic voice of a computer. "One which, I'm sure you'll admit, I've done my very best to honor."

"Yes," she said tightly, trying to ignore the rush of heat that swam through her at the mere thought of the nights she spent in his arms. If she hadn't been using her diaphragm religiously, she had no doubt that she'd be pregnant. Her mom had always said they were a fertile bunch and heaven knew Adam had certainly put everything he had into making the child they'd agreed on. "You have. As have I," she pointed out quickly.

"True."

Did his eyes warm up there for a second? Was he, too, thinking about their nights together? Or was it only wishful imagining on Gina's part?

"But," he said, capturing her attention again, "since we've been married more than two months and you're not pregnant yet, it might be time to reconsider the bargain."

"What?" She hadn't expected this. Hadn't thought that Adam would want to walk away from a deal that promised him the deed to the land he wanted so badly. But if he did want out, what could she do about it? Clearly she hadn't been able to get him to open up yet. So was she supposed to pick up her toys and go home? Forget about her time here? With him? Try to move on?

Oh, good God.

As if needing more room for this conversation, Adam stepped past her and walked into the shadow-filled barn. The mingled scents of horses, fresh hay and old wood made an almost comforting aroma. She walked to join him and kept her gaze on his even when he turned his head to stare out at the sun-washed yard beyond the open doors.

"You want to end the bargain?" she asked, and winced when her voice came out so small, so reluctant. "Because if you do, I won't agree."

She should, of course. What kind of woman would stay with a man who didn't want her? Where the hell was her dignity? Her sense of Torino pride? But the moment those questions rose up in her mind, she mentally provided the answers.

Her pride had been swallowed by her love. It wasn't as though she had a choice in this, Gina thought in her own defense. It wasn't as if you got to *choose* who to love. She had loved Adam for most of her life. Sometimes, she felt as if she'd been born loving him. And the time spent with him these last few months only confirmed her feelings.

She wasn't an idiot, though. She knew he wasn't perfect. Far from it, in fact. He could be cold and calculating. He wasn't an easy man to get along with, but he was never cruel or deliberately unkind, either. There were shadows of pain in his eyes that she only rarely caught glimpses of and his even rarer smiles were enough to melt her heart even when she was doing her best to stand strong.

Not perfect, no. But he'd always been perfect for *her*.

And wasn't that what loving was all about?

He shifted his gaze, stared at her for a long time and she really wished she could read whatever he was thinking in his eyes. But he was too good at masking his emotions. Too good a negotiator in business to let his opponent get a good read on him.

Finally, though, he spoke. "No, I don't want to end our bargain."

Gina pulled in a slow, deep breath, relief swamping

her even while anxiety hovered nearby, ready to pounce. "All right," she said. "Then what are you talking about?"

"I think it would be in both our best interests to redefine the bargain, that's all," he said quietly. "You're not pregnant yet…"

"It's only been a little over two months," she argued.

"True. But what if it takes a year? Two?"

She didn't say anything, even though on the inside, she knew she wouldn't have had a problem with it. The more time she had with Adam, the better her chances of getting through to him, making him see just how good they could be together.

"My point is," Adam said, pushing his hair back from his forehead with one hand, "I think we should set a time limit on this endeavor."

"Endeavor?"

He paid no attention to the sarcasm coloring that single word. "If you're not pregnant by the end of six months, then we end this. We each go our separate ways and—"

She shook her head and blurted, "You get your land and I get what?"

"I wasn't finished." He frowned a little, but continued. "If you're not pregnant by the end of six months, then we end the marriage and the bargain. We both lose."

"You'd give up on the land you want so badly?" Was he really so anxious to get her out of his life? Was marriage to her really so hideous? God. Hadn't she reached any part of him yet?

Yes, she had. She knew she had. She could feel it in his touch every night. See it in the flash of need and desire in his eyes when he came to her bed. Why was he fighting this so valiantly? Why was he so determined to keep her at bay? To stave off any chance they might have had at happiness together?

And *why* was she still here? How could she continue to love a man who so obviously wanted her gone?

"I'll find another way to get the land. Surely your father would change his mind eventually." He shoved both hands into the back pockets of his jeans and shook his head. "It's the only way, Gina. What would be the point in drawing this out? Making it harder on ourselves?"

"Thanks very much," she said.

At last, he gave her a very brief smile. More of a twist of the lips even than a smile, really. And it was a sad statement of fact that Gina's insides jumped when she saw it.

"I like you, Gina. Always have. And frankly, I'd prefer to end this between us while we still like each other. If you're not pregnant at the end of six months, neither one of us is going to be satisfied with this arrangement."

"You like me."

"I do."

She choked back a laugh. She loved. He liked. *Big* difference.

But he was still talking, so she focused on Adam. "I think the only fair thing to do is cut our losses at the end of six months. That way, we both have a deadline. We know there's an end in sight and we can plan around it."

"Right." She nodded, swallowed hard and tried to keep the bubble of frustration she felt rising within from spewing out her mouth. "The master negotiator at work.

Gotta have a plan. Good idea, Adam. Wouldn't want to relax into this."

"Gina…"

"No, no!" She held up both hands and started walking. She couldn't stand still another minute anyway. Honestly she didn't know who she'd rather kick more… Adam or herself. He was so damn stubborn and what was she? A glutton for punishment?

She took a few steps away from him, thought better of it and spun around to walk right back. "Do you even see how crazy that is? No, of course you don't. I'm not pregnant yet, so by putting a deadline on me, that'll be sure to take the pressure off." Gina threw her hands high then let them slap back down against her thighs. "Hey, maybe you should send a memo to my eggs? You know, something short and sweet like, *Get in line to be fertilized. What's the holdup?*"

He scowled at her. It had no effect of course, because if there was one thing Gina was used to, it was that scowl.

"Sarcasm doesn't really accomplish anything, does it?"

"Didn't know it was supposed to," she countered. "It's sort of an end all in itself." Tipping her head back, she glared up at him. "Adam, don't you get it? A deadline isn't going to help anything. What we need is to be closer, not more focused on a damn ticking clock."

One dark eyebrow lifted. "As I recall, we've been *damned* close almost every night for the last couple of months."

"That is so male," she said with a shake of her head. "Naturally you assume that having *sex* is being close."

"It's not?"

"No, it's not!" She reached up and yanked her hair in pure frustration. "What is it with your gender?"

"Just a minute…"

"No. You wait a minute." Blowing out a breath, she tried for calm and just barely managed it. "Adam, don't you get it? We're together, but not. We sleep together and then you ignore me during the day. You make love with me all night and then the next morning, you shut me out. How the hell are either one of us supposed to loosen up enough to make a *baby*?"

His features went cold and stiff again. Typical.

"In case you've forgotten, this isn't a standard marriage."

She staggered back dramatically, slapped one hand to her chest and let her jaw drop. "Really? It's not? Wow. That explains so much!"

His eyes narrowed. "If you're not willing to discuss this like a rational human being…"

"You'll what?" Gina asked, tapping the toe of her boot against the dust-covered concrete floor. "Hire someone to do my talking for me? Or no, wait. Better yet, you could hire someone to do *your* talking. Then you wouldn't even have to look at me until it was time to come to bed and do your duty for the King ranch and dynasty."

He gritted his teeth and the muscle in his jaw twitched. "You think I treat lovemaking as a chore?"

"Isn't it for you?" she countered and immediately wished she hadn't. Never ask a question if you don't think you'll like the answer. But too late now. Yes, he seemed to enjoy making love with her. But what if she was wrong about that? What if he really was doing only what he considered keeping up his end of the bargain? What if she hadn't even reached him in bed? Didn't she *have* to know? And wasn't pushing him the only way to know for sure?

"We made a deal," she accused, hoping with everything she was that he would deny what she was thinking, "and you come to me every night to check sex off your to-do list."

"Now you're not making any sense at all." He snorted a dismissive laugh.

"No? Then tell me you want me, Adam. Tell me that making love to me is more than a chore. More than just holding up your end of the bargain." She stepped in close to him, felt the heat pouring off his body and reaching for hers. "Prove me wrong, Adam," she taunted. "If I'm more than that to you, prove it to me."

Seconds ticked past as she stared into his eyes. Heat flared in those dark chocolate depths and Gina almost wondered if she'd pushed him too far.

Then he grabbed her, yanked her flush against him and took her mouth with a fierce aggression that melted every bone in her body.

Looked like she'd pushed him just far enough.

Adam couldn't breathe.

The anger that had been choking him was drowning now in a molten sea of desire. He pulled her in close, wrapped both arms around her and gave himself up to the raging need within. She opened her mouth for him and his tongue delved into her heat. He tasted and took, grabbing as much of her as he could, as if his life depended on it.

She was a contradiction in so many ways. Sweet, and yet not afraid to stand up for herself. Even to him. Sexy and warm and hot tempered, as well. She shook up his life. Brought chaos to order. Dragged strangers onto his property. Made him feel too much. Want too much.

His hands fisted in her hair and he pulled her head back, bending her back as he took all she offered. All she promised. He felt her like a drug in his system. She filled every cell. Awoke every nerve.

She was dangerous.

At that thought, he pulled himself up from the spell he was under and broke the kiss like a man surfacing for one last gasp of air before he drowned. He released her and she lurched unsteadily until she found her footing. Then she lifted one hand to her mouth and raised her glassy eyes to his.

Adam fought to bring air into straining lungs. Fought to ignore the throbbing in his groin, the near-frantic demand for release clamoring at him. When he finally felt as though he could speak again, he said only, "You're not a chore, Gina. But you're not permanent, either. You can't be."

Pain flickered in her eyes and he steeled himself against it. He wouldn't be moved by concern for her. Would hold himself to the course he'd set when he embarked on the bargain that had shattered the peaceful solitude of his world.

"Why, Adam?" Her voice was soft and sounded as bruised as her eyes. "Why are you so determined to feel nothing? You were married before. You loved Monica."

Ice flowed through his veins just as quickly as the fire had only moments before. "You don't know anything about my marriage."

He hoped she would drop it, but of course, being Gina, she didn't.

"I know that she's gone. I know that the pain you felt at losing your wife and son will never really go away."

"You know *nothing*."

"Then talk to me!" Her shout was loud enough to rattle the window glass in the old barn. "How can I know what you're thinking if you won't talk to me? Let me in, Adam."

Shaking his head, he fought for words, and couldn't find any. He didn't want her *in*. Didn't want this to be anything more than the impersonal bargain they'd first begun. His past was just that. *His*. He didn't make decisions based on guilt or pain or any other emotion that could cloud judgment, impair thought.

Adam ran his life as he ran his portion of the King business. With calm, cool reason. Something Gina clearly was unaccustomed to.

"The pictures of your family in the hall?" She looked up at him, a silent pleading in her golden eyes. "The photos all over the house? They're of you and your brothers. Your parents. Cousins. But—"

He knew what she was going to say and still swayed with the slap of her words.

"There are no pictures of Monica and Jeremy anywhere. Why is that, Adam?"

Steeling himself, he kept his voice steady, emotions hidden. "You'd prefer that I filled the house with photos? You think I want to look at pictures of my son and remember him dying? Does that sound like a good time to you, Gina? Because it sure as hell doesn't to me."

"Of course not." She grabbed his forearm with both hands and he felt the strength of her grip, the heat of her touch right down to his bones. "But how can you just shut it all out? How can you refuse to remember your own son?"

He remembered, Adam thought as an instant image of Jeremy leaped up into his mind. Small, with blond hair like his mother and his father's brown eyes. Smiling, always smiling, that's how Adam remembered him. But that was private. Something he didn't share.

Slowly he peeled her hands off his arm and took a step back from her for good measure. "Just because I don't surround myself with physical mementos doesn't mean I could or *would* forget him. But I don't run my life on memories, Gina. My past doesn't infringe on my present. Or my future." He forced himself to look at her and distance himself from the regret, the disappointment shining in her eyes. She'd known going into this that he wasn't looking for love. If she'd allowed herself to hope for more, that wasn't his fault, was it?

When she didn't speak, Adam continued. "We have a business arrangement, Gina. Nothing more. Don't expect what I can't give and we'll both come out of this with what we want."

Eleven

For days, Gina wrestled with that last conversation she'd had with Adam in the barn. She kept forcing herself to remember not only the fierce fire of his kiss, but the icy shards in his eyes.

Had she been fooling herself for months? Had she really been holding on to a childish dream that had no basis in reality? Was it time to admit defeat and bundle her heart up before it could be shattered completely?

She tugged on Shadow's reins and urged the gentle Gypsy mare down a well-worn path to the King family cemetery. As she approached, storm clouds that had been crouched at the horizon all day suddenly moved forward, sweeping across the sky like an invading army.

The temperature dropped in an instant and the sun's

light was obliterated. Grayness surrounded her and a cold wind kicked up, lifting her long braid off her shoulder, tossing it behind her back. Shadow danced uneasily beneath her as if the horse sensed the coming storm and wanted nothing more than to return to the warm comfort of the stable.

But Gina was on a mission, and wasn't going back to the house until she'd completed it. How had Adam cut his dead family so neatly out of his life? With surgical precision, he'd sliced off that part of his past and shuttered it away completely. What kind of man could do that?

The last of summer was slipping away into fall. Soon, the trees guarding the old cemetery would be awash in brilliant golds and reds, their leaves shuddering in the wind and falling to the ground in a patchwork of color. Already, the wind was colder, the days were shorter.

Shadow blew out a breath, shook her head and again tried to stray off the worn path. But Gina was determined to face the past Adam had locked away.

The scrollwork in the iron trellis fence surrounding the cemetery looked time worn yet still elegant and strong. As if it had been built with love to last generations. Like the King family itself.

Bougainvillea vines twisted through the metal work, their deep scarlet and pale lavender flowers fluttering in the wind. Headstones crowded the small cemetery that had stood in this place since the early eighteen hundreds. Some tipped drunkenly, the letters carved into their stone rubbed away by time and weather. The newer additions stood soldier straight, their stones still bright, the engraving deep and clear, hardly touched by wind and rain.

Gina swung off of Shadow, tied the reins loosely to the iron fence and cautiously as a thief, opened the intricately worked gate. A squeal of metal on metal scraped at her nerves and the wind pushed at her, as if someone or something were warning her to turn back. To stay away from the home of the dead and to return to the living.

She squinted into the wind as the first raindrops pelted her. Icy drops soaked into her shirt, snaked along her neck and down her back. The leaves on the trees rustled, sounding almost like a crowd of people whispering, wondering what she would do next.

Walking carefully across the wet and getting-wetter grass, Gina eased around the older graves and made her way back to the last row, where brilliantly white granite tablets awaited her. Adam's parents were buried side by side more than ten years ago, after the private plane they were piloting went down outside San Francisco. There were fresh flowers on their graves. Roses from the ranch garden.

But Gina hadn't come to see Adam's parents. It was two other graves, silent and chill beneath the splattering raindrops that called to her.

Monica Cullen King and Jeremy Adam King.

There were flowers here, too. Roses for Monica, daisies for Jeremy. The now-steady rain made streaks across the surface of the granite and the brass nameplates affixed there. And the silence that reached for Gina nearly choked her. Here lay the family that Adam couldn't forget and wouldn't allow himself to remember. Here was the reason he was living only a half life. Here was the past that somehow offered him more than a future with her ever could.

"How do I make him love me?" she asked, her gaze sliding from one of the stone tablets to the other. "How do I make him see that having a future doesn't take away from the past?"

There were no answers of course and if there had been, Gina would probably have run screaming from the cemetery. But somehow, she felt as though her questions were being heard. And understood.

Going down on one knee in front of the twin graves, she felt the cold wet soak into the denim fabric as she smoothed the flat of her hand across the neatly tended grass and absently picked up fallen twigs to toss them aside. "I know he loved you. But I think he could love me, too." She glanced at the stone bearing Jeremy's name and the too-brief span of years that marked the life he'd led. Her eyes filled, remembering that sunshiny boy and the devastation she'd felt for Adam when Jeremy had died.

"It's not that I want him to forget you. Either of you. I only want…" Her words trailed off as she lifted her gaze to the horizon where black clouds roiled.

"I have been fooling myself, haven't I?" she whispered finally, the wind throwing her words back in her face. "He won't risk it again. Won't risk loving when he's already paid too high a price for it."

The rain thundered out of a sky gone black and dangerous, coming down in a torrent that soaked her to the skin. A fierce wind wrapped itself around her and cold settled in Gina's bones. She knew the storm wasn't the only reason though. It was the chill realization that what she'd longed for would never happen. It was time to surrender. She wouldn't put herself through staying with a man in the hopes that he would one day love her.

Time to throw away the diaphragm.

Standing up slowly, she looked down at the graves of Adam's family and whispered, "Look after him when I'm gone, okay?"

Adam was in the barn saddling his own horse by the time Gina rode into the ranch yard, soaking wet and looking as miserable as a woman possibly could. He'd been getting ready to go out looking for her—which even he'd had to silently admit was practically useless. On a ranch the size of the King spread, it could have taken him days to find her. And still, he would have searched because not knowing where she was, if she was safe or maybe hurt or lost or God knew what else, was making him insane.

Looking at her now, though, he was torn between relief and fury. Mindless of the pouring rain, he left the barn, stalked across the ranch yard and didn't stop until he reached her side. He snatched her off the back of her mare and held her shoulders in a death grip while he looked down into her eyes and shouted, "Where the hell have you been? You've been gone for hours."

"Riding," she said and pulled out of his grasp. She

stumbled a little, caught her balance and looked around herself as if trying to remember where she was and how she'd gotten there. "I was riding. Storm came…"

Her voice drifted off and whatever else she said was lost in the pummeling thunder of the falling rain and the slam of the wind. She looked down at herself as if surprised to find she was completely drenched. The heavens were still torn open, with rain coming down in thick sheets that made it almost impossible to see clearly more than a few feet.

Adam's insides were still rattled even as he fought for the legendary calm that was normally such a huge part of his life. Damn it, he'd been going nuts wondering where she was. If she was safe. He'd spent the last two hours alternately watching the storm roll in and searching the horizon for a sign of her returning. He felt as if he'd been running all day. Exhausted and pushed to the edge of his limits.

He reached out, swiped her wet hair off her forehead and said, "Damn it, Gina, you don't go riding without telling someone where you're going. This is a big ranch. Anything could happen, even to an experienced rider."

"I'm fine," she mumbled and rubbed water off her face with her hands. Hunching her shoulders, she added sternly, "Stop yelling."

"I haven't even started," he warned, still riding the rush of emotion that had damn near choked him when she rode into the yard. Didn't she know what could have happened?

Rattlesnakes could have spooked her horse. Wildcats

down from the foothills looking for food could have attacked her. Hell, her mare could have stepped into a hole and broken a leg, leaving Gina stranded miles from help. His heart was pounding, his brain was screaming and the temper he'd kept a close rein on ever since he'd discovered she was gone finally cut loose.

Grabbing her upper arms, he shook her until her head fell back and her wide, golden eyes fixed on his face. "What the hell was so important that you felt you had to ride out with a storm coming in?"

She blinked up at him and the rain fell like tears down her face. "Never mind. You wouldn't understand."

She might as well have slapped him. Fine. She didn't want to tell him what was going on? Worked for him. But damned if he'd stand in the yard and drown. "Come on." He turned and dragged her toward the house.

She struggled in his grasp but no way was she going to get loose. "I've got to see to Shadow."

"*Now* you're worried about the mare?" He shook his head. "One of the men will take care of her."

"Will you just let go, Adam?" she argued, dragging her heels trough the mud. "I can walk on my own. I take care of myself. And I can take care of my own horse."

"Yeah?" He looked her up and down. "Looks like you're doing a hell of a job there, Gina. Nice one." Then he glanced over his shoulder, pointed and said, "There. Sam's got Shadow. He'll rub her down and feed her. Satisfied?"

She looked, too, and watched her mare being led into the warm, dry stable and it was as if the last of her strength just drained away. She swayed in place and something inside Adam turned over. She'd thrown his life into turmoil and now she was making him yell like a maniac and he *never* yelled.

"Come on," he muttered and took hold of her again, leading her behind him and he didn't stop until he'd reached the front door. He threw it open, stomped off as much mud as he could from his boots, then stepped into the house. "Esperanza!"

The older woman scuttled into the hall from the kitchen and immediately raced toward Gina. "*Dios mio*, what's happened here? Miss Gina, are you all right?"

"I'm fine," Gina said, still trying to get out of Adam's tight-fisted grip. "I'm sorry about the mess," she added, waving one hand at the rainwater and mud sliding across the once-gleaming entryway floor.

"No matter, no matter." Esperanza threw a hard look at Adam. "What did you do to her?"

"*Me?*"

"No," Gina interrupted quickly, briefly. "It wasn't Adam. I got caught in the storm."

Still, Esperanza shot Adam a death glare that clearly said, *you could have stopped this if you'd tried.* Whatever. He wasn't going to stand there and defend himself while Gina froze to death.

"I'm taking her upstairs," Adam said, already heading for the wide staircase. "We'll want something hot in, say, an hour? Maybe some of your tortilla soup, if there is any."

"*Sí, sí,*" Esperanza said. "One hour." Then she

clucked her tongue as Adam swung Gina into his arms and started up the stairs, taking them two at a time.

"I can walk," she complained.

"Swear to God, don't you say another word," he snapped. At the head of the stairs, he glanced back to see Esperanza making short work of the mess he and Gina had left behind. Time for another raise for his housekeeper.

Gina, apparently unaffected by the fury pumping through him, slapped one hand to his chest and said, "Damn it, Adam, I'm not an invalid."

"No, you're not. Just crazy," he said, sparing her only a quick look before continuing down the hall to the master bedroom. He walked inside and never paused until he reached the connected bath. A huge room, with miles of white and green tiles, it boasted a double sink, a shower big enough for an orgy and a hot tub with a wide bay window that overlooked the spectacular back gardens. Now though, rain sluiced down the glass, making the view blurry and the distant horizon nothing more than a smudge of gray and black.

"Strip," he said when he set her down.

She glared at him. "I will not."

"Fine. I'll do it for you then. Not like I don't know my way around your body." Adam reached for the buttons on her shirt, but Gina slapped at his hands. Didn't hit him very hard, since she was shaking and so cold her teeth were chattering.

"You might want to wait until you're stronger to make a fight of it," he said tightly and reached down to turn the faucets on the hot tub. He flipped up the latch to set the plug and turned back to her while hot water rushed into the tub.

He began tearing the buttons from her shirt and peeling the sodden garment off of her. "You're half-frozen." Then he undid her bra, leaving Gina to clasp one arm across her breasts in a useless bid for modesty.

"A little late for maidenly concerns, don't you think?" he asked as he shook his head at the defiant glare shooting out of her eyes.

"I don't want you here," she said, and her words might have carried more weight if her voice hadn't trembled.

"Tough," he said, kneeling down in front of her to tug off one of her boots. "What the hell were you thinking? Why did you go out today? You saw the storm. Heard the forecast."

"I thought I had time," she said, reaching out to slap one hand on the counter to keep her balance while he lifted first one of her feet, then the next. "I needed to—"

"What?" He looked up at her from where he knelt in front of her. Still furious, still relieved, still battling both sensations, he grumbled, "Needed to *what?*"

She shook her head. "Doesn't matter now."

It irritated him that she wouldn't tell him what she was thinking. Where she'd been. What had put the look of utter devastation on her face and in her eyes. He wanted to…damn it, he wanted to make her feel better. When the hell had this happened? When had he begun to care what she thought, how she felt? And how could he stop it?

Shaking his head, he tugged off her boots, then her socks and went to work on her jeans. The denim fabric was so soaked, it was hard to maneuver and he had to put some real effort into dragging them down her thighs and calves. Cold water ran in rivulets down her pale, blue-tinged skin. She shivered again and Adam fisted his hands to fight the urge to caress her, to warm her with his touch.

Instead he hissed in a breath. "You're cold to the bone."

"Pretty much."

Behind them, hot water rushed into the gigantic tub and steam rose to fog the bay window, shutting out the night, sealing them into that one room together.

"Get in," Adam said flatly.

She looked at him. "First you get out."

"Not likely," he told her and picked her up as if she weighed nothing, then plopped her down into the tub. Gina sucked in a gulp of air as warm water met her cold legs, but an instant later, she sat down and let that heat reach down inside her and somewhat ease the cold that seemed locked deep.

Gina closed her eyes and leaned her head back, focusing only on the delicious feel of the hot water surrounding her tired, aching, freezing body. She heard Adam hit the switch to turn on the hot-tub jets, and an instant later, she felt hot, steady pulses hitting her poor, abused body like tiny, miraculous blessings.

Okay, he was bossy and irritating and right now, the last human being on the face of the planet she wanted to be alone with, but he'd been right about the hot tub. And she wanted to thank him for turning on the jets.

When she opened her eyes to do that, though, she saw Adam peeling out of his own wet clothing. "What are you doing?"

He glared at her and tugged his jeans down to join the wet shirt he'd already tossed to the floor to lay atop both pairs of boots. His broad chest ran with water and droplets of the stuff fell from the tips of his wet hair. "What the hell does it look like?"

"I know just what it looks like," she said and scooted back in the tub as far from him as she could get. Yes, her body was starting to fire into life, but it wasn't as if she wanted it to happen. It was simply a biological imperative. See Adam naked, go all hot and tingly.

God, would it be that way forever?

No. Eventually if she could go without seeing him for ten or fifteen years, she'd probably be able to control her reaction to an occasional sighting. At the moment, though, she was having a hard time fighting down her body's urges. Despite the warnings and dire predictions her brain kept screaming.

He stepped into the tub, settled against the side opposite her and as the frothy water splashed at his bare chest, he looked at her and said, "I was worried."

A ping of something warm and sweet echoed inside her for a moment or two. A few weeks ago…heck, even a few days ago, she would have loved to hear Adam say that to her. It would have given her hope, made her think that there was still a chance for them.

Now she knew better.

Gina looked into his eyes and could only think that

now, it wasn't enough. The worry for her, the fear that she'd been hurt was no more than he would have felt for a neighbor. An acquaintance.

She wanted more.

And she wasn't going to get it.

"You're still cold," he said.

"I am." So very cold. Colder than she'd ever been and Gina had the distinct feeling she'd better get used to the sensation.

"I can fix that." Adam lunged forward, grabbed her arms and then swept back, pulling her up against him, stretching his long legs out in the hot tub.

He wrapped his arms around her and pulled her head down to his chest. She nestled in, listening to the steady beat of his heart beneath her ear.

"Don't do that to me again," he said, his voice rumbling through his chest.

Hot water sprayed up onto her face and the pummeling jets pounded at her back as Adam stroked her skin. She thought he might have kissed the top of her head, but Gina dismissed that notion immediately, sure she was only fooling herself.

"I won't." Not that she'd have the chance to worry him for much longer. Her time at the King ranch was definitely coming to a close. And when she left here, Adam wouldn't give her another thought. He wouldn't have to be concerned about her whereabouts. He'd have what he wanted. A twenty-acre parcel of land to make the King holdings whole again.

In a few months time, she'd be nothing more than an

inconvenient memory. Maybe he'd walk that acreage he'd worked so hard to earn and think about her. Maybe he'd wonder then what she was doing, or where she was. But then, he'd put it out of his mind. He'd lock the memory of her away as completely as he had that of Monica and Jeremy.

"At least take your damn cell phone with you next time," Adam said, stroking his big, rough hands up and down her back in long, steady caresses, a silky counterpoint to the hot tub jets. "About made me insane when I called you and heard the phone ringing up here."

"I will." She hadn't been thinking when she left the ranch or she would have told someone where she was going. She'd been raised to know better. Accidents could happen anywhere, anytime and finding someone on a ranch the size of Adam's could have taken weeks. As to the cell phone, she hadn't wanted it with her. Hadn't wanted anyone to be able to intrude on her ride into Adam's past.

"Damn it, Gina…" This time his voice was more of a growl. She heard the need in it, felt the hard, insistent throb of his erection beneath her. His body was tight, his heartbeat quickened and in seconds, his hands were moving over her with more hunger than care.

"You could have been hurt," he muttered thickly and turned her face up to his. He bent his head and kissed her, hard and long and deep. His tongue swept into her mouth, his breath dusted her cheek and the low moan that issued from his throat slipped inside her, becoming one with her own.

The rhythm of the jets pounded at her, pushing her closer to Adam, hammering home her need as if in punctuation to the raw desire rising up in her.

He was hard and thick and ready. His breath came in strangled gasps as she slid one leg over his middle. His big hands came down on her waist and settled her atop him. Their eyes met and held as Gina felt the slow slide of his body into hers. He filled her and she savored it. Relished it. Imprinted the feeling on her memory so that she'd always be able to recall with perfect clarity the feel of his hands on her slick skin. The scent of him. The taste of his kiss.

Because without her diaphragm standing in the way, she knew she'd be pregnant soon. Knew that even as he touched her, even as his body and hers became one, they were already pulling apart.

And she knew that every touch from this night on, would be a silent goodbye.

Two months later, Adam was in his study, going over reports from his brokers and projections from several of the smaller companies the King ranch held an interest in. At least once a week he was holed up in this room, going over the insane amount of paperwork a huge corporation like his generated.

The study hadn't changed much since his grandfather's time. The walls were a dark hunter-green. There were floor-to-ceiling bookshelves on two of the walls and a bank of windows displaying the wide lawn at the front of the house. A mahogany wetbar took up one corner of the room and a fifty-inch plasma television was hidden behind a copy of one of his mother's favorite Manet paintings. There were two sofas, facing each other, waiting for someone to sit down and have a conversation, along with two oversize club chairs in maroon leather. And for winter, there was a stone fireplace with a hearth big enough for a child to stand up straight in.

It was his sanctuary. No one came in here, except Esperanza, and that was only to clean. Completely caught up in the columns of figures and the suggestions on further diversifying, he didn't even notice when the study door opened quietly.

He heard it shut, though, and said without looking up, "I'm not hungry, Esperanza. But I could use more coffee if you've got some."

"Sorry," Gina said, "fresh out."

Surprised, Adam lifted his gaze and saw her look quickly around the one room in the house she'd never been. She was wearing worn blue jeans, a long-sleeved red T-shirt and boots that looked as old as the ranch itself. Her hair was pulled back into a ponytail at the base of her neck and she wasn't wearing a speck of makeup. Yet her golden eyes seemed alive with fire and emotion and he knew he'd never seen a more beautiful woman.

He felt the now all-too-familiar rush of a near electrical charge jolt through him as he watched her. Instantly his groin went hard as granite and an ache settled deep inside him. They'd been married for months and still he hadn't become immune to her presence.

Irritated by that thought, he deliberately lowered his

gaze to the stacks of papers in front of him. "Didn't know it was you, Gina. I'm kind of busy right now. Is there something you need?"

"No," she said softly, walking across the thick red Oriental carpet toward the massive oak desk that had once been his father's. "You've already given me everything I need."

"What?" Her solemn tone, more than the words, caught his attention. He lifted his gaze to her again and for the first time, noticed the sad smile curving her mouth and the gleam of unshed tears making her eyes shine brilliantly. "What're you talking about?" he asked, standing to face her. "Is something wrong?"

She shook her head, brushed away a single tear that escaped her eye to roll down her cheek and pulled a folded piece of paper from her back pocket. "No, Adam. Nothing's wrong. In fact, everything's just right."

"Then…?"

In answer, she handed him the piece of paper and watched him as he unfolded it carefully. The first thing Adam saw was one word, in chunky black lettering.

Deed.

His fingers tightened on the paper, making it crackle in the stillness. This could only mean…looking at her finally, he said, "You're pregnant?"

She gave him a smile that didn't quite reach her eyes. "I am. I did a pregnancy test on my own, then went to the doctor yesterday to confirm." She took a deep breath and said, "I'm about six weeks along. Everything looks fine."

Gina. Pregnant with his child. Emotion he didn't

want and refused to acknowledge ran crazily through his mind. His gaze dropped to her flat belly as if he could see through her body to the tiny child already growing within. Child. *His* child. He waited for the pain to cut at him, but it didn't happen and he didn't know what to make of that.

"Congratulations, Adam," Gina said, shattering his thoughts with her quiet, somehow broken, voice. "You did a great job. Held up your end of our deal. Now, you've got the land you wanted, and our bargain's complete."

"Yeah." Congratulations to him. His fingers smoothed over the paper he held and knew he should be feeling a sense of satisfaction. Completion. For five years, he'd dedicated himself to acquiring the last pieces to his ranch. And here it was. The final parcel in his hands and he felt…nothing.

"I'm all packed," Gina was saying and Adam frowned, narrowed his gaze and looked at her.

"You're leaving? Already?"

"No point in staying longer, is there?" Her voice got brighter, sharper.

"No." He glanced at the paper in his hand again. Gina was leaving. The marriage was over. "No point."

"Look, Adam, there's one more thing." She took a deep breath, then blew the air out in a rush. "It's something you should know before I go. I love you, Adam."

He swayed a little as those four words punched at him. She loved him and she was leaving. Why wasn't he saying something? Why the hell couldn't he *think?*

"Always have," she admitted and wiped away another

tear with an impatient gesture. "You don't have to say anything or do anything, so don't try, okay? I don't think either one of us could take it." She gave him a brief smile, but he saw her bottom lip tremble.

He started around the edge of his desk, not sure what he was going to do or say, only knowing that he had to do *something*. But she stopped him by holding up one hand and backing up a little. "Don't, okay?" She shook her head. "Don't touch me and don't be nice." She laughed shortly and it sounded like glass breaking. "God, don't be nice. I uh, wanted you to know, I won't be staying in Birkfield. I'm leaving. Tomorrow."

"Leaving? For where? For how long? What? Why?"

"I'm moving to Colorado." She gave him a smile that didn't fool either of them. "Going to stay with my brother Nick and his family until I find a place of my own." She was backing up toward the door, keeping her gaze fixed on him as if worried he'd try to keep her from leaving. "I can't stay here, Adam. I can't raise my child so close to a father who doesn't want it. I can't be near you knowing that I'll never have you. I need somewhere fresh, Adam. My baby deserves to be happy. So do I."

"Gina, you're throwing this at me too fast. What the hell am I supposed to do about this?"

"Nothing, Adam." Her hand fisted around the doorknob behind her. "This isn't about *you*. So anyway…goodbye."

She was changing her whole life because of him. He felt like a jerk, but couldn't quite bring himself to say it. She shouldn't have to leave. Move away from the home she loved all because of him. "Gina, damn it—"

She shook her head. "It's just how it has to be, Adam. So, have a good life, okay? Be well."

Then she was gone and Adam was alone.

Just the way he wanted it.

Twelve

"You are a fool."

Adam didn't even look up when Esperanza served his breakfast along with her opinion. Morning sunlight splashed across him as he sat at the head of the long, cherrywood table in the dining room. One man at a table for twelve.

Quite the statement on his life.

His coffee was cold, but he had the distinct impression asking for a refill wouldn't get him far. Glancing down at his breakfast plate, he noticed the scrambled eggs were runny—he loathed wet eggs and Esperanza knew it. The bacon was charred on one side and raw on the other and his toast was black.

Pretty much the same breakfast he'd been served every morning since Gina left.

Complaining about it wouldn't change anything, he knew. Esperanza had been with the family for way too long. Once a woman's paddled your backside for you when you were a kid, you no longer had any authority over her, no matter what you'd prefer to think.

"Thanks," he said, picking up his fork and wondering if he could just eat the *tops* of the eggs. Damn it, he hadn't *told* Gina to leave. That had been her idea. She'd walked away under her own power, but facts didn't seem to matter to his housekeeper.

Did they matter to him, either? Not for the first time since she'd been gone, Adam wondered what she was doing at that moment. Sitting around her brother's breakfast table? Laughing, talking, enjoying herself? Or was she missing him? Did she think about him at all?

"You are going to simply sit here and do nothing while the *mother of your child* is off somewhere in the wilderness?" Esperanza stood alongside the table, arms folded over her chest, the toe of her shoe tapping briskly against the wood floor. Her dark eyes snapped with fury and her mouth was so thin a slash, it had almost disappeared.

Adam pushed thoughts of Gina away, though they didn't go far. He blew out a breath and nibbled at a bite of egg before grimacing and giving it up. He and his housekeeper had had this same conversation for three weeks now. At every opportunity, Esperanza alternately cajoled, harangued and berated him for allowing Gina to leave him. "Colorado is hardly the wilderness," he pointed out.

"It is not *here*."

"True." Adam dropped his fork onto the plate and resigned himself to another hungry day. Maybe he'd drive into town for a decent breakfast. But as soon as he considered it, he changed his mind. In town, there would be people. People wanting to talk to him. To tell him how sorry they were to hear his marriage had ended. People fishing for more information than he was willing to share.

"You should go after her."

He finally shot his housekeeper a dirty look. She remained unmoved. "Esperanza, Gina left. She *wanted* to go. We had a deal, remember? The deal's finished."

"Deal." That single word carried so much disgust, it practically vibrated in the air. "What you had was a marriage. What you are going to have is a child. A child you will never see. This is what you want, Adam? This is the life you wish to lead?"

No, he thought grimly, looking at the chair where Gina used to sit. Imagining her smile. Her laughter, the gentle touch of her hand when she reached out to pat his arm. He hadn't even realized how much he'd come to depend on seeing her every day. Hearing her. Talking with her. Arguing with her.

In the last few weeks, life on the King ranch had returned to "normal." The Gypsy horses were gone, back at the Torino ranch until Gina sent for them to join her in Colorado. The constant stream of visitors who'd come to buy those horses had ended. There were no more vases of fresh flowers in his bedroom, because Gina wasn't there to pick them. There were no more late night movies played or bowls of popcorn eaten, because Gina had left him.

There was no more *life* at the ranch.

His world had become the stark black and white he'd once known and cherished. Only now…he hated it. He hated the sameness. The quiet. The everlasting ordinariness of his existence. It was like the breakfasts Esperanza had been serving him. Tasteless.

But he couldn't change it. Gina had gone. She'd moved on to build a life without him and that was for the best. For her. For their baby. For him. He was almost sure of it.

"She has been gone three weeks already," Esperanza reminded him.

Three weeks, five days and eleven hours. But who was counting?

"You must go to her. Bring her back where she belongs."

"It's not that simple."

"Only to a man," she pointed out, grabbing up his untouched breakfast and heading for the kitchen.

He half turned in his chair to shout after her, "I *am* a man!"

"A foolish one!" she shouted right back.

"You're fired!"

"Hah!"

Adam slumped in his chair and shook his head. Firing her would do no good. Esperanza would never leave. She'd be right here for the next twenty years, probably making him miserable at every opportunity.

But then, he wondered as he shoved himself up from the table, did he really deserve any better? He'd let Gina go without a word because he hadn't been able to risk caring for her. For their child.

Which made him, he knew, a coward.

And everybody knew that cowards died a thousand deaths.

By afternoon, Adam had irritated, angered and annoyed all of his employees and was even starting to get on his own nerves. So he closed himself up in his study, made some phone calls and started looking for new projects. After all, he had the precious land he'd wanted so badly. Now he needed something new to concentrate on.

The knock on the study door aggravated him. "What is it?"

Sal Torino opened the door and gave him such a long, level stare that everything in Adam went cold and hard as ice. He jumped up from his chair. There was only one reason for Sal to be there. "Is it Gina? Is she all right?"

Gina's father stepped into the room, closed the door behind him and studied Adam for a moment or two before speaking. "I've come because it's only right you know."

The ice moved through his veins, sluggishly headed for his heart. Adam clenched his fists, gritted his teeth and fought for control. "Just tell me. Gina. Is she all right?"

"Gina is fine," Sal said, walking slowly around the big room, as if seeing it for the first time.

Relief swept through Adam so fast, it left his knees shaking. He felt as though he'd been running in place for an hour. His heart was pounding, his breath was laboring in his lungs and his legs were rubbery. What the hell kind of stunt was Sal up to?

"Damn it, Sal. What was the point of that?" He shouted the question, as adrenaline drained slowly away. "Want to see if you could get a rise out of me? Is that it?"

"It was a test of sorts," Sal admitted, stopping on the opposite side of the wide desk. "I wanted to know," the older man said, his dark eyes narrowed, his mouth grim, "if you loved my Gina. Now I know."

Adam shoved one hand through his hair, then wiped his face. Love. There was a word he'd avoided thinking about over the last few weeks. Even when he lay awake at night, alternately planning on either flying to Colorado to kidnap Gina or burying himself in work, he'd trained himself to never think that word.

It wasn't part of his plan.

He'd tried love before and he was no good at it. Love messed people up. Ruined lives. Ended some. He wasn't going there again. Even if the heart he'd thought long dead was now very alive and aching.

Not something he was going to admit to anyone else.

"Sorry to disappoint. Naturally I was concerned for her. But if she's fine, then I don't see a reason for this visit." Sitting down in his desk chair again, he picked up a pen, lowered his gaze to the papers in front of him and said, "Thanks for stopping by."

Sal didn't leave, though. He leaned forward, bracing

his work-worn hands on the edge of the desk and waited until Adam lifted his gaze before saying, "I have something to tell you, Adam. Something I think you have the right to know."

"Say it then and get it done," Adam muttered, bracing himself for whatever news the older man had come to deliver. How bad could it be? Was Gina already in love with someone else? That thought sliced through him, even as he discounted it. It might feel like years since she'd been gone, but it had only been a few weeks. So what could possibly have happened?

"Gina lost the baby."

"What?" He whispered the word and the pen he held dropped from suddenly nerveless fingers. "When?"

"Yesterday," Sal said, his features full of pity and sorrow.

Yesterday. How had that happened and he hadn't sensed it? Felt it somehow? Gina had been alone and he'd been here. Tucked away in an insulated world of his own design. She'd needed him and he hadn't been there.

"Gina? How's Gina?" Stupid question, Adam thought instantly. He knew how she would be. She'd wanted that child so much. She would be devastated. Crushed. Heartsick.

And a moment later, he realized to his own astonishment that he felt those things, too. A profound sense of loss shook him to the bone and he was so unprepared for it, he didn't know what to think.

"She will be fine in time," Sal told him softly. "She didn't want you to know, but I felt it was only right."

"Of course." Of course he should know. Their child was dead. Though it hadn't taken a breath, Adam felt the loss as surely as he had the loss of Jeremy years ago. It wasn't just the death of the child. It was the death of dreams. Hopes. The future.

"Also," Sal added, waiting now for Adam to look at him, "you should know that Gina will be staying in Colorado."

"She. Staying. What?" Adam shook his head, trying to focus past the pain that was threading its way through his bloodstream.

"She's not coming home," Sal said, then added softly, "unless something happens to change her mind."

Adam hardly noticed when Sal left. His mind kept flashing with images of Gina until the pain in his heart was almost too much to bear. For weeks now, he'd thought of nothing but her, despite trying to shut himself off from the world. Return to the solitary existence he'd become so accustomed to.

But no matter how hard he tried, thoughts of her had remained. Taunting him. Torturing him. Wondering how she was. Where she was living. What she would tell their child about him.

Now there was no baby. Gina was in pain, so much more pain than he was feeling and she was alone in this, despite her family, she was as alone as he was. And suddenly, Adam knew what he wanted more than anything. He wanted to hold her. Dry her tears. Comfort her and wrap himself up in the warmth of her.

He wanted to fall asleep holding her and wake up to look into her eyes. Standing up again, he turned, looked out the wide window behind him at the sweep of lawn leading to the main road. The ancient trees lining the driveway danced in the wind, leaves already turning gold breaking free to twist and fly through the air. Fall was coming fast and soon, the days would be cold and the nights far too long.

Just as his *life* would be long and cold and empty without Gina.

"Esperanza was right," he muttered, turning to reach for the phone on his desk. "Half-right, anyway. I *was* a fool. But no more."

Gina laughed at the little boy bouncing around in the saddle. He was so excited at being a "cowboy," he hadn't stopped grinning since Gina had put him on the horse.

Thankfully, even though her brother Nick was technically a high school football coach, he had a small ranch outside of town. You really could take the boy off the home ranch but couldn't take the ranch out of the boy, she thought. And being here, working on Nick and his wife's small spread had been good for her. She'd spent time with her nephews and niece and had kept herself so busy that she'd only had time to think about Adam every *other* minute.

Surely that was progress.

"You're thinking about him again."

She turned to smile and shrug at her older brother. "Only a little."

"I talked to Tony last night," Nick said, leaning his forearms on the top rail of the corral fence. "If it helps any, he says Adam looks miserable."

Small consolation, Gina thought, but she'd take it. She leaned back against the fence and said, "Is it wrong to say 'glad to hear it'?"

"No. Not wrong at all." Nick tugged at her ponytail. "Tony's willing to go beat him up for you. You just say the word."

"You guys are the best."

He grinned and his golden eyes twinkled. "So we keep telling you."

She smiled again and turned to look when a car pulled into the yard behind them. She didn't recognize the bright yellow van, so her heartbeat didn't stutter until the driver opened the door and stepped out.

"What d'ya know?" Nick mumbled.

"Adam," Gina said on a sigh, straightening up and wishing she were dressed a little better. Silly, she knew. But the purely female part of her couldn't help being irritated that she was wearing worn jeans and dirty boots for Adam's surprise arrival.

He started toward her and Gina took a step before turning back to her brother. "Nick, would you keep an eye on Mikey?"

"Sure thing," her brother said with a brief nod. "But if you need me to get rid of Adam, just call out."

Get rid of him? No. She didn't want to get rid of him. She wanted to luxuriate in just looking at him. How pitiful was that? God, he was gorgeous. Even better than the dream images she saw of him whenever she closed her eyes. Her blood was humming, her heartbeat pounding and her mouth was so dry, she could hardly swallow.

Gina forced herself to take slow, even steps toward him when her instincts were telling her to run, throw herself into his arms and never let go. How long did it take, she wondered, before love faded? Months? Years?

"Gina," he said and his voice was a deep rumble that seemed to reverberate inside her chest.

"Adam. What are you doing here?"

He scrubbed one hand across the back of his neck. "I had to see you. Took one of the family jets. Rented a car at the airport—" He paused to give the van a dirty look.

"Yeah, nice color."

"All they had," he said.

She smiled. "I didn't ask how you got here. Just why you *are* here."

"To see you. To tell you—"

His eyes were flashing with emotion—more than she'd ever seen in those dark depths before and Gina wondered frantically what was going on. Hope reared up inside her and she quickly squashed it. No point in pumping up a balloon that Adam would undoubtedly pop.

Then he frowned, looked her up and down and said, "Are you all right? Should you be up and around?"

"What?" She laughed at him. "I'm fine, Adam. What's going on?"

"I brought you something." He dug a folded paper out of his back pocket and held it out to her. "This is yours."

It only took a glance to tell her it was the deed to the

land he'd wanted so badly. "What?" She shook her head. "I don't understand."

"Simple to understand. I'm breaking our bargain. The land's yours again."

She looked from him to the paper and back again. "You're not making any sense."

"Your father told me."

A niggling doubt began tugging at the edges of her mind. What had her interfering father been up to now? "Told you what exactly?"

Adam stepped close, dropped both hands onto her shoulders and looked into her eyes. "He told me about you losing the baby."

She swayed, but he kept talking.

"I'm so sorry, Gina. I know that's not enough. I know 'sorry' doesn't mean a damn at a time like this, but it's all I've got to give you." His hands moved to her face, his thumbs stroking her skin. "I'm so sorry I didn't appreciate the miracle we made together."

Her father had lied to him. And thinking she was in pain, Adam had raced to her side. That bubble of hope lifted inside her again. She sucked in a breath and despite the cold Colorado wind buffeting her, Gina felt warm for the first time since leaving California. "Adam…"

"Wait. Let me finish." He pulled her in close, held her tightly to him and stroked his hands up and down her back as if trying to convince himself that she was really there. With him. And Gina did nothing to stop him. She gave herself up to the wonder of being held by him again. To the scent of him filling her. To the feel of his strength wrapped around her.

When he spoke, his voice was quiet, torn. "You asked why I don't have pictures of Monica and Jeremy in the house."

She stiffened a little, but he felt it and held her tighter.

"I haven't forgotten them. But there's something you don't know, Gina." He pulled back to look at her. "Monica was leaving me. I was a terrible husband and not much better at fatherhood."

That explained so much. "Oh, Adam. You blame yourself for—"

"No." He shook his head now, sadly. "I don't feel guilt for the accident—though if I'd been a better husband, maybe it wouldn't have happened. No, Gina. What I feel is regret. That I couldn't or wouldn't be what they needed."

Her heart hurt for him, but there was more than grief in his eyes, there was determination, as well. And hope. Something that lifted her heart even as she wanted to soothe him.

Adam tipped her chin up with his fingertips and said, "I want to be a husband to you, Gina. I want a real marriage. That's why I'm giving you back the stupid land. I don't want it. You hold it. Give it to the next child we make together. Just give me a chance to make it up to you."

"Oh, Adam…" It was everything. Everything she'd hoped and dreamed and prayed for. All of it was here, within arm's reach. She saw what she'd always wanted to see in his eyes and knew that they would now have the life together that she so craved.

"I miss you," he said, gaze moving over her face like a dying man taking his last look at the world. "Like an arm or a leg. I miss you. A part of me is gone without you. Nothing means anything anymore because you're not with me. Gina, I want you to come home. Be my wife again. Let me be the husband I should have been to you. I do love you, Gina. I'm not too stubborn to say it anymore. Will you take me back? Will you help me try again for another baby?"

Gina was staggered by his presence, his words, by the love shining in his eyes. She could even forgive her father for interfering this time.

"I love you, too, Adam," she said, reaching up to cup his cheek in the palm of her hand.

"Thank God," he whispered and pulled her in close again. When he kissed her there was desperation and adoration and the hunger Gina knew so well. Finally, though, when they broke apart to smile at each other, Gina had to tell him.

"I'll come home with you, Adam, and we'll make that wonderful life together. But—"

He scowled at her. "But?"

"There's no need to work on another baby just yet," she said, taking his hand and laying it flat against her belly. Meeting his gaze, she smiled wider, brighter and saw realization dawn in his eyes. "Our first child is just fine."

He looked confused. "You're still—"

"Yes."

"So your father—"

"Yes," Gina said, grinning now as she went up on her toes to link her arms around his neck.

"The old fraud," Adam muttered, grinning back at her as he lifted her off her feet and swung her in a wide circle. "Remind me to buy your father a drink when we get home."

"That's a deal," Gina said.

"Let's seal this bargain right, shall we?" Then Adam kissed her and felt his world shift back into balance.

* * * * *

MARRYING FOR KING'S MILLIONS

BY
MAUREEN CHILD

To the best plot group in the known universe—
Susan Mallery, Christine Rimmer, Teresa Southwick
and Kate Carlisle. Thank you all for sharing
your friendship, your quick wit, your brilliant ideas
and your never-ending well of patience.

One

"No way. Sorry, Travis, I just can't marry you." Julie O'Hara leaned against the closed door and kept her voice pitched loud enough so that it would carry to the man on the other side.

Clearly, he heard her.

"Oh, yes you can," he said, and even through the door, his voice was all steely determination. "Now cut the dramatics and open the damn door."

Julie's head dropped back against the door and she rolled her eyes to look at the high, beamed ceiling. Sunlight slanted in through the windows across the room and the golden wash from the sun created shadows on the walls that looked eerily like the bars on a cell.

Coincidence?

She didn't think so.

This was a huge mistake. She knew it down to her bones. The bad feeling that had been taking root inside her for the last month had suddenly blossomed into big, black flowers. Ooh, there was an image.

"Travis, think about this for a minute."

"Not really the time for any more thinking, Julie," he said. "The guests are here, the minister's waiting and we *are* getting married."

Her stomach did a slow pitch and roll and she clenched her teeth together and took a few deep breaths through her nose. Didn't really help. How in the heck had she gotten herself into this? Julie's eyes flew open when Travis King's knuckles rapped on the door again and she looked around the room with a frantic gaze, futilely searching for an escape route.

But there wasn't one and she knew it. She was trapped in this plush guest room in Travis's castlelike house on the King Vineyard. Just like the rest of the house, it was gorgeous, elegant and so far away from her ordinary world she felt like a servant girl who'd sneaked into the mistress's room to try on her clothes. Bad, bad feeling. And it was all her own fault.

She'd walked into this stupid situation with her eyes wide open. "Idiot."

"Open the door, Julie…."

"It's bad luck to see the bride before the wedding," she said.

"Uh-huh. Don't think that matters so much in our case, so open up."

Our case.

Of course their case was special. Because this wasn't your ordinary, everyday wedding.

It had all seemed so simple a month ago, she thought and instantly remembered just how she'd gotten to this place in her life.

"I need a wife," Travis had said. "You need a future. It's perfect."

Julie had looked at him, sitting across from her in a red vinyl booth at Terri's Diner in the heart of downtown Birkfield, California. In a small town, the diner was the one place where everyone eventually showed up. Julie had practically grown up sliding across the red vinyl seats.

Her first date had brought her here. She'd nursed her first broken heart over four double-chocolate shakes. And now she was getting a marriage proposal here.

Shouldn't there be a plaque?

"It's not perfect," she argued, thinking that at least one of them had to be logical here. Travis had always been more impulsive than she—well, except for that one time when she'd married a man she thought loved her, only to find out too late that he hadn't. See where impulsiveness had gotten her?

Firmly, she said, "There's an easier solution, Travis. Just go find another distributor for your wines."

He shook his head, dark brown hair flopping across his forehead in a way that made her want to reach across the table and smooth it back for him. She resisted.

"Can't. Thomas Henry is the best and you know I never settle for less than the best."

True, he never had. Travis had grown up as a member of one of the wealthiest, most powerful families in the state. He'd long ago grown accustomed to being on top. Being number one. And there was nothing Travis cared for more than King Vineyards. Ever since taking it over from his late father, he'd put in the time and effort required to make King wines known all over California.

Now he'd set his sights on not only distribution countrywide, but also eventually international exports, as well. Apparently, Thomas Henry was key to Travis's plan for world domination.

"Okay, but you don't have to marry me to get him."

"No." He sat back in the booth seat with a disgusted scowl on his face. "I don't. I could marry one of Henry's hideous daughters instead. I told you, Julie. The guy's kind of eccentric. He's a self-made millionaire and now his big goal in life is to get his girls married. I'm single. Rich. Therefore, I'm prime husband material."

She smiled. "He can't force you to marry one of his daughters. This isn't the Middle Ages."

"I wouldn't put it past him to try." Travis smiled wryly. "But if I turn down his 'darlings,' he can—and will—refuse to handle my wines. I can't risk that. King Vineyards is poised for the next big step. Getting the distribution deal with Henry would put me on the right path. All I need to make it all happen is a temporary wife. If I'm already married, he won't be tossing his daughters at my feet, will he?"

"Why me?"

He grinned…and Travis smiling was pretty spectacular. She'd had a crush on him when she was a kid. But then, Travis was gorgeous, charming and his smile had been known to melt a woman's resistance at fifty feet. Good thing Julie was immune. All it had taken was marrying a jerk and being dumped. Just because she could admire Travis's smile didn't mean she was going to turn into a puddle of mush at his feet.

"A couple of reasons," he was saying and Julie listened up. "First, because we know each other and I know you need this, too. Second, because I trust you to stick to our agreement and not try to bleed me for extra cash."

She knew he was wary of most women because King men attracted gold diggers in greater numbers than the gold rush had back in the day. "But if I marry you, what makes me different from any of those other women? I'll still be marrying you for your money."

"Yeah, but on my terms," he said with a smile.

Hmm. He might think that was funny, but she didn't see the humor. Julie watched women throw themselves at Travis for years. And all of them had had one eye on his exceptional behind and the other eye on his bank account. If she allowed him to pay her to marry him, wasn't she just another member of a very large, mercenary crowd?

Julie groaned inwardly and sucked at her chocolate

shake. When tumultuous times struck, always have chocolate handy. A good rule of thumb for life's little miseries. She didn't like the idea of people thinking she was after his money.

"I don't want or need a husband," she pointed out, even though she distinctly felt herself losing the battle.

"Maybe not, but you do need the money to start that bakery you've always wanted."

True. God, she hated that he was right. She'd been working like a dog and saving every spare dime for years and still she was light years from having enough money put away to open her own bakery. She couldn't get a loan because she had no collateral, and if things stayed as they were, she'd be at retirement age before she could afford her dream shop.

But was that any reason to get married?

Hadn't she turned down Travis's offer of a loan before this? She'd known him her whole life. Her mom had been the cook on the King ranch until she'd married the gardener and hung up her apron when Julie was twelve. As kids, Julie and Travis had been friends. That had lasted until high school, when Julie'd first heard the laughter about the rich kid hanging out with the nobody. Their friendship had gradually cooled down, but they'd remained "friendly."

Now that they were grown, they weren't exactly close anymore, but the memory of that friendship was strong enough that Julie hadn't wanted to borrow money from him and muddy up their relationship.

Wasn't marrying him even worse?

"It's one year, Julie," Travis said, tapping his finger-tips impatiently against the white Formica tabletop. "One year and I'll have the distribution deal I want and I give you financial backing in the bakery. Everybody wins."

"I don't know…." She still wasn't convinced. And it wasn't just the thought of marrying for money that had her hesitating, though heaven knew, it should have been enough. Nope, there was something else bother-ing her as well. "And when the marriage ends, that would leave me a two-time divorcée."

How tacky was that? God, thirty years old and a two-time loser? Oh, if she could step back in time a year or two, she'd avoid Jean Claude Doucette like the plague. Unfortunately, she couldn't do that and that French rat was going to remain a part of her past forever.

"Yeah, but that first marriage lasted what? Two weeks? It hardly counts," Travis argued. "Besides, who cares?"

"Me."

"Don't see why. So you made a mistake. Big deal. You wised up, got a divorce…"

Yeah, she thought, after Jean Claude dumped her and arranged for a quickie Mexican divorce.

"Put it behind you, move on," Travis finished. "Anyway, he was French."

Julie laughed.

"And, I offered to beat the crap out of him for you," Travis reminded her.

"I know." She really liked having Travis as a friend. Was she ready for that to change? "And I appreciate it."

"So then marry me already."

"What would your family say? Oh, God, what would my mother say?" she wondered aloud, knowing even as she asked it that he'd have a ready answer. "This is coming out of nowhere and—"

"Hell," Travis said on a laugh. "They'll understand. We tell my family and yours the truth of the situation, but no one else. And let's remember how Gina and Adam got married last year, huh? It's not like this idea has never been thought of before."

"Yes…." Travis's brother Adam had married his neighbour Gina for all the wrong reasons, but their marriage had turned into something wonderful. Now Gina was pregnant and Adam was walking around looking like the emperor of the world. "But Travis…"

"No one but our families know the whole truth, though," he insisted, leaning across the table to look directly into her eyes. "This has got to look real, Julie. To everybody. Thomas Henry needs to believe it. So we'll play the perfect married couple. We can do it. It's only a year."

A year. A year with Travis as her husband. Oh, God, she was weakening and she knew it. Visions of a bakery with her name over the door were dancing before her eyes. Then something else occurred to her.

"What about…"

"What?"

"You know." When he just stared at her, she blew out a breath. "Sex?"

"Oh." He frowned for a minute or two, then shook

his head. "No problem. Married in name only. I swear. Trust me, I can resist you."

"Gee, thanks. Don't I feel special."

"Besides, it's only a year." He said it again as if trying to convince not only her, but also himself, that they could do this. "How hard could it be?"

She hadn't expected to get married again. Ever. Jean Claude ensured that she'd never trust any man that completely again. But this was different. It wasn't as if she was going into this marriage all starry-eyed, expecting love to last a lifetime. This was business, plain and simple. And if she was going to do it, why not marry a friend? A man who didn't expect anything from her? A man who was going to help her make her dreams come true at the end of one tiny, tiny, year.

"So what do you say?" he prompted.

"Okay," she'd said on a sigh. "Yes, I'll marry you."

"Idiot," Julie said again the memory fading. She was back in the guest room, wearing an ivory wedding dress and trying to find a way to successfully chicken out.

"Damn it, Julie," Travis implored from the other room and she heard the banked temper in his voice. "Open the damn door so we can talk about this."

She shot a look into the mirror behind her and then tossed the lacy edge of her veil over her shoulder. Steeling herself, she took a breath and flipped the dead bolt. Travis opened the door a second later and moved into the room, closing the door behind him.

He looked amazing, of course. The bridegroom of every woman's fantasy. He wore an elegantly tailored black suit with a crisp white shirt and a bold red tie. His dark brown hair was swept back from his face and his chocolate brown eyes were pinned on her. In an instant, he looked her up and down. "You look gorgeous."

"Thanks." She looked the part of a bride, even if she didn't feel like it. Her dark red hair was piled up on top of her head, with a few careless ringlets pulled free to lay against her neck. The lace-edged veil was elbow length and tickled her bare shoulders. Her floor-length gown flowed around her in a soft cloud of gossamer fabric. Strapless, the gown dipped low over her bosom and hugged her narrow waist. She knew she looked good—she only wished she felt as good as she looked.

"I don't think I can do it, Travis," she admitted and laid the flat of her hand against a stomach that was spinning and churning with nerves.

"Oh, you're *going* to do it," Travis told her and took her shoulders in a hard grip. "We've got a garden full of guests out there and the musicians are tuning up. Reporters are standing out on the drive and security just caught a photographer sneaking in over the paddock fence."

"Oh, God…." He'd always been a favorite of the paparazzi. They followed him everywhere, taking pictures of Travis with whatever woman happened to be hanging on his arm. It just hadn't occurred to Julie that now *she'd* be a photographer's target. Her whole life was about to change and she wasn't sure she could go through with it.

"You're just nervous."

"Oh, boy, howdy," she said, nodding frantically.

He tipped her chin up, stared into her eyes and said, "You'll get over it."

"I don't think so," Julie said, willing her stomach to settle. "I've really got a bad feeling about this, Travis. It's all so much…more than I thought it would be. This is marriage, Travis. Even if it's only temporary, it's *marriage.* I can't do this again."

He frowned at her. "If you think you're backing out now, you're nuts. A King wedding is big news. A King being stood up at the altar is even bigger news and that's not going to happen."

"Fine," she said, snatching at his words desperately. "Then you dump me. I don't care. I'll explain that you've changed your mind and—"

"What's this all about?" he interrupted and stared down at her.

Julie refused to be swayed by the soft brown of his eyes. Instead, she steeled herself, stomped across the room and pointed out the window at the elegantly decorated garden below. There were two hundred people, sitting in rented white chairs on opposite sides of a white carpeted aisle.

A minister waited at the head of that aisle in a gazebo draped in brilliantly shaded roses and a quartet of violinists were off to one side, playing classical music for the waiting guests. Farther in the distance, a white tent, strewn with yet more roses, awaited the reception party.

"That, Travis," she said, swallowing hard against the ball of nerves jostling the black flowers of death in the pit of her stomach. "That's what this is about. I can't face those people and *lie*. I'm a terrible liar. You know that. I get blotchy and start to giggle and then it gets *bad*."

"You're making too big a deal out of this." He strolled across the room, as if he had all the time in the world. "Think of it like a play. We're a couple of actors, saying our lines then celebrating with a party."

"A play. Great." She threw her hands high, then let them slap against the cool silk of her gown. "The last time I was in a play, I was a strawberry in the fourth grade pageant."

He sighed. "Julie…"

"No," she said, repeating herself now and not even caring anymore. "I can't. I'm really sorry, Travis."

"Oh, well, as long as you're *sorry*." His mouth tightened up and Julie frowned right back at him.

"I warned you that I was no good at this."

"You signed a contract," he reminded her.

Yes, she really had. He'd put their little agreement into writing and one of a fleet of King lawyers—or was that a herd?—had notarized her signature. So technically, she was stuck. Emotionally, she was still looking for a back door.

"This was a bad idea."

"So you said."

"It bears repeating."

"Maybe," he said and took her hand in his. "But it's the one we agreed on. So pick up your bouquet, we'll go downstairs and get this over with."

"I think I'm gonna be sick."

His eyebrows went straight up. "I believe that's the first time a woman has gotten nauseous at the thought of marrying me."

"First time for everything." Julie looked out the window again and her gaze seemed to arrow in straight on her mother and stepfather. Her mother was worried. Not hard to tell even from a distance, since she was wringing the handle of her new purse. Her stepfather looked uncomfortable, tugging at the collar and tie strangling him.

They didn't approve of what she was doing, Julie knew. But they were there for her. Supporting her. Her gaze slipped to the other side of the aisle where the King family took up the first two rows. There was Gina, pregnant and glowing, with Adam standing beside her, waiting to take his place as best man. Jackson, the youngest of the King brothers, was seated beside Gina and there were King cousins and aunts and uncles there as well.

Everyone was waiting on *her*.

But no pressure.

Beside her, Travis whispered, "Think of the future, Julie. Your future. In a year, you'll have your bakery, I'll have my distribution deal and everything will go back to normal."

She wished she could believe him. But that bad feeling inside wouldn't go away. And that, more than anything, warned her that "normal" might not be what either one of them were expecting.

Two

The ceremony was over fast and Travis was grateful. Hard enough standing there holding Julie's hand and feeling her nervous tremors rocking through her body. But as promised, when she said her vows, her voice had shaken and she got the giggles halfway through.

She really was a terrible liar, he thought, watching her dance with his younger brother, Jackson. But the deed was done now. He glanced down at the plain gold band on his left ring finger. Idly, he rubbed the ring with his thumb and tried not to feel like the small circle of gold was somehow a tiny noose shutting off his air supply.

This had been his idea after all, despite the fact that Travis had always avoided marriage. Generally, he stayed with a woman until she started getting that let's-get-married-and-make-rich-babies-so-I-can-get-a-fat-settlement look in her eye. Then he was off, moving on to someone new. It kept life interesting. Kept him footloose, which is just the way he liked it.

Now, he was married and looking at a sex-free year. Hmm…

"Second thoughts?"

Travis turned his head to meet his brother Adam's curious gaze. In the last several months, there'd been a change in the oldest King brother. Oh, he still looked the same, but his attitude had shifted. He wasn't concentrating solely on the King ranch anymore. Now his life revolved around Gina and their coming baby.

"Not at all," Travis answered and thought that he was a much better liar than Julie. What did that say about him?

"She's a nice woman." Adam glanced out to the crowded dance floor where Jackson was spinning Julie around until she laughed out loud.

"Yeah, she is." Travis reached for his glass of merlot and took a long drink. "And she knew what she was getting in to, so don't start with me."

Adam lifted both hands and shrugged. "I didn't say a word."

"Yet."

He nodded. "Fine. I'm just saying that Julie's not like your other women. She doesn't have a heart of stone, so be careful."

One of Travis's eyebrows lifted into a high arch. "I think this is where the old saying about the pot and the kettle comes into play."

Adam took a sip of champagne and let his gaze slide to the table where his six-months pregnant wife was sitting with her family. Then he looked back at Travis. "Exactly. When Gina and I got married, it was a straight-up business deal. Just like you and Julie."

"Big difference," Travis interrupted, not willing to hear a lecture or—God help him—advice. He didn't need any help here. He and Julie would do just fine. Their agreement was nothing like the one Adam and his wife had had. "Gina loved you. Always did, though God knows why."

"Very funny."

Travis shrugged. "It's different with Julie. We're friends. Hell, we're not even *good* friends. This is business for both of us. Nothing more."

"Uh-huh."

"Don't even go there," Travis warned, draining his wine and setting the glass down on the table behind him. "When the year's up, so's the marriage. End of story."

"We'll see."

Travis stared at his older brother and said, "What is up with you? Discover you love your wife and now you want the rest of us in your boat?" Grinning, he clapped one hand on Adam's shoulder and said, "Forget about it. I'm just not a one woman kind of guy, Adam. When Julie and I are finished, it's back to serial monogamy for me."

The song ended and almost before the last note drifted away, the band moved into another number. This one slow and dreamy. Music spilled from the stage, swept across the crowd and drew even more couples onto the floor.

Adam shook his head and said, "This is not going to be as easy as you think it will be, Travis. But I guess you'll find that out for yourself."

"Guess I will," Travis said, completely confident that *his* plan would work out just the way he intended.

"Now, I'm going to go dance with my wife," Adam told him. "Maybe you should do the same."

When his brother left and headed for Gina, Travis let that one word roll through his mind. *Wife.* He had a *wife.* Sounded as odd as the gold band on his ring finger felt. He turned his gaze to the dance floor and watched as a tall man with dark blond hair and a wispy moustache cut in on Jackson to dance with Julie.

Julie looked up at the blonde and her features froze in appalled shock. Something inside Travis jolted. He'd already started moving toward the couple when he saw Julie try to pull away even as the blonde leaned in closer to her, whispering something in her ear. Whatever he said had made quite the impression on Julie. She looked like a balloon, slowly deflating.

The crowd separating them seemed to get thicker as Travis moved faster. Instinct pushed him on. He slipped past people, pushed others out of his way and got to Julie's side just as she finally managed to shove herself out of the blond man's arms. She stared up at the guy as if he were a ghost and the blonde was enjoying her shock.

"Julie, you okay?" Travis came up beside her.

"Travis. Oh, God…." She covered her mouth with

one hand and kept staring at the other man as if she couldn't really believe he was there.

And just who the hell was this guy? A reporter? A photographer who'd somehow made it past security? But where was his camera? Instinctively, Travis pushed Julie behind him as he faced the tall, lanky man who was looking at him with what could only be glee shining in his pale blue eyes.

"What's going on here?" Travis demanded, keeping his voice low enough that even the other dancers around them couldn't hear him over the music.

The blonde gave him a half bow and smirked. "I've only come to offer my congratulations on your wedding," he said, his English flavored with a very thick French accent.

Travis shot a look at Julie.

She swallowed hard and shook her head. "I didn't know. I swear I didn't know."

"Know what?" Travis said, turning back to the guy silently laughing at him. Something was going on here and he was damned sure he wasn't going to like it. Hands fisted at his side, he demanded, "Who the hell are you, anyway?"

"Ahh…" The guy held out his right hand and said softly, conspiratorially, "Allow me to introduce myself. I am Jean Claude Doucette. And you must be the man who has just married my wife."

"I'm a bigamist," Julie muttered and the word tasted foul in her mouth. Well, this certainly put her "bad feeling" from earlier in perspective. Compared to now, that debilitating trepidation was like a day at Disneyland.

This was a nightmare. One she couldn't seem to wake up from. One where *both* of her husbands—dear God—were facing off like a couple of well-groomed pit bulls. Although, if she had to bet on who would be the winner of this weird contest, she'd put her money on Travis. The Frenchman who stood so calmly at ease had no idea just how much danger he was in.

"Yes, my dear," Jean Claude said, from his place beside the cold hearth. He looked suave and sure of himself, as always. His blond hair was swept back from his forehead. His pale blue eyes were locked on her and even from across the room, she read the humor in his gaze. He wore a well-tailored gray suit with a pale yellow shirt and a steel-gray tie. He looked relaxed, completely at home, as if he were enjoying himself immensely.

Julie had never hated another human being as much in her life.

Still watching her, Jean Claude leaned one elbow on the intricately carved wooden mantel. "You are indeed a bigamist. Such a shame, really. And so very…embarrassing, I think is the word. At least, it is potentially a very public embarrassment for your new husband."

It really was. The papers had been full of the wedding for the last month. Society columns were filled with speculation about the marriage of one of California's wealthiest bachelors. She could just imagine what would happen if they got wind of this news.

That distribution deal Travis was so concerned about would no doubt disappear and the humiliation would cling to him forever. Oh, God, she wanted the floor to open her up and swallow her whole.

Or better yet, swallow Jean Claude.

If her legs hadn't felt like overcooked spaghetti, she might have walked over to Jean Claude and slapped him. As it was, all she managed was a wince before she dropped into a wing-backed chair. The wide window beside her overlooked the front of the house. At least she didn't have to sit here and stare out at the wedding party.

They'd left the reception, where their friends and families were dancing and laughing, to come to Travis's study. Despite the room's size, its dark green walls, thick, colorful rugs and countless bookshelves gave the study a warm, almost comforting feel.

But it would take way more than the room's ambiance to comfort Julie at the moment. Her heart was galloping in her chest and her stomach kept twisting, as if a giant, unseen fist was squeezing it mercilessly. She shot a look at Travis and nearly groaned at the expression of pure fury on his face.

The three of them were caught together like survivors of a shipwreck. And two of the survivors looked as though they were each willing to throw the other out of the lifeboat.

Could this get any worse?

Oh, she really shouldn't have thought that question.

"I believe I saw some reporters stationed outside

this…winery," Jean Claude mused aloud. "Perhaps I should go and have a quiet word with one or two of them."

Reporters.

Julie's head ached anew and the tumult in her stomach stepped up a notch.

"You won't be talking to any reporters," Travis muttered tightly.

"This is, as you Americans are so fond of saying, a free country, is it not?"

"Not where you're concerned," Travis told him, then added, "You start talking to reporters and my lawyers will be on you so fast, they'll take everything from you but that ridiculous accent."

Jean Claude's eyes narrowed, but as Julie watched him, all she could think was that he was so far outclassed in the whole really furious competition. Anger radiated off of Travis in heavy waves that seemed to swim through the room, making the air almost too thick to breathe.

"You are in no position to dictate terms to me," Jean Claude warned.

"Mister," Travis answered. "This is my house. I do what I damn well want and right now, I want to hear everything you've got to say. So start talking."

For a moment, it looked as though the smaller man might argue, but then, he conceded and gave an indolent shrug, as if none of this was consequential at all.

"It is quite simple really," Jean Claude said in what Julie realized was a reedy, almost whiny voice. "The delightful Julie and I were never really divorced. So you have married a married woman, my good man."

Julie's heart stuttered a little, but she swallowed hard and pulled in a deep breath. She couldn't really believe this was happening, but it was hard to avoid the truth.

From a distance, the muted sounds of her wedding reception were nothing more than a soft, white noise. She glanced down at the gold, diamond-studded band on her left ring finger. Sunlight caught the channel-set stones and winked with a dazzling shine and glitter. Travis had only put it on her an hour ago. Why the devil hadn't Jean Claude stopped the wedding before it was too late? Groaning quietly, she buried her left hand in the folds of her wedding gown so that she wouldn't have to look at the ring again.

"I'm *not* your good man," Travis was saying and his voice was low, deep and threatening enough that if Jean Claude had had a brain in his head, he would have been backing up. Instead, he only picked up the glass of wine he'd poured for himself and sniffed in distaste.

"I am the injured party, *mon ami,*" he said, taking a mouthful of the cabernet and swallowing as if he'd had to force it down. The insult to King wines was unmistakable. "Surely you can see that?"

"What I see—" Travis said "—is a guy trying to work a shakedown."

"Shakedown?" Jean Claude walked around Travis, came to Julie's side and laid one long-fingered hand on her shoulder.

She flinched and ducked out from under his touch.

Jumping to her feet, she only swayed a little before locking her knees and lifting her chin. Damned if she'd let Jean Claude demoralize her again. Once in a lifetime was more than enough.

"I am only here because it is the right thing to do." He smiled, set the glass of wine down and looked around as if searching for something better.

"Oh, I'm sure that's the reason," Travis said and slanted a quick, hard look at Julie.

She met his gaze squarely and tried to tell him silently that she hadn't had a part in this. Whatever it was Jean Claude was up to, he was doing it on his own.

Smoothly, Jean Claude strolled around the room, inspecting the knickknacks, leaning in to check the signature on a painting of the vineyard, as if completely unconcerned about Travis's mounting anger. And, he probably was, Julie thought. The man was single-minded, she'd give him that. He saw only what he wanted to see.

"Why are you here, Jean Claude? Really." Julie asked the question because she wanted him gone. And the only way to accomplish that was to finish whatever he'd come to start.

"Why?" Jean Claude turned and gave her a smile most people reserved for a particularly bright three-year-old who'd managed to *not* spill his juice. "Surely that is clear, *chérie.*"

She didn't bother to glance at Travis. She knew what he was feeling, because that anger of his was still vibrating into the room. Instead, she stared at the man she'd once promised to love and cherish, and she saw only a stranger. "Spell it out for me, Jean Claude."

He sighed. "Very well. You see, when I read about the wedding of my sweet Julie to one of the powerful King family, I knew it was only right for me to come."

"Uh-huh," Travis said, moving to stand beside Julie, arms across his chest, long legs planted in a wide stance as if he were ready to do battle. "And the reason you waited until *after* the ceremony to speak up?"

Jean Claude gave him a pleased smile. "Why, speaking up beforehand might have alerted the press." He smiled. "Something I'm sure you would rather not chance."

The press. Julie could just imagine what the media would make of this. *Vineyard Tycoon Marries Bigamist.* Oh, wouldn't that be great? Or maybe *King's Queen a Counterfeit.* Her insides went cold and still. Jean Claude had come to blackmail Travis. It was the only explanation.

Travis sneered at him, raking the other man up and down with a scathing look that bounced off Jean Claude like bullets off of Superman. Clearly, Travis had come to the same conclusion Julie had. But when he turned that same sneer on *her,* she made a supreme effort to get past the disgust riddling her and find her own sense of fury.

"I had nothing to do with this," she told him, meeting his icy gaze. "Travis, you can't believe I would *help* him! You know what he did to me. How I felt—"

"Ah, *chérie,*" Jean Claude murmured. "There is no

reason for you to explain yourself to him. And what was between us has nothing to do with this man. You are after all, *my* wife."

"Oh, good God." Julie shot her gaze at the blond man who had once captured her heart, and wondered what she had ever seen in him. Now she looked at him and saw him for what he was. An oily, sneaky, evil little troll.

A troll who looked totally pleased with himself.

"All right," Travis announced, his voice commanding attention in the otherwise still room. "Cut to the chase here, Pierre—"

"Jean Claude," he corrected.

"Whatever," Travis snapped. "What the hell do you want, exactly?"

Jean Claude smiled. "My demands are small," he said with a slight shrug. "I only wish my due as an abandoned husband…."

"Abandoned?" Julie's temper finally overcame her humiliation. She charged Jean Claude and would have slapped him silly if Travis hadn't reached her side in time to stop her. Still, even with his hand on her arm, holding her in place, she hissed at the other man. "You no good, lying snake in the grass. I didn't abandon you. You left me. Remember? You said you would get a divorce in Mexico. And then you wrote me a month later and told me it was done. That you were 'free of me.' Don't you stand there and—"

"Chérie," Jean Claude cooed, his pale eyes twinkling as if he were enjoying himself tremendously. "Clearly, you are overwrought."

"Over—" She hauled her right arm back and Travis gripped both of her arms before dragging her away from the other man.

"Did you ever get a copy of the divorce decree?" Travis whispered the question into her ear.

Julie shook her head, disgusted with herself as much as with Jean Claude. She'd been a complete idiot. Not only in marrying the worm, but also in trusting him to end the marriage, too. Her only excuse was that she'd been so hurt. So totally crushed, she hadn't really been thinking at all.

"No. He told me he would make me a copy but he never did." She shot daggers at the man standing there smirking at her.

"And you trusted him."

"Yes. Damn it."

Travis's grip on her arms loosened and when he set her aside, she could see there was still fire in his eyes. His mouth was set and a tic in his jaw let her know exactly how hard he was working to keep his temper under control. "We'll talk about this later," he said, then turned to face the other man again. "How much?"

"That's very crass."

"It's expedient," Travis argued. "Let's hear it. How much for you to keep quiet?"

Jean Claude nodded once. "Very well, be it as you wish. I believe—" he said calmly as he shot his cuffs "—that one hundred thousand dollars will convince me to not seek out the press."

"One hun—" Julie gaped at him, then turned to face

Travis. "You can't seriously be thinking about paying him off. You can't do it, Travis. It's *blackmail*."

"I prefer to think of it as paying for privacy," Jean Claude mused.

"You stay out of this." Julie stabbed her index finger toward him.

"Julie," Travis said. "Let me handle this."

"No. You can't." She grabbed his forearm and felt the corded muscles in his arm bunch beneath her hand. "Travis, he won't stop. This will just be the beginning."

Travis lifted her hand off his arm and Julie could only watch as he walked slowly across the room to his desk. Opening a drawer, he pulled out an oversized checkbook and glanced at the other man. "One hundred thousand. And if you go to the press anyway, I will bury you."

Jean Claude gave him a brilliant smile. "But what reason would I have to slay the golden goose, *mon ami?* No, your—pardon, *our*—secret will stay with me, I assure you."

Not looking at him again, Travis grabbed a pen, scrawled across the check, then ripped it free. He stalked across the room, folded the check in half and tucked it into the other man's breast pocket. Jean Claude lifted one hand to his suit pocket to pat the check, as if assuring himself it was there.

"Make no mistake, Pierre," Travis said, pushing his face into Jean Claude's until the other man pulled his head back and, at long last, looked worried. "Open your mouth and you'll regret it."

"But of course," the other man said and bowed elegantly. He stepped back, then crossed the room to the closed door. He opened it, then stopped and turned to look at Julie. "I'd forgotten, you know."

"Forgotten what?"

"Just what a lovely bride you make."

"Get out," she said, fighting the darkness that was rising up inside her like a toxic spill. The coldness swamped her, cutting off her air, spreading chills along her body until she was nearly quivering. "And don't come back."

He smiled again, then left, quietly closing the door behind him.

Seconds ticked past before Julie could force herself to look at Travis. She'd known him her whole life and yet, she had no idea what she would see on his face. When she finally faced him, though, his expression was blank. His familiar features no more than a hard mask, hiding whatever it was he was feeling from her.

And the cold rushing through her turned icy.

"Let's get back to the reception," he said.

"Are you serious?"

"Damn right I am," Travis told her, coming across the room to stand in front of her. "And you're going to smile and laugh and dance like you haven't got a care in the world. Understand?"

"I don't think I can. I'm so furious—"

"*You're* furious?" He laughed shortly but there was no humor in it. Just as there was no shine of amusement in his eyes or in the hard flat line of his mouth.

"I just found out my new wife already has a husband. A blackmailer no less. And *you're* furious? Trust me when I say I've got you beat."

Yes, he probably did. Watching him, Julie felt his rage and understood what he must be feeling. But damn it, she'd been lied to, too! "I didn't know about this."

"I said we'll talk about it later." He took her upper arm in a firm grip and led her across the room to the door. "For now, we're going back to the party. We'll smile for the photographers. We'll dance and we'll eat wedding cake and we will not let anyone else even guess that there's something wrong. You understand?"

"I get it," she said, and was forced to agree with him. She so didn't need any more drama today. "More acting."

"Exactly."

"Fine." It wouldn't be easy, but with enough wine, all things were possible. "But then what?" she asked, looking up into dark brown eyes that looked as cold and empty as an abandoned well.

"When the party's over, we head to Mexico. To get you a damn divorce so we can get married again."

Three

Travis checked his wristwatch for the tenth time in as many minutes, then looked up at his brothers. Adam and Jackson stood side by side, looking so much alike they might have been twins. But then, Travis knew that all three of them were carbon copies of each other. With only a year separating each of them, they'd grown up close and had gotten even closer over the years. The King brothers were a unit. So much a unit in fact, that it was nearly impossible for one of them to hide something from the others.

For example, without even looking into their eyes, he was fully aware that they knew something was up.

"The vineyard manager, Darleen, should be able to keep things running around here while I'm gone," he said, glancing around the nearly empty garden area. The wedding and reception were over, the guests were long gone and now the catering crew was cleaning up. A veritable squad of workers was stacking the white chairs, dragging down the garlands of flowers, packing away crystal and china and whatever food was left over.

A low hum of anger still throbbed in Travis's gut. This should have been a good day. One to celebrate the fruition of his dreams for the winery. Instead, his dream was fast becoming a nightmare.

Shaking his head, he dragged his thoughts back to the business at hand and turned his gaze back to his brothers. "But if she needs help…"

"We'll be around," Jackson assured him. "Well," he corrected with a wry smile, "Adam will be. I've got a flight to Paris lined up."

Jackson ran the King-Jets operation for the family. Building luxury jets and leasing them to the wealthy of the world. They had plenty of trained, experienced pilots on the books, sure, but Jackson enjoyed taking some of the runs himself. Nothing he liked better than heading out to wherever the wind blew him. The job suited him. Jackson never had been one for staying in one place too long.

"And after Paris, it's Switzerland," Jackson continued. "Should be gone about three weeks, so Adam'll have to step in if Darleen needs anything."

"I'll be here," Adam agreed.

"Of course you will," Jackson said with a laugh. "According to Gina you're never more than five feet from her and you watch her like she's a hand grenade about to explode."

Adam scowled at the youngest of them. "Talk trash when the woman you love is pregnant. Then we'll see where we stand."

"Never gonna happen," Jackson assured him with a friendly slap on the back. Then he glanced at Travis. "Where did you say you and Julie were going on your honeymoon?"

"I didn't," Travis told him. "But we're taking one of the jets to Mexico."

"Mexico?" Adam silenced Jackson with a look. "Julie told Gina you were heading to Fiji."

"Changed our minds," Travis said with what he hoped was a careless shrug. He didn't want to get in to this with his brothers. There was no time for a long, drawn-out battle and no way would they have given him anything less. Travis checked his watch again, wondered what the hell was taking Julie so long to get changed.

"This have anything to do with the French guy who crashed the party?" Jackson's eyebrows lifted as he shoved both hands into his slacks pockets.

"Julie didn't look too happy to see him," Adam agreed. "I'm thinking he's her ex?"

"Damn it." Travis bit the curse off, low and hard. He'd hoped to just avoid all of this, since he'd rather *no one* knew about the blackmail. Especially his brothers. The Kings weren't the type to bow to extortion. And he wouldn't have gone along with it himself if he hadn't had to buy time, as well as Frenchy's silence. "Just had to be observant, didn't you?"

"Actually," Jackson mused, his features tight as he began to get the picture that something was off. "I wasn't paying attention. It was Nathan who cued me in."

"Great." So it wasn't only his immediate family that had their radar tuned in. Travis could only hope that the rest of their guests hadn't noticed anything odd.

The trouble was, there were too many damn Kings, Travis thought. His father had been one of four brothers and those brothers had spread out and created at least three sons apiece. Now they were all running different aspects of the King dynasty. Couldn't throw a rock in California without hitting at least one King cousin.

Nathan's company built personal computers and made them so well and so affordable, King PCs were threatening to take over the world. "What'd he say?"

"Nothing much," Jackson said and stepped out of the way as a catering crew member staggered past him carrying an oversized coffee urn. "Just that Julie looked like she was going to be sick and you looked like the top of your head was going to explode. Me—" he added with a sly grin "—I'm so used to seeing that expression on your face, it never registered."

"Thanks." Travis shook his head and ground his back teeth together. Nathan had noticed too much. "He tell this to anyone else?"

"Nope. Well, wait. Cousin Griffin and his twin Garret were there, too. So they know you were pissed. So what? You're always pissed about something, big brother."

He supposed that was true, but this was different and apparently, Adam sensed it. Jerking his head to the side, Travis's oldest brother shifted farther away from the rest of the cleanup crew. Adam didn't speak again until the three of them were standing in the shadows of the main house, surrounded by overgrown hydrangea bushes. "What's going on, Travis? Who was that guy? And what's he got to do with you and Julie?"

"He's an irritant." The hairs at the back of his neck bristled and Travis felt the urge to howl or hit something. His perfectly laid plans were threatening to crumble down around him. All because of one greedy bastard.

"Care to explain?" Jackson asked.

Travis glared at him. "Not really."

"Do it anyway," Adam said.

He blew out a breath and surrendered to the inevitable. "Name's Jean Claude Doucette."

Adam whistled. "So I was right. He's Julie's ex?"

"Well, that's tacky as all get out," Jackson muttered. "Why the hell did he come to the wedding?"

As the workers went on about their business, the muted sounds became nothing more than white noise. But Travis still kept his voice pitched low. "Because as it turns out, he's not as *ex* as we thought."

"Explain," Adam said.

He did. While Jackson and Adam threw astonished glances at each other and then him, Travis told his brothers exactly what had happened after the wedding. Watching their reactions, Travis felt his own anger begin to bubble fresh in the pit of his stomach.

"You *paid* the bastard?" Jackson demanded. "Are you nuts?"

"Had to," Travis said. "No choice."

"There's always a choice," Jackson told him, then paused and cocked his head. "You hear that? Sort of a low rumble?" When neither of his brothers said anything, Jackson said, "That's the sound of dad spinning in his grave."

Travis nodded. "Yeah, helpful. Thanks."

"You never pay a blackmailer, Travis," Adam said. "You should have called the police."

"Right. Because cops showing up to my wedding would look so great in the papers." Travis shook his head again and dearly wished he hadn't quit smoking two years ago. He'd only quit then to prove to himself he could do it. That his own will was stronger than the siren's call of nicotine. Well, fine. He'd proved his case. Now he wanted a damn cigarette.

"He'll only come back for more," Adam warned.

"Think I don't know that?" Travis shifted his gaze from his brothers to the remnants of the party. A tablecloth lifted lazily into the wind and a napkin skipped across the lawn, tossed by a breeze that rifled the leaves of the bushes where they stood. The sun was sliding down toward the horizon and painting the slivers of clouds in the sky a pearly sort of dark peach. And he was taking note of all of this in an attempt to not think about what his brain was chewing on.

Pointless.

Turning back to his oldest brother, he said, "I paid

him because I wanted to buy myself some time. We're going to Mexico to arrange for a divorce and a quick—quiet—wedding. When we get back, I'll take care of the little creep."

"What do you want us to do?" Adam asked and Travis was suddenly grateful for his family. Sure, they argued and fought him and let him know when they didn't agree with him, but when it counted, they stepped up to help in any way they could.

"Keep an eye on him. Watch where he goes. Who he's with." Travis had been thinking about this for the last couple of hours. Even when he stood beside Julie to cut the cake. When he'd posed for pictures he didn't want. When he danced with her to thunderous applause. During all that time, he'd been planning his next move. He'd decided to hire a P.I., but this was better. His brothers would never betray him and the fewer outsiders who knew the truth, the better for him.

He checked his wristwatch again. Whether Julie was ready or not, it was time to go. "Look in to this French guy's past. I don't care how you do it but get me some information on him. I'm thinking this isn't the first time he's pulled this stunt."

"What?" Jackson almost laughed, then sobered up again fast. "You think he marries women then goes around blackmailing 'em? Gotta be easier ways to make a living."

"I don't know about that, but I'm thinking blackmail's not new to him. He was really smooth. Wouldn't surprise me to find out it wasn't his first time."

"We'll do it," Adam said softly, shooting a look at the house behind them. "But what about Julie?"

Travis went cold and still. "What about her?"

"You don't think she was in on it, do you?"

"The million-dollar question," Travis said, turning so that he could look up to the window of the bedroom where he knew she was changing clothes, preparing to leave. "I don't know if she's a part of this. But I intend to find out."

"I don't like this a bit."

"I know, Mom," Julie said as she tried to fluff hair that refused to be fluffed. She gave herself a quick once-over in the mirror and thought that despite everything that had happened that day, she looked pretty good. Her red hair was flat, but her sleeveless, dark green dress looked great. Frowning a little, she tried to tug up the bodice, but it fell back into place again, displaying a little too much cleavage for comfort.

Too late to change now, though. She was already behind schedule and if there was one thing Travis appreciated it was a tightly run ship.

"Why was Jean Claude here?" her mother asked from her seat on the edge of the queen-size bed.

Julie looked into the mirror at her mom's concerned features and for just a minute or two, she considered confessing all. But what would that serve? All she'd do was worry her mother. It wouldn't solve the problem. Wouldn't make it go away. So, no point in opening this particular can of worms.

"To wish me luck," she said instead and forced a smile.

"Hmm…" Her mom wasn't buying it, but she wasn't arguing, either, so that was good.

"Look, Mom," Julie said, spinning around to face her. "I know you don't approve of my marrying Travis—"

"I have nothing against him," her mother interrupted sharply, getting to her feet and coming closer to Julie. "You know that. The King boys all have good hearts."

"See?" Julie argued. "It'll be fine."

Her mom wasn't finished, though. "I know the two of you were close when you were children, but people change and—"

"Mom, that was a long time ago." Julie's memories rose up in a rush, though. In seconds, she saw herself and Travis as kids, sneaking out to the barn to give the horses apples. Hiding from Jackson when he wanted to play with them. Following Adam around until he chased them off. They had been close. But that was childhood. This was now. "We're two consenting adults and we know what we're doing."

"But marrying a man you don't love and letting him *pay* you for it—"

"Wow, when you say it like that, it sounds really bad," Julie said.

"It is really bad, honey," her mother said and took both of Julie's hands in hers. "You've already had one miserable experience with marriage. I want more for you. I want you to love and be loved."

"Maybe one day that will happen," Julie said, sighing a little, since this wasn't the first time they'd had this conversation. "But this isn't about love. Travis needed a wife and I get my bakery. It's a simple business deal."

"Hmm…" Her mother's features twisted into a disapproving frown and Julie knew that Mary O'Hara Hambleton would never be okay with this situation.

But it was a done deal now. Or was it? Since she was still married to Jean Claude, she wasn't married at all to Travis, so— Oh, she really didn't want to think about any of this anymore.

"Mom, I've got to run. Travis will be waiting."

Her mother swept her up in a hard, tight hug and kissed her soundly on the cheek. Cupping Julie's face in her palms, she said, "Don't get hurt again, Julie honey. I don't think I could bear it if I had to see your heart broken like it was before."

Julie didn't want to see that again, either. As miserable a creep as Jean Claude actually was, once upon a time, Julie had thought herself desperately in love with him. And when he'd tossed her aside, the bruises had been soul deep. She wasn't interested in ever going through an experience like that again. Which is why this "marriage" to Travis would work so well. Neither of them were even pretending to be in love.

Julie hugged her mom, then stepped away and headed for the bedroom door. Her suitcases had already been loaded into the car, so all she had to carry was her slim, green leather clutch bag. Her high heels were soundless on the thick carpet and the cut-glass doorknob felt cold against her palm.

At the door, she turned to look at her mother and tried not to dwell on the worry in her eyes. "I won't be hurt, Mom. This isn't about love, remember? It's business."

Travis hardly spoke to her for the first hour of the flight to The Riviera, Maya, Mexico.

It shouldn't have surprised her any, but a part of Julie wished he would just say what he was thinking instead of sulking with a glass of scotch. Although, the fact that he was drinking expensive, single malt scotch, instead of his beloved wine, was an indicator that he wasn't looking to relax. He was looking to cloud his mind. So maybe she should be grateful for the quiet after all.

The flight attendant, who was wearing a crisp, navy blue skirt and short-sleeved white blouse, came through and offered Julie a drink. After a moment's hesitation, she ordered a margarita on the rocks. With the day they'd had, she deserved a little mind-numbing herself.

The attendant left a frothy pitcher of margaritas within easy reach of Julie, then disappeared into the cockpit to join the pilots, leaving the newlyweds alone. Great. Because being alone with a man who was so angry he wasn't speaking was sure to make the honeymoon trip a good one.

With a sip of her drink, Julie distracted herself by looking around the plane and eased back into the soft-as-butter, pale blue leather chair. The carpets were sky-blue, as well and there were two couches, as well as several wide chairs such as the one she'd claimed. At the back of the plane, there was a bedroom, complete with king-size bed, and a bathroom that made the one in her apartment look like a broom closet.

There was a plasma television screen affixed to the front wall, and a tiny kitchen tucked into a corner. There were a few paintings hung about and a vase, attached to a low table, boasted a stunning bouquet of fresh spring flowers.

It should have been ideal. Romantic. In any other circumstance.

But the quiet, broken only by the low, insistent roar of the engines, began nibbling at Julie's nerves and soon she was glancing at her new, would-be husband. Travis was stretched out in a chair closer to the front of the airplane. His long legs were crossed at the ankle and the only muscle he'd moved in an hour was his right arm, as he lifted his glass of scotch to his mouth.

She took another long gulp of her margarita and swallowed the Dutch courage before asking, "So are you permanently mute or is this just a temporary condition?"

Slowly, Travis swiveled his head to look at her then, almost lazily, he swung his chair around until he was facing her. His brown eyes were narrowed and the shadow of whiskers darkened his jaw. "What would you like to talk about?"

Good question. She didn't really even want to think about Jean Claude, let alone talk about him. But she knew that conversation was coming. No way to avoid it forever, but putting it off for a few hours didn't seem like a bad plan, either. She didn't want to talk about the money he'd paid Jean Claude, either, because that just infuriated her and she was fairly certain that Travis was still furious about it, too. Should they talk about how they weren't really married and that if that fact came out they'd both be publicly humiliated?

No thanks.

So what did that leave?

"Um, nice plane?" Lame, Julie thought. Seriously lame.

He snorted, shook his head and took a sip of his drink. "Thanks."

She wasn't willing to give up on this so soon. Now that she had him talking, she wanted to keep it that way. Julie had never been an "easy" flier. Normally, she was too busy praying frantically to keep the plane in the air to enjoy anything of the experience. Today, though, it was different. She hadn't bothered with prayer because she figured the day had been so bad already, karma wouldn't allow this plane to crash.

"I've never ridden a plane where I didn't have the guy in front of me leaning back into my lap. This is much nicer."

He glanced around at their sumptuous surroundings and shrugged in dismissal. "I haven't flown commercial in so long I've forgotten what it's like."

Wow. More than a couple of words. They were closing in on an actual conversation. "You're not missing anything. Trust me on this."

Instantly, his gaze shifted back to her. "Well now,

that's the thing, isn't it, Jules?" He was using the nickname he'd given her when they were kids, but there was nothing friendly in his gaze. "I don't know that I can. Trust you, that is."

Four

The ride to the hotel was a silent one. Travis kept his thoughts to himself, which was just as well, since they were black enough to form storm clouds inside the limousine.

Julie sat beside him, but they might as well have been in two separate cars. He felt her nerves like a living thing in the limo and he was feeling just cold enough himself to do nothing to dissuade them. She should be nervous, damn it. Hadn't been *his* fault they'd had to trek to Mexico to clear up her past before someone in the media found out.

He closed his eyes as that thought settled in tight. He could just imagine the field day the press would have blasting this little piece of news across the front pages of their rags. The King family name would be trashed and any hopes he had of moving his winery into the upper echelon of the business would have to be put on hold for years.

He simply wouldn't allow it.

He'd worked too hard, come too far for his plans to be disrupted by an oily Frenchman with a penchant for greed.

Slanting a look at the woman beside him, Travis watched her face as she stared out the window at the passing landscape. The streets of Cancún were nothing more than a colorful blur, shaded by the tinted windows as the limo sped through traffic.

But he didn't need to look at the scenery. He'd been here so many times, there was nothing new or interesting to catch his attention. Yet, Julie sat there like a kid at the circus, her gaze flitting over everything, despite her nearly palpable anxiety.

His last words to her repeated in his mind. *I don't know that I can trust you, do I?* He'd seen her face, the shocked hurt in her eyes, and still, he hadn't called those words back. It was just too neat that she had agreed to marry him so quickly only to have her soon-to-be ex-husband show up on their wedding day.

She had to have been in on it with the Frenchman.

The question was *why?*

With the agreement they'd made, she stood to make considerably more than a hundred thousand dollars at the end of their marriage. So why would she risk it all for a quick fix?

"It's beautiful here," she said now, and her voice shattered the silence.

"I guess." He didn't want to talk to her right now, but he also was tired of thinking, so he supposed he was grateful for the reprieve.

She turned to look at him and exasperation glittered in her eyes. "Y'know, Travis," she said quietly, "I'm not the enemy."

"Well now, that's yet to be decided, isn't it?"

"Apparently." Julie sat back against the seat, crossed her truly great legs, shook her head and flashed him a glare. "I've never lied to you."

"So you say," he admitted with a nod even as his gaze locked on the slide of her legs.

"That's right, I do. We've known each other since we were kids, for crying out loud. Do you really think I'd *blackmail* you?"

"We used to know each other," he pointed out, still trying to look away from the legs she kept crossing and recrossing in an obvious show of nerves.

"What I can't figure out is why you're so willing to believe Jean Claude? You've never seen him before but you're willing to take his word over mine?"

"Why would he lie?"

"He's a blackmailer and you think lying is beneath him?"

"Why bother?"

"To make you *pay* him?" she asked.

"He didn't need to name you as a conspirator to get the cash. So why would he?" He watched her and saw a flash of fire in her eyes. So she wasn't all nerves. There was temper there, too.

"Because he's a creep and he wanted to do everything he could to make sure I was miserable and you were furious." She crossed her arms under her breasts and that movement was enough to pry his gaze from her legs. Her crossed arms plumped up his already excellent view of her cleavage. His gaze lingered for a long minute, until she was uncomfortable enough to ease her arms away.

"Seems like a lot of trouble for him to go to," Travis mused.

"Didn't take much on his part at all to turn you into an *über*-jerk," she said.

Now his own temper flashed and his was a hell of a lot more intimidating than hers. "Jerk? I think I've been pretty damn considerate, considering," he pointed out. "We're here, aren't we? Going to get you that divorce and get married again so that the deal still holds and nobody else is the wiser?"

"Yes," she said, turning her gaze from him to stare out at the passing sights. "And you've been a delightful companion so far, too, so thanks very much."

He fumed silently. She wanted him to be a companion now? Friendly banter? He'd had potential disaster tossed at his feet on his wedding day and she wanted good company? To hell with that.

Thankfully, their debate ended soon after that. Travis sat up as the limousine approached the hotel. Castello de King, or King's Castle, was opulent, over-the-top luxurious and owned by family, so it would give him exactly the privacy he required.

It was a huge building, taking up half the block. The walls were a soft pink stone that seemed to shimmer in the late afternoon sun. There were round tower rooms on every corner and leaded glass panes of the windows winked with the sun's reflection. Built more than a hundred years ago by an American businessman who'd imagined himself royalty, the castle had been purchased by the King family several decades before and turned into a hotel.

But it was only in the last five years or so that the castle had been "discovered" by the famous and infamous.

Travis had always liked the place, and since his cousin Rico had taken over the castle, it had become one of Travis's favorite vacation spots.

Cameramen and tourists lined the front of the hotel, each of them trying to get a picture of someone interesting, and they all moved reluctantly out of the limo's way as the driver steered the car onto the property.

Travis imagined how Julie was seeing the place and took it in himself as if for the first time. The driveway was wide and circular, and swept past banks of tropical flowers in every imaginable color. A towering fountain stood in the center of the courtyard and water fell from its tip to dance in its base in an unceasing cascade. Doormen in full white livery waited to serve the wealthy guests who flocked here looking to be spoiled in secure, lavish comfort.

Travis could almost feel the lenses of the paparazzi

stationed on the sidewalk in front of the hotel. Their cameras were no doubt focused in to help them in their quest for an embarrassing or incriminating photo of celebrity lives. But they were kept off hotel property by a fleet of security guards, who protected the guests privacy at all costs, which was only one of the reasons Castello de King was such a popular resort for the wealthy.

The limo pulled to a stop and before Travis could get out on his side, one of the doormen had opened Julie's door and offered her a hand. She stood, turning in place and admiring the view, as Travis got out of the limo to join her.

The look on her face was one of wonder—sort of what he imagined a child might look like at her first sight of Disneyland. And he was willing to bet that the paparazzi were getting quite a few great shots of the latest King bride. As long as no reporter thought to check into her background, they might be all right. God help them both if someone got nosy and discovered the truth.

"Señor King, it is good to have you with us again." The older man had skin the color of milky coffee, snow-white hair and pale green eyes, crinkled at the corners.

Travis nodded. Over the last few years, Travis had become well known to the hotel staff. "Esteban, good to be back. Is my cousin here?"

Of course Rico was here, Travis told himself. His cousin rarely left the hotel that he'd single-handedly built into one of the most sought-after vacation sites in the world.

"*Sí*. Would you like me to call him for you?"

"Not necessary," Travis said. "But thanks." He'd look Rico up himself as soon as he got Julie settled in one of the penthouse suites always kept in reserve for visiting family.

"Hello," Julie interrupted. "I'm Julie O'— King." She held out one hand to the doorman, and he took it, surprised a little that she would take the time to introduce herself.

Travis frowned a little and she gave him a smile that told him she wasn't going to be ignored. He imagined the cameramen stationed out in front of the gates were now busily clicking off shots of he and Julie together. And they probably didn't look real happy with each other.

That thought paramount in his mind, he took her elbow, nodded at the doorman and led her into the sanctuary of the hotel—away from prying camera lenses.

"That was rude," she muttered, pulling her elbow from his grasp.

"I don't ordinarily introduce my companions to the doorman," Travis muttered and laid his hand on the small of her back.

"God, you're a snob."

"I'm *not* a snob," he whispered, irritated at the jab. "But Esteban has his job and he doesn't expect to be pals with the guests."

"I didn't say I wanted to have lunch with him, but he knew *you*. No reason why he couldn't know who I am." Her heels clicked musically on the polished marble floor until she stopped abruptly. "Unless of course, you're ashamed of me."

"Hmm," he mused, stopping alongside her. "Ashamed of being married to a bigamist. Why would that bother me? I wonder…"

Her eyes narrowed on him and her jaw went tight. "That wasn't my fault."

"So you keep saying." He glanced around and caught the eye of several people watching him and Julie with open curiosity. Perfect.

He lowered his voice even further. "I'd appreciate it if you'd just keep a low profile until things are cleared up."

"Ah. Low profile? Like the stretch limo?"

He blew out a breath and looked at her. Her grass-green eyes were practically snapping with nerves and anger. Her mouth was tight, and her chin was lifted in defiance. Her breath rushed in and out of her lungs and her breasts strained against the deep vee neckline of her dark green dress.

She looked ready for battle and so damned edible, his body went hard as a rock almost instantly.

A sex-free year with a woman who managed to turn him on even when he was furious.

Damn it.

"Look," he said, forcing a smile so no one in the lobby would guess that he and his new bride were ready to shout at each other. "We don't need to announce our presence, all right? Let's do what we're here to do and move on."

"I'm just saying, I won't be ignored."

"Fine. Point taken."

"Good." Now she smiled, curving that luscious mouth up at the corners. Only he was close enough to see that there was no answering warmth in her eyes.

Muttering vicious curses under his breath about marrying women he couldn't sleep with and couldn't kill, Travis hooked her arm through his and continued on to the reservations desk. A young woman with dark brown hair piled atop her head smiled at him.

"Señor King." She practically purred his name and beside him, Travis felt Julie stiffen.

"Welcome back to the Castello," the clerk continued, dismissing Julie with hardly more than a glance. "We have the room ready for you and your…companion. As you requested."

"Thanks, Olympia." He was polite, but completely uninterested in whatever other games she might be playing. Travis wasn't an idiot. He knew women were drawn to money and power and he'd been flirted with by the best. He'd also learned long ago that the best way to handle the situation was to simply ignore it.

The woman's coy smile and big brown eyes might have worked on any other man, but Travis was immune.

"Do you know everyone here?" Julie whispered as she leaned in close to his ear.

He smiled as if she'd said something tempting, then leaned back and murmured, "She's wearing a name tag."

"Oh."

"Will you be needing reservations at the restaurant

this evening?" The woman still avoided looking at Julie, instead giving Travis alone the benefit of her wide-eyed stare.

"No, thanks," he said, tapping his fingertips as he waited to sign for the room.

"And your…*companion,*" she asked quietly. "Will she be staying with you for your entire visit?"

"What?"

"Yes," Julie said for him, leaning one arm on the reservations desk as she glared at the girl now watching her warily. "I *will* be here for his entire visit, since I'm not his 'companion,' but his *wife.*"

"I see," the girl muttered, hurrying now with the details of check-in.

Travis bit the inside of his cheek and enjoyed the show as Julie set the little flirt down flat. There was something damned attractive about watching her sail into battle. And he couldn't help admiring the fact that she wasn't afraid to stand up for herself.

"And no," Julie said firmly. "We won't be needing your assistance with a reservation, thank you *so* much."

"Of course, señora," the girl whispered, ducking her head to avoid the icicles shooting out of Julie's green eyes.

Her point made, Julie's voice softened. "Now, if you don't mind, we're on our honeymoon and we'd like to get to our room." Then she leaned into Travis and ran her fingers over the front of his shirt for good measure.

And just like that, every last drop of amusement drained out of his body to be replaced with a heat that was powerful enough to make his eyes glaze over. Even though he knew she was putting on a performance, Travis hissed in a breath as his body tightened even further. Damn, if she kept this up, he was going to have a hard time walking to the elevator.

He looked down into her green eyes, and noted that she was completely aware of what she was doing to him. She ran the tip of her tongue over her bottom lip and everything in him fisted. What the hell game was she playing?

Sliding a glance at the clerk again, Julie smiled and said on a sigh, "I'm sure you understand that we're anxious to be…alone."

"Yes, yes of course." The last of the girl's flirtatious attitude disappeared and she hurried through the rest of the paperwork.

Julie was still plastering herself to his side and Travis told himself that two could play this game. Once he'd signed in and received his key, he wrapped his arms around her, dragged her in tight and kissed her hard and fast.

That kiss sizzled through his bloodstream, tightened his erection to the bursting point and left Julie speechless. Objective attained.

"Thanks," he said, nodding at the clerk before leading Julie toward the elevator.

Julie's mouth was still burning an hour later.

As if she could still feel Travis's lips pressed to hers.

Fine, she hadn't liked the way that woman at the desk

had been leering at Travis as if Julie weren't standing right beside him. Although, maybe she shouldn't have laid it on so thick after shutting the girl down. Teasing Travis was something like waving a raw steak in front of a hungry lion. Not surprising then that he'd kissed her in response. What *was* surprising was the quicksilver flash of heat and need that had rushed through her the moment his mouth claimed hers.

Had he felt it, too?

Or had he just been pretending?

Of course he was, she chided herself silently. He was playing his part and doing a darn fine job of it, too. She tried to concentrate on the task at hand, but once she was finished unpacking her clothes, she was free again to think about things she really shouldn't be even considering.

But could she help it if her body was on fire?

Oh, boy. She might be in some serious trouble.

Leaving the smaller of the two bedrooms in the luxurious suite, she walked into the living room and paused on the threshold just to admire the view. The room was wide and long, decorated with sheer elegance. Four low-slung white couches formed a circle around a fireplace set in the middle of the room in a stone ring. A huge flatscreen television hung on one wall. On the far side of the room, was a massive wet bar and accompanying wine cooler, and beautiful paintings adorned the rest of the soft yellow walls.

Brightly colored rugs were scattered across the glossy, honey-colored wood floor, and terrace doors leading to a balcony almost as big as her bedroom stood wide open. A cool breeze blew in from the nearby ocean and carried both the scent of the sea and the fragrance of the tropical flowers that surrounded this amazing hotel.

Standing on the terrace, Travis waited, his back to her and their room. Looking him up and down, she fought the swirl of attraction she felt. It wasn't easy. He'd discarded his suit jacket and tie and now wore only his slacks and a crisp white shirt. His dark hair ruffled in the breeze as he poured two glasses of champagne from the bottle chilling in what was probably a sterling silver ice bucket.

Steeling herself, Julie lifted her chin and started forward, the sound of her heels on the floor the only sound in the room. She stepped out onto the terrace and instantly felt the cool wind surround her. Goose bumps lifted on her arms, but she paid no attention. Instead, she focused on the lights below and the darkening sky above.

"Unpacked?" Travis asked.

"Yes," she said, accepting the champagne flute he handed her and taking a sip. The margaritas she'd had on the plane were still with her and she really should eat something before she had anything else to drink. But she glanced down at the munchies he'd ordered from room service and knew she couldn't swallow anything else at the moment. "It's a beautiful place."

"Yeah, it is."

"I guess you come here often," she said.

He shrugged. "It's a family hotel. Everyone comes here often."

"Uh-huh," she said, with another sip of the bubbly wine. "And I'm guessing you usually have a 'companion' with you?"

"Jealous?" he asked, turning his head to look at her. One dark eyebrow was arched and the wind in his hair gave him a softer, more vulnerable look.

Travis King?

Vulnerable?

"No, I'm not jealous," she said. "That would be silly, wouldn't it? It's not like we're actually—"

"Married?" His smile disappeared in a blink. "No, guess we're not. Which is why we're here. And on that subject, I'll talk to my cousin Rico tomorrow. Get the bead on who we should go to about arranging this divorce."

"Great." She walked toward the iron railing and laid one hand on the cool surface. Taking another drink of the champagne, Julie was aware that the bubbles were going directly to her head, but maybe that was a good thing.

"You're a good actress, I give you that," Travis pointed out.

"Hmm?"

"The performance you put on for the clerk downstairs almost had me convinced you were a happy newlywed."

"Yeah, well," she said, wondering why her glass was empty just before Travis reached out and refilled it. "She ticked me off."

"I guessed that much."

"And you enjoyed it," she said, taking another sip, allowing the bubbles to slide down her throat and buzz through her blood.

"I did," he said, draining his own glass of champagne in one long swallow. He refilled his glass and took another sip before speaking again. "Had to wonder, though."

"What?" God, it felt good to be out here, feeling the wind on her skin and the champagne in her blood. Looking at Travis, she felt a warmth, too. A sort of heat that was settling down low inside her. Danger, Julie. *Oh, be quiet,* she ordered that annoying internal voice.

"Well, that acting skill of yours," he said, coming around the tiny table to stand beside her.

Julie drained her champagne and licked her lips as her body began to hum. She wasn't drunk, but she was feeling pretty good. "What about it?"

"If you're that good at acting, maybe you've been playing me all along."

She blew out a breath in frustration. If he was going to continue to believe that she was in cahoots with Jean Claude then this year was going to be misery.

"I told you Travis, I wouldn't do that." She set her glass down onto the table.

"I'd like to believe you, Julie," he was saying, reaching out with a finger to play with one of the straps of her dress. "But—"

"But?" How could he really believe that about her and still want her? More, how could she be burning up with lust for him, knowing that he thought her capable of blackmail?

Apparently, though, her mind and her body were riding two different tracks. Her skin felt as if it was on fire where he was touching her. Nerves rattled through Julie's body and she knew she was in big trouble. But she didn't care.

"I'm thinking I need some convincing," he said, his dark eyes flashing with a need that her body was clamoring to answer.

"I don't know what more I can say."

"No more talking," he said and set his glass down on the table beside hers.

"Then what…"

He slid one of her dress straps down her shoulder and smoothed his thumb over her skin. Her gaze locked with his, Julie's breath caught and her blood began to pump thick and hot and urgent.

"I paid a hundred thousand dollars to marry you today," Travis said, dipping his head to kiss her bare shoulder.

Julie sucked in a gulp of air.

"Now," he said, straightening up as his finger slid along the line of her bodice, dipping down to caress the valley between her breasts. "How about you show me what I paid for?"

Five

Julie just stared at him for what felt like forever. Shock had her feeling a little stunned, but as she looked at him, she sensed that he was waiting for her response. To see if she'd take this or stand up and call him on it.

He didn't have to wait long.

His gaze was dark and hot and spearing into hers, daring her to look away. She didn't. Instead, she pulled in a deep breath, kept her gaze locked with his and said too sweetly, "Since you actually paid the hundred thousand dollars to Jean Claude…why don't I call him for you and *he* can show you whatever you like?"

Amusement flickered in Travis's eyes and one corner of his mouth lifted. "Good one. But I'm not interested in your Frenchman."

Frustration bubbled up inside her, frothier than the champagne she'd just drunk way too much of. "For heaven's sake, he's not *my* French—" She stopped because the amusement in his eyes was even brighter now. Frustration gave way to confusion. "You're laughing?"

"Not laughing, smiling."

"About?"

"About how we ended up here together, despite your Frenchman—"

She opened her mouth to protest, but he cut her off quickly. "And how we've both had too much to drink," he continued. "And how you smell so good it's driving me nuts."

Her nipples peaked.

For pity's sake, he didn't even have to *try* and her body jumped and cheered.

"Plus—" he added, dipping his index finger into the valley between her breasts again "—you look beautiful. This dress…is amazing. It tempts me to peel it off you and discover all your secrets."

She trembled. He was too close. Too warm. His breath was too soft on her face and the fire in his eyes was like an incendiary, quickening a similar blaze inside her.

When he wasn't trying to seduce her, he was nearly irresistible. When he *was* trying, he was downright illegal. His finger stroked the tops of her breasts and Julie's already fuzzy brain started clouding up completely.

"Um, Travis?" Her mouth was dry and her breath was coming in tight, short gasps that were really contributing to the whole light-headed thing.

"Yeah?" He kissed her shoulder again.

Oh, he had a great mouth.

"Um…" She was really trying to think, but it was suddenly so hard. Her nerve endings were lit up like a marquee in Las Vegas and her core was damp and hot and oh, so achingly ready that her brain probably figured it wouldn't be required anymore that night, so it had shut down.

Still, Julie tried to think. She couldn't quite remember what it was that had seemed so important a moment ago. His lips and tongue moved on her bare shoulder, the edges of his teeth scraping against her skin, sending shockwaves pulsing throughout her system. Like the aftershocks of an earthquake, everything seemed just a little off-kilter.

But at last, a solitary wispy thought flashed across her mind and Julie grabbed for it. "Right. Right, Travis…"

"Mmm…" He kissed the side of her neck and Julie tipped her head to one side to make sure he covered every square inch of available skin.

"We, uh, we agreed," she said, struggling for air while trying desperately to hold onto that one tiny thought. "Agreed to a no-sex policy for this marriage. Remember?"

"Nope," he whispered, kissing the base of her neck until Julie's toes curled. "Don't remember a thing."

Was that his tongue on her neck now? Licking,

tasting. Oh, my. "It was uh…in the uh…" What was that thing called again? "*Contract!* That's it. It was in the contract."

His fingertips smoothed over the tops of her breasts and her nipples popped even harder, each of them eagerly awaiting his attentions.

"We can always renegotiate a contract," he said, sliding his free hand up her bare back to the nape of her neck. His fingers rubbed and stroked, and slid into her hair. "If we want to…."

She groaned and closed her eyes, relishing the feel of him all around her. His body was pressed close and his erection straining against her hip was unmistakable. One hand on her breasts, the other stroking her neck, her back, he was overwhelming her with sensation. Short-circuiting her mind with deliciously seductive maneuvers that left her breathless.

"Oh, boy." She took a breath, forcing it into lungs straining for air, and when she blew it out again, she opened her eyes and looked at him. He lifted his head, his dark brown eyes locked on hers with a burning intensity she'd never seen before and she felt the heat as those flames reached for her, engulfed her. "Do we want to?" she asked. "Renegotiate, I mean?"

"Oh," he said, sliding his hand from the base of her neck all the way down her spine to the curve of her bottom. Rubbing, stroking, he leaned in and kissed her, then smoothed the tip of his tongue across her bottom lip before easing back to meet her gaze again. "I really think we do."

"Okay then," she whispered, moving against him, letting him feel that she was as electrified as he. That she wanted him as much as he wanted her. "Let's… negotiate."

"Right." He kissed her, slid the straps of her dress down and freed her breasts to his hungry gaze. Cold sea air touched her skin and Julie shivered, but it had nothing to do with the temperature. Every cell in her body was eagerly awaiting what came next.

When he cupped her breasts in his palms and bent to take her nipple into his mouth, he murmured, "Here's my first offer…."

Julie hissed in air through gritted teeth, and held on to Travis's shoulders as if without that stability she might just slide off the face of the earth. But she would die happy if he only kept his mouth right where it was.

As soon as that thought arrived though, he stopped, lifted his head and said, "Inside. Let's take this inside."

"What? What?"

He glanced around as if just remembering where they were. "You never know just how sneaky photographers can get and I'd rather not see us on the front page, if you know what I mean."

Her eyes went wide as she covered her bare breasts with her arms and scuttled back into the hotel suite. Back against the wall, she waited while Travis closed the French doors and then swept the sheers shut with a yank on the cord.

"Oh, my God," she whispered, gaze locked on him.

"Do you really think someone was out there…watching us? Taking pictures?"

He shrugged, but his eyes were cold and dark, belying his easy dismissal of the notion. "You never know."

"That's just—" She blew out a breath and tried to struggle back into her dress as if covering her breasts now could somehow erase their earlier exposure.

"Pointless to worry about," Travis told her gently. "My fault, I should have been more careful." He stroked his hand along her shoulder, stopping her from dragging the dress straps back up. "But you tasted so good. You smell so wonderful. Look so…"

Julie's body fired up again as if there hadn't been an interruption. She leaned back into the wall as Travis bent his head, taking first one nipple, then the other into his mouth. Sliding his tongue across the sensitive tip, suckling, nibbling. He tormented her with tenderness. Conquered her defenses with gentle deliberation. And when she was gasping for air and wobbling in place, he stood up, took her mouth with his and sent her flying again.

His tongue tangled with hers and everything within her went hot and wild. Her core became a molten ache, desperate to have him inside. Her hips twisted against his, and his erection pressed tight and hard to her body, letting her know that he was as hungry, as frenzied as she.

How was this possible, she wondered frantically. How could she feel so much for a man she'd known her whole life? How was there this much passion in someone she'd considered a friend? How could she slip so totally into complete abandon at his touch?

Then she stopped thinking. Stopped wondering. Instead, she surrendered to the magic rising up between them.

He wrapped a hand around the base of her neck and tipped her head to one side. He nibbled his way down the length of her throat, and then slid back up, leaving a trail of damp heat behind him as he kissed and licked her skin. She was struggling for air, but not really concerned. Who needed to breathe when there was all of *this* to feel?

But she wanted more. Needed more. Needed to feel his skin beneath her hands. Needed to touch as she was touched. Feel as she was felt.

Sliding her hands up his chest, she tore at the buttons on his dress shirt until she'd freed them all, sending several of them pinging to the floor. Then she was touching his hard, muscled skin, feeling the soft curl of dark brown hair beneath her fingers and dragging her nails across his flat nipples.

He growled in her ear and took her mouth harder, deeper. Their breaths mingled, their tongues played out a dance their bodies hungered for.

"I want you. Now." His voice was harsh, strained as if it were all he could do to squeeze out those few words. Then Travis reached down, lifted the skirt of her dress and ripped her tiny lace panties from her body.

Julie inhaled sharply and then groaned as he cupped her aching core. Sliding first one, then two fingers into her depths, he pushed her so high, so fast, her head spun. As his fingers delved inside her, his tongue continued to twist with hers in a frantic dance of need and passion.

Her body coiled tight as he rubbed one sensitive spot over and over and Julie's legs trembled violently as she tried desperately to keep her balance while giving herself over to the incredible sensations shooting through her. Again and again, he stroked her, pushing her as if he couldn't wait to feel her climax.

But she fought the feeling, wanting to draw this out as long as she could. Incredible, the way he made her feel. Overwhelming, the way she wanted him, needed him. She'd never known anything even remotely like this before and she wanted more of it. Her hands dropped to his waist and her fingers fumbled with his belt, then the snap and zipper of his slacks.

He broke their kiss as she wrapped her hand around him. His eyes briefly slid shut and he ground out one word. Her name. "Julie…"

"I want you to feel what I feel," she whispered, opening her eyes and looking into his. Raw passion and desire shone out at her and she knew he must be seeing the same things reflected back at him. She was on fire for him, her body burning inside and out. As if a fever were raging through her system.

She stroked him, her fingertips sliding up and down his length, stroking the sensitive tip of him, marveling at the soft strength of him. Travis went completely still for one long, shattering minute when their ragged breaths were the only sound in the room other than the quiet hiss and snap of the fire.

Then he looked down at her, shifted his hands to her waist and said, "Lift your legs."

She didn't ask why. Didn't think. Just went with what she was feeling, needing. Lifting her legs, she wrapped them around his hips and he leaned into her, bracing her back against the wall, cupping his hands on her bottom.

And in the next moment, he was sliding inside her, pushing himself into her body.

"Oh, Travis…" Julie sighed, twisted her hips, writhed on him as she took every amazing inch of him. An invasion of the most amazing kind, she thought, relishing the feel of his body filling hers.

He groaned tightly and began to move, slowly at first, then with a soul-splintering speed that had his hips pistoning against hers. Their bodies met and separated over and over as tension coiled and need escalated.

She felt it building, knew her release was so close she could almost touch it. The tingling sensations soared and a delicious ache rose inside until it was nearly unbearable. His strength surrounded her, his body filled her and he didn't stop. Couldn't stop. She moved with him, her body welcoming his, holding him tightly, creating a fabulous friction that accelerated the desire clawing at them both.

And when the first tiny explosions shattered within her, Julie's eyes flew open so that she could look at Travis as her body exploded in a shower of light and color and sensation like she'd never known before. His gaze was dark, hot, steady.

"Let go," he whispered.

And she did.

"Travis!" She held on to him, arms locked around his neck, legs crossed at his spine. She pulled him in tighter, closer, holding him to her as an enormous wave of pleasure crested inside her.

Her climax pushed him over that teetering edge of control and before the last of the sweeping tide of ripples had died away, Travis called her name on a hoarse shout of victory and emptied himself into her.

When the storm was over, Travis's blood was still pumping like fury through his veins. He'd thought having her would clear his head, make the wanting less, the attraction he'd felt for her less powerful.

Big mistake.

Julie nestled against him, laying her head on his shoulder and he wanted her all over again. Her heat, her touch, her explosive reaction to his lovemaking all combined to only feed the fires already quickening inside him. He hadn't eased the desire he felt for her, he'd only fed the flames.

He turned his face toward her, kissed her forehead and murmured, "I'm not done."

She lifted her head, kissed him lightly, briefly and whispered, "Me, neither."

In an instant, his body thickened inside hers, tightening, hardening. She shifted in his arms, wiggling her hips and everything in him fisted hard and tight. He wanted her. More than he had before.

Turning, he held her close, their bodies still joined,

he took the few steps to the nearest couch and laid her down. Beside them, the fire burned, and light and shadow played across her features in a never-ending shift of patterns that only served to make her more beautiful, more dreamlike.

Travis wanted nothing between them this time. He slid free of her body long enough to tear his clothes off, then he bent down over her and helped her shimmy out of her dress. Then she was naked, lying on the soft, pale fabric of the couch and lifting her arms to him.

"Do it again, Travis," she whispered as he came into her embrace. "Take me there again and let me take you."

He didn't need to be asked twice.

Covering her with his body, he braced his weight on his hands at either side of her head. Her eyes were wide and shining in the firelight, the deep green sparkling with a golden glow that intrigued and captivated him. Her mouth was swollen from his kisses and when she touched the tip of her tongue to her lips, he bent his head to capture it.

Their mouths fused as he entered her on a slow slide of languorous satisfaction. He pushed himself into her heat with a calm deliberation he wasn't really feeling. Every instinct had him clamoring to take her, to drive himself into her body, but his will kept him moving slowly, drawing out the pleasure, making each inch of her he claimed a small victory.

"Travis—" She tore her mouth from his and sucked in air desperately. Lifting her hips under him, she sought to take him in more fully, to draw him deep, high inside. "I need…I need…"

"Me, too." His words were strained, hollow, echoing with the desperation suddenly tearing at him. With each of her movements, she tore at the foundations of his self-control, his will.

He hadn't expected this lightninglike connection between them. Now, he couldn't imagine doing without it.

Travis felt her body tighten around his, felt the first velvety grip of her inner muscles and watched as her eyes flashed with wonder. Then he let himself go, falling into the green of her eyes and the warmth of her body.

The next morning, Julie was feeling completely sated and impossibly lazy. Her body ached in a very good way and just for a second or two, she stretched on the bed and let herself remember the night before.

Lying in Travis's arms. Feeling the magic that sprung up between them when they touched. Experiencing the incredible sensations caused when their bodies joined. And just for that second or two, she allowed herself to pretend that this marriage was real. That they'd really found something amazing together.

But in the next moment, that illusion was shattered.

"I don't *believe* this!" Travis's outraged shout carried from the next room.

She bolted up in the oversized bed in his room and scrambled off the mattress. Naked, she stood there for a second, wishing she had her robe. Then she shrugged and dragged a sheet they'd yanked loose during the night around her body. Tripping on the edges of it as she went, Julie stumbled into the main room.

Travis was still as a statue, standing in a wide splash of sunlight pouring through the open French doors. A room service cart loaded down with coffee, fresh fruits and an assortment of breakfast pastries stood unnoticed beside him. He held a newspaper and his features were filled with fury as he stared at the front page.

"Travis?"

His gaze snapped to hers and she watched as the anger in his eyes shifted to a different, much harder to read emotion. "We've got a situation."

"Yeah, I heard," she said, tugging the sheet out of her way as she walked toward him. "What's wrong?"

"What isn't?" When she was close enough, he turned the paper toward her.

"Oh, my G—" With her free hand, she snatched at the newspaper and tilted it so that the black-and-white picture taking up most of the front page was in the sunlight. But she hadn't really needed clarification.

The headline was large and black. *King and His New Queen.* She winced at that and wondered idly if that would be her new nickname in the press. But when she glanced farther down and took in the picture below the headline, the title *Queen* was the least of her worries.

The photograph was crystal clear and so detailed, the photographer might as well have been in the room with them. Or rather, on the terrace.

There she and Travis were, captured in the moment

when desire had leaped up between them. Her head was thrown back in ecstasy as his hands cupped her breasts and his mouth was at her throat.

They looked like an X-rated version of a vampire and his victim. Thank heaven the newspaper had thoughtfully provided a black bar across her naked breasts.

How very classy of them.

Oh, God, would her *mother* see this? Embarrassment flooded her body and she felt the heat of it swamp through her like a brushfire rushing uphill. Her gaze lifted to his. "I can't believe this."

"Welcome to my world," he muttered, then shoved one hand through his thick, dark hair. Half turning, he poured them each a cup of steaming coffee and handed one to her.

"Damn photographers." He shook his head grimly, took a sip of coffee and said, "This is my fault, Julie. I shouldn't have taken the chance of being seen, but I was caught off guard and—"

"We both were," she murmured, shifting her gaze back to the photo of Travis nibbling at her throat. She could hardly swallow her own coffee and was half afraid that the jolt of caffeine would only clear up her vision, making the photo even worse.

"Yes, but you're not used to life in the spotlight. I should have been thinking. Should have remembered telephoto lenses, damn it."

Looking up at him, Julie saw that he was both furious and frustrated. Probably not a good combination. "Wasn't your fault, Travis. Besides, it doesn't matter now how it happened. The point is, it *did*. Can't you—" she shook the paper, then tossed it to the table and concentrated on her coffee "—sue them or something?"

"Pointless," he said darkly. "It only revs up interest. If we're lucky, this will stay in the local paper and not be picked up by the bigger outlets."

"Yeah," she said, closing her eyes briefly. "I feel lucky."

He snapped her a look and seemed to notice what she was wearing—or more precisely, what she *wasn't* wearing. Moving to the French doors, he closed them, then yanked the sheers closed across them. "No more gifts to the paparazzi," he said.

"Right." She clutched her sheet tighter with one hand and held on to her coffee with the other. "So, what're we going to do about all of this?"

"I'll have my lawyers contact the paper here in town—"

"But I thought suing was—"

"Not for a suit. He'll pull out the legalese and give them a stern lecture though."

Oh, yeah, she'd always figured that paparazzi could be tamed if someone would just sit down and give them a good talking to. But no point throwing a metaphorical log onto his fire. "And then?"

"Then…" He checked his gold wristwatch. "I'm meeting my cousin Rico in a half hour. He's got some ideas on a few judges I can talk to about getting your prior marriage dissolved quickly and quietly."

"Okay," Julie said, already walking toward her half

of the suite. "Give me fifteen minutes. I'll be showered, dressed and ready."

"No need," he said brusquely, topping off his coffee. "You just sit tight. I'll take care of the arrangements."

"Sit tight?" she echoed, disbelief coloring her tone.

"Yeah." He walked to a nearby table, picked up a remote and punched a button. The big-screen television flickered to life. "Rent movies, have a massage, go to the pool. Or, there's a shopping pavilion on the ground floor. Go buy things."

Julie stared at him, amazed. He actually thought that she would trot off and play lazy rich wife while he was out dealing with her past and arranging her future? Oh, that was never going to happen.

"Uh-huh," she said. "Shopping. Massage. Is that how the other women you've brought here spent their time?"

He must have caught something in her tone because he swiveled his head to look at her, confusion clearly stamped on his face. "Yes," he admitted. "They all seemed to enjoy themselves. Why wouldn't you?"

All of them?

Of course, *all,* she told herself. Travis had probably brought dozens of women to this hotel. This suite. They'd all romped in that bed with him and— Oh, she so didn't want to think about that right now.

No wonder the desk clerk had tried her hand at a little seduction. From her point of view, Julie was no more than the latest female in a long, staggering line of Travis's companions.

Well, Julie was different. She might not be the woman of his dreams, but for now anyway, she was at least his *wife*. Well, more or less. And she wouldn't be treated like some brainless bimbo looking to get a tight grip on his credit cards.

"I didn't come here to shop. Or to get a massage. Or to do any number of the things your usual women are so entertained by," she reminded him. "I'm here to straighten out a mistake in my past."

"It's being handled," he said, glancing back at the television where a space battle was taking place in showering sparks and flashing lights.

"By you."

"Yes, by me."

Julie stared at him. "But this doesn't just concern you, Travis. This is about *me*."

"Julie, you're making too much of this. You're tired and frustrated and I'm sure the wake-up call in the paper has you upset, too."

She could almost *feel* him giving her a pat on the head. She took a long deep breath and fanned the flames of her own simmering temper. "So what you're saying is, I should just stay here, out of the way and not worry my pretty little head about it?"

He finally seemed to catch the tone of her voice, then turned to her and frowned. "I didn't say that."

"You implied it."

"For God's sake, Julie…"

"Forget it, Travis," she said, heading for her bedroom and the shower. "You may have thought you were getting yourself a temporary mousey wife, but you got one with a mind of her own."

"You'll only complicate matters," he called after her.

She stopped in the doorway to her bedroom and looked back over her shoulder at him. "Let's remember, I trusted Jean Claude to get that divorce without my input. Just look how well that turned out."

"I'm not Pierre."

"No, you're not," she said, hitching the sheet a little higher across her breasts. She felt like an idiot having this conversation while wearing nothing but a silken bed sheet. "You're Travis King, used to getting his own way and having people shout 'how high?' when you say 'jump.' Just so you know, I don't jump. Ever. So if you think I'm going to trust another man to take care of something this important without my being involved, you're way wrong. I'll be ready in fifteen minutes."

Six

"There's a car waiting for you outside. The driver will take you to Judge Hernandez."

Travis nodded. His cousin Rico King stood out in the glossy, airy lobby of his hotel like Death come to a wedding. In the middle of pale pastels and bright tropical colors, Rico wore his preferred black. Black long-sleeved shirt, black jeans, black boots. His black hair hung over his collar and his dark eyes were, at the moment, amused.

"Something funny?" Travis asked.

"To see you with a bride—" Rico said, shrugging "—entertains me."

"Happy to help," Travis muttered and slanted a look at the glass-fronted gift store where Julie was buying a pack of gum before their trip to the judge's office.

He hadn't been able to change her mind and she'd been so fast at showering and getting ready, he hadn't been able to leave before her, either. Besides, knowing Julie, she simply would have followed after him if he'd tried.

She was wearing a soft yellow dress with spaghetti straps and a slightly flared skirt. Her long legs were bare and golden and looked great thanks to the towering beige high heels she wore. In a second, his mind shot back to the night before, when those long legs of hers had been locked around his hips and just like that, Travis's body was hot and needy again.

"Your bride is a beauty," Rico said.

Travis frowned. "Yeah. I guess so."

"You guess?" Rico slapped his back. "Let me assure you that if you're regretting your hasty marriage, I'd be happy to console your grieving spouse."

The thought of Rico anywhere near Julie made temper spike inside him. "Leave her alone."

His cousin chuckled. "Do I sense a territorial streak?"

"You sense my wife. Now cut it out."

"Of course." Rico held both hands up in surrender. "My mistake."

Travis sucked in air and blew it out in a rush. As Julie walked toward them smiling, he told himself he wasn't being territorial. Though he did notice the eyes of several of the men in the lobby following Julie's progress across the shining floor. He was only playing his role as devoted husband.

That was all.

* * *

She didn't speak Spanish, Travis thought. The one saving grace in all of this.

Julie might have insisted on accompanying him, but at least she was forced to stay out of the conversation he had with a local judge. Though the man probably spoke English, Travis immediately insisted on Spanish. Not that he wasn't interested in Julie's suggestions. Actually, he wasn't. He wanted to take care of this on his own.

Rico had assured Travis that with a few donations in the right quarters, his problems could be solved very quickly and discretely. Travis could appreciate that. Hell, all over the world, money solved problems faster than anything else.

By the time he had Judge Hernandez's promise of a swift resolution to their problem, Julie was shifting impatiently in her chair and peppering him with questions.

"What was that?" She tugged at his jacket sleeve to get his attention, as if he couldn't hear her. "What did he say? Does he think he can arrange the divorce? Will he marry us? Why doesn't he speak English? People in California speak Spanish."

"You don't," Travis reminded her, with a smile for the judge.

"I could have," she muttered. "I just didn't pay attention in high school."

"Unfortunate for you."

"*¿Qué?*" The judge interrupted, a question in his eyes.

Travis took Julie's arm, drew her to her feet and in Spanish, assured the judge that all was well and that they would be at Castello de King waiting to hear from him.

They took the elevator to the street level lobby and stepped out onto a crowded thoroughfare. Sunlight stabbed down from a cloudless blue sky, glanced off the asphalt and simmered in the air.

Tourists and locals alike jammed the sidewalks and streets. Cars were practically at a standstill as people wandered in and out of shops, back and forth across the road and stopped at carts to buy everything from hats and scarves to tacos and churros, Mexican pastries rolled in cinnamon and sugar. The sounds and scents of the resort town were overwhelming.

But not to Julie.

"Tell me everything he said," she demanded.

The woman was single-minded if nothing else.

"Judge Hernandez is on it," Travis told her, gripping her elbow to steer her through the crowds. "Money talks here as well as it does at home."

"So you *bribed* him?" Shock colored her tone.

"No." He shot her a frown and shook his head. "I'm not bribing anyone. It's just that if you've got enough money to back you up, you can make the wheels turn a little faster."

"Okay. So did he say how long it would take?"

"No." Travis scowled again and stepped around a man wearing at least fifteen wide-brimmed hats on his head while he did some fast sales pitch to the people streaming past him. "But Rico figures two weeks."

"Two weeks?"

"Is there a problem?"

"No," she said, hurrying her steps to keep up with his much longer strides. "I just didn't know we'd be gone so long. Don't you have to work on that distribution deal with Thomas Henry?"

"Yes." And he didn't like the thought of putting it off. But better to have this marriage-divorce-remarriage thing taken care of before dealing with Henry. "He expects us to have a honeymoon, though."

"Honeymoon." She stumbled on a crack in the sidewalk and Travis tightened his grip on her. "So what are we really going to be doing?"

He stopped and held his ground as pedestrians slammed into him from all sides. Perfect zone for a pickpocket, he knew, so he glanced around before looking into her eyes. When he did, he heard his cousin's voice echoing in his head.

Your bride is a beauty.

She really was. Funny, but until recently, he'd always seen her as just Julie. Someone he'd known forever. Someone he once climbed trees with. After last night though, he doubted he'd ever see her as a kid again. And with that thought in mind, a slow and sure smile formed on his lips.

"We have a honeymoon."

"Are you serious?"

"Why not?" He said it with a shrug, then pulled her out of the flow of foot traffic to stand in the shade of a T-shirt shop. "We're in one of the most romantic places in the world and I think we proved last night that we're *compatible*."

"But what about our agreement?"

"Already gone, isn't it?" He smiled again and stroked the tip of one finger along her jawline. He didn't know what he'd been thinking to propose a year of no sex with a woman who could turn him on with a glance. "Look," he said softly. "We crossed over the line last night. Any real reason we ought to go back?"

"I suppose not…."

"Thanks for the enthusiasm."

"No, it's not that." She looked around, then shifted her gaze back to his. "Travis, we need to talk about something. It didn't occur to me until this morning and then we had to rush out to meet the judge and it wasn't the right time to talk to you about it, but now that we're talking about *this,* then it's the right time to bring up the other."

"What?"

She blew out a breath that ruffled the dark red curls laying on her forehead. "Can we go somewhere a little less crowded?" Her big green eyes were focused on him and didn't look happy.

"Sure. Come on." Whatever it was, he wanted to hear her out and take care of it. No more problems. He grabbed her hand, and felt her fingers automatically entwine with his. Leading the way through the crowd, he pulled her in his wake until he spotted a small city park off to the right. He headed for it and didn't stop until they were sitting on a curved stone bench beneath a shade tree.

The sun was hot, but under the tree, the temperature dropped by at least fifteen degrees. The sounds of the nearby ocean thumped in the air like a heartbeat and birdsong played counterpoint to the bustle of the crowd just a few feet away.

"Okay. Less crowded," he said, turning to face her on the bench. "Let's hear it."

"You're not going to like it."

He would have been willing to bet money on that. "Just get it said."

"Fine," she blurted, sitting back against the bench. "We didn't use any protection last night."

He stared at her, waiting for her to laugh. To tell him she was kidding and of course there was no problem. When she didn't, he felt an invisible noose tighten around his neck, trying to shut off his air. "Protection? Aren't you on the Pill?"

She gaped at him. "No, I'm not on the Pill. Why would I be?"

Damn it. "I just assumed…"

Folding her arms across her chest, she tipped her head to one side and arched both eyebrows. "And why would you assume that?"

"Because." He jumped to his feet, walked a few paces, then spun around and came back. Keeping his voice low, he snapped, "I figured you weren't interested in getting pregnant."

"Isn't that what condoms are for?"

Yes. And damned if he could even remember the last time he'd had unprotected sex. Travis was a careful

man. He liked his life the way it was. His only commitment to his work. So when it came to his women,
he practically sealed himself up with plastic wrap to
avoid being caught by a woman looking for more than
a brief sexual relationship.

So why the hell hadn't he thought of that last night?

Because he hadn't been thinking at all. He'd gone
into this marriage regarding it as nothing more than an
in-name-only bargain. They'd agreed to no sex, so he
hadn't even considered that it would be an issue. Then
last night, he'd let his hormones lead him down a path
that was turning around now to bite him in the ass.

"Perfect," he muttered. "Just perfect."

"How do you think I feel?"

He looked at her, one eyebrow arching. "Interesting question. How *do* you feel? Happy? Excited?
Visions of King bank accounts dancing in your head?"

"Excuse me?"

"Well come on, Julie," he said. "You wouldn't be
the first woman to try this."

"Just hold on one minute there, buster."

"Buster?" One corner of his mouth lifted.

"If you think I did this on *purpose,* you're way off
base."

"Is that right?"

"Of course it's right." She stood up, too, and jabbed
his chest with the tip of her index finger. "I'm not one
of the hordes of women scheming to trap Travis King
into marriage. *You* came to *me,* remember?"

One second ticked by, and then another while Julie

gritted her teeth and waited for him to be an even bigger jerk. Surprisingly enough, it didn't happen.

Travis shook his head, stared off at the fast-moving parade of pedestrians such a short distance away from them and then turned his gaze back to her. "You're right. I did come to you. And what happened last night was both our faults."

"Wow," Julie said softly. "I think we're having a moment, here."

His mouth quirked, but his eyes were flat and dark. "Doesn't change the fact that this is a serious situation."

"Why do you think I brought it up?" She'd been doing some private panicking for most of the day. What if she was pregnant? Then what would happen to their "temporary" marriage? No. She pushed those worries out of her mind and told herself to think positively.

When he didn't say anything, she took a breath and shook her head. "Look, we're worried about this for nothing. It was only the one time...."

"Four," he corrected.

"The one *night,*" she amended. "What are the chances?"

"Guess we'll find out," he muttered, then took her hand and started for the sidewalk again.

"Where are we going now?" she asked as she practically ran after him.

"The nearest drugstore," he said. "To stock up on condoms."

* * *

A week later, Julie shielded her eyes and craned her neck back to stare up at the sky. Threads of white clouds stretched across the wide, blue expanse and the red-and-yellow sail dipping and swaying in the air currents looked like a gigantic tropical bird.

Of course, this bird was her husband, who was parasailing. Travis's impulsiveness hadn't changed any from when he was a kid. He still liked to try everything at least once. And as that thought shot through her mind, her insides melted, then heated up again.

In the last week, they'd put quite a dent in their condom supply. There'd been no reason to cling to a no-sex vow when both of them were more than eager to share their nights in Travis's huge bed. And just thinking about the hours spent with him was enough to make Julie curl her bare toes into the hot, white sand beneath her.

She knew she was getting in deeper and deeper, but she couldn't seem to help herself, and she would defy any other red-blooded woman to be any different. Travis King was a one-man hormonal treat. When he had his tremendous focus aimed on one particular woman, he was irresistible. He had sucked Julie into his world and she didn't know how she'd ever get out again.

As she realized that, she felt as if someone had dropped a cold stone on her heart. God, she was an idiot. Staring up at the sky and her husband doing twirls and somersaults in the air currents, Julie felt her own stomach spin. This was the *second* time she'd married only to regret it almost immediately.

Jean Claude had been a creep, no doubt. But at least she hadn't been completely out of her element in that relationship. With Travis, their worlds were so different, they were bound to collide soon. She was the daughter of his family's cook for heaven's sake. And Cinderella aside, these things rarely turned out well.

Plus, he'd had to placate a blackmailer because of her! No, she knew that sooner or later, there was a world of hurt waiting for her. Because despite knowing that she shouldn't, that there was absolutely no logical reason for her to allow herself to fall in love…it was already happening.

"Señora King?"

"Huh? What?" She tore her gaze from Travis, who was getting lower and lower in the sky, to look up at a hotel employee wearing white slacks and a green-and-white tropical shirt. "I'm sorry. What?"

He smiled and Julie wondered if Travis's cousin Rico hired only *gorgeous* employees.

"There is a phone call for you, señora," he said and handed her a small satellite phone.

"Oh, thanks," she said, though she couldn't figure out who would be calling her here. "Hello?"

"Julie O'Hara King," her mother said in a tone Julie hadn't heard since she was sixteen and late for curfew. "Would you explain to me how a completely indecent photo of you and Travis ended up on the front page of the tabloid at my local grocery store?"

Oh, God.

* * *

"Thomas, I'll straighten this out as soon as I—we—get home," Travis was saying.

From Julie's perch on one of the sleek sofas in their suite, she turned her head to follow Travis's progress as he paced around the perimeter of the room. Ever since he'd landed and been told about the scandalous photo of them that had apparently been sold to an American tabloid, Travis had practically been foaming at the mouth.

She couldn't really blame him, though. As it was, Julie wanted to find a hole and crawl into it. Her *mother* had seen that picture. And her friends at home. And *their* parents. And strangers the world over were, even now, standing in grocery lines across the globe, looking at her blacked-out boobs.

She groaned.

"My lawyers are handling the situation," he insisted and Julie had the feeling that Thomas Henry, wine distributor, was less than impressed with Travis's assurances.

By the time Travis had returned, Julie had fielded three more phone calls, though none of them had had quite the embarrassing punch of her mother's. Still, talking to Travis's brothers, not to mention his lawyer, about the photos had pretty much sapped whatever energy she'd had left.

How was she ever supposed to look people in the eye again? Maybe she wouldn't have to, she thought frantically. Maybe they could move. To Zimbabwe or something. Yes. That would work. Run and hide until the embarrassment faded away. Shouldn't take more than ten or twenty years.

They couldn't hide though. They had to go back to Birkfield. Which was why Travis was on the phone now with Thomas Henry, trying to smooth ruffled feathers. Though what Henry had to be ruffled about, Julie wasn't quite sure. It wasn't *him* splashed across papers, sharing space with stories about headless aliens and fifty-pound newborns.

Oh, God.

"Fine. I'll get in touch as soon as I'm home. We'll work this out, Thomas." Travis hung up and tossed the phone onto the nearest chair. "This is a mess."

"You think?"

He shot her a quelling look.

She gave him one right back. "Hey, I'm in those pictures, too, you know."

"Right, right." He nodded, stuffed his hands into his slacks pockets and walked toward her. "I don't like not having control. It's not natural."

"Welcome to the real world," she muttered.

"I'd rather have my own. Where *I* make the rules."

She knew that. It was in his nature to be in charge. To take care of things himself. To protect those he cared about. Not that she was putting herself in that very select crowd. This was just a special circumstance.

Time for a change of subject. "What did Mr. Henry have to say?"

Travis scrubbed one hand across the back of his

neck. "I told you he was eccentric? Well, he's also conservative. Yeah, and don't ask me how he can be both. He just is."

"Okay…" Eccentric and conservative.

"Seeing that picture made him rethink doing business with King wines, but I think he's coming around. He admits that it's our honeymoon and hardly our fault!" Travis said as Julie took a tight rein on her runaway imagination. Pay attention, she told herself.

"If we could just settle this marriage thing and get back home, I could tie up a business deal with Henry before he has a chance to back out."

His features were tight and his eyes were narrowed as if he thought he could solve everything simply by concentrating hard enough. But for the moment, he was stalled. The future he planned was hanging just out of reach and there was nothing he could do to hurry things along.

That knowledge had to be driving him crazy, Julie thought. A man like Travis wasn't used to waiting or having zero input on what happened to him.

"My lawyer's tracking down the photographer," Travis said tightly. "And he's got a call in to the tabloids, for all the good it'll do. Now that the picture's out there, it's going to be a lot harder to get rid of."

Great. Julie stood, faced him, then quietly wrapped her arms around his middle, laying her head on his chest.

Travis just stood there. "What's this for?"

She tipped her head back and gave him a tired

smile. "I thought you could use a hug. And Lord knows, I sure could."

He sighed, then folded his arms around her. "Good point." As he smoothed his hands up and down her back, he said, "I'll take care of this, Julie."

"I know," she said softly, relishing the feel of his hard body pressed along hers. She shouldn't enjoy this so much, Julie told herself. She shouldn't get used to the feeling that it was she and Travis against the world. That the two of them were a team, united against all attackers.

Because to Travis, this team of theirs was temporary.

And when the game was over, she'd be nothing more than a memory for him.

<u>Seven</u>

Four days later, Julie's divorce came through.

That same afternoon, Travis arranged for a quiet marriage ceremony in Judge Hernandez's office. The service was brief and, thanks to the judge, safely away from the prying eyes of roving photographers.

With everything at last settled, Travis was anxious to get back to the winery. He had plenty of plans to put into motion and now that he was safely—*legally*—married, he wanted to get started. A car was called to pick them up at the hotel for the short trip to the airport, where a King jet was waiting.

Travis felt as though he were finally getting a tight grip on his universe again. He was back at the helm and now that he'd taken care of the problems facing them, everything else was sure to run smoothly. He and Julie were working well together—who would have guessed he'd find the most incredible sexual partner in his life by marrying an old friend?

Turning his head slightly, he looked at her and tried to see past the instant jolt of pure lust that slammed into him. She was beautiful, true. But was she all that she claimed? There remained a niggling doubt deep within him that perhaps Julie wasn't as innocent as she professed to be. There'd just been too many things that had gone wrong since they'd married. Jean Claude. The photos of them on their balcony. The night they'd lost control and risked pregnancy.

He'd like to think that he could trust her. But the bottom line was, Julie had entered into this "marriage" for the same reasons he had. She was being paid well for participating and who was to say she hadn't cut a side deal with Jean Claude to try to improve on the one she'd already made with Travis?

When she turned her head to look up at him and smile, Travis told himself he had nothing to worry about. But still, he'd be cautious. It didn't pay to trust the wrong people.

He checked his watch and said, "If Rico doesn't get his butt out here soon, we're going to leave without saying goodbye."

"Five minutes, Travis," she said. "Relax."

But that wasn't going to happen anytime soon.

Still, he couldn't help admiring the woman he'd married, from a purely objective perspective, of course. She was wearing white slacks, a pale yellow tank top with a peach-colored overshirt that hung open in front and white sandals on her feet. Sunlight washed through the lobby and seemed to practically glow as it gilded Julie. She looked fresh and beautiful and his body stirred hard and hot right there in the hotel lobby.

Damned if he could figure out just why she affected him as she did, but as long as they were married, he planned to make the most of it. Before he could reach out and cup her cheek, though, a voice sounded from behind him.

"Travis, I am sorry to see you go so soon."

Turning, he held out one hand. "Rico, your timing, as always, sucks."

His cousin laughed as if he knew exactly what Travis meant.

"But we appreciate the hospitality," Travis said.

"Yes," Julie added. "Thank you. Your hotel is just gorgeous and we had a—" she sent Travis a small smile "—wonderful time."

They had, Travis mused, watching her luscious mouth curve. Except for the paparazzi and the delays in the divorce and the minor crisis of photos taken at a private moment ending up on the front page of national newspapers. But she was standing there smiling, her green eyes shining, as if they hadn't had any trouble at all.

He was forced to admit that Julie had taken all of this mess in stride. Much better than any other woman he knew would have done. Hell, if it weren't for her even keel and stubborn calm, he probably would have gone over the edge himself.

Not a happy thought, he told himself. He didn't like the fact that he'd needed her to keep him calm. And thinking of that, why the hell *had* she been relatively calm about all of this? Was she really so damned easygoing? Or was it that she'd known ahead of time about all the problems that would arise because she'd been in on planning them from the start?

Hell, he hadn't *planned* to seduce her on the damn balcony. But she'd looked so blasted edible, he hadn't been able to help himself. Had she seduced him? Arranged for a photographer to catch them at an inopportune moment? But why? Hell, she'd been even more embarrassed and angry than he had. At least, he told himself, she'd seemed to be. And what about Jean Claude? How the devil had that little weasel managed to get onto the winery property on a day when Travis had had extra security measures in place? Had Julie helped him sneak past the guards?

And what about their first night of amazing—*unprotected*—sex? Why the *hell* hadn't she been on the Pill? Had she actually been trying to get pregnant and hold him up for more cash?

"Travis?" Her voice prodded at him and her tone said she'd already called his name a couple of times. "Earth to Travis...."

"What?" He came up out of his thoughts with a dark scowl on his face and suspicion crawling through his system.

She shook her head as she watched him. "Are you feeling okay?"

"Fine." The word was bitten off as he struggled to get past the misgivings still simmering inside him. "Why?"

"You must forgive him," Rico said with a laugh. "A freshly wed man has many things on his mind."

She looked as though she didn't believe that excuse, but at the moment, Travis didn't really care if she bought it or not. He just wanted to get moving. Get back to California and the winery. If Julie really were in cahoots with Jean Claude, Travis would discover the truth sooner once he was back on his own home turf.

"You are most welcome here anytime, Julie." Rico's accent flowed musically across his words as he took her hand, turned it over and kissed her knuckles.

Travis shot his new wife a look to see her reaction and damned if she didn't look charmed.

"Oh, please," Travis muttered, glaring at the other man.

"Forgive my cousin," Rico said, smiling. "He has no appreciation for the finer things in life."

"Okay," Travis interrupted, unamused by his cousin. "We'd better get a move on."

But just then, a young woman in a hotel uniform hurried up to Rico's side, and tapped his arm to get his attention.

"Pardon, Señor King," she said and when he turned to her, she leaned in close and whispered something neither Julie or Travis could quite catch.

While they waited, Travis looked at Julie, bent his

head so that his low-pitched voice was heard by her alone and asked, "Impressed by Rico, are you?"

Julie grinned up at him and something inside Travis fisted at the brightness of her eyes and the flush on her cheeks.

"He's gorgeous, and he kissed my hand," she said. "Who wouldn't be impressed?"

Travis stared into her eyes. "Just remember which King you're married to."

"Hmm…" She tipped her head to one side and pretended to have to think about that one for a second.

"Having trouble?" he asked, not liking the stir of something like possessiveness that rose up inside him. Temporary wife or not, Julie was his for the next year and he didn't want her forgetting that for a second. "Let me refresh your memory."

Heedless of the smattering of hotel guests wandering through the lobby, Travis grabbed her, pulled her up close and kissed her hard, long and deep. Every cell in his body sent up a shout of exaltation and even while he was tasting her, he knew it wouldn't be enough.

For good or bad, she'd gotten into his blood in the last week or two. He wanted her every damn minute. Something he hadn't expected. Hadn't been looking for. And, since he couldn't very well do what he wanted to do to her in the middle of a hotel lobby, he broke their kiss, straightened up and set her back on her feet.

"Wow," she whispered, lifting one hand to her mouth as she swayed unsteadily.

He smiled, enjoying the knowledge that she was as affected as he. "Better than a kiss on the knuckles?"

She licked her lips and sent an arrow of heat darting straight through him. "Yeah. Way better."

Julie felt warm all over, a deliciously wicked sensation she'd become all too familiar with in the last couple of weeks. One touch of Travis's hand, or a single kiss, was enough to make her blood sizzle with need.

Since their little "talk" in the park a few days ago, he hadn't once even hinted that he actually thought she'd tried to get pregnant on purpose. Did that mean he believed her? Or was he simply better at hiding his feelings than she was?

In fact, they hadn't discussed that wild, unprotected first night together at all. It was as if each of them were trying to pretend it had never happened. And maybe that was best. Because if she thought about it too much, she'd make herself insane.

Beside her, Travis hooked one arm around her waist and pulled her in close. His body heat reached for her even as a whisper of cool air swept across Julie's shoulders, making her shiver a bit. It wasn't a foreboding of anything, she told herself, just the excellent hotel air conditioner. But as Rico continued a whispered conversation with his employee and Julie saw the man's expression shift from charming to thunderous, she braced herself.

Ever since they'd arranged for the divorce and the remarriage, things had been better between her and Travis and she was really hoping that whatever crisis had Rico looking so concerned had nothing to do with *them.* She actually felt as though she and her brand-new, temporary husband had reached a sort of détente.

They weren't exactly a real team, but they were vaguely on the same side. Sure, Travis was still bossy and arrogant and too darn sure of himself all the time, with a real tendency to try to put her in a corner and make her stay there…but that she could handle. It was the outside problems that were making her crazy.

"Something's wrong," Travis finally said, looking at his cousin.

"I know," Julie whispered, and wondered now if that blast of air-conditioned air hadn't been more than a stray chill after all.

Rico turned to them as his employee scuttled away. His dark features were tight and furious, his black eyes snapping with indignation. Drawing the two of them to one side, he glanced briefly at Julie then turned his gaze on Travis. "There's trouble."

"Damn it," Travis muttered and his arm around her waist tightened reflexively. "What is it now?"

"Someone in the judge's office has leaked the news of Julie's divorce and your secretive marriage to the press." Rico shifted his dark eyes from Travis to Julie and back again.

"How? What? The *press?*" The relief Julie had felt only moments ago was gone as if it had never existed. Instead, there was a cold, hard knot of worry settling in the pit of her stomach. What else could possibly go wrong?

Rico spared her a sympathetic glance, but Travis was clearly too busy steaming to worry about how she was feeling. Fury literally radiated off his body until Julie wouldn't have been surprised to see ripples of heat waves rolling across the hotel lobby. She couldn't really blame him. She, too, was reeling from this latest jolt.

How could she possibly have gone her whole life being pretty much invisible to the world and have that all change in less than two weeks?

"How much does the press know?" Travis demanded.

"Everything," Rico told him, keeping his voice low. "The story broke early this morning. Should be all over the wire services by now. The idiot law clerk kept nothing to himself. It is small consolation I know—" he added with sympathy "—but Judge Hernandez has already fired the man."

"You're right. That is small consolation." Shoving a hand through his hair, Travis gritted his teeth and looked as if he wanted to kick something. "This is just great. We went through all of this for nothing."

"It would seem so," Rico said.

Julie couldn't believe it. It was like a bad dream that was stuck on rewind. Now, because of one man's greed, she and Travis had been exposed to the press. Again. But this was far worse than an embarrassing photograph. This was digging into their lives, exposing secrets. This wasn't just her breasts displayed for public consumption.

This was her *life*.

Looking up at Travis, she wondered if he was sorry

now that he'd come to her with this little bargain. Of course he was. And why wouldn't he be? Ever since they'd walked down the aisle together, there'd been nothing but one disaster after another. How could he *not* wish her to the other side of the earth?

"If I ever get my hands on that law clerk," Travis muttered.

"He is no doubt long gone already," Rico said just as tightly. "Probably counting his money."

Julie didn't care where the little worm was. She just wanted to know what they were supposed to do next. She wanted to know that Travis and she were still in this together. Would he stick with her? Honor their bargain? Or would he want to dissolve this mess before anything else happened?

She really hoped not. Because if he walked away from their oh-so-new marriage right now, she'd be all alone facing a rabid media.

"Travis?" Julie finally found her voice and when she spoke, she captured his attention. "What happens now?"

Features tight, dark eyes glinting with an anger that colored his voice, he didn't even look at her as he simply said, "We go home."

"We?"

One dark eyebrow lifted as he turned a hard look on her. "You'd rather go alone?"

"No," she said quickly. God, no. "I just didn't—"

"We're married, aren't we?" he asked, giving her a smile that went nowhere near his eyes.

"Yes, we are," she said, returning that cold smile with one of her own. They were married and even though it looked as though they were going to stay that way, at least for now, Julie felt a yawning distance open up between them.

And she didn't have a single idea how to close it.

Rico had been right, of course. The minute the King jet landed at a private airstrip near Birkfield, reporters had crowded around Travis and Julie like jackals after a particularly tasty corpse.

And as ugly as that analogy was, it hadn't gotten any better over the last week.

Leaning back in his desk chair, Travis clutched the telephone to his ear and listened distractedly to the Muzak especially designed to drive a man insane. He didn't have the option of hanging up in frustration though. He had to talk to Thomas Henry and the man had been avoiding his calls for days now.

This time, Travis was determined to reach him.

Scowling, he sent a distracted glance around his study. The walls were a deep, dark red, and white crown molding ran around the circumference of the room just below the ceiling. Bookcases studded the walls along with paintings Travis had commissioned of the vineyards. He'd always seen this room as a sort of sanctuary. He locked himself in here to work and frequently sat in one of the oversized, black leather chairs to relax in front of the fire.

Today, though, relaxing wasn't on the agenda.

"I'm sorry, Mr. King." The elevator music stopped abruptly as a woman's voice came over the line. "But Mr. Henry is still busy. Are you sure you want to hold? I can give him a message and ask him to return your call."

Busy. Travis didn't believe that for a second. Henry was dodging him. Damned successfully so far, too. Strange, but Travis had gotten married to *improve* his chances at a distribution deal. And yet, ever since he'd walked down the aisle with Julie, that elusive deal had drifted further and further out of reach.

Well, nobody stalled a King for long. And he'd be damned if he'd leave yet another message for Henry. Travis had already tried that approach twice. This time, he'd stay on the phone until the damn thing became attached to his ear if he had to. He didn't give in, never surrendered, and Thomas Henry would damn well talk to him whether the man wanted to or not.

"Thanks," he said, keeping his voice politely neutral. "I'll hold."

She sighed. "Very well."

Instantly, the music was back and Travis was left with his own thoughts again. Not the most pleasant alternative lately. He and Julie had settled into a routine of sorts, but the easy camaraderie they'd experienced in Mexico had disappeared.

Granted, he hadn't been the most approachable person over the last week. But Julie'd been just as distracted. What with reporters haunting their every step and the phone ringing nonstop, she was so on edge she jumped whenever he walked into the room. A part of him wanted to hold her, bury himself inside her and tuck the problems surrounding them into the background. But he couldn't do that while another part of him still wondered if she wasn't somehow involved in all of this.

Talking to his brothers hadn't helped any.

He stared at the far wall, gaze fixed on a painting of the winery, but he wasn't seeing the crisp colors or the subtle brush strokes. Instead, he thought back to the conversation he'd had with his brothers the night before.

"Our lawyers are working on Julie's ex," Adam had said.

"Can't we have him arrested for something?" Jackson wanted to know.

"He hasn't done anything illegal," Travis responded. "Yet."

Adam reminded him, "He blackmailed you."

"Fine. He did. And if I admit to that, it's just one more piece of news for the press," Travis replied. "No thanks. I already feel like there are photographers hiding in the vines. I don't need more of the same."

"This mess is just getting worse." Adam said.

"Really? Hadn't noticed." Travis's wry tone seemed to irritate Adam further. "I asked you to look in to the guy's past. Didn't you find anything we can use to make him disappear?"

"No." Adam said. "As far as we can tell, he's never tried blackmail before."

"Pity," Jackson commented. "Since he seems to have a flair for it."

"There's got to be something. He's playing this in the press as though he's a wounded, discarded lover."

"What does Julie have to say about all of this anyway?" Adam asked.

"What do you think she's got to say?" Travis demanded softly. "She's embarrassed and pissed off, just like me."

"Is she?" Jackson asked quietly.

Travis stared at his younger brother and fought down the anger that seemed to have become a permanent part of him. "What's that supposed to mean?"

"Don't get me wrong, I like Julie. A lot. I'm just thinking that all hell's broken loose since you two decided to get married."

"It is an interesting question," Adam pointed out.

"You, too?" Travis had asked his older brother.

"Can you say you're absolutely positive that Julie's innocent?"

Could he? No. Was he going to admit that to his brothers and have to listen to their opinions? No. He ran his own life. And he'd deal with his marriage himself. He didn't need a committee.

"Yeah," he lied. "I can."

Adam watched him for a long minute or two, before finally nodding. "All right then. That's good enough for me. You and Julie keep a low profile, for God's sake. All of this press attention is making Gina a nervous wreck and she doesn't need that with the baby due any day."

"It's not like I'm enjoying the media circus myself, you know."

Adam ignored that. "Jackson and I will keep looking for information on Jean Claude. There's bound to be something somewhere in his background."

"Yeah," Jackson said. "Maybe we can find a reporter to work for us for a change. Maybe hint that Jean Claude's not all he seems to be."

"Worth a shot," Travis said.

And it was worth looking in to, he thought as he came out of the memory like a man who'd been asleep too long and couldn't quite shake the cobwebs out of his mind.

The only thing that concerned him was if they did find something on Jean Claude, would the information implicate Julie, as well? He didn't want to think so. Not only because it would be infuriating as hell to be so completely wrong about a person but also because he'd have to live with her duplicity for the next year. He'd be damned if he'd enter into another media feeding frenzy that would ensue if he tried for a quick divorce from her.

Travis shook his head and shoved one hand through his hair. Fisting his hand around the damn phone that continued to spew hideous music into his ear, he fought down the urge to throw the phone across the room. He might not be able to straighten out one part of his life, but he for damn sure was going to iron out a deal with Thomas Henry or die trying.

"King?" A deep, brusque voice interrupted Travis's thoughts. "What is it?"

"Henry," Travis said, sitting up straight in his chair,

keeping his voice pleasantly, deliberately even. "I've been trying to reach you."

"Been busy," the other man said.

"Right. Me, too." Travis knew the older man had been reading the newspapers, following the scandal that had risen up around Travis and Julie, so the first order of business was to smooth that over. "I've been dealing with lawyers for the last week. Not the way I'd planned on spending the first weeks of my marriage."

"Yes," Henry mused. "I've been reading about you and your wife."

"I can imagine," Travis said. "But I want to assure you that there is no truth to the stories you've been seeing in the press about us."

"So she wasn't married to this…Doucette character?"

Scowling, Travis picked up a pen from the top of his desk, tapped it on the oak surface, then tossed it aside again. "Actually, yes, she was."

"Well, then—you're both getting exactly what she deserves," the man blustered, a dismissive tone in his voice that sent a blast of protective fury whipping through Travis.

"Doucette tricked my wife," he said, voice hard. Yeah, he wanted the distribution contract, but he'd be damned if he'd sit here and let someone who didn't even know her insult Julie. "She's done nothing wrong and I don't appreciate your innuendo."

"Now just one minute…"

"No, Henry," Travis said, standing up as he allowed his anger to swell inside him. "You wait a minute. It's true I want your company to distribute my wine, but I can live without it." He didn't want to. Hadn't planned to. But he wasn't going to sit back and let someone stomp on him, either.

It wouldn't be easy to find a good distributor if this deal didn't come through, but he'd find a way and damned if Travis King was going to kiss anyone's ass just to move along the success train. "You know as well as I do that a deal with King wines would serve you as well as me."

"Who do you think you're talking to?"

"I could ask the same, Henry," Travis said and shoved one hand into the pocket of his slacks. His voice was deep and dark and filled with the venom that was coursing through his veins. "I'm not some green kid just breaking in to the wine business. I've got one of the top wineries in California and you know it. King wines is growing every year. Now we can work together to build the name into something that will make us both a lot of money—" he paused, took a breath and tamped down the anger nearly choking him "—or you can utter one more insult toward my wife and I hang up and find a new distributor."

For one split second, Travis wondered if he'd gone too far—if the other man was going to hang up and forget about King wineries. Then that moment passed and the other man spoke up again.

"You're right," Henry said thoughtfully. "And I admire a man who stands for his family. I'm willing to discuss the distribution deal. Let's meet next week to talk it over."

Success. It tasted bittersweet, but Travis could choke it down. When he hung up, Travis thought about going to tell Julie the good news. Then he reconsidered. After all, it wasn't as if this was a *real* marriage.

Upstairs, Julie closed the door to the master bedroom, stepped over to the wide window that overlooked the acres of neatly tended grape vines. White, billowy clouds drifted like sails across a sky so blue it almost hurt to look at it. Sunlight slanted down on the vineyard and just for a moment, Julie took a breath and paused simply to enjoy the beauty of the scene.

But she hadn't come upstairs to admire the King winery. She'd come for a little privacy. She wasn't going to be a passive observer in her life anymore. It was time that Julie faced her past and did something about straightening out her future. Flipping open her cell phone, she dialed a number she'd tried to forget. Waiting impatiently as the phone rang, she tugged at the white sheers hanging alongside the window and almost jumped when a man's voice came on the line.

"Hello?"

God, how she hated that voice.

"Jean Claude," she said. "We have to talk."

Eight

Julie felt like a spy.

Any minute now, she half expected Travis to jump out from the shadows, point an accusing finger at her and shout *Traitor!*

"This was probably a bad idea," she muttered and carried her hot cup of coffee to the scratched-up white guardrail at the edge of the lookout over the ocean. She hunched a little deeper into her dark blue windbreaker and turned her face into the wind, letting that icy breeze blow her hair back from her face.

She was alone on the wide, half moon of asphalt, her car the only one parked on the turnout some twenty miles north of the King winery. Highway 1 traveled up the length of California, going through tiny towns, and winding along the rugged coastline. Up and down the state there were wide pullouts just like this one, where tourists could stop, park the car and take photos of the incredible scenery.

Ordinarily, Julie would be just as caught up in the beauty of the place as anyone else. But today, all she saw were the gathering dark clouds on the horizon and the never ending stretch of steel-gray sea. It was as if the whole world were suddenly in black and white. And she knew that's how Travis would see this little meeting of hers. Black and white.

Friend and enemy.

If he discovered that she'd come to meet Jean Claude of her own accord... "Oh, don't even go there, Julie," she told herself, backing away from that thought as she would have from a rabid dog.

She deliberately kept her face turned away from the highway and the forest. For all she knew, there might be reporters and photographers out there, aiming their telephoto lenses and parabolic microphones directly at her. Not that she was paranoid or anything, but over the last two weeks, she'd been dissected for public consumption almost every day.

Which is why she'd asked Jean Claude to meet her here. Even if it was a stupid maneuver, at least she felt as though she was doing *something* to try to stop all of this.

A car pulled up beside hers and Julie stiffened as she turned to watch Jean Claude park his spiffy, two-seater sports car. He climbed out lazily, a man completely at ease. His blond hair lifted from his forehead and Julie absently noted that it looked thinner than she remembered.

"New car?" she asked. A splashy one, too. Leave it to Jean Claude, to whom appearances meant more than anything else. He used to love talking about his grandfather, who had been a minor member of the aristocracy. No doubt, Jean Claude was just loving being the center of a media storm. Everyone wanted to talk to him. Tabloids and TV stations were willing to pay him to smile on camera and dish out dirt that made him look like a forgotten lover.

All he'd had to do was sell her out and make her and Travis's lives a living hell. Julie's insides twisted as she watched him shoot a loving glance at the sports car.

He trailed one finger along the shining red hood. "Yes, lovely little thing, isn't it?"

Obviously, Jean Claude was enjoying the money he'd made both from the blackmail and the constant streams of interviews he'd given.

He walked toward her, a smile on the face she'd once thought so handsome. "Julie, *ma chérie,* what a delight it is to see you."

She backed up, keeping a safe distance between them. She didn't think she'd be able to stand it if he got close enough to touch her. How could she ever have convinced herself she loved this man enough to marry him? She was *such* an idiot.

He smiled again as if he knew what she was thinking. God, was she doing the right thing by setting up this meeting? Would this only make things worse? If Travis found out about this—

"Jean Claude—"

"This is very sexy, no?" He glanced around at the empty area, then shifted his gaze back to her. "Just the two of us. All alone."

She only *hoped* they were alone and that there were no reporters or photographers hiding somewhere nearby.

"No," she said with a firm shake of her head. "I mean, yes, we're alone, but no, it's not sexy."

The wind whipped his blond hair back from his forehead, displaying a lot *more* forehead than she remembered. Apparently being a full-time jerk caused premature balding. Small consolation.

"Fine," he said with a shrug. "If you do not wish to enjoy a clandestine tryst, why did you want to meet?"

"A tryst?" Her mouth dropped open. "Are you insane?"

"Do you not remember how it once was between us, *chérie?*" His voice was low, and what he no doubt considered his "seductive" tone.

But when Julie thought back on her time with this man and then compared it to the nights spent in Travis's bed, the differences were nearly laughable. Jean Claude thought a lot more of himself than he had a right to.

Obviously, he read her expression clearly because he shrugged again and said, "Fine, then. Tell me what you want from me."

"I want you to stop what you're doing to me and Travis."

"Stop?" His eyebrows lifted and a smile pulled at one corner of his mouth. "Why would I want to do that?"

"Haven't you done enough, Jean Claude?" she asked, taking a step toward him before stopping again. "Haven't you made enough money off of embarrassing Travis and I?"

He straightened. "No. I believe there is much more to be had and I am not finished."

Her stomach felt as if an invisible someone had dropped a cold rock into it. She had known going into this meeting that he would fight her on this, but she had had to try.

"Jean Claude, you're ruining a man who doesn't deserve this. And I'm not going to let you."

"How will you stop me?"

"I'll go to the police. Travis won't, he wants to handle this himself. But I'll have you arrested. For blackmail."

He smiled at her and clucked his tongue. *"Chérie…"*

"Stop saying that!" She walked even closer, poked him in the chest with her index finger. "Back off now, Jean Claude."

"Why should I?" he interrupted with a laugh.

"I'm not the foolish woman who once married you. I'm willing to see you in jail, or deported."

"You wouldn't. Besides you have no proof."

"I can get it. Don't push me on this."

"I don't believe you." Then he bent his head and kissed her before she could jump out of the way.

Wiping one hand across her mouth as if she'd been

poisoned, Julie stumbled backward, her gaze fixed on his. "You stay away from me, Jean Claude. And you back off of Travis before you end up behind bars."

"Is that a threat?" He laughed and folded his arms over his chest. "Perhaps I should alert the papers that now Travis King is threatening me—the poor, set-aside lover."

"Travis didn't threaten you, Jean Claude. *I* did." She glared at him and it only irritated her further that he didn't look the least bit worried. "Blackmail is a crime, Jean Claude."

"Ah," he said, smiling and perfectly at ease. "Bigamy is also a crime, *ma chérie*. Do you really wish to meet me in a court of law?"

What Julie really wanted was to strangle him, but unfortunately, that was a crime, too. Though she was willing to bet that a jury of women would exonerate her. She could just kick herself for ever setting up this meeting. She'd so hoped she could somehow end this lingering nightmare. Now all she wanted was to get as far away from this man as she possibly could. She stalked across the lot to her car and when she opened the driver's side door, she stopped and looked back at him. "Don't push me, Jean Claude. Take what you have and disappear. Leave us alone."

"I will see you soon," he called back and gave her a wave.

When she left, spinning her wheels on the asphalt, Julie looked into her rearview mirror and saw Jean Claude on his cell phone.

Probably not a good sign.

* * *

Two hours later, Travis jumped down from the driver's side of his truck and slammed the door behind him. The sun was hot, but the breeze was cool. Not cool enough to take the edge off the fury currently burning his insides like a brushfire out of control, though.

Seemed he'd been angry ever since he'd come up with the insane idea of getting married. And there was no end in sight. Now he was getting phone calls from a Realtor about his "wife" looking for property she hadn't bothered to talk to him about.

He didn't see her car, but Main Street was crowded. She could be parked just about anywhere. Birkfield was small, but bustling. Local residents usually did their shopping here, rather than take the freeway into one of the bigger cities more than an hour away. Plus, the town got a good share of tourist business as well, with people driving up the coast and stopping for a little break at the many wineries nearby.

Main Street was filled with antique stores, specialty shops, restaurants and the kinds of stores small communities all required. Hardware, groceries, post office—all crowded together on both sides of the two-lane street. Birkfield was small, true, but Travis had always loved that about the place.

At least, until recently. Now there were way too many people who felt as though they had a proprietary interest in his life. And thanks to the newspapers, tabloids and weekly trashy magazines, there was plenty of fodder to feed the local gossips.

Just what he needed.

"Afternoon, Travis," a familiar voice called from the sidewalk in front of the local hardware store.

He muffled a groan, turned and forced a smile. Speak of the gossip. "Mrs. James. How are you?"

"Fine, fine. Been real exciting around here lately, thanks to you and Julie."

"Yeah." Too exciting. Just standing here, he felt as though he were under a microscope. His friends and neighbors, people he'd grown up around, people he'd known his whole life, were now watching him with avid interest.

Funny, all the times he'd gotten his picture in the paper by dating some model or actress had never gotten him the kind of attention marrying a hometown girl/bigamist had.

The older woman shook her head and gave a cluck of her tongue. "But then, you knew Julie was a caution even before you married her, now didn't you?"

He didn't get a chance to answer because the woman who had once been his fifth grade teacher just rolled right on.

"Of course, as I recall, you two used to be thick as thieves when you were children." She tipped her head back and studied the sky. "I told that nice young reporter about the time I had to chase you two out of the janitor's closet. Of course, you were both just kids then, but Julie was so sweet on you—though it was inappropriate, of course."

He'd been nodding along, just to hurry the woman

up until that last sentence caught his attention. "Inappropriate?"

"Well, you know. With her mother being your family's cook and all."

Travis just stared at her. He couldn't think of anything to say that wouldn't come out rude, so he decided it was best to just keep nodding and move along. Still, it amazed him the things people came up with.

Inappropriate? "Good seeing you, Mrs. James."

He hadn't taken more than a step when she called out, "Are you looking for Julie?"

Closing his eyes, Travis took a deep breath and said pleasantly, "Yes, I am. Do you know where she is?"

"I should say so. Didn't I see her only five minutes ago, down at the old tavern?" She clucked her tongue again in displeasure. "They ought to tear that eyesore down is what they ought to do, but does the town council listen to me?"

He sympathized with the town council.

"Thanks." He shoved one hand through his hair, nodded to Mrs. James and turned for the far side of the street.

He did a lazy run across the two lanes of traffic, lifting one hand to the cars who stopped to let him pass. At the far end of the street, he spotted a news van and hoped they hadn't spotted him. He would have thought there would be something more interesting than his life happening somewhere. But no, reporters and photographers were still dotting the streets of Birkfield, waiting for the latest installment in the King drama.

Travis kept his gaze focused straight ahead of him as he darted in and out of strolling pedestrians on his walk up the sidewalk. The scent of something delicious wafted out of the diner and his stomach grumbled in response. He'd been out working the vines all morning with his crew, just to get away from the damned phones, and his hunger marched in time with his anger.

The long-vacated bar stood between a candle shop and an art gallery featuring the work of local artists. The wide front window was covered in grime, but the door was unlocked. Travis threw a glance over his shoulder, opened the door and stepped into the dimness.

Almost no sunlight at all made it through that front window and the overhead light boasted one low-wattage bulb. Shadows clung to the walls and hid behind stacked boxes left behind by the last tenant. There was no sign of life here, but Travis could sense Julie's presence. He didn't even want to think about why that was.

"Julie?"

"Back here!" Her voice sounded muffled and he cursed under his breath as he walked toward it. What the hell was she up to, anyway?

He stepped through another open door into what must have passed for the kitchen, only to spot Julie, on her knees, sticking her head into an oven that looked older than him. "What're you doing here?"

She backed out, turned her face up to his and grinned, oblivious to the streak of dirt across her nose. "A better question, how'd you know where to find me?"

He stuffed his hands into his jeans pockets and

took the few steps separating them. "I got a call from Donna Vega. She tells me you're interested in the property."

Her grin slipped a little, but she clambered to her feet and looked around the dingy, dirty room with a gleam in her eye before she turned back to him. "I didn't think she'd call you. I was going to tell you myself later—"

"Tell me what exactly?"

She brushed her hands together in a futile attempt to dislodge the black streaks covering her palms. "I was out driving and saw the for sale sign in the window, so I stopped to take a look. I called Donna to let me in so I could explore a little."

"That explains what you're doing. Not why."

She whipped her short, curly hair off her face with a toss of her head. "I'm going to be opening a bakery, in about a year, remember? This place would be perfect."

He shook his head. "This place is only suitable for firewood."

"You have no imagination."

Travis tried to see what she did in the old bar, but frankly, it escaped him. But that wasn't the point right now anyway. "You shouldn't be doing this now."

"What?"

"Looking at property," he said with a wave of his hand to indicate the decrepit building. "Haven't we got enough to deal with at the moment?"

"Travis," she said, looking into his eyes. "This has nothing to do with any of the other stuff going on."

"No?" He cocked his head, folded his arms across

his chest and tried not to breathe. There was a very weird smell in the room. "You don't think the reporters following us around would love to print the story of King's new wife going out to open her own business? King wives don't have to work."

"What planet are you from?" Julie demanded, hands at her hips and feet braced for battle.

"Just a minute—"

"No, you wait a minute." She tipped her head to one side as if she were thinking deeply, then said, "I suppose you don't remember your mom doing ranch work every day."

"That was different," Travis argued.

"It was work. Work she loved doing," Julie shot right back.

"My mom is not the point here."

"No, she's not," Julie said. "But Gina is a 'King wife' and *she* works. She raises and trains horses."

"At the home ranch."

"Oh, so it's not the work that bothers you, it's *where* your wife works?"

Was it completely crazy, Travis wondered, that he liked that fire in her eyes? Probably.

"Not the point," he said tightly. "You're not opening the bakery until *after* the marriage is over, so why get people talking now? Don't we have enough going on at the moment anyway? Damn it, Julie, we're supposed to be a united front. How's it look to everyone if you're sneaking around behind my back?"

She flushed and her gaze shifted to one side. Her

mouth went firm and tight and she rocked uneasily on her heels. "I hate it when you're right."

"That was too easy," he muttered, wondering what else was going on in her mind. It wasn't like her to give up so quickly.

"Well, I wasn't thinking how it would look to everyone else in town. And I hate having to worry about how something looks to somebody else. Why should they care what we do? Why are we big news?"

"Hell if I know," Travis said. "Maybe people don't have enough excitement in their own lives so they need to find it somewhere else."

"Does it have to be *us*?"

"At the moment," he conceded, hating it every bit as much as she did. "Sooner or later though, some other poor fool will get into the spotlight and we'll fade away. Until then…"

She lifted her gaze to his again. "I know, I know. I wasn't sneaking, Travis. I saw the place and stopped for a look. I was going to tell you. I mean, if I'm going to tell you something, that can't be sneaky by definition, right?"

"Uh-huh." He was getting a fairly uneasy feeling about all this now. "What else don't I know?"

Nine

"You didn't mention the fact that you *kissed* him!"

Travis's voice echoed off the high ceiling in the tasting room at the winery. The gleaming oak-paneled room was empty but for the two of them and for a moment, Julie really wished for the crowd that was due to arrive at any moment.

Twice a week, the King winery hosted tastings in this room. Busloads of tourists wandered through this room, the winemaking area and the gift shop. They tasted wine, snacked on the offerings that Julie herself made for the occasions and, in general, had a lovely time while providing a nice distraction for everyone else from the everyday work of the winery.

She looked up from the elegant table set with china,

old silver and the appetizers and desserts she'd spent most of the day cooking. There were tiny, perfect shrimp, dark green sprigs of prosciutto-wrapped asparagus and gourmet crackers dotted with a feta/spinach mixture. The desserts were nearby and looking just as tempting—lemon tarts, brownie bits with hot fudge baked inside and tiny shortbread cookies dipped in an almond cream sauce. And yes, she was thinking about food because she wasn't quite ready to concentrate on her husband just yet.

Hopefully, the finger foods she'd spent hours putting together would entice their visitors far more than they interested her at the moment.

But then, the strangers headed for the winery wouldn't be facing the thundercloud of Travis's expression. Julie's stomach churned uneasily and she swallowed hard to avoid the sudden rush of nausea filling her mouth.

Watching as Travis stalked across the shining wood floor, she nearly groaned at the flash of fury in his eyes. Apparently, she wasn't going to be feeling better anytime soon. The way he shook the newspaper he held told her that she wasn't going to like what was in it.

A sinking sensation opened up inside her and she really wished she could avoid this confrontation. She didn't much care if that made her a coward or not.

Yesterday, she'd confessed to her meeting with Jean Claude and had thought that after that explosive argument with Travis, the subject would be buried. Naturally, her life just wasn't that easy.

And how strange was it that even facing Travis when he was angry, she felt a rush of heat that pushed through her bloodstream in a frantic race. He wore an expensively cut black suit, white dress shirt and a bold red tie. His dark hair was ruffled and his eyes were flashing.

The man was gorgeous. Even when he looked as though he could bite through a steel bar.

When he reached the table she stood behind, he stopped directly opposite her and shook the newspaper again in one tight fist. "When you told me about your little meeting with *Pierre*," he growled. "You neglected to tell me just how cozy it was."

"It wasn't cozy," she argued, making a grab for the paper. He snatched it back and she stared directly into his eyes, giving back as good as she got. Fine, he was mad. Well, join the club. She was more than tired of being dragged through public scrutiny by a scandal-hungry press. And defending herself to the one man who should have a little faith in her was getting to be just as irritating. "If you think I would willingly kiss that little worm, you're nuts."

"A picture's worth ten thousand words," he said, and held the paper up in front of him, showing her the front page.

"Oh, God."

There it was. In startlingly clear black and white. A picture of the moment when Jean Claude had bent down to touch his thin, nasty lips to hers. Apparently, he *had* had a photographer stationed somewhere nearby. She never should have tried reasoning with a man who had no morals. This was her fault. All of it.

"He was probably hiding in the trees," she muttered.

"Who?"

"The photographer, of course!" She grabbed at the paper again, but Travis shook his head, turned it in his hands and read the words beneath the photo aloud instead.

"Clandestine lovers?"

Shock had her jaw dropping. "Cland—"

"Jean Claude Doucette and Julie O'Hara Doucette King—"

Appalled, Julie screwed up her mouth as if she'd bitten into a lemon. "I don't still have his name, do I?"

"Meet secretly at a lookout on Highway One."

"That sounds horrible...."

His gaze lifted to hers and in those dark brown depths, she could have sworn she saw actual *flames*. "Oh, it gets better," he assured her. "The story that accompanies the picture wonders if Travis King knows that his wife is still in love with the man she never bothered to divorce before moving on to another marriage."

Now his eyes were dark, unfathomable. His jaw was clenched and his mouth was hardly more than a slash across his face. Even though he was standing directly opposite her, she felt as closed off from him as if she'd been in a sealed room.

And still, she had to say, "Travis, you can't believe that."

"What do you expect me to believe," he whispered angrily. "You set up a meeting with him."

"Yes," she said, lifting her index finger to make the point. "But I told you about it afterward."

His eyes fixed on hers and Julie felt the hard slam of his silent accusation just seconds before he said it aloud.

"You should have told me *before* you did it, so there would have been time to stop you."

She sighed a little, anger blending with frustration and sorrow. "That's why I didn't."

"Why the hell did you go to see him? What was so damned important you had to go behind my back and meet up with your ex-husband?"

"I explained this yesterday, Travis," she said, forcing patience into her being, though she actually felt like jumping up and down and tearing at her hair. He had to have the hardest head she'd ever come up against. "It was something I had to do. I had to try to reason with Jean Claude myself."

"I've got lawyers I'm paying to stop him. My brothers are looking in to it."

Frustration bubbled into a froth inside her, swamping her sorrow, drowning even the anger. "You just don't get it, Travis. I'm not the stay-at-home, wait-for-the-big-brave-man-to-take-care-of-things kind of woman." She pushed her hands through her hair then let them drop to her sides again. "Don't you see? Jean Claude is bothering you because of *me*. He's only giving you this much trouble because I was once stupid enough to marry him. It was up to *me* to face him."

"Damn it, Julie." He crumpled the paper in his fist and squeezed.

"I had to do something, Travis," she said, her voice getting stronger with every word. "I take care of myself. I always have. I don't know how to do anything else and frankly, I wouldn't want to. This whole mess was, at the heart of it, my fault. So it was up to me to fix it."

"You did a hell of a job," he said, shaking the wadded-up newspaper again.

"Yeah, well…" Her frustration bubbled a little hotter, a little thicker. "I gave it a shot. Something I had to do. I just should have remembered that I was dealing with a snake. No," she corrected herself quickly. "Something that crawls *under* snakes. Or maybe something that snakes ooze through."

"He kissed you." The words were soft, barely audible, and she watched as an emotion she'd never seen before shot across his eyes and disappeared again a moment later.

What was it? What was he feeling? Was it only anger? Or was there something more? Something deeper?

Grumbling, she admitted, "He moves pretty fast for a snake."

Travis came around the table, smoothed her hair back from her face, then cupped the back of her neck with his big palm. "I didn't like seeing him touching you."

Her heartbeat quickened and her blood felt hot and thick in her veins. One touch from this man and she was butter on a stove. "Trust me, I didn't like it much, either."

"I want to," he said.

"What?" God, she could hardly think with his hand on her.

"Trust you. I want to trust you, Julie."

Everything in her went still as glass. She looked up into his eyes and felt the threads of connection stretching between them. Could he feel it? Did he ache for her touch as she did for his? Did his skin sizzle from the contact of hers? Did he feel more than he'd wanted or expected to?

Could he see in her eyes that she loved him?

She loved him.

Julie swayed a little as that acknowledgement sank in. She had loved him almost from the start, she knew that now. Or maybe she'd always loved him and had somehow buried that knowledge deep inside. All she could be sure of was that since their wedding night, her heart had been his.

If only he wanted it.

"You can trust me, Travis."

He smiled a little, no more than a slight curving of his mouth, but it briefly lightened the darkness of his eyes. Then he moved his hand, stroked her cheek with the tips of his fingers and dropped his palm to her bare shoulder. Where their flesh met, there was heat. Electricity. And a sense of pulse-pounding urgency that told her she wanted him now. Wanted his body covering hers. Wanted to feel that intimate slide of bodies meshing, becoming one. Wanted to luxuriate in the sensations that she could only find with Travis.

But this wasn't the time. Or the place. Even as he

touched her, she felt the reserve in him. As if he were holding himself back from her deliberately.

"Trust isn't something that comes easy to me, Julie."

"Try, Travis," she urged. "You've known me most of my life and I think somewhere inside you, you know I didn't betray you. I'm not in league with Jean Claude." She reached for his hand and curled her fingers around his. "I am who I've always been."

He smiled again, softly, temptingly. "And who is that?"

"Julie," she said with a small smile. "Just Julie."

Noise sounded in the distance. Car doors slamming, a bus engine rumbling, voices lifting, talking, laughing.

"Our guests are here," he said, straightening up and moving away.

"Travis—" He was pulling back from her and only a moment ago, he'd been so close. So tantalizingly close, she'd thought for a second that he was going to kiss her. To tell her he did trust her. That he believed in her.

But the moment was gone and the shadows in his eyes smothered the light she'd seen gleaming there so briefly.

The door to the tasting room opened, allowing a slice of afternoon sunlight to spill inside. Voices trailed in the wake of that splash of gold and Julie knew the first of their guests were arriving. "Travis," she said softly, frantically, "I wouldn't betray you."

He only looked at her as though trying to figure out who she really was. But didn't he know? Apparently not.

"By the way," Travis said, his voice carrying

subtly beneath the encroaching noise. "You look beautiful tonight."

Staring at her now—her dark red hair, her green eyes wide and innocent, her luscious mouth in a hard firm line—he felt a staggering rush of desire that made him wonder what he was thinking with. His mind or his hormones?

She wore a deep yellow dress with one shoulder strap. The skirt was full and ended just above her knees. He'd seen her dressing only an hour ago and had wanted nothing more than to trail his fingertips down the line of her spine displayed by the deep back of the dress. Now, he still wanted that.

Despite the newspaper photo.

Despite everything…he wanted her.

What did that make him?

A fool?

As the voices behind them grew and came closer, Travis sucked in a deep breath, held it and then released it slowly, trying to find an even keel again. If only for a short time. Long enough to get through the tasting.

"This isn't the time," he said finally, and told himself not to notice the disappointment in her eyes. She wanted him to give her unconditional trust and belief. But how could he when everything conspired to make him think that she was in league with ol' Pierre?

"Travis—"

"Isn't this *lovely?*" a high-pitched female voice cooed from too close by and Travis shook his head.

"We'll talk about this later," he said quietly. "When we're alone."

Then he folded the newspaper, tucked it under his left arm and turned to face the winery guests. "Welcome to King Vineyards," he called out. "My wife and I hope you enjoy your evening."

Because, he added silently, *somebody* should.

Over the next several weeks, life settled into a routine of sorts. Julie worked in the kitchen, trying out new recipes, planning for the day when she would have her bakery. Although the excitement of her plans was muted by the fact that once she *had* that bakery, she wouldn't have Travis.

The ache of that thought stayed with her day and night. Every waking moment she wondered how she would spend the rest of her life knowing she wouldn't have him with her. Knowing that she would be sleeping alone, always haunted by the memories of being in his arms. And she wondered if he would miss her, too.

When they hosted the tastings together, she was almost convinced that he thought of them as a team. They worked well together, and over the last few weeks, the King winery had received more visitors than ever. Between Travis's fine wines and the delicacies Julie made and served, they were the talk of the area.

Now, newspaper articles focused more on the winery itself rather than the scandal that had surrounded them for so long. Julie wasn't sorry to see the end of that disgrace, but she was worried about what

Jean Claude might do next. He'd vowed not to stop in his harassment campaign and she had to assume that nothing had changed.

So this respite was probably nothing more than the calm before a new Jean Claude storm.

Not that that was the only thing on her mind. Or even the most *important* thing on her mind. Julie pulled in a deep breath and blew it out again slowly. As a matter of fact, Jean Claude was the last thing on her mind now.

Ever since she'd found the nerve to take a little test.

Stepping away from the cooking island, she turned and walked to the bay window overlooking the vineyard. With Travis's cook on vacation, Julie had the kitchen to herself and right now, she needed the solitude. To think. To decide what to do. What to say.

As it was, Julie felt like an idiot. With everything that had been going on around them, she'd completely forgotten to keep track of her monthly cycle. If she had, she would have noticed sooner that her period hadn't shown up when it should have.

Her gaze fixed on the horizon, she watched as the sinking sun began to paint the clouds deep shades of scarlet and gold. A wind was blowing, ruffling the leaves on the vines and sending a minitornado of dust dancing along the neatly tended rows of grapes.

And inside her, a different kind of tornado was taking shape.

She'd driven to Sacramento that morning, wanting to get as far from prying eyes and nosy neighbors in

Birkfield as possible. She'd bought the pregnancy test kit and smuggled it into the house as if she were a drug dealer. Then the package had sat beneath the bathroom sink all day, taunting her with its presence, silently daring her to take its challenge.

Finally, an hour ago, she had.

It had only taken three short minutes to redefine her life.

One little plus sign and now everything was different.

She felt more alive than she ever had and yet more subdued. Exhilarated and worried.

How could she tell Travis that she was pregnant with his child? This was a temporary marriage. They'd both agreed to that at the beginning.

Besides, even if he wanted her to, she couldn't stay with Travis simply because she was pregnant. If he didn't love her, what would be the point? They'd only end by making each other—and their child—miserable.

"Something wrong?"

Travis's voice jolted Julie out of her thoughts. She slapped one hand to her chest and whirled around to find him standing beside the cook island, watching her. Guilt slipped through her system, but she fought it back down. She was going to tell him so there was no reason for the guilt. "You scared me."

He smiled and snitched one of the tiny lemon tarts she'd taken from the oven only a few minutes ago. Since discovering they were Travis's favorites, she made them often. "Those are still hot."

"I like things hot."

She flushed. Just like that. So easy, he didn't even have to try and she felt a flash of heat inside that would have put her oven to shame. How could she ever spend the rest of her life without him? How could she raise their child without Travis's love in her life?

He blew onto the lemon surface, then took a bite, savoring the tartness. "Delicious. As always."

"Thank you."

"So what were you thinking when I came in?" he asked.

Oh, she couldn't go there. Couldn't even let the thoughts into her mind, because she didn't doubt that somehow, he would *know*. So instead, she thought about how she loved him. About how she wanted to stay with him. Have him love her back. Those thoughts, he would be oblivious to. "Nothing special."

"You're not a very good liar."

"That's a good thing, isn't it?" She forced a smile and swept a dish towel across her left shoulder. Then deftly, she moved the rest of the lemon tarts from the baking tray to a wire rack where they could cool.

"Yeah," Travis admitted. "I guess it is."

Looking at her now, Travis couldn't think of one reason to doubt her. Her hair was pulled back in a ponytail, she wore a dark green King Winery T-shirt and faded blue jeans. Her feet were bare and her toe-nails were painted a soft peach.

And her eyes met his with a simple honesty that he couldn't force himself to deny.

He kept trying to maintain an emotional distance

between them, but that was getting more difficult every day. He was drawn to her. At night, he lost himself in the feel of her, the scent of her, the eagerness she expressed when he touched her.

During the day, he found his mind wandering during meetings. He couldn't walk the vines without thinking of her, wondering what she was doing. And the nights when she stood beside him in the tasting room, he was proud to have her there with him. She was warm and friendly to their guests, making them all feel special, and as word of her talents in the kitchen spread, their tourist traffic had more than doubled. King Winery was making its mark on the state and even Thomas Henry had noticed.

Travis hadn't had to wheedle his way into a distribution deal after all. Henry had come to him with a more than fair offer and there hadn't been any more snide comments about Julie, either.

He took another bite of the lemon tart and savored the delicious mix of sweet and sour that dissolved on his tongue in a burst of flavor.

Sweet and sour. Pretty much described what this temporary marriage of theirs was like. The sweet— those moments when they were together, focused only on each other. The nights in her arms and the laughter in the mornings. The touch of her hand and the sound of her sigh when he joined his body to hers. The knowledge that she was there, in his house when he came in from the vines. It was all so much more than he'd expected to find in a marriage that had been meant to be nothing more than a business deal.

But then there was the sour and that nagged at him. There was the mess with her ex. The way she'd gone behind his back to meet him—even if her reasons had made sense to him. There was the tight feeling in his chest whenever she was out of his sight for too long and the knowledge that in less than a year now, she would be out of his life.

He could hardly imagine her not being a part of his everyday world. Who would he talk to? Who would be there to argue with him over the best way to run a tasting? None of his employees dared to oppose him. But Julie had never had a problem with it. She stood up to him. Stood up for herself. Which is why he could look back at her meeting with Jean Claude and understand the reasoning behind it. He might not have liked it, but knowing her as he did, he shouldn't have expected anything else.

And on that thought, he said, "I talked to Adam a minute ago. Actually, it was more like me listening, older brother talking."

"About?"

"Pierre, strangely enough."

He saw her flinch just before her gaze dropped to the surface of the cook island.

"What did Adam have to say?"

Travis leaned both hands on the edge of the countertop and felt that straight edge bite into his flesh. He kept his gaze locked on her as he said, "He set a plan into motion. Something that with any luck, will get rid of Jean Claude for good."

She nodded, blew out a breath and finally lifted her gaze to his. "When's this plan supposed to take place?"

"Soon."

"That's good, then."

"Yeah." She didn't look happy, though, and whether he wanted it to or not, a doubt filled whisper scuttled through his mind. *Is she happy to have the Jean Claude situation exposed and ended? Or is she worried that her compliance with him will be uncovered?* Even as that thought whipped through his mind, Travis told himself it just wasn't possible. He didn't want it to be possible.

Irritated, he frowned, straightened up and backed away. She smelled too good, looked too appealing for his own comfort level. "I just wanted to tell you. Keep you up-to-date on what's happening."

"I appreciate it," she said, but she didn't look the slightest bit happy. Instead she looked worried and a little green around the gills.

"Are you feeling all right?" Travis stopped at the doorway and looked at her closely, noticing for the first time that her skin was paler than usual. That her usually bright eyes looked a little glassy.

"Fine. Just a bit queasy." She gave him a smile that was meant to placate. "Probably tasted too much while I was cooking."

Her answer came fast and easy, but Travis went still and cold. As he'd noted earlier, she was a bad liar.

Ten

"Remember our wedding night?"

"Of course I do." Vividly. Travis stared at her, waiting. She looked nervous—the tips of her fingers plucking at the thigh seams on her jeans. She bit down on her bottom lip, shifted her gaze from his, to the wall nearby and then back again. He couldn't recall a single moment in their time together when she'd seemed nervous before. Worried, yes. Scared, pissed off and stubborn, yes. But over the last few weeks, he'd never seen her look shaken.

Until now.

As he watched her, his senses kicked in and he thought maybe he knew exactly why she seemed so on edge all of a sudden.

She opened her mouth, closed it again, then huffed out a breath.

"Just say it, Julie." Travis braced himself for hearing the only words that would explain both her queasiness and the tension that was clearly gripping him.

"I'm pregnant."

He rocked back on his feet as those two simple words punched into his gut. The words he'd somehow expected to hear. In the blink of an eye, everything had changed.

Pregnant.

His gaze dropped to her flat abdomen before lifting to meet her eyes again. She was carrying his child. Even now, that tiny life was growing, already racing toward the finish line of birth.

His baby.

Travis's brain worked frantically. He didn't know what to think. What to feel. How was a man supposed to react when he found out he was going to be someone's *father?*

Panicked, that's how.

That emotion wasn't one Travis had a lot of experience with. He always knew what to do. He never had to wonder if he was making the right decision or not. He was *always* sure of himself. And now, a tiny being the size of his thumbnail had him feeling as if he was sliding off the edge of the earth, scrambling for a handhold to stop his fall.

Scrubbing one hand over his face, Travis told himself he was a man who liked being in charge. A man who made his own choices in life. Now, though, he was a man caught firmly in the grip of a very whim-sical Fate.

Travis King…a *father?*

Boggled the mind.

He took a breath and waited a second for it to kick in, maybe air out his mind so his thoughts could clear up. But that obviously wasn't going to happen anytime soon.

"How long have you known?" The words were squeezed out from between clenched teeth. Did it matter when she had found out about the baby? Yes. It did. He had to know if she'd been keeping this from him—the thought of any secrecy irritated him. Or if she would have kept quiet about it altogether had he not asked her flat out what was bothering her.

"An hour," she said and folded her arms around her middle, as if instinctively protecting the child within her body. "I was going to tell you tonight."

An hour. She'd only just found out herself and, judging by the expression on her face, the news was as overwhelming to her as it had been to him. Her eyes looked wide and a little confused. Well, hell. He knew just how she felt.

Travis's chest suddenly tightened to the point where he was half afraid he wouldn't be able to draw another breath. He stared at her as if seeing her for the first time. Her hair shone with dark red and gold lights in the final rays of the dying sun. Her face was pale and her eyes looked huge in her face.

She was more beautiful to him in this moment than he'd ever thought her before. His instincts fired. His woman. His child. Everything in him, everything he'd been taught as a child, his belief system—or morals—railed at him to protect her. To care for her. To stand between her and the world. Hell, it was all he could do to keep from rushing at Julie, lifting her off her feet and carrying her to the nearest chair, forcing her to sit down.

But instead he just stood there, trying to come to grips with the latest wrinkle in his world. He hadn't planned on being a parent. In fact, he'd gone out of his way to insure that he wouldn't be a father. Travis had made it a point in his life to be careful with the women he spent time with. He hadn't wanted to be creating life carelessly with a woman who was no more than a brief blip on his radar.

Now he was married—albeit temporarily—and his wife was pregnant with his baby.

"I know what you're thinking," she said quietly.

"Oh," he said, with a short, sharp burst of laughter. "I doubt that." Hell, even he couldn't keep track of his thoughts. No way she would be able to make sense of them.

"You're wondering if this baby is even yours."

She'd surprised him again.

That thought had never crossed his mind.

Her arms tightened around her middle and she lifted her chin as if trying to win a battle he hadn't even engaged in yet. "It's your baby, Travis. It's *not* Jean Claude's."

He shook his head. "What are you talking about?"

"I know you've had your doubts about me." She paused for a breath. "With the trouble Jean Claude's caused, I can even understand that to a point. But this is different. This is our baby. And I don't want you to think even for a second that—"

"Stop," he said quietly, cutting off her speech because he didn't need to hear it. He hated that she felt as though she had to defend their child to him. Hated that he'd made her feel as if he would doubt her about something this big. "I know it's my baby, Julie. Our baby."

Strange, everything they'd been through the last few weeks, and he hadn't even considered that the child could have been her ex's. Almost laughable now, he thought, that he'd been so incensed by a photo of that Frenchman kissing her. He'd doubted her loyalties. Doubted her feelings.

But on this, he had no doubts.

Julie would never foist another man's child on him. It wasn't in her to be that duplicitous. She was too honest. Too straightforward.

God, he was an idiot.

How could he have ever believed that she was in cahoots with her ex? He should have trusted her. Hadn't he known her long enough to know that she had a core that was as scrupulously honest as his own? Had he really been so thrown by *Pierre's* foolish plans that he was willing to lump Julie in with the man?

It was a wonder she was still speaking to him. Julie simply wasn't the kind of woman to sink to those kinds of games. And he should have realized that simple truth before now.

She blew out a breath and nodded. "Thanks for that."

"You shouldn't be thanking me," he said tightly. "You should be furious at me for not believing in you all along."

She shrugged a little and laid the flat of one hand against her abdomen, as if she were shielding the child within. "I was before," she assured him with a small laugh that sounded strained and tight. "You've made me furious lots of times over the last several weeks, Travis. And sometimes talking to you is like talking to a wall—only the wall would probably listen better."

He winced a little at that, because he recognized it as pure truth. He hadn't been willing to listen. Too intent on his own will, his own way, he hadn't wanted to hear from her unless she'd been agreeing with him.

"But this is…different," she said quietly. "Bigger. The fact that you believe me about this makes up for the rest. Besides, it's been a weird couple of months."

"True." The last couple of months with Julie had seemed like one long roller-coaster ride. Every time he thought they were through the confusion and mess, something new had cropped up. He'd mistrusted her, and wanted her. Suspected her, and desired her.

Now, he realized, the suspicion was gone, leaving only the passion and something else…something warm and deep and… He frowned to himself and shut down that particular train of thought.

"Travis," she said, narrowing her eyes on him. "Are you okay?"

He laughed shortly. He was far from okay. But he wasn't going to admit that to her.

"I honestly don't know." Walking slowly toward her, he said, "This isn't about me, anyway. Are *you* all right?" he asked quietly, giving himself points for holding back the rush of protectiveness that was nearly strangling him.

"I'm fine. A little queasy. A little shocked." She rubbed the flat of her hand across her abdomen and Travis wondered if she was even aware of her actions. "But I'm fine—especially since you're taking this so unexpectedly well."

Didn't make him feel any better that she'd clearly expected him to both doubt her and be upset by this news. Although, now that he thought about it, why *wasn't* he upset by the news of a surprise pregnancy? Yet another thought to avoid.

"You need to see a doctor."

"I was planning to."

"Good." He nodded, his mind already skipping ahead. "I'll want to be there for it."

"Of course."

He inhaled sharply and took in the scent of lemons and vanilla. "I don't want you to worry about anything," he said. "I just want you to take care of yourself. That's the only important thing now."

She smiled as she looked up to meet his gaze. Something inside Travis turned over and tightened. His heart?

He whipped past that thought at breakneck speed. Instead, he started thinking aloud, making plans, working things out in his mind.

"We'll have to set up a nursery, but I don't want you doing any of the work." Nodding to himself, he added,

"We'll hire a designer. Architect if you'd rather build a room off of ours instead of using one of the guest rooms. Maybe that would be better. The baby would be closer to us in those first few months. We'd both probably sleep easier that way." It was all coming together for him.

Images drifted into his mind. He and Julie standing alongside their child's crib, looking down at a sleeping infant. Boy? Girl? That thread of panic wormed its way back through him and Travis started speaking again in an effort to squash it. "We could talk to the muralist who did the walls in Gina and Adam's nursery. She did a whole magical kingdom kind of thing in there and it looks pretty great—"

"Travis…"

"And I don't want you doing the cooking for the tastings anymore," he blurted. Taking her arm, he steered her toward one of the chairs at the small, round breakfast table at the far end of the kitchen. "You shouldn't be on your feet so much."

"Travis, I don't want to sit down," she said.

He hardly heard her as he gently shoved her down onto a chair. "When our cook gets back from her vacation, you can go over the menus with her. I'm sure Margaret can handle what you've been doing for the winery—"

"*Travis!*"

"What?"

She stood up to face him and he only just managed to refrain from pushing her back down onto the chair. "What're you doing?" she asked.

Baffled, he said, "Making plans."

"I can see that." She shook her head. "The question is, *why?*"

"Why? Because we're going to have a baby. We need to start thinking about these things."

"No, we don't."

Something cold and hard settled in his chest, making him feel as if a boulder had been rolled onto his rib cage. "What're you saying? You don't want the baby?"

She jerked back and stared at him as if he'd suggested she pop her head off her shoulders and set it onto the counter. "Of *course* I want the baby. How could you even think—"

"Then what's this about?"

"Travis, we don't have a real marriage. Remember?" Her voice was soft, but her words slapped at him. "This was a temporary business deal. We're only going to be together for a year."

That had been the deal.

But things had changed.

As if she heard him, she said, "The baby doesn't change that. We're not your usual expectant couple. I know we didn't plan on this," she said, her eyes shining up at him. "But I want you to know that even after our year together is up, you'll always have access to your child. I would never keep it from you."

Travis scowled as her words sunk in and rattled around his mind. Did she really think he'd let her go now? Didn't she know that their "bargain" had just changed? There was no "temporary" to this marriage anymore.

Access? To his child? Visits on weekends? Oh, no. That wasn't going to happen.

He dropped both hands onto her shoulders and held on tightly. Looking deeply into her eyes, he said, "You're wrong, Julie. Our marriage just became permanent. Think 'until death us do part.' We won't be splitting up in a year."

"But—"

"Do you really think I'd let you go now? You're having my baby, Julie."

"It will still be your baby after we're divorced."

"Not going to happen."

"Travis, I can't stay married simply because of our child. It wouldn't be right. Or good. For any of us."

"Divorce would be better?" His voice was steel. As was his resolve. There would be no divorce. Julie wouldn't be leaving him and taking his child. They could work this out together. Find a way to be happy. The three of them.

"Travis…"

"We're having a baby and we're staying married," he said, pulling her into his arms, ignoring the fact that she moved stiffly. "Get used to it."

"He won't listen." Julie sat at the kitchen table of the King ranch and watched as a hugely pregnant Gina King moved slowly across the room.

"Big surprise there," Gina muttered, reaching down four glasses from a cabinet over the kitchen counter and setting them on a tray beside a pitcher of iced tea. She shot a look at Julie. "Dealing with the King men can be cause for buying the economy-size bottle of aspirin."

Get used to it.

Travis's words echoed over and over again in her mind, as they'd been doing for the last few days. But how could she do that, Julie wondered. How could she ever settle for a marriage that was maintained simply for the sake of her child?

How could she ever live with Travis knowing she loved him but that he would never return the feelings?

"I can't do it," she whispered. "I just can't."

"It's hard," Gina said softly. "Being the one in love."

Julie's gaze snapped to her sister in law. "You, too?"

The overhead lights in the kitchen shone down on the other woman, illuminating her so brightly, she almost seemed to glow. She looked so content, so completely happy and at home, Julie felt a quick stab of envy.

Gina rubbed one hand over the mound of her child and smiled to herself. "I've loved Adam all my life. I always thought it would be one of those tragic unrequited love stories." Her smile blossomed into a grin. "But you know what? Sometimes the men we love can surprise us. Sometimes, they wake up and see what's staring them in the face."

"Sometimes," Julie admonished with shake of her head. "But Travis is much more stubborn than Adam or Jackson. He's got a head like solid cement, I swear."

"Just don't give up on him too soon," Gina told her, lifting a jug of tea to pour into the glasses. "Oh."

Julie leaped up from her chair, hurried across the

kitchen and took Gina's arm. "Are you okay? You shouldn't be on your feet like this. Let me do it, for heaven's sake." She stopped, sighed and said, "I sound like Travis talking to me."

"You think he's bad now?" Gina asked. "Wait until the baby's three days overdue. Adam practically carries me to the bathroom every morning."

"He loves you."

"He really does." Gina looked into Julie's eyes and said softly, "And here's something to think about. If Travis is that worried about you, don't you think he might love you, too?"

Julie threw a glance at the door separating the kitchen from the dining room and the rest of the house beyond. God help her, she'd like to believe that Travis loved her. But even if he claimed to now, how would she ever know if he meant it—or if because of the baby, he was only saying the words she needed to hear?

"Come on. Let's get you into the study," Julie said, putting her own worries and fears aside for the moment. "I'll carry the tray."

"You know what? I think I'll let you."

In the study, there was a fire in the hearth. Soft lighting from lamps scattered around the room added to the coziness created by the dancing shadows of the flames. The three King brothers were seated in the wide, maroon leather chairs and all three of them leaped to their feet when the women entered the room.

"You shouldn't be carrying heavy things," Travis said as he scooped the serving tray out of Julie's hands.

"It's not heavy," she argued, but had already lost the battle.

"You okay, honey?" Adam was asking as he steered Gina to a chair and lowered her down onto it with all the care of a man handling a live explosive.

"I'm fine," she said. "I'm just feeling a little tired and achy."

"Achy?" Adam's voice went up a notch. "You're in pain? Have you timed them? When did it start?"

"Not that kind of pain." Gina laughed and patted his hand. "It's just a backache."

"Are you sure—"

"Geez, Adam," Jackson said from across the room. "Let her get some air. If she's in labor, she'll tell us."

Adam shot him a look that should have fried him on the spot, but Jackson only laughed and took a sip of his Irish whiskey.

Travis frowned at his younger brother. Jackson just didn't get it. The worry. The fear. Ever since finding out that Julie was pregnant, he hadn't been able to think of anything else. And rather than laugh at his older brother's barely restrained panic, Travis completely sympathized. One part of him was terrified of what he would face in another eight months…and another part of him couldn't wait.

It was like being a split personality, he thought. He could literally stand back and watch himself be an ass. He kept a close watch on Julie at all times and worried like hell when she was out of his sight. He didn't know how he was going to make it through the pregnancy intact.

And beside the general worries was one he was sure Adam hadn't had to contend with. The concern that his wife would pack up and move out at the end of their year together. Not that she'd get far. Travis would follow and bring her back where she belonged, of course. But at the same time, he didn't want her to *want* to leave. He wanted her as committed as he now was to building their family.

He frowned, then told himself that he still had plenty of time to make her see things his way. For now, he would simply take care of her. And as Jackson chuckled again, Travis sincerely hoped that one day, the youngest King brother got a hard dose of reality all for himself, and then they'd see who was doing the laughing.

Travis got Julie into a chair, then poured iced tea for everyone but Jackson. When they were all settled, he looked to Adam. "Well? Everyone's gathered. Let's do this."

"What's going on?" Julie asked.

"You're about to find out," Travis said.

Looking very pleased with himself, Adam walked to his massive desk on the far side of the room. He grabbed a tape recorder off the surface and walked back to the group. Looking from one to the other of them, Adam started with an explanation for the ladies.

"Obviously, you two know that Travis, Jackson and I hired a P.I. to look into Jean Claude's background."

The women nodded. "As you also know, we didn't find anything that could be seen as illegal in the strictest sense."

Julie shifted uneasily, but Travis dropped one hand onto her shoulder and gave it a squeeze. "Quit telling them what they already know and get on to the rest of it, Adam," he said, wanting Julie's discomfort over as fast as possible.

"Right." The oldest King brother smiled at them all and said, "The P.I. had another idea that we all agreed was worth a try. We didn't say anything to you two—" he nodded at Julie and Gina "—because we didn't want to get your hopes up for a resolution if this idea failed. But it didn't."

"What did you do?" Julie turned her face up to Travis and he smiled down at her. It hadn't been easy not telling her this news. He'd known about it all day, but he and Adam had decided to spring it on everyone at once. Which was why the family meeting had been called so suddenly.

"Our P.I. hired a woman to cozy up to Pierre," Travis said, a tight, victorious smile curving his lips. "She was supposed to flirt, come on to him and get him drunk enough to spill his guts. I didn't really believe your ex would be stupid enough to fall for it. But turns out, he's not the freshest croissant in the bakery."

Jackson snorted.

Adam bent down, and set the tape recorder on the coffee table. "It lasts for quite a while," he said. "The poor woman sat with this jerk for over an hour, plying him with expensive booze until she hit pay dirt. I've cued the tape to the part we wanted you two to hear." Then he hit the play button.

"And her husband is going to pay you?" A throaty, female voice rolled out from the tape recorder.

"Oh, he will pay me whatever I ask." Jean Claude's voice came next. The words were slurred, but perfectly audible. *"He believes my lies about his little Julie. And he will continue to pay as long as I can keep him believing that she still loves only me."*

Beneath his hand, Travis felt Julie stiffen slightly and he squeezed her shoulder again in solidarity. He knew how hard it must be for her to listen to this, because he wanted nothing more than to hunt Jean Claude down and beat the crap out of him for all the trouble he'd caused.

"But isn't blackmail dangerous?"

"And very lu-lur-lucrative," Jean Claude said on a hiccup. *"I will tell him Julie meets me for sex and he will pay me again. And again."*

Travis scowled at the tape recorder as Julie gasped and said hotly, "He's lying."

"Of course he's lying," Adam sneered. He bent to shut off the tape. "That's enough. None of us should have to listen to more of that idiot. But believe me when I say the police were *very* interested in this tape. Soon, Jean Claude's going to be too busy covering his own ass to cause us any more problems."

"But once the police have this evidence, it'll go to court and all of this will be back in the news," Julie said softly, covering her flat belly with her hand as if trying to keep the baby from hearing any of this.

"No." Travis waited until she looked up at him before he said, "I'm going to offer Jean Claude his last deal. If he leaves the country and keeps his mouth shut, I won't press charges."

"What about the money you already paid him?"

"Doesn't matter," he said.

"So it's over?" Julie asked.

"Over," Travis said. "He won't bother you again, Julie. I swear it."

She smiled. "And your contract for your wines?"

"Sewn up," Travis said. "Struck a deal this afternoon."

"Well this is good news!" Jackson lifted his glass in salute. "Finally, the Kings can relax a little."

"Not so fast," Gina muttered, as her water broke.

Eleven

Her name was Emma.

Eight pounds five ounces of beautiful baby girl.

Gina King's hospital room was lavishly appointed and filled with so many flowers, it looked like an English garden. The air was scented with perfume and rocked with laughter and eager conversations. After eight hours of labor, Gina herself looked exhausted but exhilarated. And as she held court over the family that crowded in close to get a look at the baby, the new mother practically radiated joy.

"She's a beauty, Adam," Travis said with a grin. "Lucky for her, she looks just like her mother."

"I couldn't agree more," Adam said and bent down to kiss his wife's forehead.

Julie's eyes were blurry with tears as she watched Gina's parents, the Torinos, coo over their latest grand-child. Standing right beside them was Adam, who only managed to tear his gaze from his wife long enough to stare wide-eyed at his daughter. Jackson and Travis were both there, each of them delighted by their new niece. Julie had had a turn at holding the newborn and as she cradled that tiny scrap of life, she'd suddenly felt both a part of the crowd, and somehow distant from them all, too. When she handed Emma back to her doting father, Julie stepped back, so that she could see them all, watch the scene with an objective eye.

She didn't begrudge Gina and Adam their joy, but as she watched her brother-in-law smiling tenderly at his family, she couldn't help but wish that Travis would feel the same way toward her and the child they'd created together.

But she wasn't foolish enough to try to lie to herself about it, either. Travis was doing what he considered the right thing. Julie knew he would make a life with her whether he'd wanted one or not. He would welcome their child and love it, but he would never love *her.*

And how could she stay with a man who only remained married to her because of his own sense of duty?

The answer was simple.

She couldn't.

New tears filled her eyes, but she blinked them back. This moment wasn't about her. Or Travis. This moment, this time, was for Gina and Adam and their daughter. There would be time enough later to talk to Travis. To tell him that no matter what he did, she wouldn't be staying with him at the end of their year together.

But that decision was followed quickly by a horrible thought. What if he decided to fight her for custody of their child? What then? That thought gave Julie a cold chill that snaked along her spine and made her shiver. She wouldn't have the resources to fight him in court. So whether she wanted to stay or not, did she really have a choice?

Must she just somehow accustom herself to the idea of living a half life—loving a man and knowing that he would never return that love? She'd trapped herself in a velvet box.

A cage with no bars.

She didn't want to stay, but couldn't leave.

"Are you all right?" Travis was there suddenly, right beside her. His voice was deep and soft, so that only she could hear him. He touched her face, fingertips light on her cheek and the buzz of heat shot through her at the connection, firing up her blood, easing the ice around her heart.

"I'm fine," she lied. "Just tired, I guess."

His eyes were worried, but he smiled at her just the same. "Not surprising. And now that the show's over, I'll take you home. You should be getting some rest anyway."

She loved the way he wanted to take care of her. She only wished it was because he loved her.

"Probably a good idea," she said, suddenly so fatigued she didn't know if she could stay upright another ten minutes.

They said their goodbyes and left the private room to walk along the hospital corridor. In the middle of the night, the lights in the hallways seemed harsh. A baby wailed in the distance and two nurses huddled behind a counter, looking over a chart. Machines beeped, families paced the corridors and the sounds of their shoes clicked loudly against the linoleum.

Travis took Julie's hand in his and tried to find his equilibrium again. He'd lost it sometime during the long night they'd just passed. Watching Adam, usually a rock of emotional calm, turn into a harried, frantic man standing on the edge of panic had warned Travis of exactly what awaited him in just a few short months. He'd felt Adam's nerves, experienced the fear right along with him and then the amazing joy that had followed all the terror.

And staring down into the face of that tiny, beautiful baby girl, Travis had felt something else. Something he hadn't expected to hit him so hard. Something he was still dealing with.

Love.

Rich and full and complicated. The baby had been alive less than an hour and already, it was as if she'd always been here. She was a King. His brother's daughter. Travis knew that if it came to it, he would lay down his own life for that child.

So, he had to wonder, how much bigger would the

feelings be for his own baby? He couldn't even imagine emotions that huge.

"Quite a night," he said as he stabbed the elevator button.

Julie nodded. "Gina was amazing."

"She was." Travis tucked a strand of dark red hair behind Julie's ear and indulged himself by then cupping her cheek in his palm. "You are, too."

She laughed shortly. "I haven't done anything yet."

He shook his head and laid one hand against her belly. "Haven't you? You're *making* a child, Julie."

"Travis," she said as the elevator dinged and the doors swished open. "Are you okay?"

He wasn't sure. He only knew that as he looked down into those green eyes that had haunted him from their very first night together, that he was feeling something different. Something…

"Yeah. I'm fine." He took her elbow and steered her into the elevator for the short ride from the second floor to the first. He pushed the down button, the doors closed and a moment later, the world dropped out from beneath their feet.

Julie's scream seemed to echo forever.

Only seconds later, though it felt like hours, Travis picked himself up off the elevator floor and crawled to where Julie lay sprawled in a corner. The elevator hadn't dropped all that far. Just the one floor. But the jolting crash had sounded like a sonic boom and had clearly stunned her.

Dust drifted down from the ceiling and the elevator light flickered wildly.

Travis's head hurt, his body ached and nothing was more important to him than reaching Julie. Her eyes fluttered open when he called her name.

"What happened?"

"I don't know," he muttered, running his hands up and down her body, checking for breaks, for bruises. "Are you hurt? Can you move?"

"Everything hurts," she said, her voice catching in a way that tore at Travis's chest. "But I think I can move."

He held her as she shifted to sit upright, back braced against the wall. She lifted one hand to her forehead and a jolt of pure fear ripped through him when he saw a tiny rivulet of blood rolling along her skin.

"You're bleeding," he muttered and quickly patted his pockets for something to stop it with, even knowing he didn't usually carry a handkerchief tucked into his jeans pockets.

"Oh, boy," she whispered and rested her head against the wall. "My ears are ringing, too."

"That's the alarm," he said, glancing up and over his shoulder as if he could see the source of the sound and shut it down with the force of his will alone.

"That's good." She laughed a little, hissed in a breath and then gasped.

"What?" he demanded. "What is it? What's wrong?"

She lifted her gaze to his and in the flickering of the overhead light, shadows filled her green eyes and glistened in the sheen of unshed tears. Grabbing his hand, she held on tight and whispered, "I think something's wrong. With the baby."

The overhead light flickered again and went out, plunging them into blackness.

Hours later, Julie hurt all over.

It turned out that the elevator cable was frayed and had given way. Thankfully, they'd only fallen one floor. If they'd been on the fourth floor when the elevator had dropped, things might have been different for them. As it was, Travis had a few bruises but was mostly unscathed by the accident. Julie was still waiting to find out exactly how badly she'd been injured.

But the aches and pains in her legs and arms didn't worry Julie. The only thing bothering her now was the cramping that had her praying frantically for the safety of her child. It had taken what felt like forever for the Birkfield fire department to arrive and extricate them from the elevator car. Through it all, Travis had been there, holding her, talking to her, trying to ease her fears while they sat huddled in the dark together.

When they were finally free, Julie had been whisked off to be examined. The doctors had run tests and taken blood and now had her hooked up to an IV that made her feel as though fear was filling her, one drip at a time.

Why did she need the IV? Was the baby still with her? Had it already given up its tenuous hold on life and was even now sliding free of her body?

Tears filled her throat, choking her, making each breath a victory. Dread and worry were her constant companions. She'd been so happy earlier, enjoying the celebration of new life with the rest of the King family. Now, everything was different.

Here in her lovely, private hospital room on the medical floor, there were no babies' cries to comfort her. Only the silence of night broken occasionally by the conversations of nurses. Travis had gone—at her insistence—to tell Adam and Gina what was happening, leaving Julie alone, trapped in her bed, waiting to hear if her child would live or die.

And if she lost the baby? Grief welled up inside her. Misery both for the loss of a child she dearly wanted and the loss of Travis.

Over the last few days, since he'd found out about the baby, Travis had been amazing. He'd made her love him even more and though she'd like to pretend that his actions were prompted by his love for her, Julie knew better.

He was solicitous. Kind. Concerned.

Overbearing.

Dictatorial.

But…he didn't love her. He was only doing what he thought was right. Taking charge of the woman who was carrying his child.

And with the loss of their baby, all of that would end as well. He wouldn't want to continue their marriage once the reason for it was gone. So she would lose everything. Gently, she lay both hands on her belly, as if she could keep her child safe, convince it to stay with her.

For all their sakes.

A standing lamp in the corner threw out a puddle of soft gold light that reached for her from the shadows. The machine on her right beeped and clicked and measured each of her heartbeats.

And still she waited.

When the door to her room opened, she expected to find a dour-faced doctor standing there. Instead, it was Travis. Backlit from the hallways, she couldn't see his features, but every line of his body was tense. He walked to her side quickly, took a seat beside her bed and gathered up one of her hands in his.

"How are Adam and Gina?"

"Worried about you," he said.

"They shouldn't be," she told him, shifting her gaze to the dimly lit ceiling above. "This is a night they should be celebrating."

"We'll celebrate together after we hear from the damn doctor," Travis assured her.

Celebrate what? she wondered. The loss of everything that mattered? Would he be relieved? Sad? Was he feeling what she was at all?

"You haven't seen the doctor again yet?"

"No," she said with a careful shake of her head, that still caused an eruption of a headache.

He fired a dark look at the closed door. "What's taking them so long? How hard is it to look at ultrasounds? Why can't they just tell us?"

"They can't tell us. The doctor has to. So we have to wait."

Turning back to her, he reached across, touched the bandage on her forehead and asked, "Are you in pain?"

A single tear spilled over and rolled down her cheek. Pain? She was in so much pain it was a wonder she could draw breath. But the small cut on her forehead had nothing to do with this pain. This particular agony went soul deep. "I'm fine."

"Of course you are," he said tightly, giving her a nod that said she was definitely all right and he wouldn't accept anything less. "Everything's going to be good, Julie. You'll see."

"Travis…" She wanted to tell him she understood that he was only there because it was the right thing to do. That he didn't really want the baby that she was desperately trying to keep. That she didn't expect him to stay there with her. To not make promises he couldn't keep.

But she couldn't make herself say the words to let him go. For as long as she had him, she wanted Travis with her. When he brushed a kiss across her knuckles, she savored the contact, holding it close.

The door opened again and this time, the doctor stepped inside. Instinctively, she grabbed at Travis's hand and held on tight. The doctor walked to the end of Julie's bed, glanced at the chart in his hand then looked up at her and smiled. "Your baby's fine, Mrs. King."

Julie released a breath she hadn't even realized she'd been holding. Relief and gratitude swept through her in such an amazing rush of sensation, she was nearly blinded by her own tears. She had to blink them away to see the doctor clearly. "You're sure?"

"Absolutely. That's a tough kid you've got there," the doctor told her. "Stubborn and determined to be born."

"Naturally he's stubborn," Travis said, grinning like a loon. "He's a King."

"He or she is definitely healthy, so I don't want you worried," the doctor said, gazing meaningfully at Julie. He glanced at her chart again as if reassuring himself. "Doctor's orders."

"Thank you." She was still holding on to Travis's hand, still drawing strength from him, still relishing the touch of his hand on hers.

"Yes," Travis added. "Thank you. But what about my wife? How is Julie? Is she going to be all right?"

"Your wife is fine, Mr. King." The doctor tucked her chart under his left arm and smiled benevolently. "A little bruised, a little battered and I'll want her to take it easy for a couple of weeks…but she's going to be fine."

Travis dropped Julie's hand, jumped up, pumped the doctor's hand like a wildman and said, "Thank you. I'll see to it that she rests."

Julie watched him as Travis walked the doctor to the door. When it was closed and they were alone again, Julie realized that she'd never known a person could be both happy *and* sad at the same time. She was grateful for the safety of her baby, but now she knew she would remain trapped in a marriage with a man who didn't love her.

Her heart broke a little as she imagined the long empty years ahead of them. And she wondered how long it would be before her soul, denied love, began to die a little each day.

Travis came to her side and gently eased himself down onto the edge of the bed. He smoothed her tangled hair back from her face and leaned down to tenderly touch her lips with his. When he sat back again, he looked into her eyes and said softly, "I've never been so scared in my life. Hell, I didn't know it was *possible* to be that scared."

Touched, Julie patted his hand. "I know you were worried, Travis. So was I. But thank heaven, the baby's fine. You heard the doctor."

"I'm not talking about the baby."

She blinked up at him as if trying to understand. "But—"

"It's *you* Julie. *You* I was terrified for." He took a breath, blew it out and stood up abruptly as if he knew he was too tense to sit quietly on the edge of her bed. Stalking off a few steps, he whirled around to look at her, silhouetted by the golden lamplight. "Do you know what it was like to feel that damned elevator fall? To hear you scream? To look across the floor of the car and see you laying there in obvious pain? To be *helpless?*"

Before she could speak, he held one hand up for her silence, then stabbed that hand through his hair. Shaking his head, he said, "Of course you don't. I never thought I could feel so much. Fear so much. Always in my life, I've charted my own course. Been in charge of my own destiny. Things happen when I want them to happen."

"Travis—"

He stared into her eyes as if willing her to believe every word he said. "Suddenly, there was nothing I could do. Everything was taken out of my hands. You were hurt and I couldn't help you. I could hardly breathe until I touched you. Couldn't think until you opened your eyes and looked at me. Couldn't live until I knew *you* were alive."

A bubble of hope began to swell in Julie's chest, warming her through, filling her with the kind of wonder a child found on Christmas morning.

"My own heart stopped, Julie," he said, his words coming fast and furious in a deep whisper that shook her to her core because they were so obviously torn from his soul. He slapped one hand to his chest. "I felt it. The world stopped until you looked at me. Until I could wrap my arms around you and feel your warmth."

Tears were flowing freely now and Julie didn't even make an attempt to stop them.

He walked back to her, and when he was close enough, she could see what she'd long dreamed of seeing in his eyes.

Love. And she hardly dared to believe it.

"I love our baby, don't get me wrong," he said, making sure she understood exactly what he was saying. "And I'm more grateful than I can say that it's healthy and safe." He laid one hand atop hers, and together they cradled the child they'd made. "But without *you,* there's nothing. I need you to know this, Julie. I need you to believe me on this. I *love* you. More than I thought it was possible to love anyone."

"Oh, Travis…"

"I can't lose you. I won't lose you." He bent down, kissed her once, twice. Then he pulled his head back to look into her eyes again. "You're everything to me, Julie. I don't know when it happened, but somehow, during the last couple of months, you've become the center of my world. Without you, there's nothing. Without you, *I'm* nothing."

Smiling through her tears, Julie lifted one hand to cover his cheek. He turned his face into her hand and laid one kiss on the center of her palm. Julie's heart melted and the last of her doubts slid away.

She had everything she'd ever wanted. More than she'd ever really hoped for. Her baby was safe and so was her heart. She looked into his dark brown eyes and saw their future, a bright and shining thing, stretching out in front of them. And she could hardly wait to get out of the hospital and start living it.

"I love you so much," Travis said, capturing her hand and holding it in his. "Tell me you love me, too, or I'm going to go crazy. You have to love me, Julie."

"I do. I do love you, Travis. So very much. I think I always have."

"Thank God," he said, smiling, bending to kiss her again, as if he couldn't get enough of her. "And I'm going to personally see to it that you never change your mind."

* * * * *

FALLING FOR
KING'S FORTUNE

BY
MAUREEN CHILD

To Sarah…
for too many reasons to list here
I love you

One

"I've been stood up." Jackson King closed his cell phone with a snap. Setting his empty glass down on the lustrously polished bar top, he signaled the bartender, Eddie, an older man with knowing eyes, to fill it again.

"Well," Eddie said, "I think this is a first for you, isn't it? You losing your touch?"

Jackson snorted a laugh and leaned deeper into the cushioned back of the dark red bar stool. Swiveling it a half turn, he glanced over the dimly lit room behind him. The Hotel Franklin, the only five-star hotel between the tiny town of Birkfield and Sacramento, boasted one of the best bars in the state.

It was also conveniently close to the King family airfield where Jackson spent most of his time. He kept a suite in the hotel for those nights when he was too tired to drive home and thought of the elegant bar almost as his office.

"Oh hell no. That's never going to happen. Wasn't a woman who blew me off, Eddie," Jackson said with a grin. "My cousin Nathan canceled on me. His assistant was driving his car to his mountain place and had problems. Nathan to the rescue."

"Ah." The bartender nodded. "Good to know you're not slipping. Thought maybe it was a sign of the apocalypse or something."

He did have good luck with women, Jackson mused. Or at least, he always had. Soon enough, all of that would be over. He frowned a little at the thought.

"Something wrong?" The bartender asked.

Jackson shot him a look. "Nothing I want to talk about."

"Right. Another drink. Coming right up."

While he waited, Jackson let his gaze slide around the elegantly appointed bar. The room gleamed with a warm glow as discreet lighting reflected off the wood walls and marble floors. The mahogany bar itself curved around the room in a sinuous bend that was nearly artistic. Tall, high-backed red leather stools were pulled up to the bar inviting patrons to sit and stay awhile. Small round tables spotted the floor, each of them boasting flickering candlelight. And the soft, lazy strains of jazz piped in through overhead speakers.

In this bar a man could relax and a lone woman could enjoy a quiet drink without being hassled. At the moment, the place was practically empty. There were two couples at the tables and at the far end of the bar, a woman sat alone, like Jackson. Instinctively, Jackson's gaze fixed on the blond woman and he smiled. She gave him a long, sly look that fired his blood before returning her attention to her martini.

"She's a looker all right," Eddie muttered as he refilled Jackson's glass with his favorite, Irish whiskey.

"What?"

"The blonde." The bartender risked a quick look himself. "Saw you spot her. She's been sitting over there for an hour, nursing that one drink and acting like she's waiting for someone."

"Yeah?" Jackson took a longer look. Even from a distance there was something about the woman that made his blood start to hum. He began to think that maybe Nathan not showing up was a very good thing.

"Can't imagine anyone standing *her* up," Eddie said as he moved off to fill another order.

Jackson couldn't either. This was a woman who demanded a man's attention. He watched her long fingers move up and down the stem of her martini glass in slow strokes and his body jerked to attention as strongly as if her hand was moving across his skin.

She looked up and her gaze slammed into his. He couldn't see her eyes from here, but he had a feeling there was a knowing gleam in them. She knew he was watching her. Had probably done the whole stroke-the-crystal thing on purpose to get his attention. Well congratulations, babe, it worked.

Picking up his drink, Jackson casually walked the length of the bar, slipping from lamplight to shadow, his gaze continually fixed on the blonde who watched his approach. As he got closer, he could appreciate the view even more.

She smiled, and a blast of something hot and driving roared up inside him. He hadn't felt anything like that in…well, ever. Instantaneous heat. Even from a distance, she was affecting him in ways he never would have expected. Possibilities opened up in front of him as he closed the distance between them.

She swiveled on the bar stool as he approached and Jackson took that moment to size her up completely. She wasn't very tall, maybe five foot five, but she was wearing sky-high, black-heeled sandals that would give her an extra few inches. Her blond hair was short, cut close to her head, and small gold hoops in her ears twinkled in the light as she tipped her head to look at him. Her sapphire-blue dress had long sleeves, a full, short skirt and a V neck that dipped low enough to showcase breasts that were just the right size.

Her big eyes were blue and focused on him and one corner of her mouth was tipped up in an inviting smile as he stopped beside her.

"This seat taken?"

"It is now," she said and her voice was a whisper that sounded like long nights and lazy mornings.

He shot his cuffs, straightened his dark red tie, slid onto the stool beside hers and said, "I'm Jackson and you're beautiful."

She laughed and shook her head. "Does that line always work?"

He nodded to her in acknowledgement. "More often than not. How's it doing tonight?"

"I'll let you know after you buy me another drink."

Oh yeah. He'd have to remember to thank Nathan for blowing him off tonight. Turning, he signaled Eddie for a refill, then looked back at her. Close up, her eyes were as blue as the deep sapphire of her dress. Her mouth was tinted a deep pink and her lips were lush and full, tempting him to lean in and take what he wanted.

But he could wait. Waiting was half the fun.

"So, do I get to know your name?"

"Casey. You can call me Casey."

"Pretty name."

"Not really," she said, shrugging one shoulder. "My full name is Cassiopeia."

Jackson grinned. "Well, that's prettier."

She returned the smile and Jackson could have sworn he actually *felt* his blood start to simmer. The woman packed a hell of a punch with that smile.

"No, it's really not. Not when you're ten years old and your friends have names like Tiffany or Brittney or Amber…"

"So, you went with the short version."

She glanced up at Eddie with a murmured "thank you," as the bartender delivered her bright green Appletini. "I did," she said. "And have my father to thank for it. My mother loved Greek myths, hence my name. My father loved baseball. Hence the nickname."

Jackson blinked, then laughed, getting the connection instantly. "Casey Stengel?"

Surprise flickered briefly in her eyes. "I'm impressed that you know the name. Most in our generation don't."

Jackson eased into the conversation, realizing he was having a good time. It was more than just her sex appeal, he was enjoying talking to her, too. He couldn't remember the last time that had happened. "Please. You're talking to a man who still has truckloads of his old baseball cards carefully tucked away in storage."

She lifted her drink, put her lips around the straw and sucked. Jackson went hard as stone in an instant. His mouth was dry and his heartbeat thundered in his ears. He wasn't sure if she was deliberately trying to set him on fire, but whether she was or not, the result was the same.

While he watched, she crossed her legs in a slow slide of skin against skin and one sandaled foot began to swing. One of her hands cupped the bowl of her drink glass while the other stroked the stem, as she'd done before.

Now he was sure she was doing it deliberately. Because her dark blue eyes were fixed on his as if she were measuring his reaction. Well, he'd been playing this kind of game for years. She'd see what he wanted her to see and nothing else.

When she set her drink down, she swept her tongue across her top lip as if searching for any errant drops of liquor. Jackson's gaze followed the motion and his insides fisted even tighter. Damn, she was good.

"So, Casey," he asked idly, "what are your plans for the evening?"

"I don't have any," she admitted. "You?"

His gaze dropped from her face to her breasts and back up again. "Nothing special until a few minutes ago. Now, I can think of a few ideas off the top of my head."

She chewed at her bottom lip as if she were suddenly nervous, but he wasn't buying it. Her moves were all too smooth. She was far too sure of herself. She'd set out to seduce him and she was doing a hell of a job of it.

Ordinarily, Jackson preferred to be the one making the moves. But tonight, he was willing to make an exception. Mainly because the deed was done and he wanted her more than he wanted to take another breath. "Why don't you let me buy you dinner at the hotel restaurant? We could get to know each other a little better."

She smiled, but her heart wasn't in it. Glancing around, as if to assure herself the two of them were secluded at the shadowy, far end of the bar, she looked back at him and said, "I'm not really in the mood for dinner, thanks."

"Really?" Intrigued again, he asked, "Then what?"

"Actually, I've wanted to kiss you since the moment I first saw you."

Good. She was going to be as upfront about this as he planned to be. "I'm a big believer in going after what you want."

"I'll bet you are," she murmured.

Her voice sounded breathless and he could feel her tension in the air. A tension he shared. All Jackson could think about was kissing her. Forget dinner. The only taste he wanted in his mouth was *her*.

Oh, he *definitely* owed Nathan.

"The question," Jackson said quietly, his gaze linking with hers, daring her to look away, "is whether or not *you* believe in doing exactly what you want."

"Why don't we find out?" She leaned forward and he met her halfway, more than eager to get a taste of this woman. In mere minutes, she'd driven him to the edge of a raw desire the likes of which he'd never known before.

Their lips met and in that instant, electricity hummed between them. There was no other way to describe it. Jackson felt the burn, the rush, and gave himself up to it. There in the shadows, his mouth moved over hers, his blood practically steaming in his veins.

Her scent—lavender—filled him and clouded his mind. All he could concentrate on was the incredible feel of her mouth on his, even as he told himself to pull back. To not push this too far too fast. This was something he wanted to enjoy. To revel in. And to do that, they'd need somewhere more private than the darkened end of a luxurious bar.

But as he shifted to break the kiss, she reached up, threaded her fingers through his hair and held him in place. Her mouth opened to him, inviting a deeper kiss, even as her fingers pulled hard enough at his hair to pull out several strands.

He jerked back, laughed shortly and said, "Ow."

She blushed, bit down on her bottom lip and let her hand slide from the back of his head. "Sorry," she said, her voice a whisper of sound that tugged at his insides. "Guess you bring out the wild in me."

She was doing the same damn thing to him. Forget dinner. Forget getting to know each other. All he wanted at the moment was her under him. Over him. He'd never desired any woman so desperately as he did this one. And Jackson wasn't a man to deny himself.

"I like wild," he said and laid one hand on her knee, his fingertips sliding discreetly beneath the hem of that spectacular dress to touch her bare skin. "How wild are we talking?"

She took a breath, grabbed her clutch purse off the bar and dipped her hand inside as if she were looking for something. Then she snapped the bag closed again, lifted her gaze to his and said, "Um, I think maybe this was a mistake."

"I think you're wrong," he said and smiled to himself as she jumped a little at the touch of his fingertips moving across her thigh. "I think you *are* feeling a little wild tonight. And I know I am."

"Jackson…"

"Kiss me again."

"There are people here," she reminded him.

"Didn't bother you a second ago."

"Does now," she said.

"Ignore them," he coaxed. Not usually a man who liked an audience, he couldn't care less about the sprinkling of people in the bar. He didn't want to chance her cooling off, coming to her senses. He needed to kiss her again. To remind her what was sizzling between them. Besides, the lighting was so dim, and he and Casey were so far from anyone else, they might as well have been alone anyway. And right now, that was good enough.

Her gaze lifted to his and when he looked into her eyes, he saw her wavering. Good enough. Leaning in close to her again, he kept one hand on her leg, letting his fingers slide higher onto her thigh even as his mouth took hers again.

She inhaled sharply, deeply at the touch of his lips and an instant later, her inhibitions went out the window, just as he'd hoped they would. Her tongue tangled with his and when he leaned in closer, sliding his hand higher, she sighed into his mouth and shivered beneath his touch.

"Let's get out of here," he whispered, when he'd managed to take his mouth from hers.

"I can't."

"Yes we can," he said, fingers moving higher, higher up her thigh. She shifted instinctively, and he knew she was feeling the same burn he was. "I have a room upstairs."

"Oh…" She took a breath, blew it out and shook her head. "That's probably not a good idea."

"Trust me, it's the best idea I've had all day." Abruptly, Jackson reached for his wallet, threw a hundred-dollar bill onto the bar, then tucked the wallet away again and took one of her hands in his. "Come with me."

She looked up at him and even in the dim light, Jackson saw the sheen of something hot and needy in her eyes. She wasn't going to refuse him. A moment later, she proved him right.

Standing up, she grabbed her clutch bag off the bar, and let him lead her from the room. He walked quickly, wanting to reach the elevator before she changed her mind. She kept up with him, the sound of her heels tapping out a quick rhythm on the floor that sounded like a frantic heartbeat.

Jackson wasted no time. The elevator doors dinged and swished open and he pulled his mystery woman inside. Before the doors were shut again, he turned her back to the wall and kissed her. His tongue swept inside, tangled with hers and he felt her surrender even as she lifted both arms to hook them around his neck. She held him close and arched her body into his as he pressed tighter and tighter to her.

Again and again, he ravaged her mouth and as he did,

he shifted one hand, sliding up from her waist to cover one of her breasts. Even through the silky slide of the sapphire-blue fabric, he felt her erect nipple. Flicking its tender surface with his thumb, he listened to her moan and let that soft sound feed his own passions.

The doors opened again on the top floor and Jackson stepped back from her reluctantly. Her hair was a wild tumble, her eyes were glassy and her delicious mouth was puffy and swollen from his kisses. He wanted her desperately.

Heading down the hall, he opened the door to the suite that he kept, pulled her inside then slammed and locked the door again. In an instant, she was back in his arms.

No hesitation, no awkwardness, they came together as if they'd been touching each other for eternity. There were no games, only need. No shyness, only desire. No second thoughts, only a wild, frenzied passion blistering the air.

Jackson yanked the zipper of her dress and slid the shoulders and sleeves down her arms. He thanked whatever gods were listening that she wasn't wearing a bra. Her breasts were beautiful, just the right size and looked so tempting, he didn't wait another moment.

Covering them with his hands, he pulled and tweaked with her hardened nipples and listened to Casey's soft moans and whispers as if they were the sweetest music ever composed. He bent his head to taste first one erect bud and then the other and knew he had to have more of her.

Her hands at his shoulders tightened, holding him to her, even as she swayed from the impact of his actions.

"More," he murmured, his tongue circling her nipple. "All."

And he pushed her dress the rest of the way to the floor. It fell in a sapphire puddle at her feet and he helped her step out of it. Her fingers were at his suit coat now, shoving it off, then loosening his tie and tearing at the buttons of his shirt. His hands roamed over her amazing body, sliding over cool, lavender-scented skin again and again, as if he were trying to memorize every line, every curve.

Then her palms were on his naked chest and he felt the zing of heat slice into him. Quickly, he tore off the rest of his clothes, picked Casey up in his arms and carried her to the nearest flat surface. He wasn't going to wait another moment. He had to have her. Be in her. Had to know what it was like to be surrounded by her heat.

"Now," she whispered as he laid her down on the extra wide couch in the living room of the suite. She opened her legs for him, reached up her arms and in the pale wash of golden lamplight, her eyes burned an arctic blue. "Now, Jackson. I need…"

"Me too," he admitted, willing to let her know just how affected he was by her. No games. No secrets. For this woman, this moment, he wanted her to know that from the first moment she'd smiled at him from across the room, he'd been aching for this.

Then the talking was over and all that was left to be said was said by their bodies. He entered her with one hard thrust and she gasped, arching into him, silently demanding he go deeper, harder, faster.

He did.

Every move she made only fed his need. Every response quickened the fires inside. Every touch, every slide of skin to skin, every gasp and moan and sigh worked together to push him higher than he'd ever been before. And Jackson wanted more.

He looked into her eyes when he felt her climax nearing. He watched as pleasure flashed across her face. He heard her gasp, felt her body's tremors. Then she locked her legs around his hips to hold him tightly even as she rocked her hips and cried out his name.

Something inside Jackson burst wide open and seconds later, his body erupted, throwing him after her into the wild, surging storm.

Casey woke up in the middle of the night. Her body felt sore and stiff and, she silently admitted, fabulous. It had been a *long* time since she'd had sex. She'd almost forgotten how good it could make you feel.

Until the guilt started seeping in.

She wasn't the one-night-stand kind of girl. She'd never done anything like this in her life and she was still trying to come to grips with the fact that she'd done it *now.*

Moonlight spilled into the hotel bedroom through the glass French doors leading to what she assumed was a balcony. She hadn't really had a chance to explore the suite, after all. She'd gone from the couch to the bed and that was about the sum total of her "tour."

God, Casey, what did you do?

Turning her head on the pillow, she looked at the sleeping man lying next to her. He was on his stomach, the silk duvet pulled up just over his hips. He had one arm stretched out toward her and Casey had to curl her fingers into her palms to keep from reaching out and smoothing his dark hair back from his forehead. In sleep, Jackson looked less dangerous, but hardly vulnerable.

There was still a hardness, a strength about him that seemed to resonate around him, even when sleeping. The man was a force of nature. She was lying there, naked and well used in his bed as a testament to that fact.

She hadn't planned to have sex with him.

Although, what they'd shared couldn't be called simply *sex*. Sex was just a biological function. At least, it always had been before that night. But what she'd shared with Jackson had gone way beyond anything she'd ever experienced before. Even now, hours after his last touch, her body was still humming. And that wasn't a good thing.

Because she wasn't looking for a relationship. Heck, she'd gotten what she'd come there for while they were still in the bar. How she'd allowed herself to end up in his bed was something she still wasn't sure about.

The only thing she was certain of, was that it was beyond time for her to leave. Best she do that before he woke up and tried to stop her. Quietly, stealthily, she slipped from the massive bed and the air in the room felt cool against her bare skin.

Moonlight lay across the silk duvet-covered mattress, spotlighting Jackson's broad, tanned, naked back in a silvery glow. He shifted in his sleep, and the duvet slid down his skin, revealing a paler swatch of flesh just below his waist. Casey took a breath and forced herself to look away. She didn't need to be tempted to stay. This was not part of her plan. She'd already gone too far. Allowed her hormones and her need to sweep away rational thought.

Tiptoeing across the moonlit bedroom like a naked burglar, she hurried into the living room of the luxurious suite and in the dim light, wasted several minutes trying to spot her clothes. But she didn't dare turn on a light. She didn't want to chance waking him up. Didn't want to risk him tempting her back into his arms. Into his bed.

"You are *such* an idiot," she whispered, hardly able to believe she'd let herself get into such a situation. She was usually so much more careful. Restrained, even.

When she spotted her discarded dress, Casey grabbed it up, hitched herself into it and clumsily worked the back zipper. Shouldn't these things be on the side? Finally, she was at least dressed—minus the panties that seemed to have disappeared. She picked up her heels and searched for her clutch bag. Finding it on the floor, half under the couch where she and Jackson had first come together. Swallowing hard, she avoided looking at the couch, snatched her purse and then headed for the front door.

She turned the knob carefully, opened the door and let the hallway light fall into the room in a narrow, golden slice. Before she stepped through the doorway though, Casey turned for one last look. She'd never been in a hotel room this elegant. She'd never been with a man like Jackson. In fact, this room, this man, were so far removed from her real life, that she felt like Cinderella at the end of the ball. The magic was over. The spell was ended.

She stepped into the hall, closed the door behind her and nearly ran to the elevator.

Time to get back to the real world.

Two

"Her name is Casey. She's about five foot five, has blond hair and blue eyes."

"Well," his assistant Anna Coric mused, "at least that narrows it down. Blue eyes, you say?"

"Funny." But Jackson wasn't laughing. He'd awakened to find himself alone and if the scent of lavender hadn't still been clinging to his skin, if he hadn't found a pair of white lace panties on the living room floor, he might have convinced himself that the hours with his mystery woman had never happened.

Why the hell would she leave without a word?

Anna, a middle-aged mother of four, worked for Jackson at the King family airfield. She kept ahead of the paperwork and made sure Jackson and the pilots who worked for him were always on top of their schedules. If the military had any sense at all, Jackson had often thought, they'd have hired mothers to be generals. Anna kept his work life running like a fine-tuned engine.

Too bad she couldn't do the same for his personal life.

He thought of something, snapped his fingers and said, "Wait. She said her full name was Cassiopeia. That should help you find her."

Anna glanced at him from the cabinet where she was deftly filing last month's flight plans, gas usage records and pilot hours. She paused in her work, turned amused brown eyes on him and said, "As much as it pleases me to know you think I'm a miracle worker, I'll need more than her first name and the color of her eyes to find her."

"Right."

"Besides," she said thoughtfully, "don't you have enough women in your life already?"

He chose to misunderstand her meaning and flashed her a smile. "You're right, Anna my love. You're more than enough woman for me."

She laughed, as he'd known she would. "Oh, you're smooth, Jackson. I give you that."

Smooth enough to have managed to change the subject before Anna could start reminding him of things he'd rather not think about at the moment.

Jackson left Anna to her work and walked into his private office. Here on the airstrip, there was a tower, of course, and a main building with a room for their wealthy passengers to wait for their planes in comfort. The boarding room was lavishly appointed with overstuffed sofas and chairs, reading material, plasma TV, plus a fully staffed bar and snack area. Above that main room, were the offices. One for Jackson, one for Anna and one room that was mainly storage.

Jackson's office, like Anna's, overlooked the airfield. The walls were a tinted glass that let in light but kept the glare down to a minimum. Also, Jackson had never liked being cooped up, and having walls of glass made him feel less like he was spending time in a box when he absolutely *had* to be in the office.

Normally, he preferred spending his time on the luxury jet fleet he owned and operated. Sure, he had a staff of pilots working for him, but he enjoyed the footloose lifestyle that running his own business provided. And the chance to fly superseded everything else in his mind. Practically took an act of Congress to get him to do paperwork, but he could fly rings around most other pilots and was happiest in the air.

Today though, he walked to his desk, sat down and deliberately ignored the view. "Casey. Casey *what?* And why the hell didn't you get her last name?"

Disgusted, he sat back in his leather desk chair and stared at the phone. This shouldn't be bothering him. Not like he wasn't used to one-night stands. But damn it, in the usual scheme of things *he* was the one who did the slipping away. He wasn't used to having a woman slink off in the middle of the night. He wasn't used to being the one left wondering what the hell had happened.

He had to say, he didn't care for it.

When the phone rang, he grabbed it, more to silence the damn noise than because he was in the mood for talking. "What is it?"

"You're damn cheerful this morning."

Jackson frowned at his brother's voice. "Travis. What's going on?"

"Just checking to make sure we're still on for dinner this weekend. Julie's got her mom lined up as a babysitter."

Despite his foul mood, Jackson smiled. In the last couple of years, he'd become an uncle. Twice over. First his oldest brother Adam and his wife Gina had become the parents of Emma, now a nearly unstoppable force of nature at a year and a half old. Then it was Travis and his wife Julie's turn. Their daughter Katie was just a few months old and already had taken over their household.

And though Jackson loved his nieces, after a visit with either of his brothers, he walked into his own quiet, peaceful house with a renewed sense of gratitude. Nothing like being around proud parents and babies to make a man appreciate being single.

"Yeah," he said, sitting up to lean one arm on his desktop. What with his mystery woman, an upcoming flight to Maine and a plane in for a refit, Jackson had almost forgotten about his dinner date with the family. "We're still on. We've got reservations at Serenity. Eight o'clock. Figured we could meet in the bar for drinks around seven. That work for you?"

"It's fine. Will Marian be joining us?"

Jackson frowned. "Don't see why she should. She's not part of the family."

"She will be."

"I haven't proposed to her yet, Travis."

"But you're still going to."

"Yeah." He'd made the decision more than a month ago. Marian Cornice, only daughter of Victor Cornice, a man who owned many of the country's largest private airfields.

Joining their families was a business decision, pure and simple. Once he was married to Marian, King Jets would grow even larger. With unlimited access to so many new airports, he'd be able to expand faster than his original business plan had allowed. The Cornice family was wealthy, but compared to the King family fortune, they were upstarts. In the marriage, Marian got the King name and fortune, plus she pleased her father, who admittedly was the spearhead of this match, and Jackson got the airfields. A win-win situation for everyone. Besides, both of his brothers had entered into marriages of convenience and they'd made them work. Why should he be any different?

If an image of his mystery woman floated into his mind, Jackson told himself it was fine because he wasn't officially engaged yet. Wasn't as if he were cheating on Marian.

"If you're seriously going to do this, marry her I mean, it would be a chance for Marian to get used to the family," Travis pointed out. "But if you'd rather not, fine. I'll tell Adam about dinner. I'm driving Julie to the ranch so she and Gina and the kids can spend the day together."

"Man." Jackson shook his head and laughed a little. "Did you ever picture yourself a father, Travis? Because I've got to say, it's weird for me to think of you and Adam as being *dads*."

"It's weird to be one too," Travis admitted, but Jackson

could hear the smile in his voice, even over the phone. "A good kind of weird, though. You should try it."

He snorted. "Never gonna happen, big brother."

"Marian might change your mind."

"Not likely." Jackson leaned back into his chair again. "She's not exactly the maternal type. Fine by me anyway. I can be the world's greatest uncle, spoil your kids rotten, then send them home."

"Mistakes happen," Travis said. "Everybody gets surprised once in awhile."

Okay, Travis and Julie hadn't been trying to have a baby, but Jackson wouldn't make the same mistakes. "When it comes to that sort of thing, I'm Mister Careful. I'm so careful I'm practically covered head to toe in plastic wrap. I'm—" A hideous thought flashed through his mind, jolting him from his chair to his feet.

"You're mistake-proof, I get it…." Travis prodded, waited for a response and when he didn't get one said, "Jackson? You okay?"

"Fine," he muttered, already hanging up when he added, "Gotta go. Bye."

Careful?

He hadn't been careful the night before. Hell, he hadn't even thought of careful until just this minute. Last night, he'd been too caught up in the woman with blue eyes and a luscious mouth. Last night, he'd let himself get lost in the urgency of the moment.

For the first time in years, he hadn't used a condom.

Jackson muttered a curse, kicked the bottom drawer of his desk and ignored the slam of pain that rocketed from his foot up his leg. Served him right if he'd broken some-thing. How could he have been so stupid? Not only hadn't he been careful, but he'd been with a stranger. A woman he knew nothing about. A woman who, for all he knew, had deliberately set up the situation to try to get pregnant by one of the wealthy King family.

He shoved one hand through his dark brown hair, then stuffed that hand into the pocket of his black jeans. Every muscle was tensed. His back teeth ground together and he told himself that no matter how difficult this turned out to be, he had to find that woman.

Casey.

Had to find her, discover who the hell she was and what she'd been up to the night before.

Still furious with himself, he stared out the window at the view stretching in front of him. A few of the King Jets were lined up on the tarmac, their deep blue paint shining, their tail fins proudly displaying the stylized gold crown that was the King family logo. Usually, his sense of pride swelled when he looked down on those jets. On the empire he'd taken over at twenty-five and built into one of the most enviable in the world.

Now, as he stared, unseeing, one of those jets roared down the runway, tore into the sky and lifted off to sail into the clouds.

While Jackson stood, earthbound, feeling like he was sinking deeper and deeper into a mire.

He had to find her. Especially now. He couldn't risk losing this merger with the Cornice family.

And he sure as hell wasn't ready to become a father.

* * *

A week later, Casey held the phone in a grip so tight her knuckles were white. "You're sure? There's no mistake?"

"Honey, I checked and rechecked." Casey's best friend Dani Sullivan's voice came through loud and clear with just a touch of sympathy. "There's no mistake."

"I knew it." Casey sighed, leaned back against the kitchen wall and stared up at the rooster clock hanging on the wall opposite her. The hands went to five o'clock and the rooster crowed. Why had she ever bought such a ridiculous clock? Who needed a rooster crowing every hour on the hour?

And who cared about the stupid rooster?

"Thanks for putting a rush on this, Dani." Dani worked full-time at a private lab and she'd done the testing herself, just so Casey could not only get the results faster, but be absolutely sure about those results. "I appreciate it."

"No problem sweetie," she said. "But what are you going to do now?"

"Only one thing I can do," Casey said, straightening up and walking across the room to grab her iced tea off the kitchen counter. The old fashioned wall phone's cord was stretched to its limits and slowly reeled Casey back in. "I've got to go see him."

"Hmm," Dani said thoughtfully, "considering what happened the last time you went to see him face-to-face, maybe you should consider a phone call instead."

"You're never going to let me forget that, are you?" The whole point of a best friend was having someone you could tell your deepest, darkest secrets to. So naturally, she'd spilled her guts to Dani. The downside was, Dani wasn't shy about offering her opinion.

"The point is, you haven't forgotten it, have you?"

"No," Casey said. She hadn't forgotten. Worse, she'd dreamed of Jackson almost every night. She kept waking up hot and flushed, with the memory of his hands on her skin. And that memory, rather than fading, was only getting stronger. With only a small effort, she could almost taste his kiss again.

And she didn't want to admit just how often she expended that effort.

"But," she said, lifting her chin before taking a sip of her tea, hoping the icy drink would cool her off a little, "that doesn't mean I'd make the same mistake again. Once bitten and all that."

"Uh-huh."

"You know, a little support wouldn't be out of line," Casey said, frowning.

"Oh, I'm supportive," Dani argued, her voice low enough that no one else who worked with her could overhear, "but I still don't think it's a good idea for you to meet him face-to-face, so to speak, again. With the kind of news you're going to deliver, I really think you'd be better off making a phone call from a safe distance."

Probably. But she couldn't do that. She really resented being put in this position, but there was nothing she could do about it now. By all rights, Casey never should have had to make this decision. Things had changed though and she'd been backed into a corner. So there was really only one thing to do. The right thing.

"Nope," she said. "I have to tell him. And I have to do it while I'm looking at him."

"Never could change your mind once it was made up," Dani muttered.

"True."

"Just be careful, okay?" her friend said. "He's one of the Kings, you know. They practically own half of California. If he decides to, he could make your life really difficult."

Fear curled in the pit of Casey's stomach. She'd considered that already. But she'd done her homework. She'd done research on Jackson. She knew he was the playboy type. The footloose and fancy-free kind of man. The kind who didn't want entanglements.

So she was pretty sure that despite the news she had to deliver, he wasn't going to make trouble for her. He'd probably thank her for the information, offer to write her a check—as if she'd take money for this—and then quietly go back to his lifestyle of easy women and mega money.

"He won't," Casey said firmly, wondering if she were trying to convince herself or Dani.

"I hope you're right," her friend said. "Because you're certainly betting a lot on the outcome of this."

Oh, Casey was well aware of that.

Three

Jackson looked across the table at the woman he was planning to marry and felt the slightest buzz of interest for her. But compared to what he had felt for his mystery woman, it was the voltage of a double A battery alongside the frenzied energy of a nuclear power plant.

He'd assumed that whatever attraction there was between them would grow with time. Hadn't happened yet though and he was forced again to remember the instant chemical reaction between he and Casey Whoever during their one night together. And what kind of statement was it that he'd had a better time with a perfect stranger than he was having with the woman he was expected to propose to? Images of Casey smiling, Casey naked, reaching for him, filled his mind and despite everything, Jackson felt his body burn and his chest tighten.

His mystery woman.

What had she been after?

She'd deliberately seduced him. Gone out of her way to entice him, then disappeared without a backward look. Who did that? And why?

If he didn't get answers soon, he was going to go nuts.

"My father says you're interested in the airstrip in upstate New York," Marian said, snapping Jackson's focus back to her.

As it should be. Didn't he have the damned engagement ring in his pocket? Wasn't he planning on proposing tonight? He had plans for his life and they didn't include mystery women, so best for him to get on with this.

"Yes, it's big enough for several flights a day and I've already worked out a new schedule with my pilots," he said, lifting his coffee cup for a sip. Dinner was over and there was only dessert left on the table. Naturally, Marian would no more eat the chocolate mousse she'd ordered than she would dance naked on the tabletop.

If there was one thing Jackson had learned about the woman over the last couple of months, it was that she was far more interested in how things looked than how things really were. She was painfully thin and ate almost nothing whenever they went out. And yet, she always ordered heartily, then spent her time pushing the food around on her plate with her fork.

His mystery woman, he recalled, had had curves. A body designed to allow a man to sink into her softness, cradle himself in her warmth.

Damn it.

Marian was watching him through calm brown eyes. Her dark brown hair was tucked into a knot on the back of her neck and her long-sleeved, high-necked black dress made her look even thinner and less approachable than usual. Why was he suddenly looking at Marian with different eyes?

And why couldn't he stop?

The small velvet box in the pocket of his suit coat felt as if it were on fire. Its presence was a constant reminder of what he was there to do and yet, he hadn't quite been able to bring himself to ask the question Marian was no doubt waiting to hear.

When he felt the vibration of his cell phone, Jackson reached for it gratefully. "Sorry," he said. "Business."

She nodded and Jackson glanced at the screen. He didn't recognize the number, but flipped the phone open anyway and said, "Jackson King."

"This is Casey."

His heart jumped in his chest. Even if she hadn't identified herself, he would have recognized that voice. He'd been hearing it in his sleep for days. But how the hell had she gotten this number? A question for another time. He shot a quick look at Marian, watching him, then keeping his own voice low and level, he said, "I've been wanting to talk to you."

"Now's your chance," she said and he heard the hesitation in her tone. "I'm at Drake's coffee shop on Pacific Coast Highway."

"I know the place."

"We need to talk. How soon can you get here?"

Jackson looked at Marian again and felt a small stab of relief at being able to escape this dinner and avoid asking the question he'd come there to ask. "Give me a half hour."

"Fine." She hung up instantly.

Jackson closed his phone, tucked it into his pocket and looked at the woman opposite him.

"Trouble?" she asked.

"A bit," he said, grateful she wasn't going to demand explanations. No doubt she was used to her father bolting out of dinners to take care of business. Reaching into his wallet, he pulled out the money required for the bill and a hefty tip. Then he stood up and asked, "I'll take you home first."

"Not necessary," she said, lifting her coffee cup for a sip. "I'll finish my coffee and get myself home."

That didn't set well. Bad enough he was leaving her to go meet another woman. The least he could do was see her home. But Marian had a mind of her own.

"Don't be foolish, Jackson. I'm perfectly capable of calling a cab. Go. Take care of business."

He shouldn't have felt relief, but he did. Another small tidal wave of it splashing through him. "All right then. I'll call you tomorrow."

She nodded, but he'd already turned to weave his way through the diners seated at linen-draped tables. He hardly noticed his surroundings. His mind was already fixed on the coming meeting. He would finally see his mystery woman again. Finally discover just what she'd been up to when she'd come onto him. He'd find out if she'd been protected during their night together.

And if she played her cards right, maybe the two of them could share another night of amazing sex.

Forty-five minutes later, he was parked outside Drake's. The place was practically an institution in this part of California. Around for more than fifty years, Drake's was cheap, the food was good and they never closed.

A far cry from the quiet dignity of the restaurant he'd just left, when Jackson pulled the door to Drake's open, he was met by a cacophony of sound. Conversations, laughter, a baby's cry. Silverware being jangled into trays and the crash of dirty plates swept into buckets by harried busboys. The overhead lighting was bright to the point of glaring and the hostess, inspecting her nail polish, looked just as bright when she spotted Jackson.

He hardly noticed though. Instead, his gaze swept over the booths and tables until he found the person he was looking for. Blond hair, pale cheeks, and blue eyes focused on him.

"Thanks," he said, walking past the hostess, "I found my table."

Walking down the crowded, narrow aisle between booths, he kept his gaze locked with Casey's and tried to read the emotions flashing one after the other across her features. But there were too many and they changed too quickly.

His gut fisted. Something was definitely up.

Tonight, she wasn't dressed to seduce. Tonight, she wore a pale green, long-sleeved T-shirt and her short hair was mussed, as if she'd been running her fingers through it. She wore small silver stars in her ears and was chewing at her bottom lip.

Nerves?

She should be nervous, he told himself. He had a few things to say to her and he doubted she was going to like many of them. But damn, just looking at her made him hot and hard again. She had a way of getting to him like no other woman ever had. Not something he wanted to admit even to himself, let alone her. But it was there. A niggling tug of desire that was damned hard to ignore. He stopped alongside her table, opened his mouth to speak and then slammed it shut again.

Beside her in the red vinyl booth, was a child's booster seat. And in that seat was a baby girl. Jackson scowled as the infant—surely not even a year old yet—turned her face up to his and grinned, displaying two tiny white teeth.

And *his* eyes.

Tearing his gaze from the child, Jackson glared at Casey and ground out, "Just what the *hell* is going on?"

For just a moment, Casey wondered if Dani hadn't been right. Maybe she should have just told him her news over the phone. At least then, she wouldn't be faced with a tall, gorgeous furious male looking at her as if she'd dropped down from the moon.

Casey had watched him arrive. Watched him approach, in his thousand-dollar suit, looking as out of place at Drake's as a picnic basket at a five-star restaurant. He'd obviously been out when she called. And she couldn't help wondering who he'd been with.

Now, she stared up into his eyes—the same eyes she saw every morning when her daughter woke up to smile at her—and fought down the nerve-induced churning in the pit of her stomach. She'd known he'd be angry and she was prepared for that. Didn't mean she had to like it.

Yes, she was doing the right thing. The only thing she could do, being the kind of person she was. But that didn't mean she wanted to. Or that she was feeling at all easy about this confrontation.

She watched as he shifted his gaze from her to the baby and back again and felt his tension mount. She didn't need to see it in the hard set of his broad shoulders or the tight clenching of his jaw. She could *feel* it, radiating out around him, like flames looking for fresh tinder.

And things were only going to get worse in the next few minutes.

"Why don't you sit down, Jackson?" she finally said, waving one hand at the bench seat opposite her. *Keep calm,* she told herself. *You're two mature adults. This can be settled quickly and calmly.*

As if he'd just remembered that they were in public, he grudgingly slid into the booth, braced his forearms on the table and glared at her.

Maybe not calmly. But at least he wasn't willing to shout and argue in public. Precisely why she'd chosen Drake's to let him in on her little secret. "Thanks for coming."

"Oh, are we being polite now?" He shook his head and let his gaze slide to the baby, now happily gumming the corner of a teething biscuit.

Casey knew what he was seeing. A beautiful little girl with a thatch of dark brown curls and big brown eyes. Her cheeks were rosy from the nap she'd taken on the drive to the diner and her smile was wide and delighted with the world.

But Jackson didn't look so delighted. He looked more like he'd been hit over the head with a two-by-four. Casey could hardly blame him for being shocked. Her daughter was the best thing that had ever happened to Casey. But Jackson was being slapped with a reality that she had been living with for nearly two years.

It was a lot to take in.

Especially for someone like him.

According to her very detailed research into his background, he was a womanizer. Hence her seduction routine at the bar a week ago. She'd known that he'd respond to her if she showed the slightest interest. It was what he did. He was a man who couldn't make a commitment that lasted more than a few weeks. He was dedicated to his own pleasure and living his life unencumbered.

Not exactly prime father material.

When his gaze shifted back to hers, Casey stiffened. Accusation and reproach shone in his eyes and were very hard to miss.

"Since we're being so very civil, you want to explain to me just what exactly is going on here?"

"That's why I called you. To explain."

"Start with how you got my cell number," he said and nodded when a waitress approached with a pot of coffee. She deftly turned the cup over on its saucer, poured the coffee, then drifted away again at his dismissive glance.

"I called your office at the King airfield," she said once they were alone again. "The recording on the answering machine listed your cell number for emergencies. I thought this qualified."

He blew out a breath, took a sip of his coffee, then set the cup down gingerly, as if he didn't trust himself not to throw it against a wall. "All right. Now, how about you explain the rest. Starting with your full name."

"Casey Davis."

"Where you from?"

"I live just outside Sacramento. A little town called Darby."

He nodded. "Okay. Now, about…" He glanced at the baby again.

Casey inhaled deeply, hoping to settle the jangle of nerves rattling around inside her. She'd known this was going to be hard. She just hadn't expected to feel almost mute when the time came for her to speak.

Clearing her throat, she told herself to just say it. So she reached over and smoothed her palm over the back of her daughter's head. "This is Mia. She's almost nine months old—" she paused to look deeply into his eyes "—and she's your daughter."

"I don't have children." His eyes narrowed until they were nothing more than slits with dark brown daggers shining through. After several long seconds ticked past, he finally said, "I don't know what you're trying to pull here, but it won't work. I've never seen you before a week ago."

"I know—"

He laughed shortly but there was no humor in the sound. The harsh overhead lights spilled down over him and weirdly cast his features more into shadow than illuminating them. "I came here wanting to find out who you were, why you slipped out on me and to find out if you were trying to set me up by getting pregnant deliberately…turns out you were way ahead of me."

Casey straightened up, insulted to the bone. She was trying to do the right thing and he thought she'd— "I was doing no such thing."

"You purposely set out to seduce me that night."

"It wasn't difficult," she said reminding him easily that she hadn't exactly kidnapped him, tied him to the bed and had her wicked way with him. But at the first memory of that night, her body stirred despite her best efforts.

"Not the point." He waved one hand as if dismissing that argument. "You had an agenda and saw it through. What I want to know, is *why?*"

Picking up a napkin, she leaned over, wiped Mia's mouth despite her daughter's efforts to pull free. Then Casey looked at Jackson again. "I went there to get a sample of your DNA."

He laughed again. Louder. Harsher. "You went a hell of a long way to collect it!"

She flushed and she knew it. She could feel heat staining her cheeks and hated the fact that she'd never been able to keep from doing that when she was embarrassed. Glancing around the diner, she made sure the other customers weren't paying them the slightest bit of attention before she said in a vicious whisper, "I took strands of your *hair.* Remember when you kissed me—"

"You kissed *me* as I remember it," he interrupted.

That's right. She had. All part of the plan that had taken a seriously wrong turn almost instantly after her mouth had touched his. And there was the uncomfortable twist and burn inside her. "Fine. I kissed you. Remember I pulled on your hair?"

"Ah yes," he said, leaning back into the seat and folding his arms over his chest. "You were feeling *wild,* you said."

"Yes, well." She shifted in her seat and wished she could get up and move around. She'd always thought better when she was walking. But she couldn't very well spring out of the booth while Mia was there, strapped into a booster seat. "I needed a follicle of your hair so I could have it tested."

"Why not simply ask?"

Now she laughed. "Sure. I'm going to go up to a strange man and ask for a sample of his DNA."

"Instead, you went up to a strange man and kissed him?"

Frowning, she admitted, "It seemed like a good idea at the time."

"And what about the rest of it?" he asked. "Was that part of your plan, too? Spend the night with me to what? Trap me into something somehow? Get me so wound up that neither one of us was considering any kind of protection?"

She cringed a little. She hadn't even thought of protection that night. The way she remembered it, she'd been so hot, so needy, so completely over the edge with a kind of desire she'd never known before, the thought of condoms hadn't even entered her head. And just how stupid was *that?*

"I didn't plan any of that," she said firmly. "The rest of that night just…happened." Her gaze snapped to his. "And while we're on the subject, I'd like to assure you that I'm perfectly healthy. I hope *you* can say the same."

"Yes. I am."

One worry taken care of, she told herself.

"That's good."

"And what about the other concern?" He asked the question slowly, as if judging her reaction.

"You mean pregnancy?"

He tipped his head toward Mia. "You seem to be fertile enough, it's a reasonable question."

"You don't have to worry," she told him. "The doctors say I would have a difficult time conceiving in the usual way."

One dark eyebrow lifted and she squirmed a little. Her personal history was just that. Personal. It wasn't something she discussed with just anyone.

"And yet…"

Again, he nodded toward Mia, gurgling and now slapping that teething biscuit against the tabletop.

"Look," he said, capturing her attention again, "let's leave everything else for the moment and go back to the real matter at hand." He glanced at Mia and Casey wanted to hide her daughter from his appraising gaze. "You needed my DNA. Why? We'd never met. How could you think I'm the father of your child?"

More personal history that she would prefer not to discuss. Yet, she'd come here tonight because she'd felt she didn't have a choice.

"Nearly two years ago," she said, her voice low enough that no one could possibly overhear her, "I went to the Mandeville clinic…"

She saw understanding dawn on his features. His eyes opened, his firm mouth relaxed a little and his gaze, when it shifted to Mia, was this time, more stunned than angry or suspicious.

"The sperm bank," he muttered.

"Yes." Casey shifted in her seat a little, uncomfortable discussing this with anyone, let alone the "donor" who'd made her daughter's birth possible.

He shook his head, scrubbed one hand across his face and said, "That's just not possible."

"Clearly," she said, "it is."

"No, you don't understand." His gaze locked on hers again, silently demanding an explanation for how this could have happened. "Yes, in college, I admit, I went to the clinic with a friend of mine. We'd lost a bet and—"

"A bet?"

He frowned at her. "Anyway, I went, made the donation and didn't think about it again until about five years ago. I realized that I didn't want a child of mine, unknown to me, growing up out there somewhere. I told them I wanted that sample destroyed."

A chill swept through her at those words. She glanced at her daughter and as a wave of love rushed through her, she tried to imagine a life without Mia in it. And couldn't. Somehow, through some bureaucratic mishap, Jackson's order had gotten lost in the shuffle, overlooked and ignored. She could only be grateful. Knowing how close she'd come to never having Mia only made her treasure her daughter even more.

She smiled. "Well, I'm glad to say they didn't do as you requested."

"Obviously."

It wasn't hard to judge his current feelings. He was now avoiding looking at Mia at all. And that was fine with Casey. She didn't want him interested in her daughter. Mia was *hers*. Her family. Casey was only here because she'd felt that Jackson had a right to know he had a child.

"I thought sperm banks were anonymous," he said a moment later.

"They're supposed to be." When she'd gone to the Mandeville clinic, she'd specifically made sure that she would never know the identity of her child's father. She wasn't looking for a relationship, after all. She didn't need a partner to help her raise a child. All she'd wanted was a baby to love. A family of her own.

When she was assured that their donors' identities were very strictly protected, Casey'd been relieved. And that relief had stayed with her until about a month ago.

"I got an e-mail almost four weeks ago," she said softly. "From the Mandeville clinic. It listed my name, the donor number I'd selected and identified you as the man who'd made the original deposit."

He winced a little at that.

"Naturally, I was furious. This whole thing was supposed to be anonymous, remember. I called the clinic to complain," she told him and with the memories flooding her mind, she felt again that helpless sense of betrayal she'd experienced when she first read that e-mail. "They were in a panic. It seems someone hacked into their computers and sent out dozens of e-mails to women identifying the fathers of their children. It wasn't supposed to happen, of course, but it was too late to change anything."

"I see."

Two words, said so tightly it was a wonder he'd been able to squeeze them out of his throat. Well, fine. Casey understood that this was a surprise. But he had to understand that she wasn't happy about this, either.

"I didn't want to know the name of my daughter's father," she said firmly. "I wasn't interested in the man then and I'm not interested now. I didn't go to a sperm bank looking for a lasting connection, after all. All I wanted was a baby."

A muscle in his jaw twitched and an emotional shutter was down over his eyes, preventing her from getting the slightest impression of what he was thinking. "And you found this out a month ago."

"Yes."

He tapped his fingertips against the table. "Why'd you wait so long to tell me?"

Though his tone was even, his voice quiet, Casey had no problem identifying the anger behind that statement.

She took a gulp of her now cold coffee and grimaced as it slid down her throat. "Frankly, I'd considered not telling you at all at first."

His eyebrows arched.

"But soon enough, I realized you had the right to know if you actually *were* Mia's father."

"You doubted it?"

"Why wouldn't I?" she countered. "Just because some hacker got into the clinic's computer system doesn't mean he did a good job of it." Then she looked him straight in the eye. "Besides, you are definitely not the kind of father

I wanted for my baby. When I went to Mandeville, I specifically requested the sperm of a *scientist.*"

For a second, insult flashed across his face, then he snorted a laugh again and shook his head as if he couldn't believe they were even having this conversation. "A scientist?"

"I wanted my child to be smart."

He glared at her. "I graduated magna cum laude."

"With a degree in partying? Or women?"

"I happen to have an MBA, not that it's any of your business."

She had already known that, thanks to her research, but the point was, she knew very well what Jackson King considered most important in his life. And it wasn't intellectual pursuits.

"It doesn't really matter anymore," Casey said with a sigh. "I love my daughter and I don't care who her father is."

"Yet, as soon as you found out her father was Jackson King," he countered, "you came to me. So what's this little meeting really about?"

"I beg your pardon?" She sounded as stuffy as her late aunt Grace.

"You heard me, Casey Davis. You came here to present me with my daughter—"

"*My* daughter," she corrected, wondering why this conversation was suddenly feeling like more than a verbal battle.

"So it makes a man wonder, just what it is you really want from me? Money?" He reached into the breast pocket of his suit and pulled out a black leather wallet. "How much are you after? Looking for some child support? Is that what this is about?"

"That is just typical," she said, feeling a slow burn of anger start to build within. "Of course you think this is about money. That's how you see the world, isn't it? Well, I already told you, I don't want anything from you."

"I don't believe you."

She hissed in a breath and devoutly wished she'd never told him about Mia. "You can think whatever you like. I can't stop you. But I can leave. This little conversation is over."

Turning in her seat, she unstrapped her baby from the booster chair, lifted Mia into her arms and cuddled her close as she scooted out of the booth. Feeling Mia's warmth against her was a soothing balm to the anger churning inside her. It didn't matter what Jackson King thought or did. She'd done the right thing, now she could put him behind her. She could concentrate on her daughter.

When she was standing, her purse hanging from her shoulder to slap against her jean-clad thigh, Casey looked down at Jackson. And this time there was pity in her eyes. Because he couldn't grasp just how much he was missing, not knowing the child he'd helped create.

"I thought you had a right to know that you'd helped make this beautiful little girl possible, whether or not it was done willingly," she said, disgust pumping into her words. "But I can see now that was a mistake. Don't worry though, Jackson. Mia will never know that her father thought so little of her."

"Is that right?" He smiled up at her, clearly believing her outrage just another part of the act. "What will you tell her about me?"

"I'll tell her you're dead," Casey said quietly. "Because as far as I'm concerned, you are."

Four

She moved fast, he'd give her that.

But then, shock had slowed him down a little, too.

Jackson was only a step or two behind her, raw emotion pumping through his system. He couldn't even believe what was happening. At thirty-one years old, he was a father. To a little girl who'd been alive for nearly a year and he hadn't known it. What the hell was a man supposed to do with information like that?

His gaze fixed on Casey as she hurried across the parking lot and even as furious as he was, he couldn't stop himself from admiring the rear view of her. Her jeans clung to her behind and her legs like a second skin and instantly, lust roared up inside and kept time with the anger frothing in his gut.

Casey was already at her car, putting the baby into a car

seat when he caught up with her. A cold ocean wind slapped at him as he approached, almost as if someone, somewhere was trying to keep him at a distance.

Well the hell with that.

"You can't just drop this bomb on me, then walk away."

She flipped her head around, froze him with a hard look and muttered, "Watch me."

He glanced at the baby, who was watching them both through wide brown eyes. After being around his nieces for several months, Jackson recognized the expression on the baby's face. The tiny girl looked confused and on the verge of tears. Not what he wanted. So he lowered his voice, tried to force a smile into place and said, "Look, you surprised me. Sandbagged me. And I think you know it."

Casey paid no attention to him, instead, she struggled with the straps on the car seat. "This stupid thing always gives me fits."

He didn't want to talk about the car seat. Getting more impatient by the minute, he finally took hold of Casey's arm, ignored the instant sizzle that touching her caused, pulled her back and said "Let me do it."

She laughed. "How do *you* know anything about infant car seats?"

"I have two nieces," he muttered, not bothering to glance at her.

He'd had plenty of practice over the last year, dealing with all of the accoutrements that seemed to come along with a baby. Emma had more luggage than her parents and in a few short months, Katie's toys and necessities had completely taken over the vineyard.

In seconds, he had the buckles snapped securely. He looked at *his daughter* and tried to wrap his brain around that simple fact. Didn't work. Still, he traced one finger down the baby's cheek and got a giggle for his trouble. His heart ached with a completely unfamiliar feeling as he looked into eyes so like his own.

When he backed out of the car, he was still smiling until he caught the fiery look in Casey's eyes.

"Thanks," she said quickly, then pushed past him to close the car door and walk around to the driver's seat.

Jackson stayed right at her heels. Before she could open her car door and escape him, he grabbed hold of her arm again. "Just wait a damn minute, all right?"

She pulled free of his grasp and he let her go. Shoving one hand through his hair, he took a breath, glanced around at the full parking lot and then looked back at her. "I don't know what you want from me."

"Nothing," she said and now she sounded almost tired. "I've already said that. Now I have to go."

He slapped one hand against the car door and held it shut. Bending down, he looked directly into her blue eyes and said, "You've known about the baby—"

"Mia—"

"—Mia," he corrected, "for nearly two years. I've known for—" he checked his watch. "Ten minutes. Maybe you could cut me a break here, huh? It's not every day a man finds out he's a father while sitting in a twenty-four-hour diner that smells of corned beef hash."

An all-too-brief smile curved her mouth then disappeared again in a heartbeat.

Jackson's mind was racing. He'd just received the biggest news of his life. How the hell was he supposed to react?

"Fine," she said and he could see that the effort to be reasonable was costing her. "You need time. Take all the time you want. Take *eternity* if you need to." Her gaze bored into his. "While you get used to the idea, Mia and I will go back to our lives."

"Just like that?"

She jerked him a nod and the silver stars in her ears winked at him, reflecting off the parking lot lights. "Just like that. You needed to know, now you do. That's all."

He looked through the car windows at the back of the car seat. He couldn't see Mia's face, but he didn't have to. The image was burned into his memory. He doubted he would ever forget his first look at her.

Something momentous had just happened to him and damned if he could make sense of it standing in a crowded parking lot. So he'd let Casey go. Let her take his daughter away.

For now.

She'd find out soon enough that he wasn't a man to be dismissed whenever she felt it was time.

"All right. Take Mia home." Easing off the car, Jackson stepped aside and allowed her to open the door. He noticed the wary suspicion in her eyes, but didn't care to say anything that might ease it. Let her worry a bit. She'd put him through the wringer in a matter of a few minutes. Worrying about it now was the least she could do.

She tossed her purse onto the front passenger seat, curled her fingers over the top of the car door and looked at him. In the dim light, her deep blue eyes were shadowed. A trick of the night? Or something else?

"I guess this is goodbye," she said and mustered up a smile that only managed to tip one corner of her mouth. "I don't suppose we'll be seeing each other again, so have a nice life, Jackson."

He watched her leave, memorized her license plate number and was already making plans as he headed to his car.

"It went great," Casey lied as she moved around her kitchen, entangling herself in the phone cord as she went. She really had to get a cordless for this room. Opening the refrigerator door, she pulled out a bottle of chardonnay then went for a wineglass. "He saw Mia, we talked, then we came home and he went…wherever men like him go."

Mia was sound asleep in her room, the house was quiet and Casey was still a bundle of nerves. Seeing Jackson again had been way too hard. She hadn't expected the sexual tug to be as strong as before. And then, watching his face as he looked at Mia and realized the truth had really sucker punched her. He'd looked stunned, of course. But there was an undercurrent, too. A look of a man glimpsing something he'd never expected to find. Like he'd stumbled across a treasure—just before his eyes went cold and calculating again.

And that worried her a little.

After all, as Dani had pointed out, the King family was a powerful force in California. What if he decided to take Mia from Casey? Then what? No, she told herself instantly. He'd signed a form when he donated his sperm, giving up all rights to a baby. Though with his family's power, he could probably negate that form. He wasn't interested in having a child.

Instead, he'd actually thought Casey had come to him for money!

Was that really how he looked at the world around him? Everything solved by a checkbook or a thick wallet? Did he really believe that she would use her *daughter* to make money? What kind of horrible people did he know, anyway?

"Uh-huh," Dani said. "Your voice sounds filled with all kinds of good feelings and happy butterflies."

"Okay," she admitted, "no happy butterflies. Should have known I couldn't put one past you." Casey poured the sunlight-colored wine into a glass, recorked the bottle and only then noticed the label. *Kings Vineyard*. Perfect. Even when he wasn't here, she was reminded of Jackson. Not that she needed reminding.

She could almost feel him right now, as she stood, safe in her tiny kitchen. The man's inherent strength and *presence* was something that lingered. At least, it did in her case.

"It wasn't great and it wasn't easy. He was stunned and not in a happy way." Casey nodded firmly, forced herself to put a good spin on the night by adding, "But it ended well. I came home with Mia and Jackson went away."

"Permanently?" Dani asked.

"I hope so," Casey admitted. "He said he needed time to adjust. I told him we don't want anything from him, but I'm not sure he heard me. Either way though, the point is, mission accomplished. I told him, it's over now, and I can go back to my life. Put this all behind me."

"And you really think it's going to be that easy?" Dani paused, half covered the phone receiver and said, "Mikey, don't run the choo-choo train on your sister's head. That's a good boy."

Casey grinned. Trust Dani and her wild bunch to keep things in perspective. "Having trouble?"

"Nice subject change," Dani told her with a laugh. "And the answer is yes. I love my husband, don't get me wrong, but when Mike's in charge, the kids pretty much rule the house. When it's my turn, I spend most of my time in damage control."

Dani's husband Mike, a Darby police officer, worked nights and Dani worked days. That way, there was always a parent around for the kids. A tired parent, but at least the children were cared for by family. Of course, Dani insisted it had been so long since she'd had sex, she only had a vague recollection of it.

Casey's memories on the other hand, were clear and vivid. Which was just part of the problem.

"I don't know how you take care of Mia all alone," Dani said, switching the subject back to Casey. "I mean, Mike and I have separate shifts, but we always know there's somebody to back us up. To turn to. To *whine* to."

Casey smiled a little wistfully. She'd known going in, that she and her child would be alone. And that was okay with her most of the time. If she sometimes envied Dani's relationship with her husband, she figured that was only normal.

"I've never known it any other way," she admitted,

putting the wine bottle back in the fridge and picking up her glass for a sip. "When I decided to get pregnant, I knew I'd be doing it alone. Sure, there's nobody to help out, but I don't have to share her with anyone either."

"You don't just share the bad stuff, Casey," Dani said. "It's nice to have someone to turn to and say, 'Hey, did you just see that? Isn't our kid brilliant?'"

Casey lifted her chin. "I have you to call and brag to. Besides, Mia and I get along great."

"I love you and Mia like crazy, you know that. And nobody's saying you're not doing great on your own."

"But? I hear a but in there somewhere."

"Okay, *but*," Dani said. "I think you're being unrealistic to believe that Jackson King is going to disappear just because you want him to."

Casey's stomach did a quick flip and she took another sip of wine. She didn't want to believe her friend, but hadn't she been thinking the same thing earlier, while she'd bathed Mia and put her to bed?

Jackson came from a wealthy, powerful family. If he wanted to make trouble for her, he could. Right thing to do or not, she was beginning to wish she'd never contacted Jackson.

Casey dropped into one of the two wooden chairs pulled up to a tiny table in one corner of her kitchen. She stared out at the night beyond the windowpanes, where her postage-stamp-sized backyard lay and tried to keep panic at bay.

Shaking her head, she said, more to convince herself than Dani, "Why would he come back? He doesn't want a baby.

His whole lifestyle is built around hedonism. He does what he wants when he wants. He's got a home he rarely stays in, his business has him flying all over the world and he's not exactly a candidate for Mr. Commitment."

"That's the thing though, honey," Dani said softly. "He's never had a reason to commit to anything before, has he?"

"No. No, he hasn't." Casey set her wineglass down on the table and carefully unwrapped the curled phone cord from around her shoulders. "And by telling him the truth, I've just given him one, haven't I?"

The next morning, Jackson was at the King family ranch, having called an emergency family meeting. He faced both of his brothers and was grateful that neither one of them had brought their wives into this.

"Did you actually see the DNA report?" Adam asked.

Jackson stopped pacing the confines of the elegantly appointed room and shot his oldest brother a look. "No, I didn't."

"Well, why the hell not?" Travis demanded from his seat in a dark brown leather chair.

Shifting him a glare, Jackson snapped, "I was a little shocked, okay? Having a child you never knew existed thrown at you all of a sudden is more surprising than you might think. Besides, I don't need to see the report. You'll know what I mean when you see Mia. She looks just like Emma and Katie." He paused for effect, then added, "Prettier, of course, but then I'm the father."

Adam chuckled and shook his head. "You're sure taking this better than I thought you would."

"You should have seen me last night." Jackson had spent the entire night prowling through the home he rarely stayed in. The rooms were empty, the caretakers who lived there permanently were in their quarters and he'd listened for hours to the echoes of his own footsteps.

He'd tried to imagine the sound of a child's laughter ringing through the big house, but hadn't quite been able to do it. Hadn't really known if he'd *wanted* to do it. But even as he told himself that, he'd realized a part of him was already making room for his child in his life.

Travis shook his head and scowled into his coffee. Adam on the other hand, sat behind his desk, his feet, crossed at the ankle, perched on one corner of it. "What does she want?" he asked quietly.

"She says, nothing."

"Right." Travis blew out a breath.

Jackson walked back across the floor to face both of his brothers. "Look, she just found out I'm the father. I told you she went to that sperm bank and—"

"I can't believe you did that," Adam interrupted.

"Not the point," Jackson told him, refusing to go back over past mistakes. "Barn door open, horse gone."

"He's right," Travis said, standing up to refill his coffee cup from the thermal pot on Adam's desk. "How it happened doesn't matter. What matters is what comes next."

"What do you *want* to happen next?" Adam asked.

Hell if he knew.

He threw his hands in the air and let them fall to his sides again. This was something he was so not prepared to deal with. Something that had never once come up on his radar screen, so to speak. Now that it was there though, he had to step up and make the decision about how to go forward.

Images of Casey and Mia filled his mind. He was a *father*.

What the hell was he supposed to do with that?

"Jackson?"

Coming up out of his thoughts like a drowning man breaching the surface of a deep lake, Jackson looked at Adam and said quietly, "She's my daughter. I won't be kept away from her. Casey's just going to have to deal with that reality. Mia is a *King*. She's going to grow up knowing what that means."

Adam and Travis exchanged glances and nodding, turned back to him.

"Of course she is," Adam said.

"She's family," Travis put in.

"Her mother's not going to like it," Jackson told them.

"You'll have to find a way to work around that."

"I can do that," he said, though inwardly, he admitted that a woman as stubborn as Casey wasn't going to be easy to outmaneuver.

"There's something else to remember here too," Travis put in a moment later. He waited until both of his brothers were looking at him before saying, "You've got Marian to consider, in all this."

"Marian." Jackson whispered her name and shaking his head, realized he hadn't given her a single thought since the night before. But it didn't matter, he decided. He and Marian had a business arrangement. It wasn't as if this were a great love match, after all. He'd tell her what had happened and let her know the engagement would have to be postponed. "She'll understand."

"What makes you think so?" Adam prompted.

"Because she wants this merger. And her father wants this marriage too," Jackson told him. "Having King Jets linked to the Cornice family airfields will be good advertising for them and they know it. Our presence will bring in even more business for them."

"Still not going to make her happy to hear about the baby," Travis said.

"She'll have to deal with it," Jackson declared, unwilling to accept any other outcome. "I'll simply explain that I just found out I have a daughter."

Silence greeted him. Then he repeated the most earth-shattering part of that last sentence. "I have a *daughter.*"

Travis laughed. "I know just how you feel. Strange, isn't it?"

Strange, yes, Jackson thought as he mentally repeated the word *daughter.* A part of him thrilled to it.

Which shook him some. He hadn't planned on this happening. If someone had asked him flat out if he'd wanted to be a father, he would have said no instantly. But now, faced with the reality of Mia, he found himself wanting to know her. Wanting her to know him.

There was a kernel of something inside him that was already taking root, blossoming despite the strange situation he found himself in. There was a little girl alive right now because of him. Didn't that mean that they already had a connection, however slight?

His brothers each looked at him with understanding and he appreciated knowing that he wasn't alone in this. After all, they'd already proven they could survive fatherhood.

"Seems like the King brothers are going to produce all girls in this generation," Travis mused.

"Give me a houseful just like Emma and I'll be happy," Adam said, then frowned. "Until boys start coming around."

"We don't have to worry about that just yet," Travis said.

Jackson though, paled a little. He'd just discovered his daughter, now he had to worry about her growing up? Dating? Meeting guys like *him?*

Being a father just got a lot more complicated.

The following morning, Casey had Mia happily spending time in her walker, bumping around the floor, the plastic wheels making a whirring noise, alerting Casey to her daughter's whereabouts at all times. Mia's throaty laughter spilled into the sunshine-filled room and Casey was smiling as she bent over the graphics program on her computer.

Her home business, *Papyrus,* had really taken off lately. She designed and made exclusive brochures, gift cards, high-end stationery and invitations for every occasion from weddings to birthday parties. She had a small, but select clientele and that list was steadily growing, thanks to word of mouth.

She made her own hours, worked out of her home and had plenty of time to devote to her daughter. The best of all possible worlds. If there was a niggling seed of worry called Jackson King at the back of her mind on this beautiful morning, she made a concerted effort to ignore it.

Talking to Dani the night before had actually reinforced Casey's belief that she wouldn't have to be concerned about Jackson. Yes, Dani thought he'd be back, but Casey was sure her friend was wrong about this. Jackson was simply not the kind of man to be interested in a daughter he'd had no choice in creating. Mia did not fit into his lifestyle, for which Casey was grateful.

No doubt, Jackson was already in one of his luxury jets, flying off to Paris, or London….

"What would that be like?" she whispered, leaning back in her desk chair and staring across the room at Mia, busily chewing the ear of her beloved teddy bear. "Imagine that, sweetie, jumping into your own jet and taking off whenever you felt like it. Where would we go?"

Mia babbled, waved her arms and accidentally tossed Teddy to the ground. Before her little mouth had completely turned down to initiate crying, Casey was up and out of her chair. Picking up the lop-eared toy, she knelt down in front of Mia, handed Teddy back to her and leaned in to plant a kiss on her forehead.

"What do you think, sweetie? London? No," she said as Mia shook her head, laughing. "You're right. London in springtime, way too rainy. Okay, Paris then! We'll go to the Louvre and I'll show you all the beautiful paintings. Would you like that?"

Naturally, Mia didn't understand the question, but she loved having her mom's full attention, so she jumped up and down in her seat and babbled excitedly.

"Good! We'll go on one of those dinner cruises, too, what do you think? We'll see all the pretty lights of the city and get you some yummy French baby food?"

Mia giggled again and Casey paused just to listen. Was there any more wonderful sound than that deep-from-the-belly laugh her daughter had? Mia's big brown eyes sparkled, her wisps of dark brown hair flew about her head in a soft halo and her chubby cheeks were rosy.

"What did I ever do without you?" Casey asked, suddenly filled with so much love, she could hardly stand it. Scooping the baby out of her chair, she cuddled her close, burying her face in the curve of Mia's neck to inhale that soft scent that was so completely Mia.

Pulling back, Casey looked at her little girl and said wistfully, "I should have thanked your daddy. Whether or not he knows it, he gave me the most amazing gift ever."

The doorbell rang and Casey, carrying Mia, walked out of her cramped, makeshift office, down the short hall and through the small, cluttered living room. Evidence of Mia's presence in the house was everywhere. From the playpen tucked beneath the front window to the toys on the floor and the neatly folded clean clothes in the laundry basket perched on the love seat.

Casey shifted Mia higher on her hip and automatically leaned in to look through the peephole in the front door.

Jackson.

He looked different than he had the night before. He was wearing blue jeans today and a black T-shirt that molded itself to his broad chest. On the left breast pocket of the shirt, there was a stylized gold crown with the words

King Jets beneath it. He looked more approachable today and therefore…more dangerous.

Instantly, Casey's heartbeat raced and her mouth went dry. What was he doing here? How did he find her?

"How?" she whispered, answering her own foolish question. "You told him your name and where you lived. Of course he found you. Idiot."

The doorbell rang again and Mia squealed.

"Shh…" Casey winced, and jiggled her daughter, hoping to keep her quiet.

"I can hear the baby," Jackson called through the door.

The timbre of his voice resonated throughout Casey's body. She tried to tell herself that the shivers it created was nothing more than nerves. But even she wasn't buying it. Her body, despite what her mind would have preferred, was reacting to the man exactly as it had the first night they met.

Like a lit match set to dynamite.

"Open the door, Casey," he said, voice just loud enough to carry.

"Why?" she called back, when she knew it was useless to pretend she wasn't home. Her car was in the driveway and Mia was burbling loud enough to alert him.

"I want to talk to you."

"We said everything we had to say last night."

"You might have," he acknowledged, "but I haven't even started yet."

She chanced another look through the peephole and this time, met his stare directly. He'd bent down and was staring right back at her as if he could see her, as well.

Those dark brown eyes were filled with a quiet determination and Casey knew he wouldn't be leaving until she'd heard him out. Her shoulders slumped in defeat before straightening again with a touch of defiance. He wanted to talk? Fine. She'd let him say his piece, then they could go their separate ways.

"Your daddy's awful pushy," she whispered as she flipped the dead bolt lock and slowly opened the door.

"I heard that, too." One of Jackson's dark eyebrows arched as he gave her a cool look just before he stepped past her into the house.

Casey closed the door and locked it, then turned around to look at him. Jackson King standing in the middle of her living room somehow dwarfed her whole house.

True, the older bungalow was tiny anyway, but it had always seemed more than sufficient for her and Mia. Now though, with the strength of Jackson's presence, the house seemed to shrink substantially in size.

His gaze was on hers and she felt the heat of that stare burn right into her. His dark hair was windblown, his jaw was clenched tight and as he folded his arms across his chest and braced his feet wide apart in what looked like a battle stance, she felt a zip of something hot and undeniable.

How could she possibly keep reacting sexually to a man she should be avoiding? And how could she keep him from noticing?

"I didn't expect to see you again," she said, walking past him, and silently cursing the fact that since she had to move sideways to do it, her breasts brushed against his chest. Did he just move in even closer?

"Then that just proves you don't know me as well as you think." His voice was whiskey rough and pitched low enough to send ripples of awareness skittering along Casey's spine.

Darn it.

Determined to at least behave as if she wasn't thrown for a loop by his unannounced visit, Casey headed for an overstuffed chair near Mia's playpen. Once she was seated, she turned Mia around to sit on her lap and looked up at Jackson. He seemed to tower over her. She didn't really remember him being this tall. This intimidating.

Glancing around the room, he spotted a low hassock, gave it a shove with the toe of a scuffed-up cowboy boot and when it was positioned in front of her, he sat down on it. Elbows braced on his knees, he turned the full force of his dark gaze on her and Casey held her breath for a slow count of ten before asking, "Why are you here, Jackson?"

"To talk."

"About?"

"Mia."

She stiffened.

His gaze locked on hers, he said, "I know that neither one of us was expecting this."

She nodded, since her throat was suddenly so tight, she didn't think she'd be able to squeeze out a single word. Did he have to sit so closely? Did he have to smell so good? Did he have to have a voice that sounded like hot nights and silk sheets?

"So," he said, his tone pleasant, though his eyes were dark and unreadable. "Since we find ourselves in a unique position, I've got a unique solution to the situation."

She found her voice. It was scratchy and she was forced to clear her throat, but she managed. "I didn't realize we required a 'solution'."

"Then you were wrong again," he said and gave her a brief half smile.

"Jackson…"

"You've lived here three years, right?"

The statement was so far out of the blue, she only blinked at him for a second or two. "How do you know that?"

"You rent it."

She shifted, lifted her chin and said, "Did you investigate me or something?"

"Why wouldn't I? You show up claiming I'm the father of your child, it only makes sense to check you out."

"I can't believe this." Nerves jumped inside her and Casey suddenly felt as though she couldn't draw enough air into her lungs. She felt trapped in the little house she'd always loved so much.

"Since you rent, it'll make things easier all the way around." He nodded thoughtfully, glanced at the cramped quarters and she could guess exactly what he was thinking. He came from big, towering piles of money. He owned a mansion he rarely used and kept hotel suites ready "just in case." He had no idea what life for real people was like and she was sure he was mentally dismissing the home she'd made for Mia and herself.

But Casey had nothing to be ashamed of. The house was small, but it was clean and cute and just enough for her and her daughter. And if he had investigated her background, then he knew she was honest, paid her bills on time and that she was completely capable of caring for *her* child.

He could think whatever he liked. It really didn't matter to her one way or the other.

"That will make this easier," he said at last.

"Make *what* easier?"

"I want you and Mia to move in with me."

Five

"**Y**ou're crazy!"

"Possibly. You know, it's the oddest thing," Jackson mused as he watched her features register complete and total shock. "Your eyes change color according to your moods."

She shook her head as if she couldn't believe she'd heard him correctly. "What?"

He'd done that on purpose. Put her off guard. Off balance. Never sure what he'd do next. Besides, her eyes did intrigue him. But then, *she* intrigued him. More than he was comfortable admitting.

"Your eyes," he said. "They seem a very pale blue usually. But when you're mad—like now—or when I'm inside you…" he paused and watched his words hit home, "that soft blue becomes as dark and deep as the ocean."

She squirmed uneasily in her chair. Good. She should be uneasy. He was. Damn it, she'd thrown him for a hard loop since the moment he'd first spotted her at the hotel bar. Seemed only fair he return the favor.

Since meeting with his brothers the day before, Jackson had been in high gear. One thing you could say for the Kings, they knew how to get things done fast.

He'd placed a single phone call to the King family attorneys and within a few hours, he'd not only gained several new employees at his home and every stick of furniture an infant required, but he'd known everything about Casey Davis that there was to know. He wasn't sure how the law firm had managed it, but he assumed they had people on the payroll who could pull off minor miracles when necessary.

Even knowing that he'd come here to draw a line in the sand, all Jackson could think now was, he wanted to touch Casey again. Feel her eager response, the sigh of her breath on his neck. Drown in the heat of her body.

He shook his head, dislodging the erotic images that flooded his mind, so that he could concentrate on the problem at hand.

"You can't be serious about us moving in with you." Her arms tightened around Mia until the baby squirmed uncomfortably in her mother's grasp.

He'd expected just such a reaction. And if he were to be honest with himself, it was a crazy idea. He was supposed to be on the verge of getting engaged. Marrying a woman who was completely unaware of Mia and Casey's existence. And truth be told, he hadn't come here with the idea of moving the two of them into his house. He'd come to demand time with his daughter. But one look at the tiny rental on the ragged edge of town where his daughter lived had convinced him that she deserved better.

And she'd get it.

As for Marian, he'd talk to her. Explain that he needed more time. He couldn't go into a marriage—not even one that was a strictly business proposition—until he had the rest of his life straightened out.

And who would have thought it would need straightening? He'd always lived his life as he chose. Making his own decisions. Never factoring in anyone else's opinion.

Seemed those days were over.

"There's plenty of room. I've got a nursery completely outfitted already and plenty of help in the house for you if you need it."

"I don't."

"So you've said. Repeatedly." He shifted on the footstool and the old leather creaked with the movement. "But I've been doing a lot of thinking about this."

"And *this* is your plan?"

"That's right." He got up from the too-low footstool, not because his long legs were cramped but because he was too close to Casey. Her scent reached for him. The curve of her breasts tempted him and her mouth all but begged to be kissed.

And that wasn't why he was here. This wasn't about him and Casey. This was about his daughter.

He walked two short paces—all he could take without actually leaving the room—stopped beside the playpen and idly rested one hand on the rim. "Look, I might never have planned on being a father, but I am one now and that changes things."

Her chin lifted, her eyes narrowed and her grip on Mia tightened as if she were half afraid he was going to grab the baby and make a run for it. "I don't see how."

He laughed shortly. "Of course you don't."

She took a breath, blew it out and said, "I know what you're doing...."

"Is that right?" He let go of the playpen, folded his arms over his chest and looked down at her.

"Men like you—"

"Like me?"

"The take-charge type," she explained.

"Ah."

"Men like you see a situation and immediately jump in and start shifting things around. For some reason, you've decided that Mia and I are *your* business. We're not."

"We disagree," he said, his gaze slipping from her now dark blue eyes to the baby on her lap and back again.

She blew out a frustrated breath. "I don't know how to say this so you'll understand me. You don't owe us anything. I don't want your money and I don't need your help."

Well, that stung. True or not. And it was clearly, he thought with another rueful glance around her tiny, cluttered home, not true.

"Let's cut to the bottom line here, shall we?" he asked tightly.

Casey stood up and he silently admired the move. She wasn't content to sit there having to look up at him. Instead, she'd taken action to put them on more equal footing. Or so she thought. Her yellow T-shirt was hiked up beneath Mia's chubby leg, but her eyes were steady and her features were schooled into a carefully stoic mask. "Let's."

"I don't want my daughter living here."

She sucked in a breath as if he'd slapped her. "There's nothing wrong with our house."

"Not the best neighborhood," he said.

"We're perfectly safe."

"My daughter deserves better."

"*My* daughter is happy here."

Jackson knew this little verbal battle could go on for hours, so he decided to end it. Moving in close to her, he looked down into her eyes, inhaled the scent of lavender that clung to her and said, "We can do this one of two ways. A, you and Mia move in with me for say, six months. I get to know my daughter and at the end of that time, I'll buy you a house anywhere you want."

"I don't—"

"Or B," he said loudly, to drown out her voice and force her to listen to his counterproposal. "You insist on staying here and I make a phone call to the family lawyers. Within a couple of hours, you'll be notified that I'm suing for joint custody. And if you think I can't…remember, you contacted me. You broke the anonymity clause."

Her eyes went wild and wide. Like a trapped animal looking desperately for a way out of a dangerous situation. But there was no way out and Jackson knew it. He had her boxed in neatly.

"You…why would…"

"I'm not the bad guy here," he said.

"Could have fooled me," she muttered.

"Let's remember here that I only just found out about Mia's existence. I want to know my child. Is that really so unreasonable to you?"

"No, but expecting us to change everything about our lives, is."

"You have a choice."

"Some choice." Shaking her head, she stared up at him and the sheen of tears in her eyes threw him for a second. He hoped to hell she didn't cry. He hated it when women cried. He always felt helpless—not a feeling he was comfortable with.

"You're a bully," she whispered, willing the tears back.

"Excuse me?"

"You heard me. You're a bully. You're rich and powerful and think you can just sweep in and get anything you want."

He thought about that for a long minute, letting his gaze sweep up and down her curvy body. Finally, he said, "When I want something bad enough, yes."

She pulled in a deep breath and held the baby even closer than before. Then lifting her chin, Casey said, "Fine then. You win this one. We'll move into your house for six months. You'll get to know your daughter and then we'll leave."

"Wise choice."

"But just so you know," she said, "your tactics won't work on everything. You can't have *me*. What happened between us that first night? It's not going to be happening again. Do you understand?"

Jackson's body was hard and ready and he wanted her even more now than he had when he'd first walked through her front door. He shouldn't though and he'd do his damnedest to ignore the rush of desire that jumped through him whenever he laid eyes on her. Because he had plans for his life. And they didn't include Casey Davis, no matter how alluring she might be.

So he smiled and met her gaze as he said, "None of this is about you, Casey. This is about my daughter."

Movers arrived the following Saturday. Casey sat in a lawn chair on the front yard beside Dani, the two of them watching the kids roll around on a quilt spread beneath the jacaranda tree. A three-year-old boy and two baby girls were surprisingly loud.

"I know you don't want to hear this," Dani said as they watched two movers carry boxes out of the house, "but Mike's glad you're moving."

"What?" Casey looked at her, then reached down and pulled a stick from Mia's grip. "I thought your husband liked me."

"He does, you nut," Dani said. "But he's also a cop. And he says this neighborhood isn't a good one for a single woman and a baby."

Casey frowned. Okay, it wasn't a ritzy area, but the houses were mostly tidy and the teenagers weren't too annoying and she'd only had graffiti spray-painted on her garage the one time.

"He never said anything…."

"He didn't want you to be scared or anything," Dani

said, instantly defending the husband she was so crazy about. "But he always cruises your neighborhood at night, keeping an eye on things."

Casey sighed. That sounded like Mike. Such a nice man. Unlike some others she could name. Mike didn't push his views on her, try to run her life. He just quietly did what he could to keep her safe.

Why couldn't Jackson be more like that?

"So I'm not surprised your Jackson wanted you to move."

"He's not *my* Jackson, for heaven's sake," Casey said quickly and scowled as her insides did a quick ripple of expectation at the sound of his name. "And he's not interested in my safety, believe me. He just wants Mia."

"She is his daughter."

Casey shot her a dark look. "Traitor."

Dani laughed and scooped her baby girl up into her lap to pull a leaf out of her mouth. "I'm just saying there are worse things in life than to be scooped up by a gorgeous millionaire and whisked off to his hilltop mansion."

Sure, when you said it like that, Casey thought, it was like something out of a romantic movie. Almost Cinderella-like. Poor but honest girl meets rich handsome prince and finds love and happily ever after. But Casey knew the truth. The only thing between her and Jackson—except for some incredible heat—was Mia.

He wasn't a prince. At the moment, she thought of him more like a cartoon villain, evilly twirling his moustache.

"He threatened to take Mia."

Dani sighed. "If he'd actually meant to do that, he could have. He's probably got a fleet of lawyers on standby.

Instead, he just wants to get to know his kid. You really can't blame him for that."

"Why not?" When Dani only looked at her, Casey laughed. "Okay, I know. I'm overreacting."

"Just a bit," Dani agreed. "I mean, I get why, but you'd probably have been furious if Mia's father had turned out to be some miserable creep who wanted nothing to do with her, too."

"Maybe…" The truth was, she could understand Jackson's interest in his daughter. That didn't mean she had to like it, though.

"Casey, try not to treat this move as if it's a jail sentence. Look at it like a minivacation."

"A vacation?"

"Sure. He's got a huge place. Plenty of room for you to work and Mia to play. There'll be someone else for you to lean on once in awhile. You won't have to do it all yourself…."

She liked doing everything herself. She was used to it. She'd made her way, built a business, was raising a beautiful child. Why should she look for help she didn't need?

Besides, "Can you really see Jackson King changing diapers?"

Dani shrugged. "Guess you'll find out. But the point is, stop sabotaging this before it starts."

Was she? Or was Dani seeing only a silver lining and disregarding the huge, massive black cloud currently sitting over Casey's head? Case in point…the movers. They were carrying Mia's crib now and the rocking chair that Casey had painted herself.

"Um, didn't you say Jackson told you he outfitted a nursery?"

"Yes," Casey said tightly. Only the best for the daughter of a King. "He arranged to put my stuff in storage for six months." Without bothering to ask her. He'd just called her with the information and when she'd tried to argue that she wanted to take her stuff with her to his house, he'd simply steamrolled right over her.

"Ah…"

A cool wind kicked up, scattering twigs and lacy leaves across the lawn. Casey shivered a little. Was she making a huge mistake? Should she have stood up to Jackson? Gone to court rather than caving to his demands? She looked down at Mia and a small thread of fear wrapped itself around her heart.

"I can do this, right?"

"Of course you can."

"It'll be good for Mia."

"Positively."

Oh, God. "Is it too late to run away?" Casey wondered aloud.

"It is if that's Prince Charming in your carriage," Dani told her, pointing to a big black SUV pulling up in front of the house.

Casey didn't have to see the driver to know it was Jackson. She could tell because her body had started humming and her stomach was doing somersaults. Six months of living in his house? Being around him night and day? How was she going to manage this?

Before she could come up with an answer to that question,

Jackson opened the door and stepped out of the car. Beside her, Dani sighed heavily. Not hard to understand. Jackson was wearing black slacks, a long-sleeved white shirt with the sleeves rolled back on his tanned, muscled forearms and sunglasses that he slipped off as he walked toward them. Prince Charming? Maybe. Dangerous? Absolutely.

"Remember," her friend said, "you're going to make this work."

Casey's mouth was dry, just watching him walk across the lawn, so she nodded.

"Casey," he said, smiling. His gaze dropped briefly to Mia and even Casey saw his dark eyes warm.

"Hello, Jackson," she said when she found her voice again. "You didn't have to come by, I was going to drive to your place later."

"Not necessary," he said, turning a smile on Dani. Casey didn't even have to see her friend's face to know she was being sucked into Jackson's orbit. The man was definitely high on the charisma chart when he wanted to be.

"Jackson King," he said, holding out one hand.

"Dani Sullivan." She shook his hand, turned to Casey and lifted both eyebrows.

Casey ignored her and did her best to rise above the charm level Jackson was using. "I can't go with you and leave my car here."

"Don't worry about it. One of my guys will drive it over to the house later."

"Your guys?"

"Employees," Jackson corrected for her benefit.

"Besides, your little compact's not the safest car in the world to haul a baby around in."

Casey was stunned. "Of course it's safe. I take it in for checkups regularly."

"Not what I mean," he said, waving one hand at the pale-blue compact parked on one side of her driveway. "Look at it. In an accident, you might as well be riding a skateboard."

Dani winced and Casey stared at him. "I don't get in accidents."

"Not purposely," he conceded. "But then that's why they're called 'accidents'."

"He's got you there," Dani muttered.

Casey scowled at her friend, then shifted that same expression to Jackson. "My car is perfectly serviceable."

"Uh-huh, maybe it used to be." He turned, pointed to the black monster parked at the curb, then looked back at Casey. "*That's* your car, now."

"I—my—what?"

"I bought you a car," he said, in the same tone he might have used when saying, *I made you a sandwich.* "Had the dealer install a top-of-the-line car seat for Mia, so you're all set there, too. Much safer for you and the baby."

Casey wasn't an idiot. She could see that he was most likely right about that monstrous car/bus being safer to ride in. After all, it looked the size of a small tank. But she couldn't keep allowing him to ride roughshod on her life anymore. A line had to be drawn. Might as well be done now.

"Jackson, you can't go around doing things like that," she said, staring at the car now and trying to imagine herself behind the wheel. It was so huge it would be like driving an eighteen-wheeler. And the thought of how much it would cost simply to fill the gas tank gave her a sinking sensation in the pit of her stomach.

"Why not? You needed a safer car, I got it for you."

He really didn't get it. Didn't seem to understand that she wasn't the kind of woman to be taken over by some big strong male who thought he knew what was best for her. For heaven's sake, she was an adult. She'd been making her own way and her own decisions for most of her life.

Now, all because she'd felt it was his right to know about Mia's existence, her life was wildly spinning out of control. That old saying about *good deeds never going unpunished,* was certainly true enough.

But that ship had sailed and there was no going back. Dani was right, she'd have been furious if Mia's father hadn't wanted to know her, too. So there really had been no win to this situation and the fact that Jackson was clearly determined to be a part of his daughter's life said *something* about his character.

And even if she didn't like it, having a father would be good for Mia. That's what she had to keep in mind, here. What was best for Mia.

Still, she had to make him see that while he might be related to Mia, he had no control over Casey. So she tried again, speaking slowly and plainly. "I don't need a new—"

"It's in your name. Temporary registration and insurance information are in the glove compartment. Why don't you drive it on our trip back to my place, get used to the feel of it?" He smiled and started for the house. "I'll just check with the movers, make sure they know where to take your stuff."

"I already told them—" Her voice trailed off as Jackson walked away, clearly not trusting her to have been able to instruct movers. "Did you see that?"

"Deep breath," Dani said, putting one hand on Casey's forearm. "Okay, I see what you mean. He is a little—"

"Overbearing? Bossy?"

"Yeah." Dani gave her a pat of reassurance. "He is. But it seems like he means well."

"He's impossible."

"Honey, it's only six months."

"Six months," she repeated and thought that very shortly, she would be using those two words as a mantra.

Casey turned to look at the little house that had been hers. Where she and Mia had built so many memories. She knew she was looking at her past, because no matter what happened over the next six months, she and her daughter wouldn't return to this place. And nothing would be the same, ever again.

Jackson stepped out of the house, walked to the edge of the porch and looked at her. Across the yard, despite the presence of the movers, Dani, and the kids, Casey felt the power of his steady gaze reach out to her. Even from this distance, even surrounded by people, she felt heat building inside her. Just a look from him gave her shivers. Her body didn't seem to care that he was the human embodiment of a bulldozer. Didn't care that he was taking over her life.

All her body wanted, was *his* body.

Six

Through the baby monitor, Casey heard Mia whimpering in her sleep. Slipping out of her wide, sumptuous bed, Casey grabbed up her terry-cloth robe and headed for the door of her room.

It wasn't surprising that Mia was awake and fretful. Their day had been filled with strange people, strange places. Even Casey was finding it hard to sleep in a new place. No wonder then that the baby was feeling just as unsettled.

Skylights dotted the roof over the long hallway, letting in moonlight that guided her way along the corridor to the room beside hers. While she hurried to Mia, Casey's mind raced.

Jackson had naturally stepped in and taken over moving day. When they arrived at his sprawling hilltop home, Casey had been amazed to see just how much the man had accomplished in one week. Not only was her bedroom the

most elegant, luxurious room she'd ever set foot in, but
Mia's nursery was the sort she was used to seeing in celebrity magazine articles.

There was a mural of forest animals on the walls, a
closet stuffed with clothing, shelves filled with toys and a
crib fit for a princess. The lower half of the windows in the
second story nursery were barred for safety's sake and
looked out over the sweeping landscape that rushed
downhill toward the ocean.

Casey, on her own, never could have provided her
daughter with anything like the well-appointed room. And
though she appreciated all Jackson had done to make their
daughter a space in his life, she couldn't help feeling the
sharp sting of envy.

He was using his money to point out the differences in
their lives and he was doing a good job of it.

She reached Mia's room and the door was partially
open, as she'd insisted it remain earlier. The baby's cries
had stopped on Casey's short walk down the hall, but she
had kept going, wanting to reassure herself that Mia was
safely back to sleep. Now, Casey heard whispers just
carrying over the baby's sniffling breaths.

Curious, Casey pushed the door open silently, and
paused on the threshold. Moonlight flooded this room as
well, and the night-light that had been left burning was a
magical thing that threw patches of stars onto the ceiling.

But she hardly noticed any of it. Instead, her gaze
focused on the man standing beside the crib, holding Mia
against his chest.

"No more tears, Mia," he murmured and his already

deep voice was a rumble of hushed sound. "You're safe here. This is your new home…."

Casey's heart twisted as she watched him soothing their daughter. Clearly, he'd left his own bed to come to this room. He wore silk pajama bottoms that hung low on his narrow hips and the chest he held his daughter against was bare and gleamed like carved bronze in the moonlight. His dark head was bent toward Mia's and Casey heard his soft whispers as he soothed the tiny girl he held so carefully.

"Go back to sleep, baby girl," he said on a soft sigh. "Dream of rainbows and puppies and long summer days. Your daddy's here now and nothing will ever hurt you…."

She couldn't tear her gaze from them. There was something so sweet, so…right about the picture they made. Calling himself Mia's daddy, promising that sweet little girl that she'd never be hurt, all of it made Casey want to both smile and cry.

Jackson swayed gently, continuing the quiet rush of whispers and Mia's tiny sigh sounded gently in the room. And Casey's tears won the battle, stinging her eyes, blurring her vision until she had to fight to hold them back.

As if sensing her presence, he turned, still cradling Mia, and smiled at her. "I've got a monitor in my room, too."

Casey walked close to them and reached out one hand to smooth her sleeping baby's hair. "Of course you do."

His eyes narrowed a bit. "I am her father."

"You're right," she said, meeting his dark gaze. "I'm just used to being the only one getting up in the middle of the night."

The look in his eyes gentled some at that admission. His hand moved up and down Mia's back, soothing, stroking. "I can understand that," he whispered. "But you're not alone anymore, Casey. I'm here. And I'm going to be a part of Mia's life. I've already missed too much."

She took a deep breath and nodded. This was only their first night together. She was going to have to find a way to deal with Jackson's rights as a father.

Forcing a smile, she said, "You seem handier with babies than I expected."

Apparently realizing that she was willing to if not end their little war, then to at least declare a temporary cease-fire, Jackson smiled. "I've got two nieces, remember? Emma and Katie. Emma's a little more than a year old and Katie's about three months. I've put in my babysitting time."

Her surprise must have been stamped on her features because his smile widened into a grin that made her catch her breath.

"Didn't know that, did you?" he asked.

"No. I mean," she said, "I knew about your brothers' children, I just never thought you would—"

"What?" he challenged. "Love my family?"

Well, that made her feel small and petty. She should have known better. Should have guessed. In the research she'd done on Jackson before meeting him in person, she'd learned just how tight the King family really was. She just hadn't even thought that a man more interested in jetting off to exotic places would be so attentive to his infant nieces.

"Of course not," she said softly as Jackson turned and expertly laid a sleeping Mia back in her crib, "I just didn't think a man like you would want anything to do with babies."

"A man like me?"

She moved past him, bent over the top rail of the beautiful white crib and ran the flat of her hand down Mia's back. Listening to her child's quiet snuffles and sighs, she smiled. "You know," she said as she turned back to him. "The playboy type."

He laughed quietly. "You think I'm a playboy?"

She turned her head to look at him and almost wished she hadn't. While he'd been holding Mia, he was gorgeous, but somehow safe. Now that he wasn't…he looked much too tempting. All that bare, tanned, muscled flesh. The sleep-ruffled hair. The shadow of whiskers on his jaw. The heavy-lidded sexiness of his eyes.

Oh, God.

"I only know what I read about you," she said and moved for the door. Best to get back to her own room fast, before she did something really stupid like reaching out one hand to trace the planes of those muscles of his.

He was just a step behind her and when they moved into the hall, he caught her arm. Heat shot from his touch to rocket through her body like an explosion battering off a series of walls. She was forced to lock her knees to keep from swaying into him. His eyes were dark, fathomless and when he spoke, she had to fight for focus.

"And just what have you read?"

"I think you know the answer to that," she said, trying to tug her arm free of his grasp. "You're practically the poster boy for fast jets and faster women. So you can understand how seeing you, being so gentle, so tender, with Mia like that, could throw me a little."

He snorted. "You've got a narrow view on the world, don't you?"

"No, I don't." She tried again to get free, but Jackson wasn't ready to let her go just yet. He parted her robe and ran one hand up her arm. Even though the terry robe she wore wasn't exactly sexy, seeing the curve of her breasts beneath the soft fabric was enough to make him hard and ready and way too eager. Despite the fact that she had the ability to seriously annoy him.

"Sure you do," he said with a sneer. "You read some one-sided articles about me and decide that I'm what? Some rampaging guy, only interested in what he can take out of life?"

She stilled and chewed on her bottom lip. He'd like to help with that, but he resisted.

"Do you think the tabloids would be interested in doing a story on me babysitting my nieces? No," he answered for her. "They want sensationalism because that's what people like you want to read."

Her eyes, a dark, passion-filled blue, widened. "People like me?"

"Not fun being judged, is it?" he countered. "Yes, people like you. People who see a headline about me on a grocery store paper and assume you know me." He bent down, until their gazes were on the same level and his mouth was just a breath away from hers. "I'm not that guy, Casey. There's more to me than that, just as I assume there's more to you than the woman who seduced me just to get a DNA sample."

She tried to pull away again, but wasn't successful. Jackson stared down into her eyes and felt the tug of the attraction between them arc like a downed power line, sparks flying, hissing, through the air.

He'd leapt out of bed when he'd heard Mia crying. Hadn't stopped to consider that he'd no doubt run into Casey along the way.

It had been instinct drawing him to his crying child. Instinct to lift her from the crib and a revelation when those tiny arms had come around his neck. Love like he'd never known had dropped down on him like a thunderbolt from the sky.

Feeling the solid weight of his daughter in his arms, the slide of her tears over his skin and her tiny fingers pulling at his hair, Jackson had taken the fall. Her helplessness, her vulnerability had come together to catch him in a silken trap and hold him fast.

There was no escape for him, ever. Not even if he'd wanted one, which he didn't. He was his daughter's father and he would fight anyone who tried to keep them apart. Even if it meant going to war with her mother.

But looking down at Casey now, he knew damn well he didn't want to fight her. What he wanted was to pick her up, carry her into his room and bury himself inside her. He hungered for her touch. For the feel of her skin beneath his hands. He wanted her so badly, the need clawed at his throat, nearly choking him.

A small voice inside reminded him that he was soon

supposed to be an engaged man. But he wasn't there yet. No promises had been made, so none could be broken.

And that's when a new plan hit him. He'd told Casey that he wasn't interested in her. A lie, of course, but one that had suited him at the time. But she and Mia were here in his house, now. And that changed things. Rather than a war, Jackson decided he'd wage a different kind of battle. A battle of seduction.

The amazing chemistry between them was too hot for either of them to pretend it didn't exist. So maybe, if they surrendered to it, they could burn out the flame faster than they could by ignoring it.

He backed her against the wall and watched her eyes widen even further. The pulse point at the base of her throat pounded and her breath quickened until her breasts lifted and fell in rapid succession. She felt everything he did. He saw it in her eyes.

"Jackson, don't," she whispered, looking up into his eyes. "Like you said, we don't even know each other."

"That didn't stop us the night we met."

"That was different," she murmured even as he covered one of her breasts with his palm. His thumb slowly stroked across the tip of her hardened nipple.

She gasped and he knew it was from both desire and shock. She hadn't expected him to make a move on her and damned if he didn't like having the element of surprise on his side. And the feel of her. Even through the soft cloth of her robe, the heat of her swept into his palm, feeding the fires within until he felt as if he might spontaneously combust on the spot.

"Not really," he whispered, and kissed her briefly, gently, a featherlight touch of his lips to hers. "Besides, what better way to get to know each other?"

"It would be a mistake," she said, even as she arched into his hand.

"Are you so sure," he murmured, dropping his other hand to the hem of her robe, lifting it, sliding it up her thigh, letting his fingertips trail across her silky skin.

"Um…" She closed her eyes, moaned a little and then sighed as his fingers toyed with her nipple. "Yes?"

He smiled and shifted his hand higher on her leg, sliding inexorably toward the heart of her. The heated, silken core of her body. He needed to touch. To stroke. "You don't sound very sure to me, but then maybe I don't know you well enough to be certain."

"Exactly," she whispered, her eyes flying open again to meet his.

"Help me then," he said as he discovered she wasn't wearing panties. He stroked her heat and watched her eyes darken even further until that midnight blue looked nearly black. "What's your favorite color?"

"What?" Startled, she shook her head, whimpered and parted her legs a bit to give him easier access. "Color?"

"Your favorite," he prodded.

"Blue. Yours?"

"Black. Mountains or beach?"

"Beach. You?"

"Mountains," he whispered and slid one finger into her heat. She sighed and he asked, "Picnic or restaurant?"

"Picnic."

"Restaurant." Two fingers now, dipping in and out of her heat, sliding, pushing, stroking. Her eyes wheeled, and she bit down on her bottom lip to keep her moans of pleasure stifled. "Paris or Rome?"

She shook her head against the wall. "Never seen either." Her breath came in shattered gasps. "But Paris, I think."

"I'll take you to Rome," he promised, "you'll like it better, trust me." He watched as pleasure etched itself into her features. He felt the tension in her climb, sensed how near she was to climax and pushed her closer. His thumb stroked the most sensitive bud of flesh at the apex of her thighs as his fingers continued their ministrations.

She quivered, held onto his shoulders and dug her fingers into his bare skin. She rocked her hips into his hand, moving fretfully, anxiously, chasing the release she knew was just out of reach.

"Now we know each other," he whispered, his mouth aligned with hers. He looked into her eyes, willed her to give herself to him.

"And we have nothing in common," she told him.

"Do you care?" He touched her deeper, harder.

She groaned. "No."

"Me neither," he said. "No more excuses. So come for me. Let me watch you fall."

"I can't," she said between harsh breaths, her hips moving, her head moving from side to side. "It's too much. I can't just—"

"Let go," he demanded, his own hunger crashing through him. Gazes locked, Jackson felt her surrender and a moment later, watched as she splintered. He swallowed her moan with his mouth, taking her soft sighs and puffs of breath as his own. He felt her body contract around his fingers and continued to stroke her long after the last ripple had faded away.

Reluctant to release her, he finally picked her up, considered taking her back to her room and finally decided on his own. There at least, were condoms in the side table drawer. A few long steps and he was there. He carried her inside, kicking the door shut behind them. In his arms, her eyes were still glazed and her mouth was open, an invitation to a kiss.

He accepted and took her lips with his as he walked across his darkened room, following a swatch of moonlight that speared in through the wide bank of windows. Setting her down on the edge of the wide mattress, he wasted no time in grasping her robe and whipping it off of her, baring her body to his gaze. In the pale wash of light, her skin looked like the finest porcelain. Her nipples were hardened tips of pale pink and the thatch of dark blond curls at the apex of her thighs tempted him.

"Jackson—" Even as she sat there, naked, he could see her mind working, providing reason after reason as to why this was a bad idea. Giving her plenty of excuses to call this off. To stop him before it was too late.

"No thinking tonight," he said, shutting her down before she could get started. "Just feeling. We're in this together, Casey. Let's enjoy it."

She laughed shortly and shook her head. "This isn't why I came here. This isn't what was supposed to happen."

"This was *destined* to happen," he argued, loosening the

ties of his pajama bottoms and letting them fall to the floor.

She sucked in a breath.

"We both know it," he said. "We've known it all along."

Her gaze drifted over him and his already hard body tightened further. When she looked up, into his eyes, he reminded her, "From that first night, Casey, we were meant for this. Tell me you know it. You feel it."

"I don't know," she admitted, shaking her head, licking her lips. "I don't know what I feel anymore."

"Let me help." He set one knee on the mattress and pressed her back onto the bed. She stared up at him in the moonlight and Jackson felt a surging roar of need rise within. She touched something in him, made him crave like he'd never done before. She reached him in places no other woman had and though he didn't want to take the time to explore those feelings, he definitely wanted to enjoy them.

He wanted her over, under and around him. He wanted her legs locked over his hips. He wanted her on top, taking him inside her heat. He wanted to watch her eyes flash with climax. Wanted to hear her soft moans and desperate sighs. And he wasn't willing to wait another moment for any of it.

Reaching to one side, he yanked open the bedside table drawer, pulled out a condom and ripped the foil covering off. Then he sheathed himself, shifted until he was standing between her legs looking down at her and then he smiled.

"Jackson—"

"You want this as much as I do, I know it. And so do you."

She laughed, a tight groan of sound sliding from her

throat as he scooped his hands beneath her behind and lifted. "You're like a force of nature. You show up and take over. You're even convinced you know what I want sexually."

He quirked a brow at her. "You're saying I'm wrong?" He positioned her legs around his hips and held her there until she'd locked her ankles at the small of his back.

"Would it matter?"

"Yes," he said tightly, his fingers exploring her soft folds, caressing, dipping into her heat. "If you tell me to stop, I will."

She hissed in a breath and lifted her hips even higher into his touch. "Don't stop."

"I knew you'd say that."

"Have all the answers, do you?"

"Yeah." The tip of his penis rested at her entrance. Everything in him urged him to plunge. To take. To ravish. To pleasure. And yet he waited. "I told you before, when I know what I want, I find a way to get it."

She whimpered a little, scooted closer, claiming the very tip of him. "And when you're finished taking charge, will you tell me when I've climaxed?"

He laughed and pushed himself into her heat. "You'll know, Casey. Trust me, you'll know."

Her legs tightened around his hips and he rocked into her. Heat devoured him, sensation enveloped him. She fisted her hands in the black silk sheets and held on as he moved in her over and over again, driving them both to the edge of madness, keeping them both teetering on the very brink of release.

Each time he felt her orgasm near, he pulled her back,

deprived her of what she wanted, needed. He prolonged the pleasure for each of them, making each stroke a divine kind of torture.

He'd never known this all-encompassing wash of pleasure. He'd never felt so connected to a woman in his bed. He'd never watched her pleasure and felt it magnify his own. For a man who liked to be in charge of everything in his life, Jackson was suddenly sure that it was Casey driving this train.

Casey, whose soft groans and frantic whispers fed the fires inside him until they burned brighter than he would have thought possible. This was more than he'd found in that first night with her. This was deeper, bigger. This was *more.* Of everything. He felt her desire and stoked it. Felt her tension and created more. He wanted to be the one to take her higher and faster than any other man had before. He wanted to touch her as she had somehow touched him.

When finally, her body fisted around his, Jackson knew he couldn't delay his own release a moment longer. He surrendered to the inevitable. Gave himself up to the woman who had so completely splintered his defenses.

And when the storm passed, he stretched out on the bed beside her, gathered her close and listened to the furious beat of her heart.

Tomorrow would be time enough to figure out what the hell had just happened.

Seven

Over the next week, Jackson alternately buried himself in work and indulged himself at home. But for the first time in his life, he couldn't seem to keep his mind on business and that was a little disconcerting. It was taking all of his focus to maintain schedules, look at new routes and assign his pilots.

Before Casey, he'd spent nearly every waking moment at the airfield. Hanging with the other pilots, taking the jets up, plotting and planning the expansion of King Jets had been his be-all and end-all.

Now, everything had changed.

"I'll take the Vegas run today," Dan Stone said, leaning across Jackson's desk to point to one of the scheduled flights on their weekly roster. "And I can do Phoenix tomorrow," he added, then straightened up. "But you've got to put one of the other guys on the Maine flight Thursday."

"Why?" Jackson looked up at one of his best pilots. Most of King Jets clients were wealthy, pampered and knew what they wanted. They even had favorite pilots and Dan was one that was most often requested.

Jackson acknowledged that for some people, flying was a terrifying ordeal. He just found it hard to understand anyone who didn't love being up in the air, surrounded by clouds, with the ground no more than a smudge of green beneath you. For him, flying was about freedom. Always had been. Dan Stone was just like Jackson in that way, so the fact that the man was turning down a long flight in favor of a couple of short hops was curious.

"It's Patti," Dan said, tucking his hands into the pockets of his black slacks. "She's due any day now and she doesn't want me gone for long."

"Ah." That's right. Jackson had forgotten all about Dan's wife being pregnant with their first child. "Okay then, we'll hand off the Maine flight to Paul Hannah. He should be fine with it. Then once Patti's delivered, you can—"

"That's the thing, boss," Dan interrupted him with a wince. "Patti's a little crazed right now, talking about how she wants me to quit flying. Too dangerous."

"You're kidding." Jackson leaned back in his chair and stared up at the other man. Dan looked uncomfortable as hell.

"Wish I was," the man said with a shake of his head. He walked over to the bank of windows in Jackson's office and looked down at the airfield where blue King Jets were lined up like a military unit on parade. "She's never liked me flying. In fact, it's the one thing that almost kept her from marrying me. She's scared every time I go up. And now that we've got the baby coming…"

Jackson watched his friend. They'd been flying together for years. And he knew that Dan, more than anyone else, understood that soul-deep need Jackson had always had to be in the air. "Can you do it?" he asked. "Quit, I mean. Could you really walk away from flying?"

Dan turned his head and gave Jackson a rueful smile. "I don't know. Never considered such a thing before." He tipped his head so that he could stare up at the blue, cloud-studded sky and a sigh left him. "I do know that Patti and the baby mean more to me than anything—including flying."

Funny, but Jackson had never really thought about the inherent dangers in air travel. To him, being in a plane, behind the controls of a powerful jet, skimming through the sky—it was second nature. Something that was as much a part of him as his brown eyes. Sure, there was a risk whenever you took a plane up. But hell, he faced a higher chance of an accident just taking his car on the freeway.

And he wondered if he could walk away from something he loved so much for the sake of someone he loved more. The question had never come up for him before. Was it because the thought of crashing, dying had never bothered him much since he'd never had anything to lose? As that question resonated in his thoughts, his mind dredged up images of Mia. And Casey.

Casey?

Jackson shifted uneasily in his chair. Loving his daughter was one thing. It was to be expected. But feelings for her mother weren't a part of his game plan. Yes, he wanted her. More every damn day, despite how many times a night they came together. But anything more than lust was simply not allowed to happen. There were other considerations—*Marian.*

That name shot through his mind like a blazing comet, leaving behind a streak of fiery red sparks. Hell, he'd forgotten all about Marian over the last couple of weeks. He'd never called her back after walking out on their dinner together. He'd never bothered to check in to say he'd been busy and he *still* hadn't proposed.

"Everything okay?" Dan asked, frowning at him. "You suddenly look like you've got food poisoning or something."

Not surprising, given the thoughts rushing through his mind. But Jackson shook his head and said, "No, I'm…fine. Just have a lot on my mind."

"I know the feeling," Dan mused with a shrug. "Anyway, I've got some time still to think about this."

"Sure you do," Jackson said, preferring to think about Dan's problems than his own. "And, if you do decide to hang up your wings, I want you to know you've still got a job here." He stood up, held out his hand. "You can take charge of the ground crew, or you can move into design. You've always had a good eye and I can use a man who knows what passengers want in a plane and can look at the designs with a pilot's eye."

Dan nodded, shook Jackson's hand and said, "Thanks, boss. I appreciate it."

When the other man left, Jackson dropped back into his chair. He had to make a call. Had to go see Marian, explain about Mia and tell her they wouldn't be getting married anytime soon.

She wasn't going to be happy about it, but damned if he could bring himself to care. The truth was, it didn't really matter how Marian took the news. The very fact that he hadn't given her a single thought in two weeks told him all he needed to know. Whether the idea to marry into the Cornice family had started as a good one or not, it clearly was a bad idea at the moment.

"I've got news on your Cassiopeia."

"Huh? What?" He glanced up from his desk to find Anna standing in the open doorway of his office. Pushing thoughts of his soon to be ex-almost-fiancée out of his mind, he repeated, "What?"

"Casey? You remember. The girl with blue eyes? The woman you wanted me to locate for you? The one I've been trying to find for two weeks?" Anna lifted one eyebrow and planted a fist on her hip. "Well, I found her. She's been hiding at your house."

"Funny."

"I thought so."

Jackson leaned back in his desk chair. "Sorry. Never occurred to me that you'd still be looking for her."

"Your wish, my command," she said with a shrug. "That's how the employer/employee thing works."

"Not usually," he muttered.

"I heard that."

"Not surprising," he said with a grin.

She walked into the office, a woman completely sure of her position and not the least bit intimidated by the boss she sometimes treated like one of her own children. "So," she said, putting both hands on the edge of his desk and leaning in. "This nice woman calls, introduces herself as Casey Davis and asks me to let you know that she won't be home for dinner."

"Why not?" He straightened up, frowning.

"The funny thing is, I hear a baby crying in the background while Casey and I are chatting." Anna's eyes narrowed on him. "Care to elaborate?"

"Where's she going to be?" Jackson ignored her dig for information, as he was on a quest for his own.

Anna straightened up. "She said she had an appointment with a potential client."

"Client?" But she ran a silly little one-woman operation out of her house—his house. Why would she need to meet anyone about that? Couldn't she just do the meeting on the phone? And who was she meeting?

"That's what she said," Anna told him. "Then, she said that she would be dropping Mia off here with you about four."

He stood and immediately started looking around his office, trying to spot potential danger zones. His gaze went from uncovered electrical outlets, to long cords, to the trash can, to…impossible. This was not a baby-proofed place.

"Who's Mia?" Anna's voice broke into his thoughts.

"My daughter," he said and heard the awe in his voice as he said the words. He'd had that baby girl in his house for one week and already his priorities had shifted. Seeing

Mia's smile first thing in the morning was a bigger jolt to his system than his usual cup of coffee. Holding her before she fell asleep turned his heart into mush and seeing her tears was enough to bring him to his knees.

He was a man desperately in love with his child.

And completely at a loss over her mother.

"Your daughter?" Anna grinned hugely, sprang around the desk and wrapped Jackson up in a hard hug. "Why didn't you tell me? Why haven't I met her?"

"Yes, I just found out myself, and you will this afternoon at four," he said, answering all of her questions.

"This is great, Jackson," Anna said. Then her eyes clouded and her smile slowly faded. "Can't wait to meet the mysterious Cassiopeia and the no doubt beautiful Mia. But, what are you going to do about Marian?"

Scowling, he said, "Get her on the phone for me, will you? Guess it's time I made a date for Marian and I to have a chat."

As Casey steered the big black boat of an SUV down the road, headed for King Airfield, she had to admit it had been an amazing week.

She and Mia had, in a few short days, settled comfortably into Jackson's gorgeous mansion on the hill. It would have been difficult not to. Before she and Mia moved in, Jackson had hired a cook, a full-time housekeeper and then later offered to add a nanny to the staff. But Casey drew the line there. She didn't want strangers raising her child and Jackson had seemed pleased with her reaction.

The house itself was gigantic and though it took Casey

a couple of days to learn her way around, she had to admit that there was a warmth to the place she hadn't expected. The rooms were big, but decorated in a comfortable style. Overstuffed furniture begged to be curled up in. Window seats beckoned and shelves filled with books called to her.

And as far as her bedroom went, she'd never even dreamed of having such a lush, romantic room—not that she spent much time in it. Despite her better judgment, she hadn't been able to stay away from Jackson.

The man was completely her opposite in every way and yet, there was such a near-overwhelming magnetic attraction to him, she'd given up trying to fight it. Every night, after tucking Mia in, Casey and Jackson moved to his bedroom and there, they spent hours locked in each other's arms. In bed, their differences didn't seem to matter so much.

Which was just a little disturbing.

Casey felt herself falling for the man and even though she knew it was a gargantuan mistake, she couldn't seem to stop herself. Yes, he was bossy and arrogant. But he was also tender and sweet. He could make her insane by pushing all of her buttons and then at night, he pushed different buttons and made her crazy in a much nicer way.

But there was no future in this. She was clearly setting herself up for a huge fall come the end of six months. Jackson had no intention of falling for her and Casey knew it. Right now, she was convenient, that was all. "It's my own darn fault, too. I never should have let this start up. Idiot."

Her hands fisted on the steering wheel as she looked out over what seemed like a mile of gleaming black hood. Glancing in the rearview mirror at the mirror fastened in front of the baby seat, Casey could see her daughter's smiling face.

"You like your daddy, don't you?" she asked and Mia waved her bedraggled teddy bear in response.

Casey wasn't blind. She could see the rapport building between Jackson and his daughter. In fact, he was a much more involved father than she'd thought he would be. Which made her worry a little. The closer he got to Mia, the harder it would be for him to let her go at the end of six months. And what if he decided he didn't want to let Mia go? What then?

What if he fought for custody anyway?

"Oh, this is turning into such a big mess," Casey whispered and flipped her turn signal on at the entrance to the airfield.

The field was, as were all things King, *big*. She drove straight up to the tower where Jackson's office was located and parked. When she got out of the car, the first thing she noticed was the noise. Jet engines rumbling, men shouting, and a loudspeaker calling for maintenance.

Getting Mia up and out of her car seat, Casey walked quickly to the building and slipped inside. Worrying about tiny eardrums around so much noise put speed into her steps. The tower building itself was carpeted and sleek, with chrome-and-black furniture and an elevator tucked into the back wall. A security guard took her name, ushered her into the elevator car and just before the doors closed, gave Mia a wink.

When the doors swished open again, an older woman was standing there beaming at them. Her short brown hair was stylishly cut, her beige slacks and white shirt looked crisp and professional and her brown eyes veritably twinkled.

"You must be Cassiopeia," she said, already reaching for the baby. Mia leaned out happily, eager to explore a new face.

"Casey, please."

"Of course," the woman said. "I'm Anna. Jackson's assistant and you, you little beauty, must be Mia King."

"Mia Davis," Casey said quickly, just to keep things straight.

Anna shot her a look, then smiled. "My mistake. Well, the boss is right on through there," she waved a hand at a closed door. "Why don't you go on in and I'll take care of Mia."

Her daughter looked completely at home on Anna's hip and the older woman clearly was enjoying herself, but still, Casey hesitated. "Are you sure?"

"Oh, yes. Don't worry. I've had four of my own and I didn't break one of them." Anna paused thoughtfully. "I did consider breaking the youngest, but changed my mind at the last minute."

Casey smiled, mother to mother and felt better immediately. "Okay then, I'll just tell Jackson I'm leaving and—"

"Take your time…." Anna had already turned away and was busily pointing out all of the airplanes to a cooing Mia.

Casey knocked lightly, opened the office door and stepped inside. Jackson was on the phone and she almost backed out, but he held up a finger and motioned for her to come in.

"That's right. We'll need the fuel delivered by tomorrow morning at the latest. We've got several flights booked for the weekend. Right." He nodded, made a note on the ledger in front of him and nodded again. "Good. See you then."

He hung up, then stood up, coming around the edge of the desk toward her. Shooting a glance at the closed door, he asked, "Mia with Anna?"

"Yes. She swooped in and snatched the baby the moment we showed up."

"Well, don't worry. She's in good hands."

Casey nodded and walked around the office. She'd wondered what this place would look like. And now, she saw it suited Jackson completely. A bank of windows to open up the world for him, wide desk, comfortable furniture and on the walls, paintings of King Jets. She turned to look at him. "You don't mind watching Mia while I keep my appointment?"

"No, but who's the appointment with?"

She blinked at him. "I'm sure you don't know him."

"Him?"

Did his tone just change? She shook her head. "Yes, him. Mac Spencer. We're meeting at Drake's for coffee. He wants me to design a new brochure for his travel agency."

"I know him," Jackson said, folding his arms across his chest and leaning back to sit on the edge of his desk. "His agency's in Birkfield."

"That's right."

"So how'd he find out about you? You live in Darby."

"Not anymore," Casey reminded him, still strolling the room, inspecting the stack of flight magazines on the narrow coffee table. "Mia and I took a walk through Birkfield a couple of days ago. I passed out business cards to the shop owners. Seemed like a good idea," she said. "And clearly, it was. It's already paid off."

And it made her feel good. She might be living in Jackson's little palace, but she made her own way in the world. Always had. Once this time with him was over, she'd be back on her own, providing for Mia. The more clients she had, the better their lives would be.

"That explains it," Jackson muttered, springing up off the edge of his desk as if he had a fire under his behind.

"Explains what?"

"Mac Spencer probably took one look at you and decided to have you for dessert," Jackson said tightly.

"Excuse me?" She stared at him and was astonished to see that his jaw was clenched and his brows were drawn low over dark eyes that were flashing with heat.

"He's notorious in town." Jackson stalked across the room, took hold of her arm and Casey did her best to resist the pull of the heat she'd come to expect from his touch. "He's got so many notches on his bedpost it's a wonder it's still standing."

"Notches?"

"God, Casey," he muttered, looking down into her eyes. "You can't be seriously considering going to meet this guy one on one."

"Of course I am," she said, tugging her arm free of his tight grasp. "This is *business,* Jackson. *My* business. I was doing this before you came charging into my life and I'll be doing it long after you're gone. I'm the sole support of me and my daughter."

"Not anymore you're not."

"Do you seriously think I'm just going to stand back and do nothing for the six months Mia and I are with you?"

"Why not? Call it an extended vacation."

"If I did that," she explained patiently, "I'd lose my clients and I can't afford that. People depend on me to come through for them. I take my job every bit as seriously as you take yours."

He looked like he was chewing on that one for a second. "Fine. *I'll* hire you."

"To do what?"

"Brochures," he said. "Magazine ads. You say you're good, prove it. Work for me."

A little zip of excitement skittered through her, as she considered the possibilities of working on an account like King Jets. She'd be way out of her depth, she knew, but she was good at layout, design, color and flash. She could do a great job for him and—she looked up into his eyes, and read the victory shining in those dark depths. Instantly, Casey quashed her little vicarious thrills. He didn't mean this. Any of it. He didn't know anything about her talents or her work. He was simply doing his best to make decisions for her. Again.

"If you're serious," she said, sliding the strap of her purse up onto her shoulder, "then we can talk about it. *After* I meet with Mac Spencer."

"You're. Not. Going."

She laughed shortly. "Yes. I. Am. And you can't stop me. You don't have the right. So," she added as she marched quickly across his office to the closed door, "you and Mia have a good time and I'll see you back at the house later."

Fifteen minutes into her "meeting" and Casey knew Jackson had been right about Mac Spencer. The man was sleaze. Oh, he was good-looking enough in a sharp, on-edge kind of way. His hair was perfectly styled, swept back from a high forehead. His eyes were blue and his jaws carried just the right amount of stubble to make him look rugged.

But their coffee hadn't even been served before he'd reached across the table to take her hand in his. Casey had pulled away and opened her portfolio, determined to make the kind of business contacts she would need. If she could convince this man that she could do the job, then she was willing to put up with his not-so-subtle flirtations. After all, it wasn't the first time she'd had to peel an overeager would-be client off of her.

But he was getting irritated at the way she kept sloughing him off. He waved one manicured hand at her still open portfolio, dismissing it. "This is all fine, but I think you'd get a better idea of what I'm looking for if we went back to my office. I could show you last year's plan and you could convince me how to improve on it."

No way was Casey going to go to his office with him. She already knew it was a one-man operation, which meant that she would be alone with him. Not something she had any interest in. Much better to stay in the safety of Drake's diner.

"If you'll look at this brochure I did for the Rotary Club of Darby last year, you can see that through the judicious use of color…"

He plucked the brochure from her hand and tossed it aside. Leaning across the table, he ran the tips of his fingers down the back of her hand in a slow stroke no doubt meant to be incredibly sexy. What it was, was irritating.

"Why don't you let me buy you dinner then? Some

place nice. Some place quieter. Where we could get to know each other a little better?"

"I really don't—"

"Evening, Mac."

Jackson's deep voice thundered out around them and had Casey jolting in her seat. She lifted her head to see him standing beside their table, his black, furious gaze shifting from Mac's hand on hers to the man himself.

"King," Mac said, straightening up a little, giving Jackson an uneasy smile. "What're you doing here?"

"Came to pick up Casey," he said tightly, leaning on the table and pinning Mac with a black stare that had the man clearing his throat and looking for an escape route. "You about done?"

"Sure. Yes. I'm sure I've got all I need," Mac said, looking from Jackson to Casey and back again like a man looking for an escape and not finding one. Finally, he slid from the booth and quickly scuttled backward, out of Jackson's arm reach.

"You've got all you're going to get, that's for sure," Jackson told him.

Nodding, Mac stiffened his shoulders, lifted his chin and sent Casey one withering look. "Thanks for the information, Ms. Davis. I'll be in touch."

As Mac left, Casey heard Jackson mutter, "Like hell you will." Then he sat down in Mac's empty seat across from her and smiled thinly.

"What was that about?"

"I was saving your ass."

"Did it look like I needed saving?"

"Actually, yeah."

Maybe it had, she thought now, wondering if the distaste she'd been feeling for Mac Spencer had shown on her features. But whether or not that was the case, she could have handled the situation on her own. "Well, I didn't."

"You don't have to thank me, but you could at least admit you needed me."

"Thank you?" She shook her head as she gathered up her portfolio, shuffled all of her extra papers and designs inside and then snapped it shut. "You probably just cost me what could have been a great job. This is my work, Jackson. Do I come onto the airfield and tell you which plane to fly? Or which pilot to hire?"

"No, but that's hardly the same thing."

"Of course it is." She slid out of the booth, grabbed up her portfolio and purse and looked down at him through narrowed eyes. "I could have handled that guy, Jackson. Do you think he's the first one to think he could lay hands on me? Do you think that's the first time I've had to take care of myself in a dicey situation? Well, it's not. I've done pretty well for myself my whole life and I can continue to do it. Without your help."

The fact that she was right had little to do with anything. She had been on her own for most of her life. He'd learned that early on. She had no family. No close friends but Dani Sullivan.

But now she had him.

For however long this lasted, she damn well had *him*.

When she stalked down the crowded busy aisle, Jackson bolted from the booth to follow. He dodged around a waitress balancing a tray of soft drinks and kept his eye on Casey as he walked.

His gaze locked on the sway of her hips in that short yellow skirt and then followed the line of her trim, tanned legs down to the three-inch heels she wore to give her more height.

He'd been furious when he walked up to the table to see Mac touching her. There'd been nothing he wanted more than to plow his fist into the man's face. And damned if he'd apologize for it.

He was right behind her when she left Drake's. An ocean wind raced at him as if it was trying to push him back inside. He squinted into the wind and the dying sunlight, held the door open for an elderly woman, then trotted after Casey before she could get into the SUV and take off. "Where's Mia?" she demanded.

"With Anna," he snapped. "She's perfectly safe."

"You were supposed to be the one watching her."

"I was too busy watching *you*."

"Which isn't your job," she reminded him.

"Like hell it's not," he growled, low in his throat as he grabbed her upper arms and yanked her in close.

The sun was setting and the weird half-light made her eyes gleam and her blond hair shine like spun gold. Her breath was coming fast and furious and his own heart was pounding erratically in his chest. "You think I couldn't see what Mac was thinking, planning? You think I'm just going to stand by and watch as some guy puts his hands on you? Ain't gonna happen, Casey. *Nobody* touches you but me."

Eight

The kiss was sudden and nearly violent in the desperate passion spilling from him. Casey's brain short-circuited around a dozen dizzying thoughts. She should stop him. She should pull away and tell him he had no say in who touched her. That she didn't need him watching over her. She should remind him that their only connection was Mia. She should say that just because they slept together didn't mean he owned her.

She did none of that.

Instead, she wrapped her arms around his neck, groaned into his mouth and surrendered to the fire. His grip on her gentled but the need didn't.

The heat was all-encompassing, devouring her, body and soul. His touch as he closed his arms around her middle and held her pressed tightly to him sent waves of awakening desire pulsing through her system. It was this way every time he touched her now. Since that first night together in his house, since he'd somehow shaken her loose from the life she'd thought she knew so well. One touch and she was his. One kiss and she wanted more.

Even knowing that it would all end.

She couldn't stop the need for him. Didn't want to.

Finally, he pulled his head back and they both gasped for air. She looked up into his dark eyes and saw the same raw passion she felt reflecting back at her.

"He touched you," he said, lifting one hand to stroke her cheek. There was fire in his eyes, more than sexual heat, a kind of possessiveness that touched Casey on a deep primal level.

"He put his hand on you and in his mind, he was doing much more."

"You can't hang a man for his thoughts, Jackson," she teased, sensing rightly that the storm was passing.

"Doesn't mean I can't want to." He cupped her face between his palms and the heat of his touch sifted down into her bones. "You make me crazy, you know that, right?"

It staggered her to admit to herself just how much she'd wanted to hear him say he loved her. And that not hearing it was a kind of pain she'd never known before. Then the truth hit. How ridiculous to realize, while standing in a diner parking lot, that she was in love for the first time in her life. She loved alone, that she was sure of and the ache in her heart pulsated heavily.

Trying for reason, trying for balance, she whispered, "Jackson, what're we doing?"

"Damned if I know." Shaking his head, he looked into her eyes and she read confusion there. Well, that was something, wasn't it?

Then he took a step back, slapped one hand to the SUV and said, "I don't like the idea of you working."

"Yeah, I got that," she said, almost amused by the stubborn glint in his eye and the disgusted curve to his mouth. Maybe it was better that they don't talk about what lay unspoken between them. It was certainly safer for Casey. She couldn't tell him she loved him without risking seeing rejection in his eyes. Without the pain of watching him try to distance himself.

So in the interests of self-preservation, she kept it light. "But I do work. And I won't stop that just because I'm living in your house now."

"Right." He ground his teeth together, looked out into the distance for a long moment, then shifted his gaze back to hers. "But if you were busy enough with a big client, you wouldn't have to go out drumming up business, right?"

Wary now, she tipped her head to one side and studied him. "What are you getting at?"

"Just answer the question."

"Okay, sure." She nodded as she thought about it. "If I had a big client, of course I'd devote my time to him—or her. But the fact is I don't, so I have to spread myself around."

"Not anymore."

"Jackson…" She had a feeling she knew where this was going. And though a part of her was thinking *yippee,* another, more sensible part was warning her not to go down this route with him. If she got in any deeper with Jackson, then the eventual break would be just that much harder, wouldn't it? But even as she thought it, she knew that she couldn't get any deeper than love.

Then he started talking and Casey could feel herself getting caught up in his plans.

"I meant what I said earlier," he told her, words rushing from him as if he were half convinced if he took too long, she'd end the conversation. "I *do* need new brochures and business cards and maybe a Web site—can you do Web sites?"

"Yes, but—"

He stepped in close, ran his hands up and down her arms and gave her a half smile she was sure he meant to be charming. God help her, it was.

"Think about it, Casey. Work for King Jets and be able to cut back everywhere else. Spend more time with Mia…"

"That's cheating," she pointed out.

His grin widened. "And, I'd like to point out that King Vineyards also has a Web site that needs a redesign—trust me, Travis can't do it himself and Julie's too busy opening her bakery to worry about stuff like that. Then there's the vineyard brochures, tasting menus, event notices…" He stopped, then added, "Julie, too! The new bakery. She could probably use your help in getting notices out about the bakery."

Her brain started racing. She couldn't help herself. Being able to list working for the King family on her résumé meant she'd be able to grow her business substantially. And she'd make more money and wouldn't have to

take meetings with people like Mac Spencer anymore.
Jackson had been so right about that guy, not that she was
going to admit *that*.

Plus Jackson was right about something else. If she did
this, she would have more time for Mia. Not to mention the
fact that when their six months at his home were over, she'd
have a better chance at supporting herself and her daughter.

Because, like it or not, the truth was, whatever was
between her and Jackson wasn't forever. It didn't matter
that she was almost getting used to his dictatorial ways.
Didn't matter that the chemistry between them was off-the-
charts hot. Didn't even matter that she loved him.

The only thing that *did* matter was keeping in mind that
Jackson had arranged this as a temporary measure. To let
him get to know his daughter.

Jackson was still talking, warming to his theme. "And
then there's Gina and her Gypsy horses. She's got a Web
site too and is always complaining about how hard it is to
keep it updated when she's dealing with Adam and Emma
and the horses…."

It all sounded wonderful, Casey thought, but how much
harder would all of this make the eventual ending between
she and Jackson?

"I don't really like the look in your eyes right now," he
said softly, his thumbs tracing smooth lines over her cheek-
bones. "For a second or two, you looked excited at the idea,
then all of a sudden the light in your eyes went out."

She dredged up a smile, hoped it was plenty bright and
forced lightness into her tone. She wouldn't give him a
reason to regret their time together. She wouldn't give him

the opening to allow pity in his eyes because she'd tumbled into love where she shouldn't have.

"I'm fine, Jackson," she said, shaking her head at him. "And though I really hate to admit this to you because you're already pretty insufferable about being right all the time…"

"Yeah? Well, it's good to be right." That smile again. The one that sent shivers down her spine.

She blew out a breath. Really, how could she have helped falling in love with him? "You really are impossible, you know?"

"So they tell me."

Casey sighed and for her own sanity, stepped out of his touch and held out her hand formally.

"What's this?"

"A business deal," she said, smiling at his confusion. "You offered me a job, right?"

"Yeah, I did."

"Well then, I accept. I'll work for King Jets and for King Vineyards, and King Gypsies if Travis and Gina are interested—"

"They will be," Jackson promised as he took her hand in his and folded his long, warm fingers around hers. Then slowly, inexorably, he pulled her toward him. "But as far as sealing the deal goes," he murmured as he lowered his head to hers, "I prefer the term *sealed with a kiss*."

"Dani, when he kissed me, I swear my hair curled and you know it's too short to curl."

"Tell me," her friend demanded, her voice husky over the phone.

"We were standing there in the parking lot and he was all furious about that client making a move on me—"

"Sleaze bucket," Dani put in.

"Absolutely," Casey agreed. "Anyway, he—Jackson he, not the sleazeball he—grabbed me, pulled me up against him and kissed me so hard and so long and so deep, I'm pretty sure I felt his tongue on my tonsils."

"Wow, did it just get hot in here?"

"It's pretty damn hot here," Casey told her.

"Did he hold on really tight and just mush you in really close?" Dani asked on a sigh.

"Oh yeah."

"God, I love when Mike does that to me, but usually I have to get him really mad for that to happen."

"Jackson was mad all right."

"Worth it though, wasn't it?"

"Big time," Casey said and folded her legs up under her on the cushioned window seat in her bedroom. "But right about then is when I realized I'm in serious trouble."

"You did it, didn't you?" Dani sighed again. "You went and fell in love with him."

Casey turned her head to stare out at the spring storm. Lightning flashed behind black clouds and rain slashed at the window glass. The world outside was a blurred confusion of color that suited Casey's mood right down to the ground. And with Mia down for a nap and Jackson off at some meeting, she could indulge in the swamping emotions churning through her.

"Yeah," she said, grateful she had someone she could admit it to. "I so did. I love him."

"Oh, God." Dani's voice dropped in sympathy and Casey was reminded again of just how good it was to have a friend who understood *everything*. "Did you tell him?"

"What am I, crazy?"

A choked-off laugh shot from Dani's throat. "How does he feel?"

"I don't know." Casey sighed, watching the rain run in tiny rivers down the glass until it looked like the house was crying. "And I can't exactly ask, you know?"

"Absolutely not," Dani agreed, then half covered the receiver with her hand and ordered, "Mikey, I said we'd give the dog a bath later. Please stop squirting him with dishwashing soap."

Casey chuckled and it felt good. She'd needed this talk with Dani. In the time she'd been at Jackson's house, she'd been so caught up in him and Mia and finding time for her own work, that she hadn't called her friend as she should have. Dani might have kept her sane. Dani might have given her enough good advice to keep Casey from falling in love with the completely wrong man.

But even as she thought that, she knew that nothing could have changed the current situation. It was what it was. What had Jackson said when he first took her to bed? *From that first night, we were destined for this?* Well, maybe Casey had been destined to love him, too. That's how it felt. As if she'd finally found what she'd been searching for all her life.

For all the good it did her.

"What're you going to do?"

"What can I do?" she countered, smoothing one finger

down the windowpane, following the trail of a single raindrop. "I agreed to six months. If I tried to leave early, he'd try to take Mia."

Shock colored Dani's voice. "You think he'd still do that?"

Probably not, she mused. But how could she be sure? "I guess I'm not really sure about it, but can I afford to risk it?"

"So what's the plan then?"

"Good question. And there only seems to be one answer that I can come up with."

"Which is?"

"Enjoy what I have while I have it," she said firmly. "I may not have him forever, but I can relish this feeling, this time with him as long as I can, right?"

"Absolutely," Dani said, earning the title of Best Friend one more time. "So. Do I get any sordid details?"

Casey laughed and felt a little of the ache in her heart lift. "Sure, how many do you want?"

"How many do you have?"

"*Hundreds,*" Casey admitted, her skin heating up, just remembering all the times she and Jackson had come together.

"Oh, honey. *Spill.*"

"You have a *what?*"

"A daughter," Jackson said, watching Marian's brown eyes narrow. He'd known this wasn't going to be easy, but he'd had Anna set up this meeting with Marian because it had to be done. He'd already put off facing her with the truth for too long. "I have a *daughter.*"

As he explained what had recently happened in his life,

telling Marian about how Casey and Mia had come to be living with him, she stood there looking at him as shocked as if he'd ridden a camel into the family home. Her brown hair swept to her shoulders in a smooth, turned-under style, and when she shook her head in disbelief, he saw that hair swing out, then settle back perfectly into place again.

He blew out a breath and turning, walked a few steps to the window overlooking a formal garden. Lines of hedges neatly trimmed, trees twisted into caricatures of what they should be and flowers so rigid they marched in line like an army battalion. Hell, even the rain seemed to be falling more neatly here than anywhere else.

Nothing relaxed or easygoing about the Cornice household. The interior was just as rigid and unforgiving as the gardens. Here, stately antiques reigned. Uncomfortable chairs, spindly tables and glass knickknacks that looked so fragile, it made a man uneasy just being in the room.

Jackson turned his head to look back at the woman he was supposed to marry and tried to remember why it had seemed like such a good idea at the time. But he couldn't. Because looking at Marian with her designer clothes and her stick-figure body made him think about curvy, luscious Casey in her worn jeans and oversized T-shirts.

He must be losing his mind.

"Her name is Mia," he said. Marian hadn't been taking the news well, but then he hadn't really expected her to. Why should she? "She's ten months old, I have a picture if—"

Marian held up one perfectly manicured hand. "No. Thank you. I'm not interested in your illegitimate child."

He bristled, fought down his temper and told himself

she had every right to be pissed off. But if she took another dig at Mia, all bets were off.

He'd put off telling Marian about Mia for too long, he knew that. He should have been up front with her about the change in his life right from the beginning. But the truth was, he hadn't been looking forward to this conversation for a couple of reasons. One being that he'd known how Marian would react—not that he could blame her, and secondly, he hadn't wanted to admit even to himself that there was a part of his life that didn't include Mia and Casey.

That was a dangerous path for a man like him. He'd never thought to get tied up in knots over anyone or anything. But there was no going back now.

"And you say the child and its mother—"

"*Her* mother—" Damned if Mia would be dismissed as an "it."

"—are ensconced in your house?"

"They're living there with me, yes." He walked back to her and as he got closer, noticed the pinched tightness around her mouth. Was she just mad, or was she hurt? He'd rather not think about having hurt Marian. Hell, he'd never hurt any woman he'd been involved with. There was never a reason to go out of your way to bruise hearts. You went into a relationship, you had as much fun as you could together, then as two adults, you said goodbye. No hard feelings. No regrets.

Something slithered through his mind at that thought though and he wondered how parting from Casey was going to go. She was so deep into his blood, into his mind, she was the only woman he'd ever been with who refused to leave his thoughts. She haunted him day and night. At odd moments, her image would pop into his brain to tease him, taunt him, remind him just how badly he wanted her.

Like now, for instance.

He shut down that train of thought and told himself it wasn't wise to deal with one woman while thinking about another one.

"I need some time with Mia—my daughter," he said. "I've missed too much already and I don't want to miss any more. I have to have some time, to figure out how we fit into each other's lives."

"I see," Marian said and walked slowly toward a sideboard where she poured herself a splash of brandy and then tossed it down her throat like medicine. "And the mother?"

"Well of course she moved in too, I couldn't very well separate them, could I?" Frustrated now, because it seemed she was deliberately making this harder than it had to be, Jackson said, "It's only for six months."

"And you want us to wait to get married until they're gone."

Gone. Well, hell. He didn't really want to think about that yet. How the hell could he live in that house, walk past Mia's room and know she wasn't in there? How would he be able to walk down that hall and not see Casey pinned up against the wall whimpering in ecstasy?

Damn, this was a mess. But, one problem at a time.

"Marian, I know we had an agreement—"

"Yes, we do," she said, turning around to face him again, one long pale hand resting on the curved neck of the Baccarat crystal decanter. "One I have every intention of honoring. The question is, will you?"

That was the question, he supposed. He'd come here this afternoon fully intending to go through with the marriage merger—all he'd wanted to do was wait six months. Now, he wasn't so sure. In fact, the longer he thought about it, the less inclined he was to honor the deal they'd made what now seemed like another lifetime ago. But he'd already thrown Marian a hardball this morning. Wasn't one enough at the moment?

"We'll talk about it again in six months," he said smoothly, not exactly answering her.

She looked him dead in the eye and for a second there, Jackson was sure he was going to see her finally lose her temper. Finally see some real honest-to-God emotion coming from the woman. But true to form, she backed off, did a mental count to ten and smoothed herself out again.

"I'm not happy about this, Jackson."

He nodded. "I can understand that. But there's no way around the situation." He pushed both hands into his slacks pockets and offered, "In fact, I'll understand if you'd prefer to call the whole thing off."

Something sparked in her eyes, but it was gone before he could identify it. "Of course not," she said. "An agreement was reached and I'll certainly do my part to honor it. As you said, we'll discuss this again in six months."

It would have been so much easier all the way around if she had simply ended their arrangement then and there. But maybe she wanted a little space to do it in her own way. And if that's what she needed, Jackson would give it to her.

As for him, the relief that welled and rippled through his body at the thought of postponing a marriage to Marian

Cornice was enough to tell him that when they had their next discussion, if she hadn't ended their arrangement, he would.

Marriages of convenience didn't always work, he told himself, despite how well things had turned out for his brothers. And thanks to the appearance of Mia and Casey in his life, he'd just managed to escape a marriage that he could see now would have been a misery.

There would be no merger with Cornice airfields after all and he was suddenly okay with that. King Jets had been doing nicely up until now and would continue to do so.

"Fine then. Now, if you'll excuse me…" Jackson turned to leave. He'd only taken a few steps when Marian's voice stopped him.

"Are you sleeping with her?"

"Don't do this," he said, turning to look at her. "To either of us."

"It's just a question, Jackson."

"One I'm not going to answer." He wasn't going to discuss this with Marian. Frankly, since they weren't engaged, it was none of her business who was in his bed.

"You just did answer it," she pointed out.

"Marian," he said, thinking that maybe now was the time to end this after all. Why drag it on for another six months? Make it a clean break, he told himself. Walk away a free man.

But she cut him off before he could say anything more.

Her features went smooth as glass. "Never mind, Jackson. Forget I asked. Now, if you don't mind, I'd prefer to be alone."

He wanted to say something but what the hell was left?

Hadn't he done enough damage already? He let himself out the front door and quietly closed it behind him. Rain pelted him, but it felt damn good after being in that overheated and yet cold-as-hell house.

He paused on the front step, lifted his face to the sky to let the rain wash over his face and from inside the house, he could have sworn he heard the nearly musical tinkle of crystal shattering.

Nine

"She's got good ideas," Travis acknowledged a few days later, lifting a glass of King Vineyard Merlot. He sniffed the bouquet, smiled to himself and indulged in a sip.

Adam took a drink of his brandy and rolled his eyes at Travis's wine connoisseur behavior. "Gina's already cooing over the changes Casey suggested for her Gypsy Web site." He shook his head. "Been following me around the ranch for two days, talking my ears off about nothing else."

"That's good," Jackson said, pausing for a gulp of his favorite Irish whiskey. He felt a quick stab of pride in the fact that Casey had so easily come up with new, fresh ideas for the King family businesses. Plus, there was an extra added bonus to her working for the family. "It'll keep her busy."

"That all this is?" Adam asked from his seat on the leather couch in his study.

Jackson stood up, walked to the fireplace and stared down into the flames as they licked and curved over the dry logs stacked in the hearth. "What else could it be?" He turned his back to the flames then and looked from one brother to the other before saying, "She had a meeting with Mac Spencer a couple of days ago."

"Is that guy still trolling in Birkfield?" Travis demanded.

"Hell yes," Adam said. "I actually caught him looking at Gina when she leaned into the car to get Emma out of her car seat." The memory of it must have been enough to make him angry all over again, since Jackson saw his oldest brother's jaw clench. "Never wanted to hit a man so badly in my life."

"Did you?" Jackson asked, wondering if his brother had had the satisfaction denied him.

Adam sighed, disgusted, and took another drink. "Gina wouldn't let me. Said I'd get my hands dirty by slugging anybody that nasty."

"Would've been worth it," Travis mused. "A damn public service."

"That's what I said," Adam muttered, then shifted a look at Jackson. "Did *you* hit him?"

"Came close," Jackson admitted wistfully and silently added that he still wished he had. Just the idea of that bastard looking at Casey, touching her hand… "He ran so fast, I'd have had to chase him down though and I was too busy arguing with Casey."

"One day, some husband's going to get to lay that guy out on the sidewalk," Travis said and smiled dreamily, clearly hoping he would be the lucky winner.

Jackson looked at his brother and realized how much Travis had changed over the last year or so. Once, he'd been interested only in his wines and a string of uncomplicated beauties who sailed in and out of his life in a steady stream. Now, he was settled. With Gina and their daughter Katie.

"Hope I'm there to see it," Adam muttered.

"Me too," Jackson said, letting go of musings about his brother to savor the idea of smashing a fist into Mac Spencer's face.

"Did we care this much about that guy *before* we had women in our lives?" Travis asked no one in particular, then answered his own question. "Women sure liven things up, don't they?"

"That's one way of putting it," Jackson said, staring now into the amber liquid in his crystal tumbler.

"Not that talking about our women or dreaming about punching Mac out isn't a good time," Adam said into the silence, "but Jackson, was there a particular reason you wanted this meeting? Everything okay over at King Jets?"

"What? Oh, yeah. Fine." Jackson grimaced a little and said, "Well, I'll need to hire another pilot soon. Dan Stone is going to quit. His wife's scared and he won't let that go on much longer."

"Good man," Adam said, with a shake of his head. "I like Dan and I know he loves flying as much as you do, but it's right he put his family first."

Jackson lifted a brow. Wasn't that long ago that Adam had been devoted solely to the King ranch. But he guessed Gina had changed everything for Adam. Brought him back from the despair he'd hidden away in. His wife and daughter had given Adam exactly what he'd been lacking. Made him care about something more than the land and his brothers.

"But," Adam was saying, "I don't see how you needing to hire more flyboys has anything to do with us."

"It doesn't." Jackson stalked over to the closest chair, and dropped into it. Damn it, he didn't want to think about how much his brothers had changed. How everything seemed to be changing, including himself. For one damn minute he wanted the world to stand still so he could make sense of it again. But since that wasn't going to happen… "I came to tell you I went to see Marian this afternoon. Told her I wouldn't be marrying her anytime soon."

Both of Travis's eyebrows lifted. "You broke it off?"

"No," Jackson told him. "I didn't want to dump it all on her at once," he admitted. "I told her I needed six months. Told her about Mia and Casey and I figure I'll let Marian be the one to call it off. I owe her that much, anyway. But either way, the marriage isn't going to happen."

"Thank God," Travis said, a half smile on his face as he took another drink of wine.

"What's that supposed to mean?" Jackson looked at him and waited.

"Nothing. Just," Travis shot a glance at Adam as if for support, then looking back at Jackson, he grumbled a little and said, "But man, I never could see why you wanted to entangle yourself up with her."

Stunned, Jackson looked at both of his brothers in turn.

Adam shrugged as if to say he agreed with Travis. "That what you think, too?"

"Hell, yes," Adam said and got up to pour himself another splash of brandy. At the wet bar, he turned his head, looked at his youngest brother and said, "Jackson, the woman's about as warm and loving as a rabid polar bear."

Jackson hunched deeper into his chair, stretched out his legs and crossed one booted foot over the other. "Notice neither one of you said anything when I first suggested marrying her for the merger."

"You're a grown-up," Travis said, leaping out of his chair to join Adam at the bar. He poured more of the ruby-colored wine into his glass, chugged a healthy dollop of it then said, "If you want to make an ass of yourself, who're we to speak up and stop you?"

"My brothers?" Jackson stood up too and glared at both men. "Hell, you two had marriages of convenience and they worked out fine. You're happy aren't you?"

Both of them shrugged and nodded.

"So why shouldn't I figure the same thing would work for me?"

"Might have if you'd picked someone more…" Travis stopped short of a description of Marian.

"Or someone less…" Adam's voice trailed off and he shut up too.

Shaking his head, Jackson looked at the two men who had been the one constant in his life. His family. The Kings stood together, everybody knew that. They supported each other. Protected each other.

They always had, anyway. And now the two of them were standing there admitting that they'd been willing to let him walk into a marriage they both thought was wrong?

"This is great," Jackson said, crossing the room in a few long strides. He stepped around the bar and grabbed up the Irish whiskey. One more splash was all he could afford if he was going to drive home in an hour. "Thanks for nothing."

"You wouldn't have listened to us anyway," Travis said.

"Always did have a head like a rock," Adam added.

"My own family doesn't say anything when they think I'm making a mistake."

Adam looked at Travis. They both turned to Jackson, but Adam spoke first.

"You want an opinion?" he asked. "Fine. Here's one. If you're looking for a marriage of convenience that has a shot in hell of working out, why not marry Casey?"

"*Huh?*" Jackson set his untouched drink down on the bar and stared at the oldest King brother. "The last time I looked Casey doesn't own any airfields."

"You're either the most stubborn of us or the dumbest," Travis said with a pitiful look in his eyes. "No, she doesn't have airfields, you moron. But she *does* have your daughter."

Jackson took a breath and held it. He'd only just slipped out of a marriage that would have been, he could see now, a disaster. And his brothers wanted him to slip his head into another noose? What the hell kind of family support was this, anyway?

"You're crazy. Both of you," he said, with a look at each of them in turn.

"We're crazy?" Adam countered. "You're the one who seems willing to settle for six months with your kid. You're the one who's willing to let Mia and Casey stroll out of your life when there's something you could do to stop it."

Jackson's chest tightened. He wasn't sure why. He only knew that it was suddenly hard to breathe. Yes, he cared about Casey. And he loved Mia. But marrying the mother of his child just to get his child didn't sound like the right thing to do either.

"You know," he said, "you guys sound like you've got all the answers. You're standing there giving me advice like you're experts on this stuff."

"We *are* married," Travis pointed out. "To women we love."

"Uh-huh," Jackson countered, forgetting about the damned whiskey and shoving both hands into his jeans pockets. "And let's just think a minute about how smoothly you guys handled things with your women."

"Just a damn minute," Adam told him.

"No you wait," Jackson said, turning on his oldest brother. "Think back, huh? Didn't you make Gina so damn miserable she ran all the way to Colorado? Wasn't going to come back, was she? Not until you groveled and begged your way back into her heart."

"I didn't grovel," Adam muttered, a muscle in his jaw ticking.

"You sure as hell did," Travis said, laughing now and shaking his head.

"Just like you," Jackson told him, his gaze fixing on the middle King brother.

"Excuse me?" Travis's eyes narrowed and his laughter fell away.

"You heard me. You didn't have the guts to admit you wanted Julie until she damn near died when that elevator fell."

Travis shoved him. "You don't know a thing about what happened between me and Julie."

Jackson didn't budge. His temper jumped inside, boiling and frothing as he looked at his older brothers. Sure their lives were good now, but it hadn't always been so and damned if he'd let them forget it.

"Yeah I do. And you know what, neither one of you is qualified for the job of advice god. So back off."

In the thundering silence that followed his short speech, all three of them glared at each other. Finally though, Adam spoke up. "He's got a point."

"Don't tell him that," Travis muttered, taking another sip of wine.

Jackson laughed, temper gone as fast as it had come and reached for his glass of Irish. He took a swallow, letting the heat slide down his throat and spread through his system. Looking at his now just a bit sheepish brothers, he shrugged, point made and enjoyed the renewed sense of camaraderie. "Damn, when did life get so complicated?"

"You know exactly when," Adam said smiling, lifting his own glass. "To the women."

"The women," Travis said wryly, clinking his glass to theirs.

"The women," Jackson agreed and shared a toast with his brothers. His friends.

* * *

"This is amazing," Dani said the following Saturday. She was holding baby Lydia, jiggling her on her hip and watching as her son Mikey carefully held Emma King's tiny hand and helped her walk across the crowded lawn. "Would you look at my gorgeous son? Why isn't he that nice to his baby sister?"

Casey laughed and did a little jiggling of her own as Mia started to fret. "Because Emma's new to him, he's a sweetie like his daddy and he's nuts about his little sister and you know it."

Dani flashed her a smile. "Okay, yeah. He is. Just hope he likes the new one as much."

Casey shrieked and reached out to hug her best friend. "You're pregnant again? That's so great!" Eyes cautious suddenly, she said, "It *is* great, right?"

Dani laughed. "Yeah, it's great. Mike's excited about it. Just look at him."

Casey's gaze swung to where Mike Sullivan stood among the King brothers, laughing and talking as they drank beer and grilled steaks on Jackson's shiny new barbecue. Her friend's husband did look every inch the contented male and Casey was glad he'd been able to take the day off to join them all for the picnic Jackson had suddenly decided to throw.

Her gaze fixed on the man most in her mind and she felt her heart give a little ache. He'd come to mean so much to her in the last month or so. She hadn't expected it. Hadn't wanted it. But the unthinkable had happened anyway. She'd fallen in love with a man she knew wasn't interested in forever.

"Uh-oh," Dani said from beside her. "I see that look. And if you don't want Jackson to see it, you'd better go to your happy place."

Chuckling, Casey tore her gaze from Jackson to focus on her friend again. "The problem with that suggestion is that Jackson *is* my happy place."

"Oh, honey, that just sucks."

More laughter. "Very eloquent."

"You know, there may be more to this relationship than you think," Dani said, squatting now to sit Lydia on the quilt spread out at their feet.

"I don't think so." Casey kneeled down, set Mia on the quilt beside Lydia and smiled at her daughter before saying, "Jackson was really clear right up front. He wanted six months. Well, one of those months is gone now. And he hasn't said anything about wanting to renegotiate. Hasn't mentioned that his feelings have changed…" Her gaze drifted, as it always did whether she wanted it to or not, to Jackson.

In the bright spring sunlight, his dark hair shone and his eyes glittered. Standing with his brothers and Mike, with smoke from the barbecue twisting and swirling about him in the wind, he almost looked as if he'd stepped out of a dream. He laughed and something inside her fisted. His gaze slipped to hers and she felt the immediate swell of response in her body.

She sighed and deliberately looked at Dani, watching her. "Oh," her friend said on a sigh, "you've got it really bad, don't you?"

"Afraid so," she said.

"Not hard to understand," Dani told her, waving one hand to indicate their surroundings. "This place is awesome. Jackson's gorgeous and he's crazy about your kid. You'd have to be made of stone to not be affected by it all."

Casey nodded and turned to smile up at the two women approaching them. "You're absolutely right about all of it, but let's change the subject, okay?"

"Oh. Right."

"Hi," Gina King said as she plopped down onto the quilt beneath the shade of an ancient elm tree. "Julie and I thought we'd join you two here, if that's okay."

"Of course it's okay," Casey said and smiled as Julie, nestling her infant daughter to her chest, sat down beside her.

"Your son is just the cutest thing," Gina said, grinning at Dani. "The way he acts with Emma just touches my heart."

Naturally, the surest way to win Dani's friendship forever was to praise one of her children. And as she settled in to talk babies with Gina, Casey watched as Julie opened her shirt to feed baby Katie.

"She's beautiful," Casey said softly, reaching out with one hand to trace a fingertip across the tiny girl's forehead. Already, Mia was growing up and Casey could see the day ahead when her little girl would no longer be her baby, needing only her. She would have liked to have more children, she thought longingly. But having Mia had been so expensive, the chance of repeating the experience was slim and she already knew that conceiving any other way was nearly impossible. But as she considered that, a new thought whispered through her mind and disappeared again when Julie started talking.

"Thanks, Travis and I think she's gorgeous, of course." Julie hissed in a breath when Katie latched onto her breast, then grinned and said, "I wanted to tell you again, how much I *love* your ideas for the bakery Web site."

Pleased, Casey smiled back, pushing regrets and worries out of her mind for another day. "I'm so glad. I think it's going to be fun getting the King family sites up and running."

"A woman after my own heart," Gina crowed. "Someone else who thinks work is fun! I swear, to hear Adam grumble you'd think I'm the only wife in the world who has a job. And I work right there on the ranch! He sees me every day."

"Mike does the same thing," Dani put in, "but some of that might be because we've become ships that only occasionally bump in the night!"

"Travis hates it too," Julie agreed with a small laugh. "He used that bakery of mine as a tempting offer to get me to marry him in the first place and now he grumbles because I want to spend so much time there." She laughed delightedly. "But then I remind him how hard it is to pry him out of the tasting room at the winery."

It felt good to be with these women, listen to them all complain lovingly about their husbands. But it also brought home a simple truth to Casey. She could complain all she wanted about Jackson, but she didn't really have the right, did she? He wasn't her husband. He was her lover.

Her *temporary* lover.

No matter how much she felt at home here, with these women, with the King family, at this amazing hilltop mansion, none of it really belonged to her.

"I'm thinking when this one's born," Dani was saying slyly, "that I just might come to Casey for a job." She slid a hopeful glance at her friend. "That way I can stay home with the kids and maybe Mike and I can see each other for more than a mumbled greeting in the hallway as we change shifts!"

"What a great idea," Gina put in. "I've got lots of plans for Casey's time, so I think she'll be needing the help."

"You've got plans?" Julie said with a laugh, shifting baby Katie from one breast to the other. "Back off, sister-in-law of mine, I've got the bakery getting ready to open and I want those menus done before the next tasting at the winery—"

Enjoying herself immensely, Casey gave them all a broad smile and clapped her hands. "As much as I love being the center of attention," she said, "there's plenty of me to go around." Then she shot a look at Dani. "As for you…we're going to have to talk, because if you're serious, I could use you *sooner* rather than later."

"Seriously?" Dani's eyes sparkled at the thought of being able to stay home with her kids.

"Definitely," Casey told her. With all the new work she had lined up, she was going to need the help. Who better than her best friend? "And as for the menus for the winery," she said, looking at Julie again, "I came up with an idea yesterday that I think you're going to love."

"Excellent!" Julie whooped with excitement and just for good measure stuck her tongue out at Gina. "I win. Can I see them now?"

"Sure." Casey stood. "Keep an eye on Mia and I'll run upstairs to get them."

With the women in charge, Casey sprinted across the

lawn toward the back door of the big house. She ran over the flagstone patio, pausing only long enough to wave at Jackson, then she slipped through the open French doors and into the shadowy coolness of the state-of-the-art kitchen.

The cook had the day off since Jackson was busily burning dinner on his own and so the house felt empty and quiet as Casey ran down the hall and up the stairs. From outside, the wash of voices and laughter floated to her on a soft wind and she smiled to herself as she ran down the hall to Jackson's bedroom. Temporary or not, she liked being a part of a big family. Since she'd been on her own for so many years, the idea of being surrounded by those you cared about was a delicious one.

She'd been showing Jackson the new design for the King Vineyard menus earlier that morning and she was sure she'd left the papers on Jackson's dresser. She entered the big room that smelled of him and saw what she was looking for right away. But out of the corner of her eye, Casey also noticed a new, economy-sized box of condoms lying in the middle of his neatly made bed.

"Oh, perfect," she muttered, shaking her head. If anyone in his family came upstairs for any reason, that would be the first thing they spotted. Just what she needed. Sure, they all had to know she and Jackson were lovers. That didn't mean she needed to draw them a picture, though.

Picking up the box, she opened his bedside table drawer to put them away. But the world stopped and the condoms fell from suddenly nerveless fingers when she found a small, dark-blue velvet jeweler's box tucked inside the drawer.

Mind racing, heart pounding, she held her breath, picked it up, opened the lid and stared down at a diamond that was so big it deserved its own zip code. It flashed in the light as if it had been waiting for someone to give it the opportunity to shine and Casey's mouth went dry at the implications.

Was Jackson going to propose?

Her heart leaped in her chest and an unexpected joy sent so many sharp, jagged shards of happiness through her it was nearly painful.

"Hey," Jackson said from the doorway, "what's going on? I saw you running and—"

She turned around, heart in her eyes and held up the box she'd found. And joy died as his smile faded.

"Oh, God," he whispered. "That's Marian's."

Ten

"Marian?" Casey's voice sounded so small, so hurt, Jackson felt her pain like his own.

He hadn't thought about that damned ring in weeks. If he had, he would have taken it to the bank, put it in the safety deposit box. But no, he'd been so wrapped up in Casey and Mia that he'd tossed the three-carat diamond into a drawer and forgotten all about it.

Until it had shown up to bite him in the ass.

"Damn it," he muttered, walking toward her. He took the velvet box from her hand, snapped it shut and dropped it back into the drawer. Then he slammed that drawer closed and looked into blue eyes that were so pale, so *wounded,* he felt like a first-class bastard.

"Um," she said, taking a sidestep away from him and looking everywhere but directly into his eyes, "I'm sorry. I didn't mean to pry. I was only putting the condoms away and—"

"Casey, let me explain." He reached for her, but she slipped away like mist before he could actually touch her. And just for a second, he wondered if it was a sign of things to come.

"Explain?" She choked out a laugh and backed up even further. Shaking her head, she walked quickly to his dresser and snatched up the pages she'd left there earlier. The designs she had for the King Vineyard menu. The ones she'd been so excited about that morning.

He remembered her showing them to him, with her eyes alight and her imagination on high gear. And even then, he'd felt a small twinge. He'd set her up with his brothers and their wives more for his convenience than for her sake. He'd wanted her safe. There. In the house.

Now, even her joy in the direction her business was taking had dimmed. Because of him.

"There's nothing to explain," she said and as she talked her voice got firmer, stronger. "You've got an engagement ring for another woman in the same drawer where you keep the condoms you use with me. What could be clearer? I'm the bedmate, she's the wife material." She headed for the door. "Trust me, I get the picture."

"No you don't," he snapped and cut her off before she could get out of the room, away from him.

From outside, he heard the rumble of his brother's voices, the laughter of the women clustered together beneath the tree and even the call of seabirds swooping low, looking for a handout.

But inside, all was cold and quiet. Looking into her eyes, Jackson felt the distance between them and damned if he could find a way to close it. He hadn't meant for her to find out about Marian. If everything had gone according to his plan, she and Mia would have stayed here for six months and then they all would have gone on with their lives.

But somewhere along the line, things had changed. He wasn't sure how, wasn't sure when and he for damn sure didn't know what to do about it. But Casey was staring at him and he had to say something.

"Yes, I had planned to marry Marian," he blurted when nothing better came to mind.

He saw her wince and if it had been possible, he'd have kicked himself. He'd never planned to hurt her. Yet it seemed he couldn't now avoid it.

"It was a business decision," he told her, trying somehow to lessen the sting of the surprise she'd just had.

She closed her eyes briefly, shook her head as if she were tired and said, "Business."

"Yes. A marriage of convenience. A merger really, more than a marriage," he added. Then he took a deep breath and kept talking because he sensed she was shutting down. Shutting him *out*. And suddenly, he very much wanted to be *in*. "Look, both of my brothers married women for the wrong reasons and wound up so damned happy they're annoying with it. I figured I stood at least the same chance they'd had and it was a good call for King Jets. Marian's father owns several well-placed airfields around the country. By marrying her, I guaranteed King Jets landing space and new routes."

"Good for you," she said, folding her arms over her

chest. "Congratulations. I'll be sure to get all the new routes correctly when I redesign your Web site."

He groaned with frustration himself. "The damn ring's here, remember? It's not on her finger because I'm not marrying her."

"Really. Why not?"

Why not. A loaded question if he'd ever heard one. And hell, he wasn't completely sure of the answer himself beyond the fact that he couldn't face the thought of a lifetime with a woman who wasn't Casey.

Damn.

When he didn't answer, Casey looked up at him, waiting. "It's a simple question, Jackson. Why are you not marrying the fabulous Cornice airfields?"

"Because of you and Mia," he said, tightening up in self-defense. The woman was glaring at him like he'd just told her he was personally responsible for the new sport of puppy kicking. "I told her I needed time. Time with Mia. Time to get my life together."

"So you're not marrying her *now*."

"Ever," he corrected, more certain of that fact now than he had been before.

"That's not what you told her though, is it?"

"No," he admitted, shoving one hand through his hair and wondering how the hell to get out of this mess he was slogging through. "I told her we'd talk in six months," he admitted. "I wanted to give her the chance to call it off herself."

"How very noble of you," she said and tried to step past him.

He cut her off again and she blew out a frustrated breath.

"It's not noble," he argued, trying to figure out how to explain to her what he didn't completely understand himself. "It's—"

"It's what, Jackson?" she asked and he actually *saw* her eyes go from pale to dark blue and he felt a wary twinge echo inside him. "Expedient? You don't want to be engaged to one woman while sleeping with another? Well, that just makes you a candidate for Man of the Year, doesn't it?"

Her hurt was quickly swallowed by fury and Jackson, being a wise man, took a step back.

"You used me," she said tightly, raking him up and down with a gaze that should have turned him to ice on the spot. "You used me for sex while keeping the no doubt eminently suitable *Marian* in the wings."

He was willing to let her blow off some steam, but damned if he'd stand there and let her insult both of them. "We used each other for sex, babe," he said and saw his verbal dart hit home. Quickly, instinctively, he followed it with another. "I never promised you anything."

"So that makes it okay, hmm?" Her whisper was nothing more than a hiss of sound. "Don't make promises and then it doesn't matter what you do? Who you hurt?" She walked in close, jabbed her index finger at his chest and said, "What about Mia? Were you going to push her aside once you married *Marian?*"

"Of course not! Mia's my daughter. She's always going to be my daughter."

"That's something, I suppose," she said under her breath.

"Casey…" He reached out and grabbed her shoulders,

holding onto her tightly when she tried to slip out of his grasp. He didn't know how to put things back together and it irritated hell out of him to have to admit that to himself. Always before, he'd known what to say. What to do. Now, when he needed that ability the most though, it had deserted him. "Don't do this. Don't do this to us. Don't ruin what we have."

"What we have?" she repeated softly. "You can't ruin what you don't have." When she lifted her gaze to his, he saw the furious dark blue of her eyes had faded to a nearly impersonal pale blue stare. "Besides, I didn't do any of this, Jackson. You did." She pulled away from him, tightened her grip on the papers she held in one fist and said, "Now. Julie's waiting to see these menus."

"She can wait a few more minutes," he said, not willing to let her go. Not when there was so much left unsaid between them. Not when he could still see pain he'd caused shining in her eyes.

"No, she really can't." Casey ran one hand over her short, shaggy hair, and said, "I'd rather your entire family and my friends didn't know anything was wrong, so if you don't mind, I'd like to see some of your fabulous acting skills when you go back downstairs."

"Casey—"

"No reason the day has to be spoiled for anyone else," she said and walked out of the room without a backward glance.

When everyone had left, Casey still was in no mood to talk to Jackson and since she needed to make a trip into town, she left him with Mia and took off. The drive in the big black bus he'd purchased for her at least shifted her concentration away from the fool she'd made of herself. She had to focus on the road, on other drivers, rather than on the lancing pain stabbing at her heart.

"It's your own fault," she murmured, steering the lumbering SUV into a diagonal parking slot in front of the drugstore. She slipped the gearshift into park, set the brake and turned off the key. Then she leaned her forehead on the steering wheel and closed her eyes. "You knew going in that this was temporary. That all it was for Jackson was a chance to know his daughter. You're the one who let sex become more. You're the one who started daydreaming…."

She blew out a breath, lifted her head and stared through the windshield at the store in front of her. A sinking sensation opened up in the pit of her stomach as she thought about why she was there. What she'd come to buy. And the fact that if she was right, everything was about to get much more complicated.

Jackson tried to talk to her when she got home, but she breezed right past him as if he weren't there. So he decided he'd give her a little space. A little time. Work things through in her head, then he'd talk to her again and she'd damn well listen.

He'd just spent the longest damned afternoon of his life, talking to his brothers and Mike Sullivan, pretending nothing was wrong, when he could *feel* Casey's misery hanging over him like a black cloud dripping rain. No one else had noticed, of course, because she'd plastered a smile on her face and had done just what she'd set out to do. Kept everyone else in the dark about what had happened between them.

"But what exactly did happen?" he muttered as he stared through the living room windows at the night beyond. "She found a ring I didn't use. Big deal. It didn't *mean* anything," he argued with himself, his voice a low mutter of disgust. "I told her I broke it off with Marian, why can't she understand that?"

Logic was lost on women, he thought. They were too busy being hurt or wounded or angry to listen to reason. Well, he told himself, she'd listen tonight, whether she wanted to or not.

He listened hard and heard Casey singing to Mia as she bathed the baby then put her to bed. Then he listened to the sounds of Casey moving around and realized for the first time that the reason he'd never spent much time in this house before now was that it had been too quiet. Too big for one man. Too filled with a silence that only seemed to get bigger when a man had time to think about it.

But with Mia and Casey here, the house seemed alive, somehow. And so, damn it, did *he*.

He finally gave up on trying to work out a new flight schedule, assigning pilots to fill in the gaps left by Dan, who had indeed quit right after the birth of his son. He'd worry about the logistics of flight time tomorrow. Jackson was definitely going to need to hire someone else, but until he did, he himself would have to pick up some of the slack.

Since Mia and Casey had come into his life, flying had taken a back seat. He hadn't been on a run himself in weeks and up until that very minute, he hadn't even realized it. Hadn't missed it.

Maybe his brothers were right, he thought suddenly. Maybe he should ask Casey to marry him. It would sure as hell solve a lot of problems. They shared Mia. And they shared an incredible chemistry that would make living together no hardship at all.

He smiled to himself as he warmed to the idea. Hell, Adam and Travis might have hit on the solution he needed. A marriage of convenience. But with the *right* woman.

"Jackson?"

His head whipped around and he jumped to his feet. As if his thoughts had conjured her, Casey stood in the open doorway of the living room. He hadn't heard her come downstairs because he'd been lost in his own thoughts. But now that he saw her, standing there in the wash of golden lamplight, she looked pale and her eyes seemed huge. Wide and shocked.

"What's wrong?" Before he even realized he'd taken a step, he was moving toward her.

"Nothing—" she waved him away, but he wouldn't be put off.

Dropping one arm around her shoulders, he steered her to a chair, pushed her down into it and tried to ignore the fact that she'd been so stiff and unyielding beneath his touch. Still mad, then. Well, fine. He could bring her around. In fact, as soon as he told her his idea, he had the feeling that she'd be so damn happy, all thoughts of this afternoon's confrontation would fall away.

He fell to a crouch in front of her and looked up into

her eyes. Eyes that were swimming in a sheen of tears she was fighting desperately to keep at bay. Worry rose up in him, nearly choking him and Jackson pushed his own plans to one side for the moment.

"Damn it, Casey, something's wrong," he said. "I can see it on your face. If this is still about what happened earlier, I want to talk to you about it. I've been doing some thinking and if you'll just hear me out—"

"Stop." Casey shook her head, scrubbed both hands over her face and then met his gaze with a grim determination that filled Jackson with a kind of dread he'd never known before.

"What is it?" he asked, reaching out and taking one of her hands in his. She was trembling. Damn it, what was going on? "Just say it, Casey."

"I'm pregnant."

Casey watched as shock, then wonder, then relief flashed across his eyes. She pulled her hand from his and sat quietly, waiting for him to say *something*.

Taking the home pregnancy test half an hour ago had solidified for her what she'd begun to suspect only that afternoon. Talking with the other women about babies and pregnancies, Casey had realized with a start that her period hadn't arrived on schedule. There had just been so much going on in her life lately, she hadn't paid the slightest bit of attention to the fact that her period simply hadn't shown up. And even if she had, she wouldn't have worried. After all, a doctor had told her that it would be nearly impossible for her to conceive the old-fashioned way. That's why she'd gone to a sperm bank in the first place. Why she'd had an in vitro procedure. How she'd come to be here, with a man who didn't love her.

The father of *both* of her children.

"I thought you said—"

She nodded, knowing what he was going to say. "My doctor told me it would be nearly impossible—" She laughed shortly and felt the sound scrape at her throat. "I guess the key word in that phrase is *nearly.*"

"So that first night when we—"

She nodded. "Apparently, your little swimmers have no trouble finding my womb."

He almost looked pleased, but maybe that was just her imagination working overtime.

"How long have you known?"

"Since about a half hour ago." She jumped up from the chair, suddenly unable to sit still a moment longer. Rubbing her hands up and down her arms, she paced aimlessly around the room. She could *feel* Jackson's gaze on her, and wished more than anything that she could throw herself into his arms and celebrate this…miracle.

She'd had no one but Dani to celebrate news of her first pregnancy. And this one was such a triumphant thing, such a one-in-a-million shot, that she wanted to shout, to laugh, to cry. But this time, she would do all of that alone, despite the fact that the baby's father was in the same room with her.

Casey couldn't fool herself any longer. She'd wanted to pretend that somehow, Jackson would one day come to love her. But the simple truth was, he didn't. Wouldn't. And it wasn't as if he were incapable of love. He loved Mia, that was obvious to anyone with eyes. So it was only Casey he couldn't love. And the addition of one more child wasn't going to change that.

"Casey."

She stopped, turned and looked at him from across the room.

"Don't you want the baby?"

"Of *course* I want this baby," she said, cupping both hands over her abdomen as if she could prevent the tiny life nestled inside from hearing any of this conversation. "This is a gift, Jackson. One I'll always treasure. It just…" she sighed and shook her head "…makes everything that much more complicated than before."

"No." He walked to her side, stopped directly in front of her and looked down at her. His eyes were shining, his smile was wide and when he spoke, Casey could hardly believe what he was saying. "This just makes things simpler," he said.

"I don't see how."

He ran his hands up and down her arms until finally sliding them up to cup her face between his palms. "That's what I wanted to talk to you about. I've got the solution to this, Casey. Marry me."

Eleven

"What?"

He'd surprised her, Jackson thought. Good. Better to keep her a little off balance. Better to force her to go with her instincts than to give her time to consider all options. Of course, when she finally *did* consider them, she'd see he was right. This was the absolute best decision for all of them.

"Marry me," he repeated, astonished at how easy the words fell from his mouth. Hell, he'd had an arrangement to marry Marian and he hadn't been able to talk himself into making the actual, formal proposal. But saying the words to Casey was different.

Right.

"You're crazy," she said, shaking her head and moving back, out of his touch, away from him.

So maybe keeping her off balance wasn't the best

option, he told himself, thinking fast. Maybe he should lay it all out for her. Clearly she was too muddled in her head right now, due to finding out about the coming baby.

Another baby.

Joy filled him. And pride. And a sense of expectation he never would have believed possible. He'd missed so much with Mia, Jackson couldn't wait to experience everything with this baby. He wanted to be there for all of them. He had to make Casey see that doing things his way made sense.

"It's perfect, don't you see?" He grinned and threw both hands high before letting them slap down against his thighs again. "We both love Mia. Now we've got a new baby coming. There's plenty of room in this house as you well know and you and I get along great."

She shook her head, staring at him as if he were speaking Greek. So he talked faster.

"You and I, Casey, we've got something good going. We can build a family here, with neither one of us being a weekend parent." He took a step closer and felt hope notch a little higher inside him when she didn't step back. "You've got all the new work for the King family and we'll add on to your office here at the house. Do it up however you want it. We can do this, Casey. We've got chemistry together, you have to admit that. We work well together, we both love our daughter, what could be better?"

She lifted one hand to her mouth, shook her head and looked at him as if he were out of his mind entirely. Why the hell wasn't this making sense to her? It was all perfectly logical. Reasonable.

"Love could be better, Jackson," she finally said on a tired sigh. "You were going to marry Marian—"

"Don't start on that again—"

"But you didn't think of marrying me until you found out I was pregnant. You don't want a wife, Jackson. Not really. You want company in bed and you want to be a father."

He frowned at her. This was not going the way he'd expected it to. "Even if you were right," he countered, "how does that make me any different than you? You said yourself you wanted to be a mother, that's why you didn't wait for a perfect relationship. You went to the sperm bank and got the child you wanted. Well, I *have* the child I want, right here. And now you tell me I'm going to have another one. So why wouldn't I want to be their father?"

"You're right," she said, but he didn't feel any better. "I wanted to be a mother. But the difference between us is, I didn't marry someone I didn't love to do it. Jackson, don't you see? The fact that you love Mia—that you will love this baby—isn't enough to base a marriage between us on."

"Why the hell not?" It sounded great to him. A ready-made family. Two people who liked each other, enjoyed each other.

"Look, you were all set for a marriage merger—"

"Will you leave her out of this? I told you, Marian doesn't mean a thing to me."

"Neither do I," she countered quickly. "This is just another convenient move for you. Before, you were going to use your marriage to expand your airline. With me, you'll expand your family. It's just another merger."

"With a hell of a lot better chance for survival," he told her.

"No, no it wouldn't work."

"Give me one good reason why not." He stared at her, completely lost as to her reaction. He'd been so sure she'd see that this was the right thing to do. So positive that he'd made the right move. That a marriage between them would solve all of their problems.

"Because I love you, Jackson." She gave him a sad smile. "I didn't mean to, and believe me when I say I wish I didn't, it would make things much easier."

He wasn't an idiot. He'd known that she had feelings for him. He hadn't really thought about her being in love with him, but since she was, why couldn't she see that it made even *more* sense for her to marry him?

"Now I'm really confused," he admitted with an under-the-breath curse. "If you love me, you should be *happy* with this solution."

"Happy to marry a man who loves my kid, but not me?" She shook her head. "Happy to live a lie? Happy to deny myself the hope of being loved in return? No, Jackson. Your idea doesn't sound like a bargain to me."

"Damn it, I *care* about you!" He took another step forward and she lifted her gaze to his. Her eyes were pale blue. No passion. No anger. No dark, churning emotion changing that color to a deep-sea blue. There was only regret shining in her eyes and Jackson felt as if he were standing on a slippery slope, skidding relentlessly downhill toward an abyss he couldn't avoid.

His chest tightened and everything in him went hard and

still. He felt as if he were fighting for his life. Why couldn't she just take what he had to offer her? A life with him and their kids? He cared more for Casey than he had ever allowed himself to care for anyone. Why couldn't it be enough?

He grabbed her shoulders, pulled her to him with a yank and folded his arms around her. She stood still for him, but she didn't wrap her arms round his waist. Didn't yield her body to his. Didn't lean into him. She was simply *there.*

"Caring isn't loving, Jackson," she whispered against his chest, her voice muffled so that he barely heard her words. "I deserve more."

"It's all I've got to give," he said.

"I know," she told him. "That's the saddest part about this."

He let her go then and his arms felt empty without her. *He* felt empty, damn it, and there was no reason for it. All she had to do was accept his proposal and they'd be fine. They'd have everything.

Why couldn't she see that?

When she walked past him, headed for the hallway, he called out and she stopped. "Where are you going?"

She turned her head to look back at him. "Upstairs. I'm tired and I need some time alone."

When she was gone and the only sound in the living room was the hiss and crackle of the fire in the hearth, Jackson thought that "alone" was overrated.

Early the next morning, Casey sat in the dining room, Mia tucked into her high chair, cheerfully mashing banana slices in her tiny fists. While watching her daughter have breakfast, Casey drank tea and wished for caffeine.

Laying alone in her bed had felt so strange. She was used to Jackson's touch, his heavy sigh as he settled into sleep. The drape of his arm over her middle as he pulled her up close. She'd come to rely on having him there beside her and now that he wasn't—she was lost.

Mia squealed, lifted both banana-covered hands and kicked at her high chair. Without even turning around, Casey knew that Jackson had come into the room. No one but he ever got that kind of reception from his daughter.

"Good morning." His deep voice rumbled through the room and seemed to reverberate around her. Instantly, Casey's heartbeat quickened and she felt a slow build of heat swirling inside her. God, would she always feel this way about him? Was she destined to spend the rest of her life in love with a man who only "cared" for her?

Steeling herself, she nodded. "Morning, Jackson."

"Sleep well?" he asked.

"No, you?"

"Great."

Disgusted, she shot him a look as he came around the table, bent down to kiss Mia and slid his gaze to hers. Instantly, she felt better. He was lying. There were shadows under his eyes that were every bit as dark as her own. Somehow, she enjoyed knowing his night had been long and miserable, too.

Sunlight slanted through the windows. Mia cooed and gurgled. And still Casey and Jackson stared at each other, each waiting for the other to speak first. Finally, Jackson did.

Pouring himself a cup of coffee from the carafe on the table, he said, "Last night you told me you needed some time to yourself."

All the alone time in the world wasn't going to solve the problems facing her. But she had to think. And being around Jackson was not conducive to thought. "I still do."

"Well, that's what I want to talk to you about." He paused for a sip of coffee. "You know I'm shorthanded at the airfield." She nodded. "Well, I've decided I'm going to take one of the flights myself. Give us both a little breathing room for a few days."

"A few days?" Strange, she'd wanted alone time, but hearing him say he was leaving wasn't making her happy. Apparently she wanted alone time with him nearby. God, she was a mess.

"Yeah," he said softly, "I'm heading to Paris this afternoon. I'm flying a couple over there, then I'll stay and take care of some business."

"Paris?" He was leaving. For days. The ache of loneliness settled in, but she told herself it was probably for the best. She wanted him to love her as much as he did their children. And the fact that he didn't made her feelings too raw and painful for her to be around him.

His voice dropped and Casey looked up into his dark eyes as he added, "As I recall, I once promised you a trip to Rome."

That night in the hall, she thought. The first night in this house with him, when they'd set the path they'd followed ever since. The night she'd discovered that her body could erupt in flames and she could survive to tell the tale.

"I remember." But fantasies and great—amazing—sex

didn't take the place of love. He wanted her, she could see it in his eyes. But want was a poor substitute for need. So it was good he was leaving, she told herself.

He set his coffee down onto the table, leaned both hands on it and speared her gaze with his. "Say the word and I'll stay. Marry me and we'll take that trip to Rome."

"I can't."

He pushed up from the table and she didn't know if he was disappointed or annoyed. Probably both. "Fine then. Do all the thinking you want while I'm gone," Jackson said. "When I get home, we'll settle this." Then he bent to kiss the top of Mia's head. When he straightened up, he looked right at Casey again. "When I get home."

Jackson came home early. He'd rousted his co-pilot out of bed, fired up the jet and set a new personal record for flight speed on the trip back to California. How the hell could he be expected to take care of business in Paris when his head was full of Casey? He'd tried, damn it. He'd wandered the streets of Paris, visited old haunts and never did find the enjoyment he usually experienced when he was wandering the world.

None of it mattered.

Nothing mattered, because he felt like his heart had been scooped out of his chest. She hadn't even answered the damn phone when he'd called. She was avoiding him and he'd had enough. Now it was the middle of the night and he didn't care if she was sound asleep. She was *going* to listen to him. She was *going* to marry him. And they were *going* to be happy, damn it.

He parked his car in the driveway, jumped out and trotted up the narrow walkway to the front door. He stepped inside and the silence hit him like a blow. Taking the stairs two at a time, his own footsteps echoed in the stillness like a heartbeat. He passed his own room, went straight to Casey's and opened the door.

Her bed was empty and the first tendrils of uneasiness began to slip through his system. Turning fast, he crossed to his own room, thinking that maybe she'd come to her senses and had wanted to be in his bed—their bed. But she wasn't there, either.

Across the hall from him was Mia's room and her door stood open. No night-light was burning, though. There were no magical stars shining in the darkness to keep his baby girl company. There was only more silence. He walked across the threshold, and moved through the darkness to the crib, though he knew he'd find it empty. His heart fisted in his chest and the uneasiness quickened into a deeply felt fear like he'd never known before.

Casey had taken Mia and left. He glanced into the baby's closet. Empty. As empty as the house. As empty as his soul.

"Where the hell did they go?" Fear and fury tangled together in the pit of his stomach as he answered his own question. "Dani's."

"Don't tell him anything!"

Jackson looked past a sleepy Mike Sullivan to his wife, standing on the stairs, wearing a pink fluffy robe and a dangerous gleam in her eye. "Dani—"

"Haven't you done enough?" She came down another step and glared at him. "Leave her alone."

Mike moved to block Jackson's view of his wife and planted one hand on the threshold, preventing him entry. "She's not here," he said.

Jackson had been so sure. So positive that Casey would turn to her best friend, he had no idea where to turn now. He looked at the other man and saw sympathy on his face. Jackson responded to it. "Tell me where she is."

Mike shot a glance over his shoulder and winced. Lowering his voice, he looked back at Jackson and said, "I feel for you. I do. But Casey's a friend. And if I want to keep living with my wife…"

"Just tell me if Casey's okay."

"Unhappy, but safe."

Jackson's heart felt like lead in his chest. He didn't want her unhappy. He just wanted *her.* Shoving one hand through his hair, he turned around and looked at the quiet, suburban street. Houses were shut up tight, lights were few. Families were in those houses. Together. And Jackson felt more solitary in that one bleak moment than he ever had before.

"I don't know where to look," he murmured, more to himself than to the man behind him.

Lowering his voice, Mike offered, "You might try talking to your brother."

Whipping his head around, Jackson stared at him. "Which one?"

"Adam."

Turning, Jackson jumped off the porch and ran through the night to the car parked at the curb.

Twelve

"**W**hat the *hell* are you doing pounding on my door in the middle of the night?" Adam stood on the threshold, bare-chested, wearing pajama bottoms. His hair was sleep-ruffled and his eyes looked furious.

"Casey's gone." Jackson pushed past his brother, stalked across the foyer straight into Adam's study. "I've got to find her and I don't know where to look." He wasn't used to feeling panicked and he didn't like it. Felt like he was beginning to unravel at the edges and there was nothing he could do about it. "I went to her friend Dani's and her husband told me I should check with you." Facing his older brother, Jackson said, "So? What do you know?"

"I know it's the middle of the night and I'm tired." Adam walked past him to the wet bar, poured himself a brandy and asked, "Do you want one?"

"No, I don't want a damn drink. I want Casey." He shoved both hands through his hair again and gave a good yank. "I'm wasting time just standing here. I should be looking for her. But *where?*"

Adam took a sip of brandy and leaned one elbow on the bar. Studying his brother he asked, "Wherever she is, maybe she doesn't want to be found."

"Too bad," Jackson snapped. He felt as if he were hanging off the edge of the world, the only thing keeping him safe a quickly unraveling rope. "I'm not going to let her leave me. Just walk away like what we have is nothing."

"Uh-huh. Why not?"

"What?" He shot his brother a hard look. "What the hell's that supposed to mean?"

"Simple question. If you don't love her, why do you want her?"

Jackson winced. "Did Casey talk to Gina?"

"You could say that," Adam muttered darkly. "Gina's been talking my ear off about nothing else since. She's not real fond of you at the moment."

Gina wasn't Jackson's problem. Casey was. "I asked her to marry me and she turned me down!" He shouted the words as if he'd been bottling them up for days.

"This surprises you?" Adam snorted a laugh.

Astonished, he said, "Hell yes. She's pregnant with *my* baby. We've already got a daughter. She *should* marry me. It's the only sensible solution."

Adam shook his head, walked across the room and turned on a single standing lamp before sitting down. "God, you really are an idiot."

"Excuse me?"

"Gina's been calling you one for days and I've been defending you, but I can see now, I was wrong."

"How am I the bad guy here?" Jackson asked, defending himself since it was clear as hell nobody else was going to do it. "I wanted to marry her."

"Not because you love her."

"What's love got to do with anything?" Jackson prowled the dark room, shooting the occasional hot glare at his brother, so comfortable in his own house. "Love just complicates things. You get in so deep you don't know which end's up. Who the hell needs that?"

"Everybody," Adam mused, taking a sip of his drink.

Jackson stopped and scrubbed both hands over his face. "I wanted this to be simple. To live with Casey and our daughter. To be together. Happy."

"How's that workin' for you?"

"Not well."

"Tell you anything?"

"Yeah," Jackson said, dropping into the closest chair. "It tells me I'm in deep trouble here. Hell, I've been in deep trouble since the night Casey walked into the hotel bar and smiled at me. I knew it then. I've just been fighting it. Tonight just caps it. I walked into the house and she was gone and I felt like I died. Like there was no air in the world."

"Congratulations," Adam said softly. "You're in love."

"Damn it." Jackson looked at his brother. "I didn't plan on loving her, you know."

"Hell, none of us plans it," Adam said, giving him an

understanding smile. "But you should know…she didn't leave just because of you."

"What else happened?" Jackson took a breath and held it. What else could possibly have gone wrong in a few short days?

"The day after you took the flight to Paris, Marian went to see her at your place."

"Ah, God. What did she do? What did she say?" Jackson jumped to his feet.

"I got all of this from Gina," Adam said on a sigh. "And let me warn you, none of the King women are big fans of yours right now."

"Great."

"Seems Marian tried to buy Casey off. Apparently she offered her a nice little nest egg if she'd leave and agree not to marry you."

"I should have been there. Shouldn't have left. I wanted her to think. To miss me. Backfired big time. I'm the one who missed her." Jackson let out a sigh. "I already know she wouldn't take the money."

Adam scowled at him. "Damn right. According to Gina, Casey told Marian what she could do with her money, said that you and Marian deserved each other and that she wouldn't be a problem anymore."

"We deserve each other? What the hell…why would she—how could—" Jackson had never been more furious. Or more frustrated. Things were happening. Beyond his control. Beyond his ability to fix them. Arrange them into the right kind of order. What the hell was going on with his world?

"You should have called me."

"Casey didn't want us to."

"You're *my* brother."

"And I have to live with *my* wife, who's completely on Casey's side in all this, so no thanks."

Jackson though, hardly heard his older brother. His mind was too busy, racing down several different paths, trying to find the one that would lead him to Casey. Trying to figure out how he could dig himself out of the mess he was now in. She'd taken off, but where would she go? She said she loved the beach, right? So he'd start there. A lot of beach in this country though. This could take awhile.

"I've got to find her. Explain. Talk to her. Maybe the airport in Sacramento. She probably wouldn't want to stay around here and her old house is gone. She's not with Dani, so she's probably headed off somewhere new. Somewhere she thinks I won't be able to find her. Somewhere on the beach."

"That narrows it down."

"Gotta start somewhere."

"Not going to be easy."

Jackson looked at his older brother and smiled grimly. "Nothing about Casey is easy. And you know what? Easy's overrated. I'll find her. You can count on it. And when I do, I'm dragging her back home with me. Where she belongs."

He was halfway across the foyer when Adam's voice stopped him. "Jackson."

"I'll call you from the road, Adam. I'm wasting time here."

"Jackson, stop."

He did. And when he looked over his shoulder at his

brother, Jackson felt the first faint fluttering of hope inside. "You know where she is."

Adam sighed. "If you screw this up, Gina's gonna kill me for telling you."

"*I'll* kill you if you don't."

"I guess we men have got to stick together sometimes," Adam said with a half smile. Then he jerked his thumb at the stairs. "Gina gave Casey your old room on the second floor."

Jackson didn't even pause long enough to thank him. He hit the stairs at a dead run, moving through the darkness on memory alone. He'd grown up in this ranch house. He could find his way blindfolded. And now, knowing that Casey was waiting for him, he knew that nothing could have kept him away.

Outside his old room, he paused, taking a ragged breath and letting it slide from his lungs in an effort to calm himself. But he was as calm as he was going to get, so he turned the knob and slowly opened the door.

Moonlight shone through the windows in slants of silvery light that illuminated the woman asleep on the bed. Her short, blond hair was tousled, the deep red duvet was pushed down to her waist and he smiled when he noticed she was wearing one of his T-shirts to sleep in.

Maybe there was still hope. Maybe she still loved him. Maybe he could bring himself back from the edge he'd blindly walked out on.

Crossing the room with quiet steps, he listened to the sound of her breathing and felt his own smooth out and begin to move in time with hers. She was here. She was safe. And he was in love for the first and last time in his life.

* * *

Casey dreamed of him and in that dream, she caught his scent and inhaled deeply. When he called her name, she turned toward him, even in sleep, reaching for him.

Then he kissed her and the dream was so real, she tasted him, savoring the feel of his lips on hers. So warm, so soft, so… Her eyes flew open and she gasped. "Jackson? How did you—"

He was sitting on the edge of the bed and when he grabbed her before she could scoot back and away, he pulled her across his lap and wrapped both arms around her. She knew she shouldn't lean into him, but she'd missed him so much, pined for him so deeply that the feel of his heart-beat racing in time with her own was too much to resist.

"You scared about ten years off my life tonight," he whispered. "When I got home and you weren't there…"

"I had to leave," she said and remembering why gave her the strength to push out of his arms and scramble back onto the bed. She folded her arms over her chest and held on tight. Just looking at him melted everything inside her. Her heart ached for him. And a voice in her mind whispered, re-minding her to be strong. To not settle for less than love.

"I know." Jackson reached out, smoothed her hair, then let his fingertips trail down the side of her face with a touch so light she might have still been dreaming.

He took a breath, looked around the room and asked, "Where's Mia?"

"Sleeping in Emma's room."

"Good," he said. "Good."

"Jackson—"

"No, let me talk first, okay?" He shifted on the bed, getting comfortable, but he didn't reach for her again and Casey wasn't sure what to think about that. "I thought when I left," he said softly, "that you'd miss me so much you'd cave in and marry me. I figured I'd teach you a lesson." He laughed a little, but there was no warmth in the sound. "Turns out, I'm the one who had to learn."

She scooted back, higher against the pillows. Keeping her gaze fixed on Jackson, Casey tried desperately not to let a small bubble of hope become so big that its popping might destroy her.

"I missed you. I missed looking at you, listening to you laugh with Mia. I couldn't *sleep,*" he added with a shake of his head, "because you weren't there to hog the blankets."

"I don't—"

"When I closed my eyes, I saw you. When I walked down the streets in Paris, all I could think was, I wished you were there."

As if he couldn't stand still another minute, he pushed off the bed, walked across his old room to stand beside the window. Moonlight fell on him and Casey couldn't tear her gaze from him.

He turned his head to look at her. "I didn't want to fall in love, Casey. Never planned on it. Never was interested. Love makes life messy. Gives the one you love too much power over you."

She held her breath, waiting, hoping.

"The thing is," he said, "I fell in love anyway. You slipped up on me. You came into my life, knocked it all around, and it shocks the hell out of me to know I like it better that way.

I don't want to go back to my old life, Casey. I want a life with you. With Mia and with our new baby."

Joy rippled through her with such staggering force, Casey thought for a moment she must still be dreaming. Surely it was impossible to be this happy. To have everything she'd ever wanted right in front of her.

Walking back to her side, Jackson sank onto the edge of the bed beside her and looked deeply into her eyes. "Marry me, Casey. This isn't a merger—I'm not trying to build my fortune here. You, Mia and the baby *are* my fortune. The only one I'll ever need."

"Jackson…"

"It isn't convenience, either," he said, talking faster now, wanting to say it all. "This is love, Casey. I can't live my life without you in it. So maybe it's simple after all. I love you. I need you. And if you don't marry me…"

"You'll what?" she asked, already moving toward him, a smile in her eyes.

"I'll…keep asking. I'll tell you I love you every day. Until you're so sick of hearing it you'll marry me just to shut me up."

"I'll never get sick of hearing it," she assured him, sliding onto his lap, wrapping her arms around his neck, trailing her fingers through his thick, soft hair. "Say it again."

"I love you."

"Again."

He buried his face in the curve of her neck. "I love you."

"I love you too, Jackson. So very much."

He held her fiercely, squeezing her until she lost her breath and didn't care if she caught it again.

"So is that a yes?" he demanded.

"It's a yes, Jackson." She grinned at him, her heart whole, her soul singing. Everything was just as it should be. She was in Jackson's arms and the future looked bright. "Of course it's a yes. I love you."

"Thank God," he whispered and held her even tighter.

"Welcome home, Jackson," Casey said, losing herself in the magic of love.

Epilogue

Eight months later...

They named her Molly.

She looked just like her big sister. Just like her cousins.

And her mommy and daddy couldn't have been happier.

Jackson leaned down, kissed Casey and released a breath he felt as though he'd been holding for months. "You're amazing," he said, smiling down at the woman who had made his life absolutely complete.

"As long as you keep believing that, honey," she said, cupping his cheek in the palm of her hand, "everything's going to be great."

"After seeing what you did in here today, I'm convinced," he said. He looked tired, but then, they'd been in labor and delivery for the last nine hours. He'd never left her side and Casey couldn't believe how much easier everything had been because she'd had the man she loved with her through it all.

The King brothers and their wives had already been by, cooing over Molly, promising to keep Mia happy until her parents came home. And now, it was just Casey and Jackson. Molly was asleep in the hospital nursery and the glow of having accomplished another miracle was riding high in Casey's heart.

"I love you," Jackson said, amazement still shining in his eyes as he pulled a small, blue velvet jeweler's box from his pocket.

Casey eyed it warily and even managed a smile. "The last time I saw a box like that, it caused all kinds of trouble."

"I don't know what you're talking about, gorgeous," he said with a grin just before he bent down and dropped a kiss on her mouth. "I'm a married man, desperately in love with my wife."

"Well, in that case..." She took the small box from him, flipped the lid open and gasped. A huge, square-cut sapphire glittered on silk and from either side of the deep blue stone two diamonds winked at her. "Oh, Jackson!"

He took the ring from the box, pushed it onto her right-hand ring finger and said softly, "The sapphire is because it reminded me of your eyes. The twin diamonds are for our girls. The gold ring…that's eternity. With you. Thank you, Casey. For finding me. For loving me."

She lifted her face for his kiss and felt, as she did every day of her life, that her dreams had finally come true.

* * * * *

A sneaky peek at next month…

By Request

RELIVE THE ROMANCE WITH THE BEST OF THE BEST

My wish list for next month's titles…

In stores from 18th April 2014:

❏ Indecent Arrangements – Mira Lyn Kelly, Anna Cleary & Julia James

❏ The Lost Princes: Darius, Cassius & Monte – Raye Morgan

3 stories in each book - only £5.99!

In stores from 2nd May 2014:

❏ Las Vegas: Scandals – Nina Bruhns, Loreth Anne White & Carla Cassidy

❏ Single Dad Needs Nanny – Teresa Carpenter, Alison Roberts & Cindy Kirk

Available at WHSmith, Tesco, Asda, Eason, Amazon and Apple

Just can't wait?

Visit us Online

You can buy our books online a month before they hit the shops! **www.millsandboon.co.uk**

0414/05

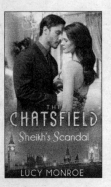

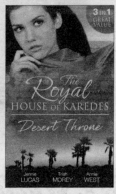

24 new stories from the leading lights of romantic fiction!

Featuring bestsellers Adele Parks, Katie Fforde, Carole Matthews and many more, *Truly, Madly, Deeply* **takes you on an exciting romantic adventure where love really is all you need.**

Now available at:

www.millsandboon.co.uk

The World of Mills & Boon®

There's a Mills & Boon® series that's perfect for you. We publish ten series and, with new titles every month, you never have to wait long for your favourite to come along.

By Request

Relive the romance with the best of the best
12 stories every month

Cherish™

Experience the ultimate rush of falling in love
12 new stories every month

Desire™

Passionate and dramatic love stories
6 new stories every month

n o c t u r n e™

An exhilarating underworld of dark desires
Up to 3 new stories every month

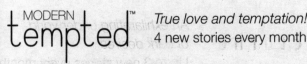